PRAISE FOR THE TAKEN TRILOGY

LOST AND FOUND

"Amusing . . . intriguing . . . consistently entertaining."
—*Locus*

"Foster excels at comic adventure, and this tale is no exception. . . . A promising start."   —*Romantic Times*

"Foster has an amazing ability to not only tell a great story, but to make even alien squid and mountainous fuzzy monsters believable."

—*Baton Rouge Advocate Sunday Magazine*

THE LIGHT-YEARS BENEATH MY FEET

"Alan Dean Foster is a master of creating strange, yet understandable, alien cultures."   —*The SF Site*

"Sometimes humorous, sometimes serious, and always entertaining."   —*Library Journal*

THE CANDLE OF DISTANT EARTH

"Stunning."   —*Jive Magazine* (4.5 stars out of 5)

"Foster creates alien characters and races with awesome expertise. . . . In the end, Foster delivers a neat little twist and a thoroughly pleasing conclusion that had me sighing with satisfaction and regret that the tale was over. This trilogy is a wonderful read."   ns.com

D1366693

By ALAN DEAN FOSTER
Published by The Random House Publishing Group

The Black Hole
Cachalot
Dark Star
The Metrognome and Other Stories
Midworld
Nor Crystal Tears
Sentenced to Prism
Star Wars: Splinter of the Mind's Eye
Star Trek* Logs One–Ten
Voyage to the City of the Dead
. . . Who Needs Enemies?
With Friends Like These . . .
Mad Amos
The Howling Stones
Parallelities
Star Wars: The Approaching Storm

Stories:
Impossible Places
Exceptions to Reality

The Icerigger Trilogy:
Icerigger
Mission to Moulokin
The Deluge Drivers

The Adventures of Flinx of the Commonwealth:
For Love of Mother-Not
The Tar-Aiym Krang
Orphan Star
The End of the Matter
Bloodhype
Flinx in Flux
Mid-Flinx
Reunion
Flinx's Folly
Sliding Scales
Running from the Deity
Trouble Magnet
Patrimony

The Damned:
Book One: A Call to Arms
Book Two: The False Mirror
Book Three: The Spoils of War

The Founding of the Commonwealth:
Phylogenesis
Dirge
Diuturnity's Dawn

The Taken Trilogy:
Lost and Found
The Light-Years Beneath My Feet
The Candle of Distant Earth

Books published by The Random House Publishing Group
are available at quantity discounts on bulk purchases for
premium, educational, fund-raising, and special sales use.
For details, please call 1-800-733-3000.

THE CANDLE OF DISTANT EARTH

ALAN DEAN FOSTER

William E. Anderson
Library of Penn Hills
1037 Stotler Road
Pittsburgh, PA 15235-2209

BALLANTINE BOOKS • NEW YORK

Sale of this book without a front cover may be unauthorized. If this book is coverless, it may have been reported to the publisher as "unsold or destroyed" and neither the author nor the publisher may have received payment for it.

The Candle of Distant Earth is a work of fiction. Names, characters, places, and incidents are the products of the author's imagination or are used fictitiously. Any resemblance to actual events, locales, or persons, living or dead, is entirely coincidental.

2007 Del Rey Mass Market Edition

Copyright © 2006 by Thranx, Inc.

All rights reserved.

Published in the United States by Del Rey Books, an imprint of The Random House Publishing Group, a division of Random House, Inc., New York.

DEL REY is a registered trademark and the Del Rey colophon is a trademark of Random House, Inc.

Originally published in hardcover in the United States by Del Rey Books, an imprint of The Random House Publishing Group, a division of Random House, Inc., in 2006.

ISBN 978-0-345-46133-9

Printed in the United States of America

www.delreybooks.com

OPM 9 8 7 6 5 4 3 2 1

For Amos Nachoum
Fellow explorer . . .

1

For the eleventh time, Ussakk the Astronomer pored over the most recent collated readouts while trying to decide how best to kill himself. Whichever method he chose, it would be faster and cleaner than what was coming. While the last time the Iollth had ravaged Hyff had been well before his birth, abundant records were available to illustrate in gruesome detail their appetite for destruction. Given the history of their visitations to Hyff, it was remarkable that any of the populace would continue to resist. Yet invariably, outraged at the periodic demands for tribute and treasure, some did. And just as invariably, they died deaths that were as horrible as they were futile.

That much could be tolerated, if not for the disagreeable Iollth habit of slaughtering out of apparent boredom the occasional batch of innocent civilians.

Ussakk felt he would be as fated to be among the latter—that is, if the authorities did not kill him outright as the bearer of bad news. He sympathized in advance with their probable reaction. There was always the hope among his people that the Iollth would tire of their cyclical visits to Hyff, that they would seek to enrich themselves at the expense of others elsewhere and leave the Hyfft to their peaceful, widespread communities and to the tending of the crops of which they were so proud.

A fool's dream, Ussakk knew. So long as the Hyfft fashioned beautiful objects out of rare materials, so long as their mines produced rare and unsynthesizable raw materials, the Iollth would return: to plunder, and not to buy.

The astronomer knew they could not be put off with excuses. A hundred years ago, the Great Government had decreed that the production of objects of beauty and the mining of gems was to cease. Despite the temporary harm this inflicted on Hyfftian culture, it was hoped the absence of such things would discourage the Iollth. After all, one cannot ransack that which does not exist. It was a defensive maneuver predicated on a rational reaction.

Unfortunately, the Iollth did not respond in a rational manner. In their fury and frustration, their unopposed ships laid waste to a dozen of Hyff's largest communities. Tens of thousands died. After that, there were no more attempts to discourage the visitors with clever subterfuges.

Occasionally, there came together bands of Hyfft who were still determined, somehow, to resist. Sadly, having evolved from sedate bands of farmers who had known nothing but greater and greater cooperation that had eventually resulted in the development of the present state of high culture, the Hyfft were emotionally and psychologically ill-equipped for warfare. Even thoughts of acquiring an armed starship from one of the other space-traversing species who paid the occasional rare visit to Hyff fell by the wayside when none among the Hyfft could be found who were bold enough to leave the Nesting World long enough to travel between the stars to arrange the actual acquisition.

Though technologically advanced, the Hyfft could not find it within themselves to manufacture weapons. Psychologically crippled, they could not muster enough individuals to make use of such weapons even if they managed to buy them from elsewhere. Located far from the fringes of galactic civilization, they did not attract the attention of those who might have offered them protection.

Besides, it was rationalized, the Iollth did not threaten genocide. They came only to plunder and ravage, and that only once every hundredth-passing or so. Hardly sufficient reason for distant species with a surfeit of their own problems to take the time and expense to interfere. Especially when most of Hyff never even suffered beneath the heavy foot of the visitors, except to witness and weep over their sporadic depredations via relayed images.

That the fast-moving signatures Ussakk had detected emerging from deepspace belonged to the Iollth there was no question. The infrequent and uncommon traders or explorers who occasionally found their way to Hyff always arrived singly. There *was* one atypical report from three hundred-passings ago of two such vessels arriving simultaneously in orbit around Hyff, but that was only the result of coincidence. They had not been traveling in tandem, and were as surprised by each other's appearance in Hyfftian space as were the Hyfft themselves.

No, without question, a triple signature could signify the imminent arrival of nothing other than the dreaded Iollth.

As the senior astronomer on duty, he had the obligation to deliver the bad news to the local Overwatch, who would then pass it along to all the individual elements of the Great Government. Composed of hundreds of local Overwatches, the Great Government would then dictate an appropriate response. The best that could be hoped for, Ussakk knew, was that the Iollth would take what they wanted, murder for entertainment as few citizens as possible, and be on their way after causing a minimal amount of damage to Hyfftian civilization. It might be, he reflected as he began to make inviolable recordings of the relevant readouts, that with luck he would not be expected to kill himself.

As soon as the necessary recordings had been prepared, he stored them in his body pouch and prepared to leave his post. There was no thought of transmitting such sensitive information electronically. It was his responsibility, his personal *cura,* to deliver it in person. Coworkers were bemused by his nonresponsiveness as he departed. Such glumness was not usually associated with the bright and chipper senior astronomer. But no one pressed the limits of what was culturally acceptable. Though concerned, they left him to his private dejection. That was just as well, since if they had asked what was troubling him, he would have been compelled to answer.

Let them dwell in happiness and contentment a little while longer, he decided as he exited the observatory and ambled toward the nearest conveyor. Horror was now in the neighborhood and would arrive on their mental doorsteps soon enough.

The Escarpment of Lann dropped away behind him and his speed increased as the terrain leveled out. Racing toward the city, he was forced to slow repeatedly as his vehicle bunched up behind other conveyors. Each held, at most, no more than a single family. Hyfft did not travel in groups. On a world as heavily populated as theirs, even though that population was evenly dispersed, personal privacy was at a premium. So was courtesy, which was why the anxious Ussakk waited his turn until one by one, those in front of him reached their exit points and left the main conveyor route. Only then did he accelerate again.

There was no road, the conveyor route being only a line on a map that was duplicated in actuality by perfectly spaced sensors buried in the ground. The route Ussakk was following ran through fields of *pfale,* whose dark green fruit burst from the center of a spray of bright blue-green leaves. Enormous in extent, this particular field was nearly ready for harvesting. For a moment, the color and anticipation took his mind off the dreadful news he was about to deliver. *Pfale* was famed for its piquant taste, and for the ability of master cooks to turn it into a variety of elegant dishes usually supplemented with a quartet of *semell* condiments. Descended from wholly herbivorous ancestors, the Hyfft were masters of vegetarian cuisine.

An alien observer might have wondered why the agitated astronomer did not simply accelerate his levitating personal conveyor and pass the slower travelers in front of him. He could easily have done so, to the right or to the left. But such a move would have been an unforgivable breach of manners. On Hyff, one politely waited one's turn. The queue was a way of life, and woe betide any who violated it. Rules such as waiting for those in front to finish whatever they happened to be doing were not merely a matter of unspoken courtesy; they had been officially codified.

Exceptions were tolerated only for extreme emergencies. Unable to see how delivering his bad news a few morning-slices earlier would make things any better, Ussakk preferred to take his time and follow custom. Officialdom might soon berate him as the harbinger of doom, but no one would be able to accuse him of being impolite as part of the process.

The family ahead of him finally turned off, allowing him to accelerate afresh. Once within the outskirts of the city, he was able to take advantage of the much greater multiplicity of available conveyor routes. Like most urban concentrations on Hyff, Therapp was not large. With few exceptions, the majority of structures were built low to the ground in traditional fashion. Such buildings might cover considerable stretches of ground, but that was how the Hyfft preferred it. They did not like heights, and they favored open spaces.

Therapp's administrative center was housed in one such complex, which extended for several *midds* from the center of the city and across the meandering river that cut through it. Slotting his conveyor in a public receptacle, he quickly swapped it for its much smaller in-house counterpart. Within the vast structure, municipal workers dashed to and fro along clearly designated routings, never so much as nudging any of the pedestrians they passed. Without the internal conveyor, it might take him half a day to walk to the sector he sought.

Like the spokes of a wheel, the adjuncts to the office of Overwatch Delineator fanned out around a central core. As custom dictated, there were twenty-four such offices. Today the office of Delineator was held by number nine. Tomorrow it would be ten, and so on until next-month changeover. In this way the city's administration had twenty-four heads, among whom both responsibility and credit could be divvied up collectively. With only one day in charge each next-month, no one official had time to accumulate power over another. Occasionally, number twelve might swap day-work with the official occupying office twenty-one. Like everything else on Hyff, the system made for an administration that was both civil and efficient.

Today's Delineator was Phomma, of office nine. An unlucky number, Ussakk reflected as he stepped off his conveyor and snapped it into the nearest unoccupied recharger. Unlucky, because she would be the one to have to receive and deal with the dreadful news he carried with him.

When he entered, office nine was occupied by a pair of subordinate administrators engaged in debating the merits of expanding the city's southernmost recreation facility. Both looked up at his entry.

"Devirra li Designer," declared one. "Zubboj vi Procurer," added her companion.

"Ussakk ri Astronomer," he responded. While on business, the Hyfft did not waste time on extended formalities. They were an efficient folk. "To see today's Delineator."

The Designer's reply was prompt and inflexible. "Delineator Phomma qi Administrator sa Nine is not seeing visitors or supplicants until last two afternoon-slices. We respectfully suggest you return to request a meeting at that time." Small, dark, fast-moving pupils regarded him hesitantly. "Unless you already have arranged a meeting time for this morning."

"No, I haven't," he replied, "but I must see the Delineator immediately. It is a matter of global importance."

"Global?" Long, feathery white whiskers twitching to emphasize his amusement, the Procurer eyed his fellow subordinate administrator. "From an astronomer I would expect nothing less than galactic." They shared a casual touch, he clicking his prominent incisors against hers.

Ussakk was as well-mannered as the next person, but today he had no time for sarcasm. "You are more right than you say. The Iollth are returning to Hyff, and will be here within a two-day."

Later, though he could easily justify it, he regretted his bluntness.

A look at his face—eyes staring evenly, whiskers unquivering, short round ears perfectly erect and forward facing—being all that was necessary to convince them that the visitor was not joking, the change in attitude among the pair of subordinate administrators was shocking in its abruptness. The Designer's hairless eyelids fluttered once, twice, before she collapsed. Trembling visibly, the Procurer bent over her and began to tug on her short arms in an attempt to reestablish normal breathing. He was so badly shaken he could not sustain his grip, leaving it to Ussakk to take over and maintain the procedure until the psychologically stunned female finally regained consciousness.

"I apologize," he murmured. "I did not mean to cause shock. That is why I did not use public channels to communicate the information, for fear it might get out before it could be appropriately reviewed. But it must be delivered now, here, so that means of dissemination to the rest of Hyff can be decided upon, and propagated accordingly." His tone, normally relaxed and carefree as that of any of his kind, was unnaturally solemn.

His seriousness seemed to steady the Procurer. "Go on in, quickly," the subordinate administrator told him as he resumed working the Designer's upper arms.

With an acknowledging twitch of the whiskers to the right of his nose, Ussakk hitched up the cross-straps of his formal work attire, turned, and strode toward the inner wall. Sensing his approach, number nine of twenty-four ceremonial panels slid aside to admit him to the circular inner office.

It was beautifully appointed, the citizens of Therapp and the surrounding district being proud of their accomplishments and those of their local artisans. A conical central skylight of synthetic crystal flooded the interior with sunshine lightly tinted gold by the swirling, stained panel attached to it. Directly beneath the skylight, a round desk sat embedded in the mosaic stone floor. There the Delineator of the Day of Therapp sat and worked. Placing the desk slightly below floor level compelled each of them to look up at approaching citizens. In this manner, humility was enforced on the Overwatch's principal public servant.

Delineator Phomma qi Administrator sa Nine looked up and chittered a polite traditional greeting, followed by, "I specifically asked staff to grant me a two day-slice period of privacy. You must have considerable influence to have gained admittance in spite of that." Her long, drooping whiskers inclined toward him as she spoke, the aggressiveness of their posture belying the civility of her words. Unusually, he noted, they were tinted a pale red.

"I am Ussakk the Astronomer, and I have no influence: only bad news."

"Proceed forward." Rising from her seat, she stepped away from the trio of readouts that floated in the air before her. They started to follow obediently until she thought to wave them away. "What news can simultaneously be so bad and so influential?"

He descended the six short ceremonial steps, each corresponding to one of the whiskers that dominated the Hyfftian visage. "This morning I regret to say that I was forced to reconfirm certain previous significant observations made by my facility's instrumentation. Three starships have entered our system from deepspace. Though it has not happened in my lifetime, I know from history that infrequent visitors to our world invariably arrive in only one such vessel. One time, by coincidence, two such marvelous craft arrived at Hyff." He blinked meaningfully. "The presence of more than that can mean only one thing."

As an educated person, the Delineator Phomma knew what it meant, too. To her credit, she neither fainted nor shook. But moisture did begin to appear at the lower edges of both eyes. She wiped it hurriedly away.

"This leaves no time for advance lamenting. That will have to come later." Turning, she moved purposefully back to the seat she had been occupying when he had arrived. Her hovering tripartite readouts had to move fast to hold their positions in front of her eyes. This time she did not dismiss them. "The Great Government must be notified immediately. You will provide all details. Work must be started to minimize the inevitable panic that will greet the official announcement." As her hands moved, the four short fingers on each waving instructions at the readouts, she glanced over at him. "Who else knows?"

Ussakk considered for a moment. "Only the two sub administrators whose permission I had to seek to enter here. Their personal reactions," he added thoughtfully, "were as might have been expected. Otherwise, not even my colleagues at the observatory know. Yet."

She chirruped an acknowledgement. "Then this can be handled appropriately. Or at least, as well as can be hoped." He thought he saw tears begin to rise again, but the Delineator shut them down before they could dampen the neatly trimmed brown fur under her eyes. Leastwise, the formal face paint that streaked and speckled her plump cheeks did not run.

"If you do not require my presence any longer," he murmured, "I should be getting back to my work."

She replied without looking up at him, her hands busy with

the readouts. "Your work is here now. As Delineator of the Day for the Overwatch of Therapp, I am requisitioning your services to city administration. When your coworkers have been notified, they can monitor the approach of the . . ." She could not choke the name out, did not want to get the name out. "Of the incoming vessels," she finally finished.

Ussakk was appalled. "I am an astronomer, not a bureaucrat or civil servant. I answer to the Great Science, headquartered in Avvesse. Of what possible use could my extended presence be to the city government of Therapp?"

She paused in her work to study him. His whiskers quivered slightly under her suddenly intense stare, but he held his ground. "It is clear you are not a politician, either. Very well; if you need a reason, I feel that your continued presence in an urbanized area will in itself help to provide some small modicum of reassurance to the general populace."

His small black nose twitched. "How can that be?"

"By showing that you have not run away." She returned to manipulating the readouts. "In the coming days, that may prove critical. I don't suppose you can tell by the angle of approach of the Iollth ships where they intend to put down on Hyff?"

He reminded himself that this was not a fellow scientist he was talking to. "Angle of approach means nothing. They may decide to go into extended orbit around Hyff before choosing a place to—put down. Or they may decide to land at three different places. History shows that—"

"I know what history shows," she barked irritably. He took no offense at the sharpness of her response. Helplessness bred frustration, and frustration bred anger. He felt like doing some yelling and screaming himself. As a scientist, he realized the futility of such reactions better than most.

A tenth of a day-slice later, she waved both hands simultaneously, and the readouts that had been hovering before her vanished. With a weariness not even her elaborate ceremonial makeup could dispel, she turned back to him.

"The appropriate authorities have been advised. The Great Government is now in motion." Eyes as red as her whiskers met his. "All continental representatives are to meet here tomorrow. That is as fast as travel allows. Each of the eight continental Overwatches will determine how best to respond should an Iollth vessel set down in their territory. If all three approaching craft send their landers to one place, a worldwide response will be coordinated." The tearing started again, and this time it did not stop. "As we have throughout our history, we can only hope to minimize the destruction."

Stepping forward, Ussakk took her in his arms. The fact that she was the day's Delineator and he a research astronomer, and that they had never met before this moment, meant nothing. The Hyfft were a species as emotional as they were demonstrative, among whom close physical contact was not only commonplace but expected. Anyway, Ussakk was glad of the opportunity to embrace someone.

He needed the warming physical contact as badly as she did.

They traveled to Therapp from all over the continent of Vinen-Aq, Delineators who under the newly imposed regulations of emergency had found their terms of office extended indefinitely beyond the usual one day. It was not certain that each was the best of their kind to deal with the crisis at hand, but there was no time to process extended evaluations. If you were Delineator on that dire day, you found yourself chosen.

Having come from far and wide, they assembled the following morning in the circular chamber of Therapp's administrative center. Informed of Ussakk's discovery, his scientific colleagues had promptly dropped all other work to devote themselves to the single task of monitoring the approach of the three ships. That left Ussakk free to exhibit himself to the general public. True to Phomma sa Nine's observation, his presence did seem to have a reassuring influence on public opinion.

That did not prevent some panic from spreading as word slipped out. At least by the time it did, the efficient and fast-moving Hyfftian authorities had been given a breathing space in which to prepare. The worst of the panic was quickly contained. But nothing could stop the consequent rush of city dwellers toward the countryside. Every conveyor route out of every conurbation was soon jammed with desperate, would-be refugees. Even so, the lines were orderly. The few seriously unbalanced individuals who actually ignored the designated routes in favor of taking off across private property were quickly apprehended and suitably chastised.

The Hyfft might be prone to panic, but they did so in an orderly fashion.

Within the chamber, designated Delineators from dozens of Vinen-Aq's largest communities milled and conversed. There was no yelling, no piercing echoes of raised voices. Administrators were not allowed that kind of emotional release. But the general conversation was certainly borne along by an uneasy edge.

Nestled in one ear, a communicator kept Ussakk in constant touch with his associates at the observatory. Every similar installation on Hyff had likewise abandoned its regular work schedule to focus on the incoming craft. Thus far there had been no attempt at communication. If history was any guide, Ussakk knew, that would come once the Iollth had settled themselves in orbit and chosen the unfortunate location or locations for their landing. In the past, they had been known to destroy a city center or two from orbit, just as a preliminary object lesson. Or perhaps for entertainment. On that aspect of Iollth psychology, there were few details.

All across peaceful but tense Hyff, ten billion individuals now spoke one thought with one mind, albeit usually in private so as not to offend their neighbors. *Please don't let them land here.* In silently wishing this, Ussakk unashamedly had to admit that he was no different from his less scientifically inclined fellows.

No one thought of mounting an active resistance. Confined to their planet and happy to be so, at peace among themselves for thousands of years, the Hyfft possessed no weapons of advanced destruction: nothing more offensive than nonlethal police gear. Nor did they need any such—except when the Iollth came calling. Discussion of developing such weaponry, which was certainly within the technical ability of Hyfftian science, had come to naught. The one time such a thing had been tried, over a hundred years earlier, an Iollth landing craft had actually been destroyed. Its three companion vessels had escaped to orbit, one badly damaged.

Safe high above the surface of Hyff, their mother ships had proceeded to kill some two hundred thousand Hyfft. After that, their subsequent visitations had met with no further resistance.

Wandering among the dense crowd of visiting, apprehensive Delineators, Ussakk had the opportunity to eavesdrop on numerous ongoing discussions. All he could do was listen, having nothing tangible to contribute. He would much rather have been back at the observatory, even if there was nothing to do there but monitor the rapid progress of the three incoming starships and agonize about possible landing sites.

There was one good thing. Given the speed at which the Iollth vessels were traveling, they should arrive by tomorrow, thus putting an end to all the increasingly nerve-wracking speculation. He felt himself to be as ready as any of his kind for whatever might come. His elderly parents had been sent out of the city, to a (hopefully) safe refuge deep in the agricultural countryside. He was not mated and not courting. He had no offspring. If anyone was suitable for sacrifice at the hands of the Iollth, it was him.

But he didn't want to die.

2

"It very puzzling." Sobj-oes's neck frill flexed repeatedly as she stared out the port at the beautiful, lush world above which the three Niyyuuan ships had entered orbit. "Is ample evidence here of large population having achieved an advanced level of technology. Seaports, carefully laid out urban cores of modest dimension, atmospheric travel, very advanced and widespread agriculture. Local electromagnetic spectrum is full of noise. But communications specialists say despite repeated attempts, is no response to any of our transmissions."

Relaxing in Marcus Walker's arms so that he could see out the port, George used one paw to dig at a persistent itch, then sneezed effusively. Walker's expression furrowed.

"You could at least cover your mouth."

The dog glanced up at his friend. "Why? Most of it comes out my nose. And paws don't provide much coverage anyway." He looked over at the Niyyuuan astronautics specialist, meeting wide, gold-flecked eyes. "Maybe your people just haven't hit on the right frequency yet."

Using one long, limber arm whose tip terminated in two digits that pinched together forcefully, Sobj-oes responded with a negative gesture that reflected personal as well as professional disappointment. "I assured that everythings have been tried. Most obvious reason for noncommunication from surface is that we now well outside boundaries of accepted galactic civilization. Is entirely possible that, despite obvious high level of local technology, has been little or even no contact with any of the civilized species."

"Does that explain why they haven't come up to meet us?" Walker found himself asking.

Straightening her kilt-skirt around long, silk-skinned lower limbs in a manner that reminded him uncomfortably of the distant but not forgotten Viyv-pym, Sobj-oes turned huge, yellow-gold eyes on the human. "Are many communications satellites in multiple orbits around planet, but is no evidences of even a single spaceport. Are large facilities for atmospheric travel, but nothings to suggest locals venture into zone of no air. Not a habitable satellite, no installations on either moon or on outer planets. Nothing."

"Homebodies," George hypothesized thoughtfully. "Found an alley they like and keep to themselves. I can sympathize with that." As Walker set him down, the dog employed a hind foot to scratch at one ear.

"Maybe they have social reasons for not wanting to step off their world." Walker spoke while gazing out the port at the attractive planet below. "Maybe they're shy."

"Spatially speaking," Sobj-oes told them, "this system comparatively isolated. Are no other inhabited or habitable worlds nearby. Indigenous population may think selves isolated, intelligence-wise. This also help to explain why maybe no knowledge of numerous galactic methods of communication."

"We can always communicate with gestures," Walker pointed out.

"*If* the locals have limbs," George put in, choosing to overlook the fact that his kind were similarly lacking in such useful accoutrements as an opposable thumb.

"*Couhgh,*" the astronomer rasped. Ear-grating Niyyuuan expressions were, if anything, even harsher sounding to the human ear than their wince-inducing language. "We may yet have to resort to something that basic. But to do so means must have face-to-face contact." Her round, muscular, painted mouth expanded and contracted as she coughed slightly to indicate amusement and her foot-tall, tapering ears inclined in George's direction as she addressed the dog. "*If* the locals have faces."

"If you're talking about sending down a landing party, I'd like to come along," Walker told her.

She returned her attention to him. "Is realized that by historic mutual decision of multiple realms of Niyu that you nominally in command of this expedition, Marcus Walker. However, in lieu of specific recommendation from you or science staff regarding this unusual situation, Commander-Captain Gerlla-hyn already think it best you accompany any landing group." Glancing past him, she eyed the sitting dog. "Also yous three friends, if they so wish."

Walker frowned slightly, not understanding. "Why all of us?"

"Perhaps if this world previously visited by Tuuqalian or K'eremu representatives, locals will recognize and be able to make suggestions toward helping find respective home-worlds that we seeking."

Tongue lolling, George shrugged diffidently. "If it's a nice breathable atmosphere full of interesting smells, I'm game."

"Braouk loves open spaces," Walker put in. "After having been cooped up on this ship for so long, I don't think you could prevent him from coming along. But Sque—I don't know." He cast a meaningful glance in the direction of the port and the planet below. "I see oceans. If a landing site could be chosen that's near a shore, it might help me to convince her to participate."

"Unresponsiveness to our arrival being universal," Sobj-oes replied, all four tails twitching slightly, "I see no reason why cannot select local atmospheric craft port near coast for site of first contact."

"Good." Walker nodded approvingly. "I'll talk to her."

George sucked his teeth. "I'd think the scientific contingent would want to put down near the biggest city."

"Is very interesting," the astronomer told him. "Are no urban concentrations over a certain size. Is as if a limit on such expansion proscribed by local custom." She took the opportunity to peer out the port for herself. "All indications point to a most interesting culture, even if it one that has not pursued interstellar travel."

"Maybe they've tried and just couldn't lick the problem of other-than-light speed," George opined.

"When we meet them," Walker commented with a smile, "we'll have to be sure and ask. Wonder what kind of greeting we'll get?"

Not elevated enough to see out the single port now that Walker was no longer holding him, George could only nod in its direction. "If they're indecisive, you can always cook something up for them," he reminded his gastronomically talented human friend. "It's the same among dogs as among humans: when you go visiting, it's always polite to bring food along."

"Like a bottle of wine," Walker reflected, wishing he had one.

George nodded approvingly. "Or a dead rat," he added, wishing he had one.

Sobj-oes indicated confusion as she fiddled with the translator clipped to her right ear. "Not sure I understanding. No matter." She turned to go. "Notification of time of down-going will be forthcoming. Interpretation of preliminary data suggests climatological requirements to be minimal."

Walker nodded knowingly. "I'll change clothes anyway. Want to look my best. First impressions are always important."

Ussakk was compiling statistics when Eromebb the Assistant rushed in and interrupted the work. The face of the younger male bristled with brown and white fur that had not yet begun to curl downward. Whiskers half the length of Ussakk's stuck straight out to the sides of his short muzzle, stiff as needles. He was breathing hard in the short, quick gasps of his kind and his eyes were wide with a fusion of fear and fascination.

"The Iollth are coming!"

Emitting a soft whistle of acknowledgement, Ussakk turned resignedly away from his work. "That is known. It was too much to expect that they would simply arrive in strength, sit in orbit for a while, and then leave. I as well as others *told* the representatives of the Great Government that failing to respond to their landing requests would not work. You cannot make a threat go away by ignoring it." He whistled again; the equivalent of a soft sigh. "There was no harm in hoping, I suppose. And history teaches us that responding with surface-based weapons only brings immediate reprisal." He gathered himself for the inevitable. "*Where* are they coming?"

"They have signaled their intention to land a small vessel at Pedwath Port. Because of the terrain, much of Pedwath's landing site is constructed atop shallow reclaimed sea bottom. What this signifies, if anything, no one knows."

"It may connote nothing in particular," Ussakk told him. He considered. "Pedwath is on the west coast. I could be there in a couple of hours."

"Less." Eromebb eyed him with the look one reserved for the incubator of a fatal disease. "The Great Government is putting together a team to meet with the invaders, in the hopes of restricting their depredations as much as possible. A police aircraft is already standing by and waiting for you at Therapp Port to transport you to Pedwath." He puffed out his cheeks, a nervous gesture that inflated the lower half of his face to twice normal size. "That is the message I was sent to deliver to you. I'm sorry, Astronomer Ussakk. I've always liked you personally, as well as working with you, and have been proud to labor in the same work-warren."

Rising from his backless seat, Ussakk leaned forward so

that the tips of his whiskers curved toward the younger re-
searcher and lightly brushed his face. "I'm not dead yet,
Eromebb."

In reassuring the other male, Ussakk was expressing a
confidence he did not feel. As near as he could recall from
what relevant history he could remember, few Hyfft survived
personal contact with the Iollth. They had a habit of engaging in killing demonstrations, just to remind the local populace of what they were capable.

Well, except for not having formally bred, he had lived a
good life, marked by professional achievement and relative
contentment. And his lack of a mate meant that he had sired
no offspring, so there were no family or warren connections
there to be broken. No doubt some sharp eye among the authorities charged with putting together a sacrificial pack to
meet the initial wave of Iollth had noticed that and had taken
it into consideration. Coupled with the fact that Ussakk had
been the first to track the incoming ships, it made him ideal
for the purpose.

The farewells of his coworkers at the observatory were
marked by strong feelings. Plainly, they did not expect to
ever see him again. Not all was emotion and angst, however.
Among the tears and touchings and uneasy tail twitchings
were hopeful, even desperate requests for him to do his best
to try to mollify the Iollth. Perhaps, if the sacrificial greeting
pack was inordinately persuasive, the invaders might confine
their traditional demonstrative rampaging to the west coast
of Vinen-Aq, and depart satisfied with the tribute and plunder they would demand. In that event, the rest of Hyff would
be spared all but the cost of cleaning up afterward.

He was understandably distracted as an official conveyor
bore him toward the airport. His escort, consisting of two police, said nothing, concentrating their attention on attaining
the highest safe speed possible. All other traffic, from commercial to individual, was efficiently shunted aside to allow
the law enforcement conveyor to rocket past. He had not even

been given time to pack. No doubt the authorities who had consigned him to the greeting party had not bothered to take that into consideration.

After all, a dead Hyfft would have no need of personal paraphernalia that would only be left behind.

As he was rushed through the small terminal reserved for official business, there were few who did not turn to regard him with a mixture of hope and pity. He wanted to speak out, to reassure them, to settle their nerves in the traditional communal Hyfftian manner. Unable to ease himself, there was no way he could reassure them. The best he could do was try to project an aura of calm and not add to the already widespread sense of hopelessness.

Much to his credit, he did not throw up until he was on the aircraft.

Little more than an hour later, he arrived in Pedwath with nothing on his back and little in his belly. Officials were there to meet him and escort him to the terminal that had been chosen as the site of contact. There was no mistaking the sense of growing dread among everyone he passed. Fear permeated the air like farts. Glimpses beyond the corridor down which he was being hustled showed no activity outside.

"Ever since it was determined that the Iollth planned on landing here first," the female on his right informed him in response to his query, "all public facilities were immediately shut down. Historians said they would not put it past the invaders to shoot down any and every aircraft within abovecurvature range of their spacecraft. So none have departed Pedwath Port since notification was received." Moving closer, she lowered her voice to a conspiratorial chitter.

"The government is releasing only meager amounts of information. Some reports say there is only one Iollth ship. Others say a dozen." Dark eyes beseeched him. "You are Ussakk the Astronomer. Ussakk the Revealer."

"There are three ships." No one had told him not to speak on the subject, nor did he see any reason to withhold so basic a piece of information. Everyone would know the details soon enough. "Not many."

"Too many," the female officer responded. "Three. I'd hoped it was only one. Are they very big?"

"Big enough," he admitted.

"We are here," she announced, suddenly resuming her official demeanor. But despite her best efforts she could not completely hide her anxiety. No one could.

The assembly-warren he was introduced into was already crowded. A few of those present wore senior police uniforms, the Hyfft having no military. They had no need for one. Nor was it a problem.

Except when the Iollth arrived.

Among those not in uniform Ussakk recognized several prominent scientists. There were also a few community representatives from across Vinen-Aq. Whether they were volunteers or had been ordered to participate by the Great Government he had no way of knowing, though he fully intended to ask.

As he was handed a two-piece translator, one part to drape around his short neck and the other to insert into an ear, a distinctive face jumped out at him. White of fur as well as whisker, bent forward at the upper spine like a cub's mistreated toy, Yoracc the Historian was struggling to insert his translator's receiver into his left ear. Ussakk moved to assist.

"Allow me, honored elder." Carefully, he worked the small, silvery unit into the older Hyfft's hearing organ.

"Thank you." Eyes once replaced regarded him thoughtfully. "You are Ussakk the Astronomer, who first detected the Iollth intrusion."

Ussakk chirruped an affirmative. "I would have preferred it had been someone else."

"We all have our preferences," the historian agreed, "which are now to be ignored. Albeit that it is all secondhand and gleaned from historical records, I am here because of my knowledge of Iollth conduct and behavior." His whiskers trembled slightly but were no longer capable of rising or pointing. "Your presence I find less understandable."

Ussakk whistled softly. "As the bearer of bad news, I suspect that this is my reward. More logically, the authorities must believe I have something to contribute."

Yoracc snorted, both nostrils curling slightly up and backward toward his face. "Sacrificial distraction. You have just arrived?"

The astronomer chirruped an affirmative. "I was rushed out of Therapp without even a chance to settle my personal affairs."

The older male blew empty air. "It was much the same with me, though I am no longer so easily rushed." Raising a short arm, he gestured not at the crowd that milled about within the warren but at the sweeping transparency that revealed the first fringes of urbanization beyond the outer limits of the airport. "It has been bad here. The Overwatch authority has done its best, and is to be commended for doing so, but there was still considerable panic. There were injuries; some serious, all impolite. I would imagine it is ongoing. You did not see evidence of it?" Almost instantly, he answered his own question.

"No, you wouldn't, having arrived directly by aircraft. I am told there is an assortment of some damage within the city itself, but the greatest harm has come from those utilizing conveyors who in their panic have strayed from the designated, marked routes. Without sensors to guide them, they have slammed at high speed into fixed objects as well as one another." His unhappiness showed in his face, in the way in which his ears and whiskers drooped all the way forward. "Already the Iollth have caused many deaths, and they have not yet even arrived."

As fretful, restless chatter rose and fell around them, Ussakk and the historian spent a moment commiserating in silence. "What is it we are expected to do?" the astronomer finally asked. "What does the Great Government want of us?"

"You mean, besides serving ourselves up as an initial sac-rifice, in the event the Iollth should arrive in a foul mood?" Plainly, Yoracc the Historian held no illusions about the probable fate that was in store for him. "I imagine we are ex-pected to find out exactly what they want and to try to mini-mize it. Fortunately, if any part of this can be said to be fortunate, precedence provides us with reasonably clear guidelines. The modern history of Hyff records six separate Iollth incursions. Although serious harm was inflicted each time, it was in direct proportion to the degree of defiance our kind offered." Accepting a drink pipe from a passing auto-mated server, he waved it in the general direction of the eerily deserted airfield beyond the curving transparency.

"Since it has been decided by the present Great Govern-ment to offer as little resistance as possible, we may be ex-pected to avoid the worst of Iollth depredations. That there will still be some, history also shows us." With an effort, his whiskers fluttered slightly upward, a sure sign of impending sarcasm. "They have an apparent fondness for reminding the Hyfft what they are capable of inflicting, if our people should be so obstinate as to annoy them."

Ussakk brooded, though not for long. The Hyfft tended not to dwell in moodiness. "How bad will it be, do you think?"

The historian blinked several times in rapid succession; a visual shrug. "That, I am afraid, history does not tell us. The Iollth are not wholly predictable. Certainly some Hyfft will die. Whether the number will eventually be countable on one hand or whether a calculator will be needed to render the final tally, only time, luck, and diplomatic skill will tell."

Having nothing more to ask, and finding the conversa-tion's direction wearing more and more on his spirit, Ussakk bade the senior historian farewell and moved off to a corner of the room that allowed him to press his nose and whiskers up against the curving transparency. Like all such, it was flexible, and allowed him to push his face slightly into it. When he drew back, a slight bas-relief of his visage briefly remained, a rapidly shrinking echo of his appearance. In a little while, it was entirely possible that he would be disappeared just as quickly, and efficiently. He raised his eyes to the clear, blue sky of Hyff.

Most of all, he would miss seeing the stars.

"It all go crazy below."

Sobj-oes strode alongside Walker, her long legs (though not as long as Viyv-pym's, Walker reflected) easily maintaining the pace as they headed for the big cargo shuttle that would carry the landing party down to the surface. George trotted confidently alongside his human. As for Sque and Braouk, they had preceded the two Terrans and were awaiting departure.

"Surface imaging show clear signs of population abandoning not just area of selected landing site, but entire city. Several fires also breaking out." Wide yellow-gold eyes gazed into his much smaller brown ones. "Evidence of widespread panic is compelling."

"Must be us," George commented blithely. "We'll soon straighten them out. They'll relax as soon as they learn that all we want to take away from here is directions."

"Possibly." Walker was trying to make sense of the astronomer's words as they turned into the shuttle bay access corridor. "I wonder if they react like this every time a visiting spacecraft arrives in their system."

"Maybe they don't get many visitors." George effortlessly hopped over a conduit rise in the floor. "They haven't exactly been welcoming. If they don't want company, you'd think somebody down below would at least have the courtesy to ask us to get lost."

"They may not think they're in a position to do so. After all, insofar as Gerlla-hyn's staff has been able to determine, they have no space-going capability of their own." When trading commodities, he reflected, those unable to make a purchase sensibly kept the inability to themselves. You didn't advertise weakness.

But weakness was one thing, the kind of regional panic the Niyyuu were observing from orbit another matter entirely. Something else had gripped the denizens of the planet below.

Well, if the locals wouldn't communicate with ships in orbit, perhaps they'd be more inclined to do so in person.

Commander-Captain Gerlla-hyn was taking no chances. As preliminary surveys had shown, the natives were technologically advanced. Just because they had thus far shown themselves to be noncommunicative didn't mean they were helpless, much less friendly. As nominal "commander" of the expedition, Walker had reluctantly agreed that under such confusing circumstances it was always more sensible to deal from a position of strength. So the landing party would disembark armed, in the hope that there would be no shooting but in the realization that anything was possible.

Sque had tried to veto the decision. "There is always the danger our appearance may be misconstrued by the no doubt equally primitive locals, and result in a typically primal aggressive reaction." Her silver-gray eyes had squinted even tighter than normal. "There is also the fact that the Niyyuuan warriors who accompany this expedition are overly eager to make use of modern weaponry, having been on their own benighted world restricted to the use of ancient and traditional devices."

But the K'eremu was overruled, both by Gerlla-hyn and Walker. Better for their appearance to be misconstrued than to be subject to a fatal ambush. Despite the signs of apparent panic below, it was possible the city was being cleared of its population to save it from an anticipated battle. George, certainly, understood that the Niyyuuan Commander-Captain could not take chances.

"You don't trot into another dog's territory wearing a muzzle," the mutt had declared firmly.

Commander-Captain Gerlla-hyn was not among those

slated for the landing party, Walker noted as he entered the big shuttle. Besides himself and his friends, Sobj-oes was present, as were several Niyyuu who had been to other worlds such as Seremathenn. There was the agreed-upon contingent of warriors, all of whom had volunteered to participate in the great expedition. And the appointed (perhaps anointed would have been a better term) representatives of the worldwide media of Niyu, chattering hoarsely and expectantly among themselves as they prepared to record the encounter for later broadcast to enthralled viewers back home.

Assuming they got back home, Walker found himself thinking. In its scope and expectations, no Niyyuu had ever envisioned anything like this attempt to return himself and his friends to their respective homeworlds. Unlike their heroic hosts, he and George, Sque and Braouk, had nothing to lose by trying.

Maybe, with luck, we'll all get home, he mused as he found a too-narrow Niyyuuan seat and tried his best to secure himself firmly for the coming descent. But he had been away for so long now, several years, that that hope grew fainter by the day.

Luck would be needed, he knew, if the seemingly unsettled sentients whose acquaintance they were about to make were going to be of any help at all in that increasingly desperate quest.

Sobj-oes settled herself into the landing seat beside him.

"Still no response from below?" he asked halfheartedly.

Something powerful *whanged* far behind them and the shuttle shuddered slightly. "Nothing," the visibly bemused astronomer told him. "Latest observations confirm locals continue to stream out of city. I am told by military people that it almost as if they expecting an attack. But if not talk to us, how can they find out we only here to ask questions of their astronomers, try some restocking of edible organics, and let Niyyuu who have been confined within ships stretch legs on planetary surface?"

Conversation ceased briefly while the shuttle disengaged and dropped out of the main ship's bay. Artificial gravity faded. There were no ports, but heads-up views of their destination drifted throughout the main cabin, available for anyone to scrutinize.

"You don't think maybe that they're planning to ambush us when we land?" Walker found the awkward possibility unsettling. He was not armed, and unlike on Niyu, any hostile action here would involve weapons embodying more destructive potential than the traditional Niyyuuan swords and arrows.

"In absence of communication, is imperative not begin relationship with miscommunication," she told him. "But must be ready for anything." She waved a twin-digited hand at the image floating in the air before her. "If left up to us, I and fellow scientists would make landing without weapons. As would attached official representatives of media of Niyu. But we not charged with responsibility for protecting and preserving this expedition. Commander-Captain Gerlla-hyn is, and he not send contact force into unknown situation without suitable protection."

Peering around the sizable compartment, Walker noted the presence of two dozen volunteer troops drawn from the many semi-independent realms of Niyu. They had been fitted out with modern arms and body armor—a considerable change from what they were used to using against one another in the traditional realm-against-realm battles that supplied both entertainment and political sway on their homeworld. As only the best had been chosen to accompany the expedition, he had no doubt they were proficient in the use of such arms.

Were their counterparts awaiting their arrival on the planet below? And if so, were they prepared to shoot first and query later? He tried to convince himself that was unlikely. Intelligent species, he had learned, tended not to shoot on sight, but to talk first. To seek commonalities rather than differences.

Hostilities were expensive. One had to have sound economic reasons to make war rather than peace.

Besides, unless the survey that had been ongoing ever since the Niyyuuan force had arrived in the system had been badly mismanaged, the inhabitants of the world below had not traveled beyond their own atmosphere, much less between star systems. Surely that put them at a disadvantage in matters military. It was akin to one football team playing another without shoes. Range, mobility, and tactical options were greatly reduced.

The shuttle shuddered as it entered atmosphere, its descent guided by automatics and only monitored by the pilots on board. Chatter among the soldiers that had been almost constant since his arrival began to fade. The Niyyuu were not afraid of fighting, but any sentient was sensible to worry about the unknown.

Hovering before him, the three-dimensional heads-up view of clouds gave way to green rolling terrain tinged here and there with fields of yellow and brown. In places, hills gave way to mountains, none of them daunting. The shuttle passed high over several small cities, none comparable in extent to the larger municipalities of Niyu, far less the extensive modern conurbations of advanced Seremathenn. The shuttle's combat gear was fully activated, but nothing gave chase, nothing tried to bring them down. The nearest anything came to interfering with their descent was a flock of thousands of small winged creatures that appeared on the heads-up as brown-bodied dots. The shuttle flew through and past them far too fast for its external sensors to resolve individual zoological details.

Then they were over ocean and slowing rapidly. A number of watercraft of appealing and functional design flashed by beneath. Once, something large and streamlined burst from the water and glided for an unlikely distance above the surface before sinking once more beneath the waves. Walker saw little evidence of foam. Perhaps the water oceans of this world were less salty than those of home. Thinking of foamless waves made him remember lazy days spent on Lake Michigan. He forced them from his mind.

A voice sounded in the compartment, apprising them of their imminent arrival. The shuttle struck ground, slid some distance on its specially treated skids, and came to a halt. The heads-up showed their immediate surroundings: open tarmac, buildings not far away, a few multi-winged parked aircraft of local design. For a while after that, nothing.

Then the view displayed on the heads-up shifted toward one multi-story structure. Figures were beginning to emerge, approaching the motionless landing craft. As Walker stared at them, intrigued by the short, single-garmented shapes, George nudged his leg. From the seat alongside his human, the strapped-in canine nodded at his own heads-up.

"Kind of cuddly-looking, as aliens go," the dog observed. "Except for the guns they're carrying."

3

Ussakk stared at the alien vessel. Its dimensions loomed all the more impressive when one realized that it was but a fraction of the size of the smallest of the three great starships that were in orbit high overhead. It did not help knowing that had his kind chosen to make the effort, their technological prowess was probably equal to the task of constructing similar vessels.

Something that was unlikely ever to happen, he knew. The Hyfft were too homebound, too attached to their own comfortable, congenial, familiar world to want to cast themselves out into the vast, cold reaches between the stars. There was no need, the authorities declared whenever such proposals were tentatively put forth by the more audacious members of the scientific community. A waste of time and resources. Besides, even if such craft were designed and built, who would use them?

What it all came down to, Ussakk knew, was that when the Hyfft emerged at night from their sophisticated, technologically advanced warrens and looked up at the curving bowl of the universe, they were both awed and afraid. Over the years, he had learned not to judge his kind too harshly. His profession placed him in that exceptional, small group of individuals who felt differently from the majority.

Besides, he reminded himself, the Hyfft had reason to fear the great darkness. When the universe came calling, it was all too often in the form of the Iollth.

A stirring in the crowd of officials and police caused him to tense. He did not have to look far for the source of the unease. A vertical gash had appeared in the side of the landing craft. Like a tongue from the mouth of hungry *dyaou,* a ramp was descending silently from its base.

The figures that emerged were tall, exceedingly so. Well-formed and comfortingly bipedal, they hurried down the freshly extruded rampway in a manner suggestive of disciplined chaos. Those officials standing close around him chittered nervously and shrank back as the big-eyed aliens raised an assortment of unfamiliar tiny devices. The short, stubby fingers of the Hyfftian police tightened grimly on their weapons.

But if the devices the swiftly descending aliens wielded were weapons, they were quickly trained not on the crowd of greeters but on the very same opening from which their manipulators had just emerged. What peculiar manner of Iollth protocol was this? Ussakk found himself wondering. Surely they were not preparing to shoot their own kind? Perhaps the instruments they were so energetically fingering were not weapons after all, but instead served some other as yet unknown purpose. Signs of further movement appeared in the dark recesses of the alien craft. He inhaled sharply. More figures were emerging from within. Shapes that were far more impressive, regimented, and threatening than the group that had preceded them outside.

Unlike the group that had exited first, these newcomers exposed very little bare flesh. They were almost completely encased in form-fitting, nonreflective material of gray and brown. It looked soft, but Ussakk suspected it was designed to repel all manner of hostile intent. While most of the marchers carried long metallic/plastic devices, two advanced slowly under the burden of large backpacks whose contents were a mystery. The astronomer decided he would be quite content if they were to remain so. He cast a glance in the direction of the police. His own escort was already clearly intimidated, and not a shot had been fired.

Not that he blamed them. The shortest of the arrivals was more than twice the height of the average Hyfft. Though slim of build, they had long, no doubt powerful limbs. Surprisingly, each of these terminated in only two digits while the Hyfft could boast four on each hand and three on each foot. He smiled wryly to himself. A small claim to superiority somewhat mitigated by the fact that the newcomers could each boast of four longish tails to the Hyfft's short, stubby one.

The Hyfftian delegation and the new arrivals faced one another uncomfortably across the narrow stretch of flat pavement. One of the few armored invaders who was not carrying one of the ominous-looking long instruments stepped forward. After surveying the half-paralyzed, half-fascinated delegation, each of whom had mentally and emotionally prepared to have his or her life extinguished at any moment, the visitor removed a small, oblong device from its waist and raised it to mouth level. Proceeding to speak into it, visitor and machine delivered a rising and falling stream of incomprehensible gabble to the bewildered crowd.

Without a doubt it was an attempt at communication. It was also a failure, as none of the specialists in the crowd of onlookers recognized so much as a single word. Even the speech patterns were unfamiliar, the cadences jagged and unfathomable.

As the futile effort continued, Ussakk moved to stand close to Yoracc the Historian and dared to essay a whisper. "Tell me, venerable one: Do you have any idea what the creature is saying?"

The historian replied without hesitation. "Not only do I have no idea what the creature is saying, I must confess that I have no idea what the creature *is*."

To show his confusion, Ussakk blinked speedily several times in succession. He would have accompanied the rapid-fire eye gesture with a sharp chirp-bark of uncertainty, except that it would not be appreciated by those near him and might also be misconstrued by the visitors.

"I'm afraid I don't understand. Do you mean you are unsure if it is a male or female Iollth?"

"I mean," replied the historian testily and a bit too loud, "that I don't know if it's an Iollth. In fact, I am fairly certain it is not."

Ussakk eyed the towering, menacing armed and armored figures arrayed before them. "That makes no sense, honored elder."

"I quite agree, querulous youth. In their weapons and bearing they have the general aspect of Iollth, but I am not senile. I remember quite well the imagery that survives from their previous visits, and while there may be some superficial similarities of size and shape, there is much else that does not conform. To begin with, these are tall and slender, while images of the Iollth show them to be shorter and much more thickly built through the lower portion of their bodies, their legs, and especially their feet."

Ussakk's thoughts were crackling like *betimp* leaves in cooking oil. "Then if they are not Iollth, what can they be?"

"The possibilities are as wide ranging as they are worrying, my young star-gazing friend." The dour historian scratched under his chin, where the hairs had turned as white as his long whiskers. "My first thought, I am afraid, is that they may be something worse than the Iollth."

The astronomer swallowed hard and tried to keep from trembling. "How could that be?"

The older scientist was unrelenting in his speculation. "It could 'be' in many forms. For example, these intimidating visitors could be friends of the Iollth, sent to prepare the way for a later arrival of the Iollth themselves. Or perhaps," he continued morbidly, "the Iollth have informed allies of theirs of the gentle nature of Hyff, have told them what a rich world awaits and how defenseless are its inhabitants."

Accustomed to being surrounded by friends and family, Ussakk found himself being dragged down into the mire of despair by his knowledgeable yet pessimistic companion. Hyfft were by nature buoyant and cheerful. Yoracc was an exception, and not a pleasant one: a grim, brooding, almost bitter store of remembrance. He was also, unfortunately, a realist, Ussakk appreciated. That did not make the elder's listing of possible catastrophes any easier to take.

As if to confirm Yoracc's view of the situation, the lines of heavily armed aliens parted to make way for still more visitors. Though apparently unarmed, they included among their number two creatures who were as different from their predecessors as they were from the Hyfft. One of them was slightly shorter than the alien average, but much, much heavier of build. Other than being bipedal and bisymmetrical, it differed in a bewildering variety of ways from its companions. Interestingly, it displayed five digits on each hand instead of two.

Even more captivating was its companion: a short, quadrupedal, unclothed being covered in ragged fur. Its most notable features were bright black eyes that seemed to miss nothing, and a flat pink appendage that hung loosely over one side of its parted jaws. It too did not appear armed, though its open mouth revealed a set of sharp teeth. Among the Hyfft, intelligence tended to favor slightly smaller individuals. Ussakk wondered if this could be true among the aliens as well.

Then he felt himself being urged forward. Looking to his left, he saw that Yoracc the Historian was also being pushed and shoved in the direction of the alien craft. They were the unhappy recipients of a traditional and concerted community push. In pre-civilized times, such mass compellings were intended to sacrifice those on the outside of a Hyfftian multitude to whatever carnivore happened to be assailing the communal warren. Over time, it had evolved into a time-honored means of thrusting to the forefront those the community felt best qualified to address a particular problem, be it a rampaging untamed carnivore or something more problematical.

In addition to himself and Yoracc, a third individual was being carried forward on the crest of the insistent Hyfftian wave. Fighting to stay on his feet (in ancient times he might have been trampled), Ussakk proffered a hurried introduction.

"I am Mardalm the Linguist," she replied to him over the susurration of shoving and encouraging soft whistling. As she spoke, she fussed with her translator gear, a wearable setup that was far more elaborate than the hastily provided ear-and-chestpiece arrangement that had been given to Ussakk and to the historian. "They expect me to talk to these creatures." With her free hand, she gestured at the aliens they were nearing all too rapidly. "My department was unable to understand their attempts to communicate from orbit. Now they somehow expect me to talk to them in person."

"I know what to do," declared Yoracc blithely from the other side of Ussakk. "Don't make them mad."

Since the historian seemed disinclined to introduce himself to the linguist, Ussakk performed the necessary service. Even in such moments of dire peril, he believed Hyfftian courtesy should remain in force. They might not know who their visitors were, but they should not forget who *they* were, he felt.

Then they were almost upon the first of the creatures, and there was no time left for comforting thoughts.

Close up, the aliens were even more intimidating than they had been from a distance. Stood on end, the weapons many of the creatures carried would be taller than himself. Visitors and Hyfft stood staring at one another. Clearing her throat with a polite *chuff,* Mardalm began speaking through the equipment draped around her upper body. A bizarre assortment of sounds came out of an aural projector. None of them made the slightest sense to Ussakk. Nor, apparently, to the aliens, several of whom exchanged glances while commenting in their own incomprehensible and incredibly harsh-sounding language.

Feeling something against his leg, Ussakk looked down and nearly jumped out of his fur. The undersized, four-legged alien was methodically passing its nostrils over his lower body, sniffing with unconcealed interest. Ignoring the nose, Ussakk remembered the teeth. After analyzing his smell, would this peculiar yet strangely affable creature next decide to sample his taste? And if so, how would, how should, he react? There was something oddly unthreatening about the activity, though Ussakk knew he could not attribute Hyfftian characteristics to a being so utterly alien.

The other singular visitor came forward. Unlike the small quadruped, however, this individual was far more menacing. It loomed over the three resolute if apprehensive Hyfftian scholars, its mass nearly blocking out the sun. When it knelt, they instinctively retreated several steps backward. But it was not reaching for them. Instead, it placed a hand (all five digits were triple-jointed, Ussakk noted) on the spine of the quadruped and began to stroke. Some form of nonverbal communication, the astronomer quickly decided. Was the kneeling creature somehow deciphering the quadruped's observations, or urging it to continue with its examination? A frustrated Ussakk no more knew how to interpret the aliens' gestures than he did their language.

The second alien rose to its full, intimidating height and looked back toward the opening in the vessel from which it had come forth. Ussakk followed its stare, as did his companions. Two more aliens were emerging.

At the sight of them, a number of the assembled dignitaries cast aside any and all pretense at dignity and the need to present a united front in the face of alien challenge. Chittering unashamedly, they broke and ran for the perceived safety of the nearest terminal. Shaken by the sight of what was advancing toward them, the rest of the crowd wavered. Mouth agape, Ussakk could only stare in shocked silence. Mardalm the Linguist reacted similarly. Then, without any warning, Yoracc the Historian broke from his position and ran, too.

Straight toward the newly emerging aliens.

Had he not been frozen to the spot, Ussakk might have tried to reach out and grab the crazy old historian. By the time the notion that he ought to do so bloomed in his brain, the elder was already out of reach, having scrambled forward past both the quadruped and its massive companion. Expecting Yoracc to be squashed flat on the spot, if for no other reason than because he had violated some unknown alien protocol, Ussakk and Mardalm looked on in horrified fascination as the historian came to a halt at the bottom of the access ramp.

Looming above the elder like a monstrous mechanical excavator was something like a nightmare out of an infant's worst dreamings. Two nightmares, if one counted the second creature that rode like a hereditary potentate atop one of the giant's four flexible, tree-like limbs. Both gazed somberly down at the single elderly, diminutive, bewhiskered native biped who had halted before them. Then, without a sound, they resumed their descent.

If anything, the already diverse gathering of aliens appeared as confused and uncertain by this improbable confrontation as did Yoracc's fellow Hyfft. There was much stirring on both sides, but neither intervened. The aliens were hardly fearful of anything the lone Hyfft might do, while the assembled dignitaries and representatives of the collective Overwatches of Vinen-Aq could only alternately marvel and gape at the manic boldness of one of their own. The unspoken consensus was that the historian had gone mad. A consequence, perhaps, of advanced age. Or possibly by his exhibition of untenable bravado he was sacrificing himself in a futile attempt to show these allies of the Iollth, or whoever they were, that his kind could not be easily intimidated. A few hands within the crowd fingered weapons, but no more. There was no point in firing until the venerable historian was directly threatened, and by then it might well be too late.

The two monsters—one immense, the other a mass of squirming limbs—halted at the bottom of the ramp. If it was so inclined, the gigantic alien could kill the unmoving, staring Yoracc simply by stepping on him. Instead, it sank down on its four supporting limbs, the better to bring its frightening tooth-lined vertical jaws closer to the historian. The better to converse, an edgy Ussakk wondered tensely, or to consume?

Yoracc proceeded to sputter something in a strange singsong voice. The giant's reaction was immediate. In a far deeper voice, it responded. At the same time, the bizarre being it held aloft with one upper limb writhed its own coils. After several dumbfounding moments of this mystifying vocal byplay, the historian turned and shouted to Mardalm. Despite Ussakk's hurried attempt to restrain her, she responded by rushing forward to join the historian. Revealingly, her attitude was one not of fear but of expectation and even delight.

More impenetrable droning ensued between the two Hyfft and the two aliens. All of it without, a captivated Ussakk noted, the use of Hyfft translators. If the aliens possessed similar devices, they were so small as to not be visible. This went on for some time until the visiting Delineator of the northern city of Andatt spoke up from within the depths of the thoroughly mesmerized crowd.

"If it would not be too much trouble," she blurted loudly, "could the honorable historian and noted linguist let the rest of Hyff know what is going on?"

Yoracc turned while Mardalm continued the animated conversation, for that surely was what was taking place. "Hyfft! Know that this imposing organism standing before you is not Iollth, nor an ally of the Iollth, nor even a passing friend of the Iollth. Neither it nor its associate being nor any of their consorts has ever even heard of the Iollth. Or, for that matter, of Hyff. I myself only finally recognized it from old records. It is a representative of a species that has previously visited our world. Only once, and then many year-days ago. His kind, and it is a he, came this way as explorers and traders. Visitors with whom our ancestors exchanged kind words. That visit took place well before this one's time as well as before yours and mine, so just as we did not immediately recognize him, he did not recognize us." He gestured to his left, where Mardalm hardly paused to look away from her conversation.

"Mardalm the Linguist has the record of their language. But there is only one of these creatures, a Tuuqalian, among the crews of the three vessels that currently orbit Hyff. Those who dominate them are called Niyyuu, a race that until now has been unknown to us. And until recently, I am informed, the Tuuqalia were unknown to them." As he spoke, he was gesturing energetically with both short arms. "Therefore, in all their attempts to contact us from space, the Niyyuu never thought to try the language of Tuuqalia. Never having visited here himself, and not knowing that his own kind had done so long ago, this lone Tuuqalian saw no reason to suggest that the Niyyuu do so."

Pivoting, Yoracc turned away from the intimate conference and back toward the milling crowd. As they slowly digested the historian's knowledgeable and reassuring words, their fear began to give way to curiosity.

"Your translator units are all interleafed with one another as well as with the omnipresent broadcast control. If you will set them so"—and he proceeded to detail the very simple, basic instructions—"the indicators to allow you to receive and speak through your devices in the language of Tuuqalia will be provided." He looked back toward the busy Mardalm. "I am certain that the means to do so in Niyyuuan also will be forthcoming."

Even as he worked to adjust his own equipment, Ussakk

was advancing toward the historian, gesturing as he did so. "What then of these other aliens? They are manifestly neither Niyyuu nor Tuuqalia. Nor for that matter is the many-limbed creature the Tuuqalian carries."

Yoracc chirped acknowledgement. "One is called a human; the small quadruped a canine, or dog. They are citizens of still another world that is unknown to us, as is that of the K'eremu that rides high upon the Tuuqalian's limb." Black eyes gleamed. "I am as curious as you to know why there is only one of each of them among this general crewing of Niyyuu. Unless, of course, there are more of them aboard the ships in orbit."

A wave of sound made them both turn. Unlike anything either of them had ever heard, it was at once sonorous and soothing. It boomed and rolled across the tarmac, washing over the assembled luminaries of Vinen-Aq in waves of deep, droning noise. Having set his translator unit according to Yoracc's instructions, Ussakk found he could understand the words contained within the drone. Braouk had chosen that moment to recite part of a saga, and it left his newest audience simultaneously stunned and rapt.

Those who did not cover their ears or disconnect their translators, that is.

It was quite a sight to see Braouk lumbering toward the terminal building, surrounded by locals above whom he towered like Godzilla over Tokyo. Walker had to smile. Several of them chattered concurrently at him as he and George trailed in the wake of the big Tuuqalian and the leaders of the Niyyuuan landing team. Who would have thought, he mused as he strode along, that the one language visitors and locals would stumble upon as a commonality for conversation would be Tuuqalian? If the price of mutual understanding was having to listen to Braouk repeatedly recite, it was one he and his companions would have to pay.

Once the initial contact confusion had been cleared up, he

found himself abashed at hearing of the effect he and his friends had had on the locals. Setting down with the intent of only asking a few questions, they had inadvertently terrified the entire population. The reason for this had all been explained by the native called Yoracc the Historian. In turn, researchers among the Niyyuu were able to reconfirm that they knew nothing of the species the locals referred to as the Iollth. From the time the Niyyuuan craft had first entered the Hyff system, it had all been a case of mistaken identity, compounded by the fact that the Hyfft were not space-traversing and knew nothing of sentient species save those that had visited their world.

With everything now clarified, a wave of relief had spread swiftly around the planet. Inquisitiveness had replaced alarm. The immensely relieved Hyfft now wished to learn everything there was to know about their genial visitors. There were to be presentations, feasts, official welcomings. Everyone wanted to greet the travelers, to show them the hospitality of the Hyfft, and to meet them in person. At the very least, Walker realized, they would have no trouble refreshing their ships' stores here. Spared the expected devastation and destruction, their new hosts were almost embarrassingly eager to please.

While expansive by Hyfftian standards, the terminal's interior ceilings were barely high enough to allow Braouk to stand without bending. Even so, he had to watch where he walked. If he grew forgetful, there were always Sque's insults to remind him. The Hyfft were as fascinated by her as by the Tuuqalian who carried her. Choosing to interpret their curiosity as appropriate adoration, the K'eremu was correspondingly content.

As for Walker and George, they found themselves surrounded by chattering Hyfft. So fast did their hosts talk that both sides had to be reminded to wait for their respective translating devices to catch up. It was during one of the brief interludes in these ongoing friendly interrogations that Sobj-

oes managed to make her way through the crowd of Niyyuu
and now welcoming local dignitaries to confront man and
dog. Her great yellow-golden eyes were shining and her neck
frill was not only fully erect, but flush with blood. Visibly,
she was more than a little excited about something.

She wasted no time in sharing the cause. "Is great news for
yous, friends Marcus and George." Turning slightly, she gestured with one limber arm at the milling mob of chattering
sentients. "Was long odds to find place where one of yous
kind was known. Came this way hoping. Now hopes is
confirmed. This indeed region of space where mention of
Tuuqalia was sourced. Now we find world where Tuuqalian
species has actually visited. I have made acquaintance of local
called Ussakk. Is astronomer like myself. He will arrange
meeting with others of his kind. With luck, may actually be
able generate a vector between this system and that of yous
companion Braouk!" Her frill bobbed up and down with her
excitement. "Is this not great news?"

"Yeah, great." Somehow, George was unable to muster the
same degree of enthusiasm that was being exhibited by the
Niyyuuan astronomer. "I don't suppose they've ever heard of
Earth?"

All four of Sobj-oes's tails drooped as one. "Are only just
beginning to converse with these people. Do not be so quick
to give up hope. Must provide what details we have of yous
home and yous kinds to local scientific establishment."
Looking over the top of the crowd, an effortless task for any
tall Niyyuu, she located Braouk and the tentacle-waving
Sque. "Needs to do same for the K'eremu. Relax your frills
and . . . hope that best possible news may yet be forthcoming."

In lieu of an immediate response to their promising in-
quiries, what *was* forthcoming was the kind of hospitality
Walker and his companions had not experienced since their
sojourn on Seremathenn. As soon as word spread around the

planet that the arriving starships were crewed not by plundering Iollth but by friendly travelers, one of whom was a member of a species whose trading ancestors had actually called at Hyff long ago, the collective sigh of relief was almost strong enough to perturb the atmosphere. What ensued was a battle (a courteous one, of course, this being the Hyfft) among different regions and Overwatches to see who would be allowed to play host to the visitors.

In the end, unable to decide among several deserving locales, the authorities used precedence as an out, and chose to house the visitors where they had landed, on the outskirts of Therapp. Conscious of the honor that had been bestowed upon them, the inhabitants of the city and its surrounding agricultural provinces threw themselves into the opportunity to show off their region. Not at the expense of others, however. To have done so would have been distinctly un-Hyfftian.

A goods warehouse was immediately cleared and proper accommodations, insofar as the Hyfft understood them, were thrown together with an efficiency and skill that left the visitors more than a little impressed. It was necessary to adapt the warehouse because, with the exception of the single K'eremu and one lone dog, none of the visitors could squeeze through the opening of a Hyfftian warren even by bending.

Nothing seemed to faze their hosts, Walker marveled as he considered the results of their hasty efforts. Not even a need to fashion temporary furniture to accommodate not one but five different body plans.

When their makeshift quarters were ready, it was left to Walker and his friends to decide, in concert with Commander-Captain Gerlla-hyn and his staff, if they should actually make use of them.

"The decision whether linger here or not rest with yous," he told Walker and his friends. "This yous journey. I and my crews charged with conveying yous where and when yous desire. We will comply with your decision in this matter."

George was all for continuing on as soon as possible. So was Sque, who thought no more of the accommodating Hyfft than she did of any species that had the misfortune to be not-K'eremu. But Braouk found himself rather taken by their eager, would-be hosts, not to mention their ability to tolerate and even enjoy his interminable recitations. As for Walker, he confessed to taking pleasure from just walking on solid ground again, beneath a clear and open sky (if one that was a bit more yellow than usual) instead of the hard, cold ceiling of a ship corridor.

Furthermore, it was clear that their hosts were eager for them to stay awhile. They were almost painfully grateful that the visitors were something, anything, other than Iollth, and wished to have the chance to express those feelings. From years of trading on the Exchange, Walker was nothing if not sensitive to the need of others to express gratitude. He considered.

There was no rush to be on their way. Earth, K'erem, and certainly Tuuqalia would not change their positions—assuming the Niyyuuan astronomers led by Sobj-oes and her Hyfftian counterparts could actually locate any of them.

The scientists needed time to do their work. Despite Gerlla-hyn's assertions, Walker suspected that if polled, the Niyyuuan crews of the three ships would have voted en masse for the interstellar equivalent of shore leave.

"I think it would be a good thing all around if we stayed here awhile," he told the Commander-Captain.

Gerlla-hyn's verbal acknowledgement of Walker's response was terse and formal—but from the way his frill erected and his tails coiled, Walker knew that the Commander-Captain was as pleased as anyone by the human's decision.

It was two days later, after they had been installed in their hastily but stylishly modified temporary quarters, that Walker encountered Sque sitting alone in the rain outside the building. Since even Hyfftian commercial-industrial areas were artfully landscaped, there were tri-trunked tree things and a

peculiar reddish-gold brush all around. Woven more than excavated, a small stream caressed the northern edge of the
warehouse boundary. That was where he found the K'eremu.

She was sitting in the shallow stream, letting it flow over
her ten limbs, her upper body erect and clear of the cooling,
moistening water. She did not even care if it carried industrial effluents or agricultural runoff. Under the dark sky, her
maroon skin glistened almost black. Closed when he appeared, her recessed, silvery eyes opened at his approach.
Even today's selection of the brightly colored bits of metal
and ceramic that decorated her person seemed unusually
subdued.

Making his way carefully down the slick side of the em-
bankment, he halted just beyond the edge of the lapping
water and crouched, the better to bring himself closer to eye
level with her.

"What do *you* want?" Her tone, as conveyed through the
Vilenjji implant in his head, struck him as even more bitter
than usual. There were overtones, he thought, of depression.

"Just checking on you," he replied. "This is a new world,
after all."

"A harmless world," she hissed. "While of moderate intelligence, the inhabitants are inoffensive to the point of banal-
ity. I am in no danger here." She did not thank him for his
concern. Nor, knowing her as well as he did now, did he expect her to.

Even the rain here was agreeable, he decided. Warm and
refreshing; not cold, not stinging. "Enjoying the water?" he
asked conversationally.

Since she could not twist her upper body far enough
around, she had to turn to face him, her limbs utilizing the
purchase they held on the smooth rocks that lined the bottom
of the manicured stream.

"I would have preferred to remain by the local sea. But it is
best we all stay together. More important for you than for me."

"I agree," he said, hoping to mollify her. One hand gestured at the stream. "What are you doing? Just moistening up?"

She looked away from him. "I am lamenting. Quietly. Or at least, I was until you showed up."

"Sorry," he told her, genuinely apologetic. "What's wrong?"

This time when she looked back over at him, her horizontal pupils had expanded to their fullest extent. "What's wrong? What's *wrong*?" From her tone, it was apparent that his comment had finally exceeded even her capacity for sardonic reply. Nevertheless, she tried.

"I am alone, lost with and wholly dependent upon inferior beings. I have none to engage in intelligent discourse with, none with whom to debate issues of real importance. Never again will I be enfolded in the soothing, damp embrace of K'erem."

Her manifest misery was so palpable that had it been expressed by anyone other than the redoubtable Sque, Walker would have been moved to tears. As a visual expression of sympathy, they would have been ineffective in the rain anyway.

"This doesn't sound like you, Sque. Well, not entirely like you. You've always shown so much confidence in our chances, even when it seemed we were going to be stuck on Seremathenn for the rest of our lives."

Alien though they were, those metallic gray eyes could still convey the emotion that lay behind them. "And you've thought all along that I believed that. Lesser lifeforms are so easily deceived." Her tentacles stirred sand from the streambed. "Such expressions of sanguinity as I may have declaimed over the past years were for your benefit, and that of your companion and that saga-spinning oaf of a Tuuqalian. Since you have all been necessary to my survival, it was necessary that I keep your own feeble, faltering spirits up." She looked away, down the stream that did not lead to home.

"I have from the beginning never been anything other than realistic about our chances. I believe you yourself, in your simple, uncomplicated way, are equally aware of that reality."

He refused to be disheartened by her despair. He knew nothing of other K'eremu, but this one, at least, he knew was subject to wild mood swings. Rather than go on the defensive, he tried as best he could to raise her spirits.

"Essentially, then, every expression of hope you've put forth has been for our benefit. I'm surprised you'd be so concerned for our mental welfare, even if such efforts were self-centered at heart."

"I am equally surprised," she retorted. "It is a sign of my advancing weakness in the face of utter despondency. I am losing my true K'eremu nature." Tilting back her head and upper body in a single, supple curve, she regarded the benign but leaden sky. Rain fell in her open eyes, but did not affect her. "I will never get home. You will never get home. It is possible, just possible, that the Tuuqalian will get home—if these chittering, chattering, childlike natives with mild pretensions to intelligence can actually coordinate their primitive science with that of the only slightly less primitive Niyyuu. But you and I? We will never see our respective homeworlds again, except in dreams."

They were both silent then, the only sound the tap-patter of gentle rain falling on and around them, plinking out piccolo notes in the mild flow of the stream. After several minutes of mutual contemplation of time, selves, and the alien yet comforting elements, Walker rose from his crouch, scrambled and slid down into the shallow brook, and sat down alongside the startled Sque. When he reached out an arm toward her—a heavy, human, inflexible, bone-supported arm—she started to flinch back. He waited until she was ready. Then he let his arm come down. Since she had no shoulders, and her upper body was one continuous smooth shape from head to lower torso, he let it rest against the place where two of her ropy limbs joined to her body. She did not move it away.

Later, two more of her own appendages writhed around
and came to rest atop his wet, hirsute arm. He did not move
them away.

With nothing better to do at the moment, George went
looking for his friend. It took a while and several exchanges
with busy (were they always so busy? the dog wondered)
Hyfft before he was directed to a drainage canal outside the
converted warehouse.

Through the steady but tranquil drizzle he finally saw
them, sitting side by side in the middle of the drainage ditch,
Walker's arm around the base of the K'eremu, a couple of
Sque's serpentine limbs lying across the man's arm. The dog
watched them for a moment, pausing only once to shake accumulated rain from his shaggy coat. Not knowing what was
going on but deciding in any case not to interrupt, he turned
and trotted back toward the dry shelter of the big warehouse.
He would find out what it was all about later. Walker would
tell him, whether he wanted to know the details or not.

Meanwhile, if nothing else, at least the acid-tongued,
barely tolerable, know-it-all ten-legs had finally discovered
the one thing humans were really good for.

4

Artfully efficient though they were, it still took the Hyfft several days to properly prepare an appropriate greeting for their unexpected but most welcome multi-species visitors. While the initial, hastily adapted warehouse was continuously upgraded to provide better temporary living quarters for the guests, a second structure nearby underwent feverish preparations for use as a center of celebration. Most pleased of all by these developments were the ever-active agents of the Niyyuuan media, who found kindred spirits (if not equivalent fanatics) among those Hyfft charged with relaying the details of the forthcoming gathering to the rest of their utterly engrossed society.

Inexpressibly relieved to learn that the newcomers were neither Iollth nor allies of the anticipated marauders, and in fact had never heard of them, the population of Hyff prepared to put forth the very best of their ancient, extensive, and admirable culture. The best singers and callers were flown in from all across the multiple continents, while specialist chefs made preparations to provide the visitors with the finest local victuals their systems could tolerate. In this Walker found himself, once again, something of a minor celebrity. Nominal leader of the expedition or not, he possessed gustatory expertise that was in constant demand by those seeking to satisfy the appetites of Niyyuu, Tuuqalian, K'eremu, and canine alike. He almost forgot to request certain foods for himself.

The Hyfft being strict vegetarians limited his input somewhat, but he was still able to surprise their hosts with some of the tricks of which the modern culinary technology he had mastered was capable. So it was that he found himself simultaneously enjoying the fruits of Hyfftian cuisine while helping to prepare it. It was more real work than had been required of him since they had left orbit around Niyu.

He enjoyed every bit of it immensely.

For one thing, the Hyfft were not only easy to work with, they were a delight to be around. Averaging a meter in height, with rounded furry bodies and darting black eyes, they reminded him of active bear cubs, though with saturnine faces, complex attire, and dexterous four-fingered hands and three-toed feet. They acceded readily to his suggestions. Nor was the exchange of culinary information exclusively one-way.

The official festivities, which local media broadcast around the globe and contented Niyyuuan monitors recorded with barely restrained glee, began on a worldwide holiday that the current (and much relieved) planetary Delineator had just established by executive fiat. It was to continue for an entire local four-day. Work did not stop entirely, but there was no question the locals were enjoying the unprecedented celebration at least as much as the visitors. Rotating crews by thirds allowed every Niyyuuan technician, soldier, and general crewmember to enjoy a day of it while also participating in basic ground leave. It was something to see one of the slender, graceful, two-meter-tall Niyyuu loping lithely through Therapp surrounded by an aurora of adoring, awestruck locals.

Sated with celebration, Walker and George decided to take some time to trek the city's extensive botanical gardens. These were garlanded with a riot of alien growth that, other than containing a passing affection for the local variety of photosynthesis, were more different from the flora they were familiar with back home than a saguaro was from a sequoia. Taking the tour also allowed them to bring along their own food. After three days of nonstop ingesting of vegetable matter, no matter how superbly prepared, omnivore human and carnivore canine both craved meat. Or at least, meat products. By not attending the day's festivities, they were able to enjoy food from their ship without offering insult to the Hyfftian population at large.

Among their guides (or handlers, as George continued to insist on referring to them) were the astronomer Ussakk, the linguist Mardalm, and a senior, darkly furred government representative who went by the euphonious moniker of Sehblidd.

Trotting alongside the diminutive civil servant made George look bigger than he was. "So tell me, Sehby: What are these Iollth really like and how often do they show up to pick on your kind?"

The bureaucrat's eyes were deeper set than those of the majority of Hyfft, giving him an atypically severe appearance that was belied by his effusive personality. The subject of George's inquiry, however, was enough to dampen his customary enthusiasm. Brushing past a grove of diminutive trees, whose brown trunks were striated with startling streaks of bright orange, he considered how best to respond.

"They are a terrible folk." The delegate's tone was devoid of the usual cheerful chirps that characterized Hyfftian speech. "Of course, I myself have thankfully never actually seen one. The last Iollth raid on Hyff occurred before the time of my birth." Breaking off from a protruding branch what appeared to be a four-petaled flower but was actually more lichen-like, he inhaled its sharp fragrance and passed it along to Walker. Tentatively, the human sniffed the odd-looking growth and was rewarded with a noseful of tingling bouquet not unlike crushed pepper.

"It is very peculiar," Ussakk put in, joining the conversation. "Though we ourselves shy away from interstellar travel, the economics of it are not difficult to assess. As it seems impossible any raid by a few starships on another developed world could justify the expense incurred in doing so, our mental analysts propose that the Iollth must obtain more than just fiscal profit from their wicked enterprise."

Short arms behind his back, Sehblidd let out a terse whistle of revulsion. "It has been suggested that they make these occasional forays for the purpose of plundering and destroying because something in their racial nature compels them to do so."

"In other words," George observed sagely, "because they enjoy it."

The delegate's whiskers rose noticeably, signifying his agreement. "It's difficult to imagine how any species calling itself civilized can embark on such a vile endeavor. But what other reason could there be?"

"Excuse me for saying so," Walker put in, "but this kind of motivation relates pretty closely to what I do—to what I used to do—for a living. It's been my experience that sometimes individuals or groups will go out of their way to get something, even paying more for it than it's worth, that they can't acquire any other way but that they desperately want."

"Yes, yes." Sehblidd gestured absently. "We know that is the case with certain minerals. At least, we assume it is the case. It is almost too much to imagine that the Iollth would rather cross the void between the stars to obtain something they could otherwise acquire by simple mining."

Tail metronoming as he walked, George shrugged expressively. "Hey, I know a couple of dogs just like to fight. They'd rather steal your food than go find their own. To their way of thinking, it's more rewarding." He glanced up at Walker, then away. "I'm not above snitching somebody else's bone myself, if I can get away with it without losing a piece of ear in the process. Humans, of course, never do anything like that."

"Don't insult me until I've admitted to something," Walker

chided his friend. He looked back at Sehblidd. "Your people have weapons. Advanced ones, from what little I've seen and learned about such things. You have local and planetary entities that are organized to handle law enforcement. Seems to me you could put together an army pretty quick."

Sehblidd tilted his head back to meet the eyes of the much taller human. "It would be counterproductive. Small arms are little use against weapons that can be launched from space. There have been, in the past, discussions about building armed satellites with which to surprise our tormentors. That technology is not beyond us. But the one time we offered armed resistance, we were badly defeated. The consequences were terrible. If we were to try to employ something like mobile, weaponized satellites and even one Iollth ship were to escape such a counterattack, it could rain incalculable destruction down on Hyff that we would not be able to defend against." His dark eyes glistened. "Or worse, it could flee, and return with a much larger force that would not be surprised a second time, at even greater cost." He looked away, letting his short arms fall to his sides.

"The general consensus is that it is better to allow the Iollth their infrequent incursions, tolerate their brief depredations, and fulfill their demands, than to risk devastation on a far greater scale."

"I'm familiar with that philosophy," Walker murmured softly. "It's part of the history of my kind, too. Sometimes it works, sometimes it doesn't."

"We have adapted to the necessity," Mardalm told him, speaking up for the first time. "That is the situation now. It has been stable, if uncomfortably so, for many thousands of day-slices."

"And you're overdue for a visit from these merry marauders?" George inquired again.

Sehblidd gestured positively once more. "Hence our reaction at your arrival in our system. We are visited so rarely by space-going species, and it has been so long since the last

Iollth incursion, that we were certain you were them. Or their friends, or allies."

"What you folks need," George declared as he sniffed intently at an aromatically attractive bush before a frowning Walker nudged him away, "are a couple of big dogs of your own. The technomilitary equivalent of a mastiff on one side of you and a rottweiler on the other."

Confused, Sehblidd and Ussakk fiddled with their translating units. It was left to the linguist Mardalm to try to interpret. "I believe the quadruped George is referring to large, powerful creatures from his own domain. The analogy is clear, even if the biology is unreferenceable."

They were approaching the shallow artificial lake that lay in the center of the gardens. Search as he would, Walker was unable to espy a plant or blade of growth that was out of place. Even in their landscaping, it seemed, the Hyfft were orderly to a fault.

"Of course," Sehblidd ventured unexpectedly as they continued their stroll, "if we were to have the aid of the aforementioned 'big dogs' in the form of armed space-going craft that had the ability to confront the Iollth on their own terms, resistance might be possible. As you already know, we have no such vessels, nor the ability to construct them, nor the inclination to pilot them." Bright black eyes locked onto Walker's own. "Other species, however, do."

Walker halted and stared down at the diminutive delegate. Ussakk the Astronomer and Mardalm the Linguist were eying him with equal intensity, he noted. So was George, though more out of casual curiosity than with intensity.

"Are you asking for our help?" were the first words out of Marcus's mouth.

Ever the diplomat, Sehblidd kept his whiskers carefully parallel to the ground. "It was *your* companion who brought up the need for the weak to seek out strong allies."

"My companion has a big mouth." Walker glared down at

George with an expression that said clearly, *That's right—put me in the middle.*

"In the first place," he told the trio of suddenly very attentive Hyfft, "we're trying to get home. Involving ourselves in an ongoing armed conflict between two other species wouldn't exactly hasten us on our way."

"Certainly true," agreed the respectful Sehblidd.

"In the second place, this isn't a military expedition."

"But you travel with individual weapons and armor. Surely your ships carry armament as well?" Ussakk asked.

"Yes, they do, but they're for defensive purposes only," Walker countered protectively.

"Understandable," agreed the ever-amenable delegate, whiskers locked rigidly in place.

"And lastly," Walker concluded, "that kind of decision isn't up to me. It lies with Commander-Captain Gerlla-hyn and the captains and staff of the three Niyyuuan starships who are trying to help us find our way home."

"Of course," Sehblidd acknowledged without argument.

"Besides which," George added forcefully, intrigued at the direction the conversation had taken, "you don't even know when these Iollth are liable to hit you again. Could be next week, could be next century. Even if we and our pack friends had a collective attack of temporary insanity, we can't hang around here waiting for them to put in an appearance. When I suggested you needed strong allies, I meant allies who'd be available to assist you all the time. Not casual passersby like ourselves." He looked up at Walker. "After the celebrations and the exchange of mutual howdy-dos are over, we're out of here. Right, Marc? *Marc?*"

"What? Oh, sorry, George. I was just thinking."

"Well, don't," the dog instructed him. "It tends to get us into trouble. Unless you're thinking about cooking. And sometimes that gets us into trouble, too."

"Then you won't help us?" Sehblidd murmured. Three

pairs of dark eyes continued to gaze mournfully up at the tall human.

"Look," Walker finally told them, after what an increasingly uneasy George felt was far too long a pause, "even if the decision was made to do so, what makes you think we'd have anything to defend? Your own people would have to agree to stand up and fight. You just said that your people had 'adapted to the necessity.' "

"Adapted, yes," Sehblidd told him, and this time the tips of his white whiskers arced noticeably forward. "But that does not mean any of them are happy about it. It is an accommodation that was forced on us because we have not been able to see any other alternative. Offered one . . ." He let the implication hang in the air.

"We're on our way home," Walker informed them decisively. "We've no idea how long it's going to take us to get there, or even if we'll be successful in the attempt. We may have to give up and return to Niyu, the world of our hosts. We can't stay here, waiting to help you defend yourselves against an assault that may not come in any of our lifetimes."

"You could train us," Ussakk declared.

"What?" Walker turned to the astronomer.

"You could train us. Show us how to best organize ourselves for a planetary defense against what is a technologically superior but small attacking force. Perhaps leave us with some advanced weapons, or the schematics for the same that we could try to build ourselves. The Hyfft are not innovators in such things, but we are very good copyists and fabricators." Moving close, he rested one small four-fingered hand on the human's right wrist.

"I am not saying such an effort would make any difference. It may very well be that the Great Government would decide not to employ the results of such training and gifts, and choose to continue appeasing the Iollth. But it would at least provide a possible alternative. We would reward such an effort on your part with everything at our disposal."

"You've been wonderful hosts," Walker told him. "But as I've said, a decision of this magnitude isn't up to me." He glared warningly at George, but this time the dog stayed silent. "Training and the designs for advanced weapons, hmm? Supplying both would still take time. I don't know . . ."

Both Sehblidd and Mardalm came up to him. Echoing the gesture of the astronomer Ussakk, each placed one hand on his left or right wrist. "Please, at least put the matter before those in a position to make such a decision," the bureaucrat implored him. "If you cannot do this, we will of course understand." He stepped back, as did his two companions.

They continued their tour of the gardens. Nothing more was said about the request that had so unexpectedly been put forth. It didn't have to be. Both of Walker's wrists tingled with the memory of those small, clutching fingers.

If only, he thought angrily, the Hyfft weren't so damn selfless.

"Madness!" Tentacles fanned out neatly around the base of her body like the spokes of a wheel, Sque focused silvery eyes on Walker and edged closer to the rear of the landscaped pond that had been installed in their quarters solely for her use. "Can it be that your simple mind has so soon forgotten the very reason for our presence here?"

"I agree with the squid." Brusque as always, George promptly plumped himself down on a nearby pillow.

Walker eyed them both. "I'm as anxious to be on our way as both of you are. But if we're going to ask these people for their help in finding Tuuqalia, how can we turn down their request that we help them?"

"Watch me." Rolling over on his pillow, George commenced snoring; loudly, pointedly, and mockingly.

Sque was more fulsome, if less visual, in her objections. "They are not the same thing, Marcus. You know they are not. In nowise is asking for assistance in preparing a vector equivalent to helping an entire species prepare for war."

"For defense," Walker argued. "You've seen some of this world. These are good folk. They don't deserve what these Iollth do to them on a regular basis."

The K'eremu raised four appendages. "None of us deserved to be forcibly abducted from our homeworlds, but we were. None of us deserve to live in a universe that is, save for the occasional pinprick of a partially oxygenated world, harsh, cold, and deadly—but we do. Had we not come along, life here would have proceeded, for better or worse, exactly as it always had. It is not incumbent on us to expend time and effort to change that." Metal gray eyes searched his face.

"Oh, I don't know." Not for the first time, Walker found himself thoroughly irritated by the K'eremu's unrelenting assurance. "Maybe it is because it's the right thing to do."

"Ah, so now the truth comes out." Maroon tentacles waved in the air. "Ethics trump practicality. A noble, but ultimately misplaced gesture."

"Not from the standpoint of the Hyfft," he shot back.

She crawled halfway out of her pond, water dripping from her tentacles and turning her slick skin shiny under the overhead lights. "Might I have the temerity to remind you that we each of us have our own viewpoints regarding this matter, and that they do not necessarily coincide with the needs of the fatuous aliens who happen to be our present hosts?"

"I can't get you to agree to this," he muttered unhappily.

"That's for sure." George had rolled onto his back and was regarding his friend unblinkingly.

"And it's true," a disappointed Walker conceded, "that Gerlla-hyn and his staff would also have to agree. They might balk at a proposal like this no matter what we here decide."

"I think we should help these Hyfft, without question."

All eyes turned to the back of the single, expansive chamber. Braouk reposed there, his massive body squatting on four tree-like lower limbs, his eyestalks fully extended in opposite directions.

"Why?" George demanded to know, sitting up on his haunches. "Because 'it's the right thing to do'?"

"That," the giant Tuuqalian admitted, "and also because it will inspire our hosts to work as hard and as long as possible to discover the information we seek."

The dog snorted. "Easy for you to say, when it's your world they have by far the best chance of locating."

"Find Tuuqalia and it becomes easier to find your Earth," Braouk reminded the dog. "And," he added as one stalk-mounted eye swiveled slightly, "K'erem."

"Perhaps," admitted Śque as she climbed fully out of her pond. Drawing herself up to her full height of a meter and a third, she focused her attention on the lone human. "It might also get us killed. According to our hosts, these near-mythical Iollth are overdue to lavish their inimical attentions on this world, are they not?"

Walker nodded, knowing that the K'eremu was now wholly familiar with the gesture. "That's what the Hyfft have been telling us."

"Then it is not inconceivable that should we linger among them for a while, we might still be here when they arrive, and find ourselves caught in the middle of a resultant conflict that is none of our business and is not in our interests."

George nodded shrewdly. "That might just be what our furry little friends are counting on. That Sehblidd character already as much as asked us to intervene directly. I don't trust him. Too clever by a tail."

"We already declined to do that," Walker reminded him. "Sehblidd immediately downgraded their request to one for training and the loan of arms or armament schematics. That shouldn't take very long to supply."

"Long enough to get us killed," Sque pointed out, "if these beings arrive while we are still here." Her eyes glittered. "You fail to make your case, friend Marcus. I believe you would fail to make it to Commander-Captain Gerlla-hyn and his staff as well."

They were evenly divided, Walker saw, with himself and Braouk arguing for lending assistance while Sque and George stood against it. It was time to put forth more than words on behalf of his position.

Turning, he extracted a small communicator unit and spoke into it softly. "You can come in now, Ussakk."

"More begging?" Sque hissed derisively as she scuttled unhurriedly back into her pond. "More pleading?"

"No," Walker countered as he watched the Hyfftian astronomer enter from the far side of the refurbished warehouse. "I think, a little history."

Halting before the much larger human, Ussakk had to crane his neck to meet the other biped's eyes. "I thank you for this opportunity. Sehblidd explained to me what was needed, and helped to requisition the pertinent materials." Gesturing with his whiskers toward the other occupants of the high-ceilinged chamber, he began unlimbering the equipment strapped to his back. "This should only take a day-fragment to prepare. Please bear with me."

George sniffed, but this time as much out of curiosity as disdain. "As if we were in a hurry to go somewhere."

True to his word, the astronomer soon had a small device assembled in the center of the spacious compartment. In response to his verbal urgings, it began to project images above and between the small audience. The imagery, Walker noted, was as sharp and three-dimensional as any he had seen generated by Niyyuuan or even Sessrimathe equivalents. Truly, the Hyfft were not backward: they were simply isolated from the mainstream of galactic civilization. Isolated, and pacific.

The historical recordings showed Iollth landing ships hovering low over neatly laid out Hyfftian cities and towns, manipulating physics in assorted inimical ways to rain death and destruction on the helpless communities below. Though sophisticated in their own right, Hyfftian aircraft armed with little more than improvised weaponry were no match for the invaders, who when annoyed by the attention could simply ascend to heights the Hyfft could not reach. From orbit, missiles and energy beams poured down on the helpless defenders. Only faint outlines of the main Iollth vessels were available, taken from ground-based imaging instruments.

When queried about this deficiency, an apologetic Ussakk explained, "My people tried to obtain better images, but whenever an attempt was made to shift a satellite closer to the invaders' starships, it was immediately destroyed. None of our satellites was armed because, as you already know, there is usually no need for them to be. And also because the Iollth would regard such a development as a provocation that would stimulate even harsher response than usual."

The presentation wore on, until everyone was sickened and appalled at the seemingly senseless destruction. Only Sque did not appear touched by emotion.

"If this is an attempt to horrify, it fails. The extent to which many non-K'eremu species pervert their tiny quotient of presumed intelligence is well-known, and constitutes only one more reason why my kind prefer to be left alone. Any half-sentient who travels widely quickly discovers that 'civilization' is a relative term—usually relative to whichever militarily superior species happens to be defining it at the time." Multiple flexible limbs gestured at the waning projection and the last of its disturbing images. "I have seen nothing that surprises me, nor moves me to change my opinion."

"It only mine, reinforces much more strongly, to help," declared Braouk melodiously. A pair of powerful upper appendages moved in the direction of the dire imagery. "To assist those, who help us all, is rightness. Rightness personified." The bulky body swelled with a sudden intake of air, and both eyestalks went vertical above it. "I could not return to the beckoning plains of Tuuqalia knowing I had abandoned such a cry for aid from the very folk who proved responsible for providing me with a direction homeward."

The K'eremu's gray eyes turned to the huge Tuuqalian. "They have as yet provided no such thing."

"Working on it, with all possible speed, they are," her far more massive companion countered. Ussakk added confirmation to the Tuuqalian's claim.

"Theory is not fact, good intentions not conclusions," Sque lectured him.

"I'm still inclined to vote to help," Walker put in.

George looked up at his friend. "Even if it means delaying our journey? And at the risk of imposing on the hospitality and friendship of our friends the Niyyuu?"

Walker nodded. "That's a risk I'm willing to take."

The dog snorted. "Be interesting to see your reaction if the Niyyuu simply decide they've had enough and head home one day without us. That would leave us stuck here permanently." The dog cocked his head sideways. "You've changed, Marc. Time was you'd be a realist, be focused solely on getting back home. What's happened to you?"

Walker watched as Ussakk quietly deactivated his projector and prepared to disassemble it. Despite the mortal danger his people faced, he did not plead for their assistance, was not begging. Physically, the Hyfft was small. But in dignity, he exceeded everyone in the room.

"You're right, George. I have changed. The past several years have changed me." He eyed his friend evenly. "I've learned there are more important things to do with one's existence than trade orange juice futures at a profit." He raised his gaze to the astronomer. "So even if it entails the risk of displeasing the Niyyuu, I'm going to insist that we stay awhile and try to help these people."

Sque waved a tentacle. "Two in favor of continuing on, two in favor of wasting time here. We are evenly divided. How shall we fairly decide this matter?"

Walker hesitated. He could have tried to pull rank on his friends, however artificial it might be, but that was something else the past years had taught him. The corporate structure in which he had been immersed for so long and to which he had contentedly adhered notwithstanding, it was clear that consensus was better than command. Each of them had struggled to survive the same trauma, the same strains. Therefore each had an equal voice in their shared future.

"We'll put all arguments, on both sides, to Gerlla-hyn and his staff, and let them decide."

One tentacle fed a local food bar laced with si'dana from her private stock into her extended, pinkish mouth, subsequent to which Sque blew several contented bubbles. "You'll find no comfort there. I hear everything. Already there is dissention among crews. Despite the call of adventure and the opportunity to visit spatial realms new to their species, many among our tall escorts are beginning to express a desire to return to their own homeworld."

Knowing what she said to be true, Walker did not respond. What he did not know was that he and Braouk would find unsuspected allies among the large Niyyuuan contingent who not only would support their desire to aid the fretful Hyfft, but would actively encourage it. In fact, they would fall all over themselves to encourage such a development. Not because they were inherently altruistic, not because they felt any particular sympathy for their diminutive, furry hosts, not even because it was morally the right thing to do.

They would support the time and effort necessary to lend such aid because it would be good for their business.

5

Scenes of Niyyuuan warriors training selected Hyfftian police in military tactics made for excellent pictures. So did portraits of Niyyuuan technicians instructing other Hyfft in the use of advanced weapons, some of which could be spared from the arsenals of the three orbiting starships. And images of Niyyuuan engineers working to transfer the design schematics of other armaments to their Hyfftian counterparts for the purpose of hasty manufacture were far more interesting to observe in person than they sounded like they would be at the time the measure was finally acceded to by Gerlla-hyn's staff.

All of them would make for excellent viewing by rapt and image-hungry Niyyuuan audiences when the fortunate media representatives of that world eventually returned home with the recordings they were engaged in making. It was that small but critical and highly vocal contingent of Niyyuu who turned the tide in favor of helping rather than abandoning the Hyfft. Where Walker and his friends were divided as to whether or not to render such assistance, where the Niyyuuan military and technical staff were uncertain, the media representatives who had been given the task of recording the great and unprecedented voyage made the difference.

Helping another sentient species in such a manner would

demonstrate the ethical superiority of Niyyuuan principles, the media reps argued. The crews of the three great starships would return home much enhanced in honor. Little actual expense was involved, and not a great deal of time, much of which the ships' crews could expend enjoying the hospitality of the grateful Hyfft and their congenial world.

Above all, this morally commendable exertion would make for great pictures.

Demonstrating admirable, even astonishing energy, the enthusiastic Hyfft proceeded to turn the industrial outskirts of Therapp into the nearest thing to a military base their world had ever seen. Though their domestic police force was characteristically well-organized and extremely efficient, it was rarely called upon to deal with any disturbance more far-reaching than a riot at an arts festival. Preparing for warfare, much less warfare on a planetwide scale, was completely outside their experience. Their racial history was generally devoid of applicable examples, the Hyfft having been an exceedingly cooperative species from the very beginnings of their civilization.

Nevertheless, the police force, at least, possessed weapons in the form of small arms and knew how to use them. Elite units were equipped with what the Niyyuu could spare from their onboard arsenals and trained as rapidly as was feasible in their use. Meanwhile, such devices were scanned and dissected by the Hyfft's own instruments and replicated in factories all across the planet, with the result that within weeks they were being churned out at an impressive rate.

Small arms would be useful only in countering any Iollth who chose to set foot on the surface, however. To deal with invading spacecraft, should the Hyfft prove determined and decisive enough to do so, various commercial satellites had to be converted for offensive use. In this the Niyyuu proved more knowledgeable than Walker had expected. Not that they had used them against their own kind, but like every space-traversing species, the Niyyuu had long ago learned to prepare to defend their homeworld against potential attack from beyond.

Hyfftian satellites proved amenable to the necessary conversions. The sophistication of their technology surprised the Niyyuu who participated in the work. If one excluded their inability to travel beyond the bounds of their own solar system, the Hyfft were quite accomplished. Yet again, it was shown that their lack of the ability to travel in deepspace was due more to failings of culture than of science. Even Ussakk the Astronomer, who might have been expected to jump at the chance to travel beyond the bounds of his local star system, expressed no desire to do so, and was content to carry out his observations with the aid of ground- and satellite-based instrumentation only.

Throughout it all, the attitude toward their visitors of individual as well as groups of Hyfft bordered on the worshipful. Walker and his friends found that they were unable to go anywhere without attracting hordes of locals eager to meet the benign and compassionate travelers from the stars.

Growing bored with Therapp and the surrounding countryside, he and his companions had asked to visit the area around Pedwath, where they had initially set down. Sque all but insisted on it. Gerlla-hyn raised no objection, any security concerns having long since been obviated by their hosts' unadulterated hospitality. Since the local passenger conveyors were far too small to accommodate the much larger visitors, cargo vehicles were used to transport them to the coastal city. There the travelers were forced to endure several days of civic feting and thank-yous before they were finally able to escape the attentions of a grateful officialdom.

Now Marc and George found themselves strolling down an alien beach of fine pink sand. To their right, the dual-realm inhabitants of Hyff's oceans seemed to spend as much time aloft as they did in the water. On their left, a natural preserve was bordered by hedges of bright orange-green plants that sucked sulfides from volcanic soil and turned them into sugars while respiring oxygen that stank mightily of its un-usual origins.

As they walked, their privacy was respected, but only to a certain extent. They found themselves being trailed by half a hundred Hyfft, who were careful to maintain a respectful and polite distance behind the honored visitors. Having learned over the past several months to distinguish among Hyfftian expressions, Walker could only interpret those of their current followers as bordering on the reverential.

When he and George paused to enjoy the ocean view, or to examine the strange arthropods or coelenterate-like creatures that had washed up on or were wandering the beach, their admiring retinue promptly also halted. When the two dissimilar aliens resumed walking, so did their polite yet attentive followers. To be the unwavering subject of so many intent unhuman eyes was simultaneously flattering and unnerving.

"They think we're going to save them. From the Iollth," Walker commented as he turned back to the path ahead. From the midst of the brightly hued bushes off to his left, something erupted into the air with a squawk like a startled chicken. It had neither feathers nor wings, and propelled itself slowly upwards into the blue-green sky by means of several frantically flapping translucent fleshy flaps that sprouted from its crest.

"They'll have to save themselves." Trotting alongside his friend, George sampled the seawater through which he was walking. It was noticeably less saline than he expected, though not nearly as tasty as the familiar waters of Lake Michigan. "This was meant all along to be nothing more than a quick stop on the way home. Pop in, ask directions, and continue on our way." He looked up at Walker, black eyes gravid with augmented soul. "I'm tired of this, Marc. It's all been real exciting, but I'm tired. I want out. I want to move along."

"You're not the only one." As he continued walking, Walker eyed the first of Hyff's two moons, which was just beginning to show itself in the northeastern sky. "I'm thinking of getting out of the commodities trading business when we get home, George. Lots of opportunity, but too much stress." He examined his friend closely. "I'm thinking of opening a restaurant."

"Oh, now *there's* a stress-free business," the dog commented sarcastically. Something rippled under his foot and he gave a little jump. Cautiously, he lowered his snout toward the sand to sniff at the ribbon-like, almost transparent burrowing creature that had startled him.

"Nothing too big." Walker continued to muse on future possibilities. "I wouldn't have access to the tools or ingredients that I do now, of course. But with what I've learned, I think I could make something of a name for myself. That would be worth tolerating some start-up stress. You can't really make a name for yourself trading commodities, you know. But a good restaurant, especially in Chicago . . ." His voice trailed off as he fantasized, the dream a small glint in his eyes. Meanwhile, fifty or so meter-tall Hyfft, black of eye and mottled of fur, continued to trail behind at a respectful distance.

The two aliens were about to turn back when movement up ahead caught George's attention. "Something's going on in front of us." He glanced up at his companion. "Want to check it out?"

Walker glanced at his faithful watch, still keeping time across parsecs and planets. "Getting late."

George's nose was high in the air, sampling. "Smells interesting. Come on—it'll only take a minute."

Letting out a sigh, Walker moved his legs. They couldn't get lost, he knew. All they had to do was follow the beach back to the point where the Hyfftian conveyor had dropped them off. And if they needed help—well, there were half a hundred supplicants following close on their heels who would eagerly provide any assistance needed.

An astonishing sight awaited them on the other side of the

next pink dune. Hyfftian soldier-police were making their way ashore, removing compact underwater breathing apparatus as they did so. They were armed, though it was impossible to tell if the weapons they carried were charged. Tight-fitting camouflage suits compressed their fur against their bodies, rendering them not only more hydrodynamically efficient underwater, but nearly invisible. But what really drew the attention of the human and dog were not the dozens of dripping wet, incipient Hyfftian commandos, but the figure in charge of the exercise.

Clutching a wave-worn boulder above the landing beach, Sequi'aranaqua'na'senemu was deep in conversation with a pair of senior Hyfftian officials. As Walker and George approached, it was plain to see that she was not present merely as an observer, but was an active participant in and critic of the proceedings. Within their horizontal recesses, her sharp silvery eyes were alert. Multiple limbs waved and gesticulated as she delivered herself of a steady stream of commentary.

She was also patently surprised to see them.

"Marcus, George: I thought you two would still be aestivating at a more popular location, letting your minds vegetate while our charmingly unpretentious hosts waited on your every biological need."

Walker halted nearby, towering over the two Hyfftian police officials. "And George and I thought you'd be somewhere offshore Pedwath, soaking in the sea." He gestured toward the beach, where nascent Hyfftian fighters emerging from the water began stripping themselves of their new, specially fabricated gear. "What are you doing?"

"Yeah," George added, grinning at the obviously uneasy K'eremu. "You wouldn't, uh, have volunteered to *help* these people in their time of need, would you? Wouldn't that be un-K'eremu? Wouldn't that be engaging in an activity that has nothing to do with getting your supercilious self home?"

Her tentacles contracting defensively around her, she drew

herself up to her full height. "What would be un-K'eremu would be refusing to respond when a lesser lifeform appropriately recognizes one that is their superior." In a huff, she turned away from the dog. "My limited activities here are merely designed to confirm that which our hosts already know."

George was not in the least diverted by her protestations. With a nod, he indicated the beach full of budding Hyfftian commandos. "Speaking of knowing, I got the impression that K'eremu tended to keep to themselves. That would seem to rule out a knowledge of military tactics."

"We do indeed prefer our own company," the K'eremu replied sibilantly. "However, circumstances sometimes dictate a need for communal action. Mutual defense is one of these." A tentacle tip brushed clinging water away from one eye. "You should know by now that there is no area of knowledge that is foreign to the K'eremu. While I am not expert in such matters, my understanding of such strategies exceeds that of our hosts by several orders of magnitude. And your own as well, I would suspect."

"Don't bet on it," the dog shot back. "You've never been in a pack fight, whereas I—"

They were interrupted by the arrival of none other than Sobj-oes. While the lanky Niyyuu came loping down the nearest dune, her companion Ussakk the Astronomer paused to chat with the two Hyfftian police officials who had been taking instruction from Sque.

The constant movement of all four tails coupled with the fact that her crest was fully erect indicated that the Niyyuuan astronomer was in a state of great excitement. Indeed, the words spilled so swiftly from her perfectly round, painted mouth that Walker and George's Vilenjji translator implants were unable to keep up, and they had to indicate via gestures that she slow down.

Swallowing, she composed herself and began again. "We

have it!" she exclaimed in a voice grating enough to put teeth on edge.

"That's swell," declared George phlegmatically. "*What* do you have?"

"That which we been seeking on yous behalf." Walker had to lean back as one excitedly waving two-fingered hand nearly accidentally smacked him in the face. "Thankings to Guild of Hyfftian Astronomers"—and she turned just long enough to wave in Ussakk's direction—"we have been able to lay out likely vector leading toward homeworld of great storyteller Braouk."

A sudden surge of mixed emotion tore through Walker. "You've actually located Tuuqalia?"

The rapid twitching of her tails slowed and her crest half collapsed. "Well, not world itself. Hyfftian astronomers not know that star's location for certain. But are confident is correct stellar neighborhood. We take yous there, should not be difficult locate Tuuqalian system. More than probable, less than impossible." Reaching out, she rested one hand on Walker's upper right arm and stroked him in the familiar, reassuring Niyyuuan manner. "Is best news have had for you since triangulation of original electromagnetic waves alluding to location of Hyff, yes?"

"I'm happy for Braouk" was all the dog would mutter.

Walker tried to raise both their spirits. "We should be more than happy, George. If we can find Tuuqalia, not only can we return Braouk to his people, but based on the time each of us spent on the Vilenjji capture ship, we can hopefully calculate backward and find indications of Earth. And K'erem," he added hastily. "Also, for all their adherence to ancient traditions, Braouk insists that his kind are a scientifically advanced species. They might know right where to look for Earth and K'erem."

"I know, I know," the dog muttered, rubbing his backside against Walker's right leg. "But there's no guarantee of it, either." Tilting back his head, he looked up at the newly energized Niyyuuan astronomer. "Nothing personal, Sobj-oes. You've been a great friend. But there's no denying we're locked in a race between finding our homeworlds and the inevitable steady increase in homesickness among the crews of your ships. Given eternity, we'd for sure find our way home. But none of us have that luxury. And besides discontent among the crews, there's the matter of finding a way back to Earth within our individual life spans. I don't know if I mentioned it before, but dogs don't live as long as humans." He looked to his left. "Or K'eremu, or Tuuqalians." He dropped to his belly and put his head down on his forepaws. "It's an inequitable universe, Marc."

"Don't I know it," his friend concurred with feeling. "I once placed an advance order for ninety thousand liters of pineapple concentrate at twenty-two cents a liter, only to have the price halve over the weekend before I could dump the stuff."

Raising his head, the dog snapped at something small, hard-shelled, and airborne. "That's terrible, just terrible. How can the threat of being lost forever among the stars possibly compare?"

Walker ignored his friend's sarcasm. "Show some faith, George. We're on our way again, and this time we've got a destination. A real destination."

"Uh-huh, yeah. Somewhere in space probably light-years across, where the homeworld of a race of oversized saga-spinning sometime-berserkers may or may not be waiting to be found. I'm aquiver with anticipation."

Refusing to let himself be baited, Walker let his gaze wander back to the beach below where they were standing. The Hyfftian commandos who had emerged from the water were chittering and chirping excitedly among themselves, comparing notes and swapping suggestions. Nearby, their two officers continued in animated conversation with Sque. The K'eremu was only too happy to deliver herself of her superior knowledge.

They might not exactly be going home, Walker told himself as he looked on, but for the first time since leaving Niyu, at least they were going *someplace.*

Month-slices later, as they prepared to board the shuttlecraft waiting on the tarmac of Pedwath Port for their final departure from Hyff, Walker found himself overcome by his surroundings. Given the way the Hyfft had treated them from the beginning of their relationship, he and his friends had expected some kind of formal send-off. But nothing like this. Not on such a scale.

On Earth, a similar formal ceremony of departure might have involved a brass band and massed salutes from ranks of smartly uniformed soldiers. While the Hyfft possessed sophisticated musical instruments, their tradition favored something closer to a cappella singing. Except that it wasn't singing.

But it surely was enchanting.

Standing shoulder to furry shoulder, two thousand elegantly attired Hyfft brought forth from their small throats a meticulously modulated harmony that sounded like a cross between a gigantic covey of songbirds and an equal number of enthusiastic kittens all clamoring together in chorus. The resultant exquisite sound waves induced delectable vibrations in his inner ears. Nearby, the massive Braouk was swaying almost gracefully in time to the lilting tones while Sque's undulating tentacles were nearly as upright and alert as George's ears. Only the Niyyuu, as personified by Sobj-oes and the last of the departing warriors of her kind, seemed variously immune or indifferent to the mesmerizing drone. That was not surprising, Walker realized, if one knew that their "music" tended as much to dissonance as did their language.

A deeper roar began to overwhelm the magical vocalizing. Arising in the east, it drew steadily nearer and more profound, until a hundred Hyfftian aircraft roared by overhead in a formation so precise and tightly packed it would have left a comparable gathering of human aviators openmouthed with awe. As they thundered past, they released something from their internal holds. The drop darkened the sky. It consisted of small objects in every shade, in all colors of the rainbow.

As the components of the release reached the ground, Walker reached up and out with a hand to catch a few of the first flowers. Perhaps the massed aircraft also sprayed the airport area in passing, or possibly the attendant perfume that now filled the air arose only from the flowers themselves. Whatever the source, the mild tang of Hyff's sea air, milder than that of Earth's oceans, was rapidly suffused by a diversity of aromas that bordered on the sensuous. Walker felt himself growing dizzy with the all-pervading fragrance. George had to cover his besieged nostrils, while Sque was largely immune to the effect. Braouk, however, was all but floating on the runway. The sight of the hulking Tuuqalian tipsy with sensory overload brought a broad smile to Walker's face.

Surprisingly, there were few speeches. Some succinct, well-considered words from the local dignitaries they had worked with: the Delineator of the Day for Pedwath, her counterpart from Therapp, the representative of the Great Government itself, and a few more, and then the official farewell finished in a flurry of final refrains from the massed chorus of costumed chanters, visitors and hosts alike drenched in perfume both olfactory and sonic.

Walker had turned and was making his way together with George toward the boarding ramp of the last shuttle when several figures came scurrying toward them out of the crowd of assembled dignitaries. Still sated with pleasure from the effects of the farewell ceremony, he maintained his smile as he identified Yoracc the venerable Historian and Ussakk the Astronomer among them. The other two, whom he did not recognize, wore the practical and readily recognizable garb of officialdom. In contrast to the rest of the crowd, they looked neither happy nor sad. Only oddly unsettled.

Out of breath, they slowed as they approached Walker and his friends. At this point the four Hyfft exchanged glances, as if trying to decide who should be the first to speak. Though in an irrepressibly ebullient mood, Walker was more than ready to depart.

"Come on, then," he chided them fondly. "If this is a last-minute presentation, let's get it over with. Time favors the punctual."

"Time favors no one, least of all the unlucky Hyfft," Ussakk chittered via his translator. Reaching into his pouch, he removed a small piece of equipment. Though its lensor was small, the image it generated filled the space between Hyfft and visitors.

At first, nothing was discernible but stars. Then the resolution improved, the field of view shrank, and a small dot in the upper left-hand region of the projected image resolved itself into a gas giant of modest proportions.

"Avuuna, on the outskirts of the system of Hyff," Ussakk explained.

"Avuuna, we'll be passing you soona," George crooned—but no one was paying any attention to him. The atmosphere around the little knot of Hyfft and visitors had quickly turned solemn.

"This was recorded only a few day-slices ago by the automated scientific station that orbits Avuuna." Ussakk adjusted his equipment one more time.

There were five of the ships. They were sleeker than those of the Niyyuu, and considerably more so than that of the highly advanced Sessrimathe. Their comparative slenderness was only relative, since every starship design Walker had seen, including that of the Vilenjji, involved combining different sized and shaped sections to create the final vessel. In space, there was no functional reason to streamline enormous craft that were never designed to touch down on a world's surface.

Even within the sharp resolution of the three-dimensional projection it was impossible to estimate the relative sizes of the incoming vessels, since there was nothing familiar to measure them against. Walker was assured by Ussakk that readings made by the automatic scientific station indicated they boasted approximately the same dimensions as the starships of the Niyyuu. Though some superficial changes were visible, they were irrefutably the descendants of their predecessors. As to fighting ability, neither Ussakk nor the pair of officials who had accompanied him and Yoracc could say. Never having been able to confront the Iollth in space, the Hyfft had no knowledge of what the invaders' combat capabilities might be in such an environment.

"I not a military person," Sobj-oes observed thoughtfully, "but as yous know, all Niyyuu participate in traditional fighting between realms. From what little I know, it seem unlikely such a force, representing such an aggressive society, would travel unprepared to defend selves against advanced as well as more primitive societies." She gestured in the direction of the attentive Hyfft. "No insult to yous selves is meant by this observation."

"We are aware of our psychological as well as our technological deficiencies," Yoracc snapped back. "The question before us is, what do we do about them?"

"You're sure they are Iollth?" Walker queried the historian.

"No question." Shoving a stubby, four-fingered hand into the projection, the historian stirred starships. "Despite some apparent modifications, the basic designs are unmistakable, and correlate accurately with the pertinent historical records." Retreating slightly so he would not have to crane his neck as sharply, he looked up at Walker. "You've trained many of our people. You have provided us with some weapons. Unfortunately, the designs for more effective devices have yet to be fully implemented."

"What will you, bereft of further assistance, do now?" Braouk rumbled from behind Walker.

The mordant historian snorted and turned away. "Pay. Do what we have always done—give the Iollth what they want. Some Hyfft will die. That is how it has always been. If we had more time, time to build some of the more powerful weapons whose designs your Niyyuu have provided to us, we might be able to give them a surprise." Tired, he rubbed first one ear, flattening it against the top of his head, and then the other. "Either way, I'll be dead before that happens."

While the historian had been replying to the Tuuqalian's question, Sobj-oes had been conferring with an officer of her own kind. Now she leaned apologetically toward Walker.

"Word has come down from the *Jhevn-Bha,*" she explained, referring to the Niyyuuan command ship. "The five incoming vessels now also been detected by instruments on board our own vessels." Her muscular, toothless round mouth paused fully open for a moment before she continued. "If our instruments can sense them, it reasonable at minimum suggest theirs can now also detect us. Gerlla-hyn urges conclusion of this ceremony and return to *Jhevn-Bha* with all possible speed."

"I'm there," barked George tersely as he started for the beckoning rampway. Having preceded him, Sque was already at the top. Only Braouk and Walker, together with Sobj-oes and a couple of Niyyuuan officers, had yet to board.

As he started to turn, he was struck by a sudden change in the atmosphere. Hitherto politely boisterous, the assembled multitude of Hyfftian performers, delegates, and dignitaries had gone eerily hushed. Plainly, word of the Iollth's arrival in their system had seeped out and worked its way through the crowd. A morning of radiant happiness was dissolving into an afternoon of silent despair.

Dozens, then hundreds of silent faces turned from their neighbors. Not all, but a great many, came to rest on the few figures that were bunched together beside the Niyyuuan landing craft. Walker had to force himself to turn away. They were alien visages, all of them. Unthreatening to be sure, but also unhuman. He was not responsible for them. Ultimately, and especially these past few years, he had come to be responsible only for himself, and perhaps to a certain small extent for George.

"We really must go." Shorter than the average Niyyuu and therefore no taller than the human standing beside her, Sobjoes was able to reach a flexible arm around his shoulders without having to bend over to do it. "Nothing can do here. Not good be caught on this surface when these Iollth arrive."

"Why not?" Walker muttered even as he let the astronomer lead him toward the waiting shuttle. "We have nothing against the Iollth, and they have nothing against us."

"That true enough," she agreed softly. "But is likely to be some fighting, however short-lived, and munitions not particular about who happen to be standing in their vicinity when they go off."

Reluctantly, he allowed himself to be urged toward the landing ship, up the ramp, and into the portal. Pausing there, he looked back. From the slightly higher vantage point he was able to see better over the heads of the crowd. It was slowly, silently, and efficiently disbanding, each individual Hyfft shuffling toward specified departure points or waiting conveyors. There was no panic; no screaming and wailing, no flailing of limbs or pounding of diminutive chests. The air that had settled over the tarmac and nearby buildings was one of poignant acceptance. Having suffered the same impending, destructive fate multiple times previously, the Hyfft were sadly and stoically preparing to meet it and survive it once more. The attitude of the crowd was heartrending in its resignation. No doubt some among them, like the bitter historian Yoracc, expected to die in the coming day-slices as part of the customary carnage wreaked by the Iollth.

Then he was inside the landing ship. He was still staring

out at the civilly dispersing throng as the door cycled closed. A concerned Sobj-oes guided him to his modified thrust chair. Moments later, engines thundered as the shuttlecraft lifted from the surface of doomed Hyff, carrying him and his friends and the last of the visiting Niyyuu toward their waiting starships, and to safety.

6

For all its spaciousness and modern galactic comforts, the *Jhevn-Bha* no longer seemed quite so welcoming. It had been home and refuge to Walker and his friends for many months, but after so much time spent on the surface of Hyff, among the congenial inhabitants of that world, the interior of the great starship now seemed cramped and cold. The novelty of both the vessel and its method of travel had become little more than commonplace.

From what little he knew of the motion picture business, Walker found himself comparing travel by such means to the making of movies. With film, he had read, actors spent most of their time standing around waiting for a scene to be set up. Then a minute or even less of filming was followed by more hours of set adjustment, makeup, camera positioning, and so on. It was the same with interstellar travel: long weeks of travel cooped up in a ship, during which nothing happened, until one reached the next destination. There wasn't even a chance of hitting an iceberg.

How quickly we humans become jaded, he found himself thinking as he made his way through the access corridor. The Incas were startled and amazed to see men riding on horseback, and thought at first that man and horse were both part of the same outlandish animal. Today their descendants mounted and rode horses without thinking. Later there was the automobile; a shock and wonderment at first, now nothing more than another tool, like a hammer or a screwdriver. Then came air travel; initially restricted to the rich and powerful, today as ordinary a means of transportation as the car. And how had civilization survived without the computer and the internet?

Now here he was, a few years removed from taking taxis and trains to get around Chicago, and already he was bored with interstellar travel. A means of transportation that any scientist on Earth would have given years of their life to experience if only for an hour or so, and he was living it every day. Of course, he didn't have a clue how it worked, and was not even particularly interested in the details. As the old movie said, you turned the key, and it goes.

I've changed, he thought as he turned a corridor, and not just because his professional specialty was now food preparation instead of commodities trading. It struck him that he also no longer thought much about the aliens among whom he now lived. Not as species, anyway, but only as individuals. Tuuqalians, K'eremu, Niyyuu. The Hyfft. The vile Vilenjji and the sophisticated Sessrimathe. All the different, diverse, sometimes bizarre races he had been compelled to encounter and deal with. No other human being existed in such circumstances. There was only him, Marcus Walker of Chicago, son of George Walker the retail salesman and Mary Marie Walker the schoolteacher. The closest thing he had to human companionship was his dog, George. Or as George would have put it, the closest thing he had to canine companionship was his human, Marc.

It's all relative, he told himself. What mattered was not size or shape or color or number of limbs, or whether one breathed twenty-one percent oxygen, or thirty, or pure methane. What was important in a galaxy full of intelligence was how one related to one's fellow sentients. Discrimination existed, but had nothing to do with appearance. While discouraging to learn that it existed beyond the boundaries of Earth, at least it was based on something other than one's outer shell.

Having been forcibly torn from his homeworld, he wanted only to return there. Since then, circumstances had conspired to place him in a position to have an effect on the destiny of others. It was something he had not sought. At least his former profession had schooled him in dealing with important decisions, even if they had only involved money. How trite that seemed now. How utterly insignificant and unimportant. Nickel prices. Cocoa futures. How severely a lingering drought might affect the soybean harvest in central Brazil. Before his abduction, he had lived a life dominated by inconsequentialities and trivial pursuits. As did the great majority of human beings. But at least he had an excuse.

He hadn't known any better.

Now he had to participate in a discussion that would decide whether or not he and his friends ought to risk their lives to aid a people whose very existence they had been unaware of up until a short while ago. To try to help, or to continue on their course. For better or worse, they now had a destination: a real vector that should lead them to the stellar vicinity of the home of one of his now closest friends: Braouk's homeworld of Tuuqalia. It seemed an easy choice.

Certainly George thought so. The dog spoke up without waiting to be prompted.

"We've come a long way from months lost as captives on the Vilenjji ship," the dog declared to the assembled group. "We lost more time on Seremathenn, pleasant as our stay there might have been. Then there was our little diversion on Niyu." He nodded in the direction of Gerlla-hyn, the Commander-Captain's first assistant Berred-imr, and the astronomer Sobj-oes. "The flow of time is continuous, don'tcha know. The universe makes no exceptions for individual biological clocks." Turning, he peered up at his human, eyes wide, and rested his front paws on the seated man's knees.

"Don't look at me like that," Walker warned him. "I know that look. It won't work. You're no puppy anymore, and neither am I."

"All right then." With a bound, George jumped up onto the conference table and began to pace purposefully. "Consider this. I'm ten years old. With luck and care, I might have another ten or so in me." Turning, he strode back to Walker, nearly at eye level with him now. "You've probably got half a century, bonobo-bro, maybe more. So excuse me if I seem like I'm in more of a hurry to get home. I know I'll be food for worms one day, but I'd like them to be familiar, homey, terrestrial-type worms. Not some slithering alien glop whose shape is more twisted than its DNA." He smiled thinly. "Call me traditional."

"That something we can all understand." Gerlla-hyn spoke from the far side of the circular, double-topped table. "As you know, tradition is of great importance among my kind." The Commander-Captain's huge yellow-gold eyes focused on the only human in the room. "But sometime, tradition must make space for improvisation. Question before us remains: Is this one of those times? I know what matter to me. But I am, within reason, at disposal of yous." His frill lying perfectly flat against his neck, he leaned forward slightly. "How now wish yous proceed?" Clasped together, the two fingers of one hand indicated George, presently recumbent on the upper table-top. "Already know, I believe, opinion of small quadruped on this matter."

Having already struggled with the question, Walker was ready with an answer. "If we decide to try to help, we first need to determine if it's even feasible. That's a matter for military analysts, not us. Gerlla-hyn, your staff has had a chance to study the accounts compiled by the Hyfft. What do they portend?"

The Commander-Captain turned to the elderly female seated on his left. Berred-imr promptly consulted a portable readout. "Unless unforeseen technological developments present selves, is possible effective defense might be concocted. As in many potential clashes between opposing forces, much depend on intangibles such as tactics. Of these Hyfft know nothing, since historically all fighting take place on surface of Hyff or at least within planetary atmosphere. Hyfft can provide no information on type of Iollth strategies and weapons systems designed for use in free space." She lowered the readout. "Any proposed action on our part must take these unknowns into consideration."

A response that might have been anticipated, Walker realized. Also not an especially encouraging one.

From the far side of the table, Sque emerged from between the two tops to wave a trio of tentacles. "Do you want my opinion, or do you all still remain so low on the intelligence scale that it does not occur to you to ask?"

"Yes, Sque," Walker replied with a measured sigh, "we want your opinion. As always."

Mollified no more or less than usual, the K'eremu clambered up onto the upper tabletop. "Leaving aside for the moment the ethics of this situation and focusing solely on matters military, you are all obsessed with capabilities these Iollth—another inferior species, I have no doubt—may or may not possess. I should like to point out that irrespective of these unknowns, we already have one advantage over them."

"What that be?" a curious Berred-imr demanded to know.

"We know far more about them than they know about us," the K'eremu reminded her matter-of-factly. "Even if they have detected our presence here, they do not know if the technology available to us is superior to theirs or inferior. They do not know if these three ships represent harmless visitors or aggressive warcraft. Their ignorance exceeds ours."

"They'll find out, though," George pointed out from the other end of the table. "The Hyfft will tell them—after we've left."

"That is one possibility." Sque continued to wave several

tentacles, apparently under the impression that the constant undulating motion somehow kept her audience in a state of enduring fascination. "Another is that we do not leave, but that we remain to render what assistance we can to our recent hosts."

George lifted his head in surprise. Walker was openly astonished. From the back of the room, hunched low against the ceiling, Braouk thrust both eyestalks toward the table.

"Not like Sque, this sudden unexpected declaration, of help. Is most refreshing, to hear something unselfish, from you."

The K'eremu flashed metallic gray eyes at the hulking Tuuqalian. "I agree. But I have reasons. Perhaps one is that I'm in no hurry to get to your world, which I know from all too much experience is nothing if not aurally polluted." Pivoting on her tentacles, she turned to face Gerlla-hyn and Berredimr. "Among my kind the ready acceptance of the observably superior, be it collective or individual, is recognized as a sign of high intelligence. As the Hyfft accorded me that status early on in our relationship, I would find it bad-mannered to flee precipitously while they are so grievously threatened."

A slow grin began to spread across Walker's face. "Why, Sque—you *like* them."

"I do not 'like,' " she corrected him coolly. "I *appreciate* the Hyfft. They demonstrate the kind of courtesy and respect that is all too often lacking among the inferior species." Her stare left the commodities trader in no doubt to whom she was referring.

It didn't bother him. With an effort, he fought back the smile that threatened to spread across his face. "However you wish to define it." He returned his attention to the two Niyyuu. "They've got five ships; we've got three. We know little about them; they know nothing about us."

"Sounds like a good recipe for leaving," an increasingly glum George ventured hopefully. He could tell which way the wind was starting to blow, and it wasn't toward him.

The Commander-Captain and his first assistant conferred. When they had concluded their brief private conversation, Gerlla-hyn looked back at his guests. His frill remained flat and his tails stilled. Not a good sign, Walker felt.

"While we are at yous disposal in yous attempt return home," he informed them, "I still charged with safety of many hundreds of my people. All else being equal, where 'else' remains unknown quantity, three against five not good odds—and we not know if all *is* being equal. In absence of additional information as to Iollth capabilities, I compelled to urge against remaining here, much less participating in any active defense of this pleasant but unallied, unaligned world."

"Out of the mouths of aliens, sanity." Relieved, George let his head slump back down onto the table.

"That could be taken as an insult by some," an increasingly confrontational Sque shot back.

"Please to understand, friend Sque," the Commander-Captain pointed out, "that in military situation, superior individual intelligence no substitute for lack of same about potential enemy. Cannot risk fighting blind. Not three against five." Respectful of the K'eremu's acumen but in nowise intimidated by it, he thrust all four tail tips in her direction. "Unless can find way change this assessment, I must order departure from this system."

"The Hyfft have survived these incursions before," Berred-imr added. "Will survive again."

"But will Ussakk the Astronomer?" Walker asked pointedly. "Or Mardalm the Linguist? Yoracc the Historian? And all the others with whom we became good friends, who gave of themselves on our behalf without having hardly to be asked?" Turning slightly in his too-narrow chair, he peered across the room at Braouk. "Can we just abandon those who helped find a vector to the vicinity of Tuuqalia?"

The Tuuqalian bestirred himself, and for a moment, the

Commander-Captain and his first assistant looked suddenly uneasy. But all Braouk flailed them with was words.

"We are divided, on this contentious issue, between selves. In such situations, is often much better, query others. Put decision making, to those who require, danger chancing. They will insist, that we stay here, to help."

Gerlla-hyn's mouth contracted visibly as his tail tips twitched. Walker frowned while Sque looked on impatiently. Even George, who had already made up his mind, was newly intrigued.

"And who might that be?" the dog asked curtly.

Eyes the size of soccer balls swung around on their flexible stalks to focus on him. "The Niyyuuan media," Braouk reminded them all, this time eschewing verse.

Ki-ru-vad turned from his position at the Gathering station to contemplate the rest of the Dominion chamber. Among the Iollth there was no captain, no commanding individual. Decisions were made communally and rendered by instantaneous collective vote.

"New information has come available regarding the three strange vessels that were detected in orbit around Hyff upon our emergence into this system."

"Show us," chorused his fellow operators from their positions on the inside circumference of the circular chamber.

Obediently, Ki-ru-vad turned back to the ethereal instrumentation hovering before him and swept his tiny hands through it as he sat back on his powerful haunches. Occasionally, the long, flexible toes of one unshod foot would adjust the lower set of controls, their actions coordinating smoothly with the fingers of his much smaller hands. As the Iollth had no need of chairs, there were none in the Dominion chamber.

Dozens of repetitive images formed, one in front of each of the operators present. Each image was identical to the one that hovered in front of Ki-ru-vad, so that each ship's techni-

cian could simultaneously evaluate the same information
and imagery for him- or herself.

The images provided icons for the three ships that had been
orbiting Hyff. Had been, because indicators now showed
them heading outsystem, packed as close together as drive
fields would safely allow. Their identity was a mystery, and
would doubtless remain so. They did not originate from
Hyff, of course. The Hyfft had no ships.

Everyone in the Dominion chamber was able to follow
the progress of the departing vessels until they made the
Jump. Once the indicators signifying the locations of the
strange craft vanished, in concert with their Jump, speculation abounded as to their origin.

"The Hyfft could have bought ships," one operator pointed
out.

"One does not just buy a starship from another species and
instantly make use of it," another operator argued. "Much
education in its functions and maintenance is required. One
certainly does not buy three."

"It does not matter." Ki-ru-vad was already putting the
brief appearance of the unexpected vessels out of his mind.
"If they were Hyfft, they have fled, as all Hyfft would doubtless wish to do when we arrive. No matter what they may be
carrying away, a whole world awaits us. An amenable world,
where we shall relax and sate ourselves, in accordance with
ritual." The small, sharp teeth that lined the interior of his
wide, flat mouth glistened in the dim light of the Dominion
chamber.

"I suspect they were most likely visiting traders, or possibly explorers." Another operator spoke with confidence as
she worked at her own instrumentation. Narrow dark eyes reflected back the light from hovering devices. "It may have
been time for them to leave. Their departure need not have
been sparked by our arrival, and may be wholly coincidental.
Or they may have been warned away by the Hyfft. Or, detect-
ing our approach, they may simply have decided against so-

cializing with the unknown." The latter, she knew, would reflect a wise decision on the part of the recently fled. Her kind were not above appropriating the occasional alien vessel and its contents.

"No matter," commented Ki-ru-vad. "Whoever they were and whatever their purpose, they are gone." Leaning back, he used one foot to adjust a readout that was shading toward an unacceptable green. "Dear Hyff lies before us. Its productive and submissive people await our arrival, though not with raised feet."

The soft, sharply modulated whispering that was the Iollth equivalent of laughter passed around the Dominion chamber. Da-ni-wol spoke up. "It is proposed that since it has been longer than usual since our last visit, we should stay longer this time, the better to lavish our attentions upon the sorely neglected Hyfft. It is not meet that they should forget us."

"That is unlikely," responded another operator, without a hint of sarcasm. "Even though additional time has passed, there is not one visit in our history that has been less than memorable." Tiny, thumb-sized ears twitched at the sides of the oval, hairless skull.

Ki-ru-vad indicated agreement. "We should strive to ensure that our forthcoming visit is no less so, and that it lives up to the criterion established by those who have preceded us here in The Work. I myself am looking forward to equaling if not surpassing the labors of my ancestors."

A chorus of approval issued from the circle of operators. Elsewhere within the ship, their contemporaries were preparing for the arrival. All five ships would go into close orbit around Hyff. Advanced weapons activated, landing troops at the ready, they would first contact the authorities, the so-called "Great Government" on the ground, and issue the traditional list of demands. Once the government responded, landing parties would go down, to begin The Work. Any resistance would be met with the customary ruthless and overpowering force.

Though he did not show it outwardly, Ki-ru-vad felt the excitement rising within him. Like all his equals on the five ships, he had already killed and plundered elsewhere. Hyff lay at the farthest limit of their traditional prowling. Once they were finished with The Work here, it would be time to return home. All of them had been away from Ioll for nearly two years now, and were anxious to return, though none begrudged the individual expenditure involved. To do The Work properly required time. Every Iollth knew that.

Only rarely did they encounter any kind of resistance. Their reputation was usually enough to smooth The Work among the lesser species. Personally, he looked forward to such exceptions. The Work was much more stimulating when actual fighting, as opposed to the token ritual slaughter, was involved. He slowed his respiration. They were unlikely to encounter any such from the Hyfft. They were not a warlike people. Even their boring history was largely devoid of actual war. Like the rest of his colleagues, he would have to satisfy his personal desires through the exercise of ritual.

Though with luck, an atypical Hyfft or two might dare to raise an objection to the forthcoming depredations, and that would allow him the pleasure of engaging in formal butchery outside custom.

The good feelings he had been experiencing ever since they had arrived in the Hyff system were confirmed when he was among the fortunate ones whose identity was randomly pulled to participate in the initial landing party. Though no resistance other than the usual nonviolent protests was expected, every member of the landing team drew fully powered sidearms from stores. History had shown that crazed and foolhardy individuals, and more rarely, organized groups of rogue citizens, occasionally attempted to exact revenge on the visitors from Ioll. One had to be equipped for the unexpected.

When the last of final preparations was concluded, five

landing vessels broke simultaneously from their orbiting mother ships and descended toward the beckoning surface below, each heading separately for one of the five largest Hyfftian communities. As it had in the history texts, Hyff appeared inviting. Not all the worlds visited by the Iollth were so pleasant. Like everyone on board, Ki-ru-vad wore a mask designed to filter out potentially harmful gases and particulate matter, as well as to reduce his oxygen intake. Used to an atmosphere that was sixteen percent oxygen, any Iollth who breathed Hyff's twenty-three percent for very long would suffer the effects of oxygen poisoning. That which gives life can also take it away, he mused as the landing ship made first contact with the outer atmosphere. Just like his own kind.

He had never set foot on Hyff, of course. The last Iollth visit had taken place prior to his birth. In accordance with Iollth philosophy, visited worlds needed to be given time to recover between incursions. Too many demands imposed too often would encourage sullenness, noncooperation, and even futile resistance among the populace. So each visit was mounted by a new generation or two. And each, he knew from the texts, was as successful as those that had preceded them.

Anticipation ran through the assembled troops like free-flowing hormonal supplements. This battle group had already called on two other worlds, in two different, far-flung systems. Each visit had been successful. Hyff lay at the extreme edge of Iollth influence. Once they had finished their work here, the five ships would at last turn homeward, pausing at two more worlds before returning to Ioll in final triumph. Then there would be a long pause to allow the five unlucky chosen worlds to rest and recover while work on Iollth commenced in anticipation of the next expedition.

Word that the landing ship was on final approach came to him via the communicator inside his skullcap. Touchdown followed not long thereafter. There was no rush to exit the landing ship. Ki-ru-vad and his dozens of colleagues took their time, marching out in good order.

As always, it was wonderful to breathe something besides ship air, even if it did have to be filtered through a reduction mask. In line with the directives that had been broadcast from orbit, the airport was suitably deserted, all native aircraft having been shifted elsewhere. Not that a disgruntled Hyfftian pilot was likely to try to crash one of the primitive local aircraft into the landing ship, or into the disembarking landing party, he knew. Firstly, it would never succeed. The predictors and defensive weaponry on board the ship would vaporize any aircraft that came within a proscribed radius. Secondly, even if by some miracle of nature a local pilot did succeed in striking such a blow, he would have to know that it would result in severe repercussions being enforced against the civilian population. Aware of this, any resistance was defeated before it could get started.

As per historical protocol, a small delegation of local officials was waiting to acknowledge, if not welcome, the first shuttleload of Iollth. False pleasantries would be exchanged, whereupon the Iollth would be conveyed to the lavish temporary quarters they would be inhabiting for the duration of their visit. These would comprise the best the Hyfft could provide, of course. It would not do to displease the delegation. Reprisals were possible for all manner of error, including conscious oversight. Two visits previous, the Hyfft had made such a mistake. By way of showing their displeasure, the Iollth had razed to the ground a small ocean-farming community of several thousand souls. Ever since that incident, the Hyfft had been especially attentive to the demands of their visitors.

As was appropriate, the members of the Hyfftian deputation arrived wearing suitable translators. Between theirs, which Ki-ru-vad had to admit appeared to be of quality manufacture, and those built into the skullcaps and masks of the

Iollth, communication proceeded swiftly and without confusion.

"We welcome our guests the Iollth to Hyff," the leader of the delegation intoned as unemotionally as possible. Since there was not a single Hyfft on the planet who would do so willingly, any attempt at false jollity was set aside. This did not trouble the Iollth. They had not returned seeking the hand of friendship, and did not expect their hosts to smile as they were plundered and abused.

A shot split the air. A few members of each species turned to follow the sound. A single neatly attired Hyfft lay prone on the pavement, facedown, a neat hole drilled through the furry skull from front to back. A pair of Iollth stood over the body, peering down. The one holding the activated pistol put a foot on the dead native's head. From heel to toes, the flexible, unshod foot more than covered the motionless head.

Some perceived slight had no doubt drawn the illustrative response, Ki-ru-vad knew. Perhaps the Hyfft had stepped out of line. Perhaps it had looked at the massed Iollth and made an importunate gesture. It did not matter. It was only a Hyfft.

The official welcome had now received a response.

The Iollth were escorted toward the nearest airport building. There conveyors would be waiting to transport these first arrivals from the airport to the special place of residence that had been prepared for them. As soon as the landing area was cleared, the shuttle would lift off and return to its mother ship, there to wait while the next lot of soldiers and the first of property-acquiring technicians boarded for descent. The same scene was being repeated across the planet, in four other major conurbations.

They were nearing the building when thunder behind them signified liftoff of the landing ship. It was only by coincidence that Ki-ru-vad happened to be looking back in time to see the half dozen Hyfftian aircraft come plummeting out of the clouds. His eyes expanded as the ascending landing ship let loose with its full complement of defensive armament.

All around him, startled Iollth were whirling to take in the shocking and wholly unexpected development. Outrage began to boil within the hearts of every soldier present.

First one Hyfftian aircraft went down, trailing smoke and flame. A second, caught head-on by a disrupter, simply shattered into a miniature starburst of splintering particles. A third caught a seeker and blew apart with a satisfying bang. But the other three . . .

The remaining three each launched something. The tiny white trails that materialized from beneath their graceful curving shapes converged on the landing ship. Near-instantaneous defensive weaponry engaged the trails.

The trails dodged.

It was impossible. Ki-ru-vad knew it was impossible even as he watched it happen. The established texts were very clear: the Hyfft possessed nothing in the way of advanced military technology. Nor did even sophisticated species suddenly originate the means for doing so. To defend against something like the landing ship's weapons' integrated systems, you first had to have an understanding of how they functioned. Having had little in the way of exposure to such systems, how could the Hyfft have, in so short a time, developed effective countermeasures?

One trail terminated itself on the exterior of the landing ship. There was a loud explosion. The concussion shook those standing outside the terminal building below, and not just physically. A second trail impacted, then the third. The landing ship seemed to quiver for a moment, its ascent faltering. Then, engines sputtering, it fell backward, picking up speed as it descended. When the crippled, smoking, but still impressive vessel slammed into the runway, the resulting detonation excavated a considerable crater.

The Hyfft were not displeased.

And where were the Hyfft? Ki-ru-vad wondered as, stunned, he turned away from the roaring flames and plume of rising black smoke that marked the spot where the landing ship had crashed and exploded. The official greeting party had disappeared inside the building. Overhead, the three surviving native aircraft circled ominously.

"Inside! Kill them all! Leave none alive!" The orders came rapidly, one after another, relayed to him via the communicator built into his skullcap. Teeth grinding together as jaws flexed, he drew his own weapon and allowed himself to be borne forward by the now livid, furious mass of fellow Iollth.

They poured into the terminal building, dozens of armed invaders looking for something to kill. None of the treacherous Hyfft would survive. And once they had disposed of every member of the official greeting party, Ki-ru-vad knew, they would move on to the city itself. Pedwath would pay for the loss of the landing ship, and pay in such a way and to such a degree that none on Hyff would ever again think to perpetrate such a duplicitous act.

"There!" someone near him shouted, pointing with a small hand. Movement was visible at the far end of the wide hallway that led to the airport's nexus. Immediately, a dozen weapons were raised. A couple of soldiers wielding heavier armament immediately swung around the rifles on their backs and steadied them with one powerful foot as they prepared to aim. Fire poured down the corridor. And for the second time on that inconceivable morning, the utterly unexpected occurred.

The Iollth's fire was returned.

7

It was all quite impossible, of course. The texts drawn up on the basis of previous visits stated clearly that while Hyfftian civilization maintained a force of police equipped to deal with a broad range of domestic difficulties, they had no military capabilities whatsoever. Nor had they ever, in their modern history, displayed any inclination to pursue them. The fire that Ki-ru-vad and his companions were now taking was not only devastating in its effectiveness, it showed a knowledge of tactics that was as unsettling as the use of advanced firepower itself.

Where had the simple, inoffensive Hyfft acquired such devices? Surely they had not experienced a sudden burst of insight into the methodology of weapons manufacture, much less a desire to pursue it? As the stunned Iollth took cover behind what little protection the terminal interior offered, it was clear they were up against an opponent who understood more than crowd control. Where and how had the short, furry denizens of this congenial and wide-open world learned military tactics?

He would have ordered a retreat to the landing ship, except that the landing ship was a smoking ruin outside the building in which they were currently pinned down. The sequence of events implied planning and a good deal of forethought. His thoughts raced even as he tried to aim and fire. Why not destroy the shuttle when it had been on its descent? To lull the visitors into a sense of false security?

Something ionized the air above his head as it thrummed past to punch a hole in the wall well behind him. Whatever had made the sound and drilled the subsequent hole was not something designed for arresting unruly celebrants, nor was it likely to have been derived or modified from such. All around him, soldiers of Iollth were dying. They were trapped. More astonishingly, they were losing; being outshot, outguessed, and outmaneuvered. And this without the locals employing any heavy weaponry. Perhaps they wanted to try to save as much of the Pedwath terminal complex as possible. Possibly they wanted to take prisoners. Ki-ru-vad was unsure whether to be frightened or outraged.

In the end, which came very soon thereafter, he surrendered.

He could see the shock writ large in the faces of those around him as, singly and in small groups, they tossed their weapons into several piles on the attractively mosaicked floor. Only when the last sidearm and rifle had been discarded did their opponents begin to emerge from cover down the corridor and advance toward them. It was mortifying to see the Hyfft, those weak and inoffensive sentients, marching up the passageway to take control of what remained of the landing team. His anger was only partly tempered by his amazement at the sight of the weapons they carried. Fashioned like jewels to fit the small Hyfft's hands, they were like nothing he had ever seen, either in person or in any text.

Then he saw the others.

Tall and slim, they carried themselves like warriors. Their body armor fit their slender forms as if it had been molded onto their lean muscularity. Limber arms and two-fingered hands supported weapons of a design as foreign to him as their bearers. Enormous, curving battlefield lenses covered huge eyes. Backpacks concealed unknown instrumentation and advanced weapons engineering.

As several of the willowy giants moved to stand guard over the growing heaps of surrendered guns, Ki-ru-vad observed several Hyfft (armored Hyfft!) conversing with them. This simple act clarified a great deal. Somehow, from somewhere, and by means unknown, the Hyfft had acquired allies. Aliens who were militarily sophisticated and, again for reasons unknown, willing to put their lives on the line for their much shorter, furry hosts. Professional mercenaries, perhaps. He almost felt sorry for them. They had no idea what they were getting into. And they were about to find out.

Accompanied by a particularly elderly male Hyfft, the female Hyfft turned and came toward him. Instinct, not to mention desire, demanded that Ki-ru-vad kick out with both feet, wrap his powerful legs around her neck, and snap her spine. He did not do so because the two Hyfft were joined by a pair of the tall aliens. Alert and ready, this escort focused on him and his nearby companions. Behind red-tinted transparent battle lenses, their impressive eyes were active and searching. Whoever these tall, interfering strangers were, they were used to the ways of warfare.

Not only that, they had somehow managed to train the formerly innocuous Hyfft in fighting tactics. Being taken by surprise and defeated by tall militaristic aliens was bad enough. Being taken prisoner by armed Hyfft was humiliating. If not from beam weapon or explosive shell, Ki-ru-vad felt he might well die of embarrassment.

Halting before him, the female made some adjustments to the two-piece translator system fastened to one ear and around her neck. Pushing back the battle goggles that protected and concealed her eyes, she looked up at him. He fought the urge to kick her small, flat teeth out through the back of her skull.

"I see by your insignia that you are of a high caste, therefore I address myself to you. I am Delineator Joulabb qi Administrator sa Twelve of Pedwath." She indicated the elder standing next to her. "This is Yoracc ve Historian. He is present to observe, to record, and to comment."

The Iollth muttered something uncomplimentary.

"Make an effort to be civil," Joulabb chided him. "You are defeated. Though we Hyfft are not by nature a vengeful species, there are still those living who are old enough to remember the tales told by their immediate relations of your last visit to our world. It would not take much to convince the populace to dispense with diplomatic niceties and simply kill you all."

Her words burned into him via the translator that was part of the instrumentation banded across the top of his head. Several of Ki-ru-vad's fine, pointed teeth splintered and broke inside his mouth as his jaws clenched. The loss was of no significance, as the lost dentition would soon be replaced by his efficient physiology.

"Those who so reminisce should also remember the consequences of defiance," he growled through his mask. "You are correct about one thing, though: much killing is going to follow this. Once word of what has happened here is digested and confirmed aboard the five ships, there will be such slaughter on Hyff as to make the visits of our predecessors seem like year-end celebrations of birthing."

One of the tall aliens spoke to the Delineator. As Ki-ru-vad's translator was unfamiliar with the creature's language, he was unable to comprehend what passed between them. The female Hyfft helpfully explained.

"Djanu-kun wants to know if I can let him kill you. He doesn't like your attitude."

More curious than afraid, Ki-ru-vad squinted up at the alien. "It understands my speaking?"

Joulabb indicated in the affirmative. "All the Niyyuu were given access to your language, which has been programmed into their own translation apparatus. So he can understand your threats, yes."

Lifting his left foot, the Iollth brought it down hard, smacking the floor with the tough, leathery sole. "Then it understands that it is going to die, along with everyone in this building?"

The alien's reaction was worthy of note. It emitted a series of short, staccato coughs, as did its companion. Unfamiliar as he was with the species standing guard over him, Ki-ru-vad did not learn until much later that this singular respiratory response constituted Niyyuuan laughter. It was just as well. He was already frustrated and infuriated enough to threaten the coordinated pumping of his two hearts.

Again the insolent Hyfft conversed with one of the aliens—the Niyyuu, he told himself. He had never heard of them. It would be interesting to enter that name into the sacred texts and search for a match.

"Djanu-kun begs to disagree. He says that you and your companions fought well, and compliments you on your martial skills."

Ki-ru-vad leaned back slightly and eyed the Niyyuuan warrior anew. If not common sense, at least these creatures were capable of showing proper respect. His opinion of the Hyfft's allies, if not the Hyfft themselves, rose another degree.

"But he and his friends are not going to die," Joulabb continued, "nor is anyone else in Pedwath, or anywhere across the whole expanse of Vinen-Aq. Fighting on this world has ceased." She eyed him evenly and without rancor. "I am in contact with the forces of Hyff across the world. The same fate that has befallen you has overcome the landing parties from your other four ships. All have surrendered." One furry hand adjusted the hearing unit that fit neatly over her other ear as she paused a moment to listen to something.

"No, that is not entirely correct. The landing party of Iollth that set down in the center of Cirelenn refused to lay down their weapons, and had to be completely destroyed." She lowered her hand. "The loss of life is to be regretted."

"It will be regretted far more when devastation such as this generation of Hyfft has not known and cannot imagine begins to rain down from the sky." With one diminutive hand Ki-ru-vad indicated the nearest pile of surrendered armament. "These are toys compared to the weapons that are carried on the five ships themselves. You here may survive. Your proximity to myself and my companions offers you some degree of protection. But other cities, other communities where no Iollth are in danger, will feel the heavy heel of obliteration." He gestured toward the curiously watching Niyyuu. "No contingent, or multiple contingents, of off-world mercenaries is going to save you.

"As for the vessels that brought them here," he added, remembering what had been observed as the Iollth had entered the Hyff system and drawing the most reasonable conclusion, "they have departed. They were observed leaving this system and making the Jump before we entered orbit around your world." He turned his attention to the silently observing Yoracc. "If you know your people's past well, Historian, then you know that no Hyfftian aircraft or surface-based weapons can harm an Iollth spacecraft. As for any small local artificial satellites that may have been modified for military purposes, those are as easily dealt with."

Having listened in silence to all that the unrepentant invader had to say, the elder Hyfft now gestured imperceptibly. Tilting back his head, the fur of which was white with age, he gazed thoughtfully skyward.

"No doubt all that you say is true, soldier of Iollth. We of Hyff and our new friends as well stand before you utterly at your mercy. There is no hope for us."

Oddly, in direct contrast to his words, the historian did not seem especially unsettled. Nor did the Delineator Joulabb. As for the pair of mercenaries, or whatever they were— Niyyuuan warriors—they had not even bothered to follow the elder's lead and look upward.

They just started coughing again.

* * *

On board the orbiting Iollth flagship *Am-Drun-za-div,* one inconceivable report after another passed swiftly before the incredulous eyes of the affiliates of the dominion caste. Sa-ru-vam reacted so sharply to the abrupt flood of disbelief conveyed by the tenuous yet precise instrumentation hovering before her that she nearly lost her skullcap. Large but agile toes worked in tandem with small, delicate fingers in a frantic search for confirmation. The results were undeniable. She knew they had to be so as the chamber came alive with a zephyr of confirming whispers.

"How could this have happened?" she demanded to know of her colleagues. "What of our detectors?"

"All aimed toward the world below," another operator declared, "and aligned to monitor the primitive but efficient artificial satellites of the inhabitants. Nothing directed outward."

And why should there be? she reflected as she stared in dumbfoundment at the increasingly somber readouts. The Hyfft could barely and only occasionally mount even the most feeble opposition from their own world. There was no reason, none whatsoever, to expect an attack from behind, from the reaches of extraplanetary space to which the locals had never aspired, and which they had only cursorily explored with simple automated scientific instruments.

Yet the threat was there, undeniable and immediate. An entire array of self-propelled devices, a potent mix of atomics and kinetics, were poised to close the remaining gap between themselves and all five Iollth craft. Awaiting, no doubt, only a reversion of the command that had halted them just short of their targets. Their origin was clear, now that detection fields had been adjusted to reach out into space and sweep the firmament *behind* the orbiting vessels.

There were two of the strange ships. Extensive in size, alien in design, and perfectly positioned, they had launched their weaponry immediately after emerging from concealment behind the largest of Hyff's moons. With targets now in range, the Iollth were situated to respond—except that their own weapons would take notably longer to reach the two attacking vessels than the latter's already launched devices would to reach theirs. Assuming the efficiency of the latter matched their stealth, the result would be five Iollth ships and their crews completely annihilated, with no guarantee of destroying their assailants. Electronic predictors repeatedly confirmed what direct observation had already proposed.

Like many battles in space, the end of this one was determined before it could be started.

"The fleeing traders," observed a thoroughly muted Aj-kilwon as he turned around, his feet preceding him. "Or explorers. One is forced to wonder now at their true purpose, their real intent." A small hand gestured at his own floating instrumentation. "Simple traders and explorers do not carry this kind of weaponry. Nor do they deploy it with such tactical skill and efficiency. What interests me at the moment is not how, but why? We have no quarrel with these folk, whoever they may be. Why are they doing this?"

Sa-ru-vam had already given the matter some thought. "Absurd as it may seem, it appears that our Hyfft have somehow, through means unknown and unimaginable to us, acquired powerful allies." Raising one foot, she indicated the lower levels of her own suspended readouts. "Whatever the reason, one thing is unmistakable. We are defeated."

She knew that the soft murmurs of incredulity that echoed through the Dominion chamber were likely being echoed elsewhere throughout the flotilla. There were no records, none, of the inoffensive, harmless, isolated Hyfft ever making use of allies, or attempting to acquire them. This development was unprecedented. Had it not been, it was unlikely the Iollth would have been so swiftly and completely taken by surprise.

Their instruments had shown the three visiting starships fleeing the Hyff system prior to the Iollth's arrival. Developments now revealed this apparent flight to have been a sham, a clever diversion. Somehow, one of the alien craft had managed to simulate three departing drive fields, leaving the other two to conceal their presence behind the bulk of Hyff's largest moon. And in fact, as she contemplated the most likely scenario, her own instruments revealed the presence of a new approaching signal: the absent, and deceiving, third alien craft.

Bitterly, she condemned the certitude and overconfidence that had allowed her kind to be overcome without a fight. The question now was: *Why* had these mysterious newcomers involved themselves in a confrontation that was none of their business, and what did they intend to do with their victory? She suspected that she and her kind were likely to find out very soon.

Meanwhile, there was nothing for them to do but surrender.

"There's nothing for thems to do but surrender." Commander-Captain Gerlla-hyn's observation might have been obvious to Berred-imr and the rest of his staff, but it was far less so to the one anxious human and curious dog who stood in the command room off to one side and out of the way.

"I don't understand. Nobody's fired a shot." Walker looked to his left, to where Sque squatted on her tentacles, as bored with the proceedings as she was with any that did not orbit around her.

"Nobody's even barked." Tail wagging energetically, eyes alert, George stared in fascination at the schematic that floated in the air before them all. It showed clearly the surface of Hyff, the five Iollth ships, the two Niyyuuan vessels, and a scattering of bright pinpoints of light, each one representing a lethal, self-propelled weapon.

It was left to the hulking Braouk, leaning up against one wall as he did his best to avoid stepping on any of the participants, to explain. As he did so, he gestured with both eye-stalks as well as all four upper limbs.

"No valid reason, to pursue a clash, already won." Both eyes rose at the end of their stalks to study the glowing schematic. "Niyyuuan weapons systems, in excellent position to, finish fight. Whereas the Iollth, have not even commenced, weapons deployment. For them to, do so now would, be suicidal." While one eye remained on high studying the projection, the other dipped down low to regard Walker. "The tactics of advanced armaments, Marcus. Combat in space, between ships, is not like limb-to-limb fighting on a solid surface. Preparation is more important than execution. Outcome is often, foretold before anyone needs, to die."

"Communication is coming in." Everyone turned to where Gerlla-hyn was speaking aloud. There was a pause, but only verbally. Around the command center, Niyyuuan technicians and crew were actively at work.

"The Iollth have surrendered," the Commander-Captain announced. "The battle is now formally as well as tactically won." Strident whistles of satisfaction filled the room.

Some battle, Walker thought. Not even insults had passed between ships. "What now?" he wondered aloud.

"Why now," Sque commented, "we discuss with the Hyfft how they wish to treat with their former tormentors." One tentacle reached up to clean an eye. "Civilized folk would come to some peaceable, mutually satisfactory arrangement for future relations that would not involve the subjugation and exploitation of one species by another. Revenge being a term employed only by the primitive, I would expect the Hyfft to demand it in some measure." Other tentacle tips quivered. "I do not expect, but would be delighted, to be surprised. I am especially glad that our intervention was able to be accomplished with no loss of life on either side."

Walker frowned at her. As was often the case, the K'eremu's words left him with the distinct impression that there was more she could say, that she knew more than she cared to share, if only she would choose to do so. And as was often the case, she remained silent and offered nothing more on the subject at hand. He tried another tack.

"We still don't know what happened to the Iollth landing parties," he pointed out.

"That is so," she admitted. "One can only hope word was received from on high before much violence was committed."

Trotting over to the K'eremu, George sniffed one extended tentacle. It promptly coiled sharply away from him. It was clear to Walker that his four-legged friend also suspected Sque was holding something back. "What do you care, squid? These Iollth have plagued and mistreated the Hyfft for centuries. Sounds to me like it would do them collectively good to have the crap kicked out of a few of them."

The K'eremu's silvery horizontal eyes withdrew even farther into their sockets. "That is typical of the scatological appraisals that I have come to expect from lower lifeforms such as yourself. Simply because the Iollth are militarily superior to the Hyfft and the latter have been courteous to us does not automatically mean that the Hyfft are superior to their invaders in all other ways. We know nothing of these aggressive visitors other than what the Hyfft have told us. Truly, enough to induce us, or at least you and the Niyyuu, to decide to help them. I maintain that is insufficient grounds for condemning the Iollth unreservedly."

Walker frowned down at the K'eremu. "How can you side with them, Sque? You saw the same horrific historical documentation as the rest of us."

Tilting back her upper body, she looked up at him. "I side with no one who is not K'eremu. I am simply saying that while the Hyfft have grounds for abhorring the Iollth, the rest of us do not." A pair of tentacles gestured at the massive floating image. "It may be that our hosts will wish to execute a sampling of their tormentors. There is no compelling reason why that should be our wish. The Iollth have done nothing to us. It is one thing to intervene to settle a quarrel. It is another to take permanent sides."

She was right, Walker realized. Having been exposed to the historical evidence of the Iollth's depredations, he was pained to admit it, but there was no reason why he and his friends should take an active interest in punishing the invaders.

Or did the K'eremu have something else in mind, as she so often did? If that was the case, she was not volunteering her thoughts. He saw no reason to try to draw them out, as they would only be revealed in her own good time.

Certainly the Niyyuu seemed happy with the outcome. Once the surrender had been recognized and accepted, Gerlla-hyn left the necessary follow-up details in the capable hands of Berred-imr and came over to join them.

"There to be a formal ceremony of surrender on surface." One limber, two-fingered hand indicated the hovering schematic. "All our weapons to remain in position until then, and maybe for some time afterward, until we certain of Iollth intentions. Knowing nothing about them, cannot trust them so easily." Wide, golden eyes gazed down at them while Braouk in turn regarded the Commander-Captain from on high.

"Should alls be most pleased at success of strategy. Could not work second time since Iollth now aware of our stance, but that is good thing about such tactics. Need only work one time. Is some regretfulness among crews. Not have opportunity in historical times to utilize modern weapons."

Haughtily superior, Sque turned away in disgust, surrounded as she was by inferior minds. Only accident and circumstance had caused her to fall in with these Niyyuu, not to mention a Tuuqalian, a canine, and a human. It could just as easily have been with these Iollth. How she longed for home and intellectual surroundings that, however fractious, were steeped in common sense!

Addressing himself to Walker, Gerlla-hyn continued politely. "As nominal director of forces, is decided you must attend surrender ceremony."

Walker looked startled. "Me? But this is something for the Hyfft to handle, and for your people to oversee." He spread his hands. "I wouldn't know what to do or say."

"That goes without saying," Sque put in, but by now no one was paying attention to her.

"Not need do or say anything," Gerlla-hyn assured him. "Only needs you provide presence." Now that the "battle" was concluded, his frill was completely relaxed, as were his quadruple tails. "Is useful defeated Iollth see that Hyfft have support of not just Niyyuu but four other sentient species as well." His gaze shifted beyond Walker. "Yous all should attend." Both eyes settled on Sque. "Perhaps even K'eremu deign to grace ceremony with presence, so as to demonstrate innate superiority of at least one species among victors."

Sque, who had turned away, now pivoted in place. A few desultory bubbles emerged from her pink speaking tube as she idly jiggled some of the garish metal ornaments that decorated her smooth frame.

"I suppose it is necessary. For purposes of efficiency, if nothing else. These Iollth should cooperate more easily once they see that there is at least one superior mind among their vanquishers. Very well, I will come along. If nothing else, it will provide the opportunity to visit the local ocean once more."

8

As Walker hoped, the Hyfftian capacity for tolerance far exceeded any desire for revenge. While there were certainly elements among the population who sought such, especially among those who had directly lost ancestors to incursions by the invaders' predecessors, they were compelled to mute their feelings in favor of the Great Government's decision to conclude a formal and permanent treaty of peace between their species and the Iollth. Whether understanding would follow peace was something only the progress of future relations could decide.

The official ceremony of surrender was more low-key than Walker had anticipated. A comparably important agreement on Earth would have taken place amid a certain pomp. On Hyff, a handful of representatives of the defeated Iollth filed silently into the official gathering chamber of the Overwatch of Pedwath. Accompanied by her daily equivalents, the city's Delineator of the Day was present, as were envoys of the Great Government.

The chamber itself was large but not awe-inspiringly so. Among the Hyfft, representatives of the government felt no need to intimidate those from among whom they had been chosen. The chamber was big enough to accommodate citizens and civil servants engaged in business. Fortunately, the bowl of the slightly curved ceiling was two Hyfftian stories high. This allowed all the participants in the ceremony to enter and file toward the sunken center without having to bend, though Braouk had to do some squirming to make his way inside via the main entrance. Just as Sque pined for the damp and cloudy surroundings of K'erem, the Tuuqalian wished fervently for the wide-open spaces of his own world. Though he was far too polite to say so, he was tired of dwelling among midgets.

Deliberately, he turned his eyestalks away from one of the many Niyyuuan media recorders who sought to document his reaction. They filled the chamber, roving purposefully among Hyfft and Niyyuu alike, their presence and purpose as well as their evident freedom of movement a continuing bafflement to the already disoriented Iollth.

The uniforms of the invader were quite spectacular, Walker observed. Layers of clashing colors clothed their bottom-heavy attire while small stripes of metal adorned their fronts and massive thighs. They did not hop, but rather lifted first one side of their bodies and then the other as they advanced. Under other circumstances their style of personal locomotion would have prompted a smile. Any amusement he and his companions might have felt at the sight was mitigated by their knowledge of the history of Hyfftian-Iollth relations. Given the opportunity, he knew that the funny-striding aliens entering the chamber would happily have slaughtered everyone within.

Instead, badly duped and overcome by Niyyuuan tactics, they had been brought to this moment. There would be no elaborate ceremonial signing of documents, Walker had been told. Such archaisms were unnecessary. Terms had already been agreed upon. The Iollth would cease their raids on Hyff. Any future visits would take place under the aegis of the peace agreement that had been agreed upon by the two species.

Looking askance at the Hyfftian chairs that had been pro-

vided for them, the four members of the Iollth delegation finally arranged themselves in a line on the lowest level of the
multi-level chamber, settling back on powerful haunches.
Overhead lights shone flatteringly on their uniforms. Though
it was always difficult to interpret alien expressions, George
voiced the belief that to him the visitors looked uncomfortable but far from beaten.

"Tough bunch of fatties," the dog commented from where
he stood atop a seat.

"They're not fat," Walker corrected him. "They just taper
toward the top. Big legs and lower bodies; small upper limbs,
necks, and heads." He gestured. "Look at the muscles in
those legs. You can see them through the clothing."

"Even a Chihuahua could run circles around them." Letting out a derisive snort, the dog settled himself back on his
own haunches. "Soon as this is over with, we're out of here."

"Yes," Walker admitted. "The Hyfft helped us; now we've
helped them. We're even." Reflexively, he glanced toward the
transparent center of the ceiling. "Tomorrow we leave for
Tuuqalia." *And hopefully we'll find it,* he added by way of
silent prayer. Not only for Braouk's sake, but for their own.
He didn't care to think what their next step would be if the
Tuuqalian's homeworld could not be located.

Below, Ki-ru-vad's attention drifted from the high-pitched
chirping of the Hyfft who was presently speaking, to the upper
levels of the chamber. Not one but four non-Hyfft aliens
stood or sat there, observing the proceedings. He was at once
intrigued and confused by their appearance. None of them
bore the slightest resemblance to the Niyyuuan allies who
were responsible for the defeat of his kind. Where had they
come from, and what were they doing here, at this significant
and degrading moment? Were they simply friends of the
Hyfft, or the Niyyuu? Observers? Or something more? It was
important to know, because of the Commitment.

Obviously, the Hyfft were unaware of the Commitment.
Nor did their ferocious and admirable allies the Niyyuu give

any indication of being aware of its reality. Certainly neither representative of either species exhibited any indication of recognition. Ki-ru-vad sighed inwardly. The Commitment could be ignored, of course. But that would be unworthy not only of the dominion caste as a whole and of the many castes that supported it, but of himself personally. Pains would have to be taken to dispel the evident ignorance.

To a certain degree, he was looking forward to it. Whenever the Commitment had been made in the past, it had only led to the elevation of the Iollth. He believed strongly that it would not have to be made to the Hyfft. That in itself was a relief. Bestowing the Commitment was difficult enough. Granting it to the Hyfft, who for hundreds of years had been nothing more than pitiable victims of the noble Iollth, was almost unthinkable. The Niyyuu, now—that he could see doing. It was likely to be the Niyyuu, he knew. But one could not be certain. Where the kind of unexpected tactics that had been used against his people were concerned, nothing could be taken for granted.

As for himself, personally, he fully expected to be killed, and hoped only that his demise would present itself in a concise and forthright manner. There was nothing in the history of Iollth-Hyfftian interaction to suggest that the victors were inclined to the use of torture. Still, he had steeled himself for whatever might come.

The summit went well. When not being slaughtered and abused, the Hyfft were quite efficient. Aside from having to endure some vociferous chiding for multiple past wrongs committed, nothing was said to the assembled quartet of Iollth about taking revenge. Not even on Ki-ru-vad and his colleagues, who had been chosen by their peers as much for their suitability as sacrifices as for the prestige they conferred on the occasion.

"None of us are to be killed?" he finally felt compelled to ask.

The Delineator of Pedwath regarded her ancient enemy

out of small, dark eyes. "What would that gain? An entirely nonproductive response. We prefer that you return, all of you, to your homeworld, to convey the news of what has transpired here." The reaction of the other Hyfft gathered around her was proof that hers was not a response that had been decided individually.

Ki-ru-vad looked over at Sa-ru-vam and the others. They were equally as resolved as he to follow through with tradition. Being of dominion caste, they had no choice.

"We cannot do that," he told the Hyfft.

Confusion engendered animated discussion among the locals until one, whom Ki-ru-vad knew as Mardalm the Linguist, stepped to the fore, fingering her translator gear as she did so.

"There seems to be some confusion in translation. You have agreed to the provisions of treaty. What is it you cannot do? With what element of the surrender terms can you not comply?"

"We cannot return home," Sa-ru-vam told her. Among the Hyfft no one said as much, but it was clear all were thinking, *"Well, you certainly can't stay here."*

"Why not?" inquired a curious elderly historian from among the pack of suddenly uneasy natives.

Ki-ru-vad explained patiently. "It is a matter of the Commitment. A custom among the Iollth that extends backward for eons, to the time when our ancestors first emerged from the harsh hills of Ioll and set to fighting among themselves. The Commitment is one of our oldest traditions. On those exceedingly rare occasions when soldiers of Iollth are overcome, practice demands that the defeated pledge themselves and their fealty to the one responsible for their defeat." His attitude and tone showed that he did not believe the individual in question to be among the multitude of gaping Hyfft.

That was fine with the Delineator. Receiving allegiance from a host of the Hyfft's ancient enemies was not a condition she was anxious to accept, though she was prepared to do so. All the Hyfft wanted, now that peace and security had been obtained, was for the Iollth to go away and never come back. It had never occurred to the Delineator, nor the astronomer Ussakk standing nearby, nor even Yoracc the Historian, that their erstwhile tormentors might not wish to leave.

No, the Delineator corrected herself. That was not what the horrid, if overcome, Iollth had said. The bottom-heavy alien invader sought the one most responsible for the defeat of his kind. To her relief, she knew that praiseworthy individual was not to be found among the Hyfft.

Uncertainty followed the dissemination of this unexpected development. The commander of the visiting force of Niyyuuan soldiers was put forth as a logical candidate to receive the resolute Iollth commitment. He promptly declined the honor, and not just because he felt himself unworthy.

"Was not I who propounded strategy that led to victory," the officer explained honestly. Lifting a limber, armored arm, he gestured skyward. "Devising of tactics employed originates with senior command."

Word of the unanticipated conundrum was dutifully passed along to the ships in orbit. It stimulated energetic debate among Gerlla-hyn and his staff.

Gazing down at the milling throng of Iollth, Hyfft, and Niyyuu, George strained for a better look. "Wonder what they're deliberating down there? I thought this ceremony was supposed to be pretty much cut-and-dried."

"That's what I thought." From where he had been uncomfortably seated on a Hyfftian chair alongside his friend, Walker rose and leaned forward. "My translator doesn't work at this range, but it sure looks like they're arguing about something."

"Inconsequentialities." Behind them, Sque clung to the back of her seat and thought fondly of rain. "The lower orders worship mindless babble for its own sake." Behind her, scrunched down beneath the curving ceiling and up against the rear wall of the chamber, Braouk murmured verse under his breath, his vertically aligned jaws opening and closing silently in time to his thoughts.

"I not responsible for this development." Gazing out the port at the world below, his senior officers arrayed behind him, Gerlla-hyn was adamant. "None here can claim credit for such. For elaborating tactics that led to victory in battle, yes. But persuasion to do and therefore ultimate source of causality arose from other source." Neck frill erecting, tails twitching in unison, he gestured at the port. "Credit for initiating alliance with Hyfft lies elsewhere. True responsibility belongs to those who first propounded it." He glanced over at a technician. "Is only proper, I think, to so inform senior Hyfft as to who is nominal commander of expedition, and with whom final decision making on any course of Niyyuuan action ultimately rests."

George frowned as a pair of Hyfft approached. Ussakk the Astronomer was one of them. The other, clad in the finery of a Hyfftian administrator, eyed the canine with the kind of fawning adoration usually attributed to the dog's own kind.

Reaching the level where three of the four aliens reposed, Ussakk made sure his translation gear was fully operational before beginning. Glancing only briefly at George and Sque, the astronomer directed his attention to the lone human, who at the moment was looking more than slightly bemused.

"Your presence is required below," he announced politely.

Walker frowned. "Is there a problem with the surrender?" He looked past the much shorter Hyfft. "I thought the Iollth had already agreed to the terms of the treaty."

"They have," Ussakk informed him. "This is something else. Something in the nature of a post-surrender complication. There is some awkwardness. The Niyyuu have been in touch with their superiors." A small, furry hand gestured cryptically. "It appears only you can resolve the quandary, friend Walker."

"Me?" The commodities trader blinked. "What about the surrender could possibly involve me?"

"Maybe both sides need you to bake surrender cookies," George quipped tartly. With a sigh, he dropped off his seat and started down the ribbed walkway. "Come on. The sooner we find out what they want, the sooner we can head out for Tuuqalia."

The rendering of the Commitment was no small matter. Having been conquered, Ki-ru-vad knew that he and his kind had no choice in the matter. But one could hope for a respectable recipient. Ki-ru-vad studied the human intently. Appearance-wise, the creature was certainly an improvement over the inoffensive Hyfft. While not as tall as the Niyyuu who had done the actual fighting against his kind, the nearly hairless biped was considerably broader and presumably more muscular. Its eyes bespoke a certain intelligence, though less so than the slick-skinned decapod that spread out across the floor behind it. Most promising of all was the tentacled monster that loomed impressively over every other sentient in the room.

But it was the biped that the Hyfft and a Niyyuuan officer had urged forward.

"Wait a minute," Walker protested. What was happening here? "What's going on? What's this all about?" His questions ceased when Ki-ru-vad raised his right side and took a heavy, ceremonial step toward him.

The top of the defeated alien's slim skull came up to the level of the human's chest. Extending its short arms, the Illoth turned them bony side down in a gesture that meant nothing to Walker. One massive foot slid forward, to slide atop the commodities trader's right foot. At that, each of the three members of his caste who accompanied him raised a right foot and placed it behind their neck, balancing easily on their other broad foot. Walker's translator received the alien's words as Niyyuuan speech and efficiently translated them into English.

"Know, all present, that we of the dominion caste, and those of all the lower castes aboard the Five, do thus offer fealty to the architect of our defeat."

Walker swallowed hard. "Excuse me?"

Wide, powerful feet returned to the floor. Ki-ru-vad slipped his own off of Walker's. The alien's foot had not pressed down hard, but neither did it exhibit the disgustingly gracile touch of the Hyfft, either.

"We are yours," the Iollth repeated more succinctly. "All castes, all ships. This is the might of the Commitment. So it has been since the beginnings of Iollth civilization. So it will be until the last of my people breathe their last."

"No. Oh no." Backing up, Walker waved both hands, palms outward, at the alien. Ki-ru-vad strove mightily to grasp the meaning of the energetic but incomprehensible gesture. "We don't want that. *I* don't want that. There's been some mistake."

Next to him, an amused George was slowly shaking his head from side to side. "You make a decent cook, Marc, but a lousy pack leader." He grinned, showing white teeth. "I guess the Niyyuu don't want the responsibility, either. Gerlla-hyn and his staff must have fingered you once again as the titular leader of the expedition. Carrying that logic to its conclusion, I guess that makes you the ultimate 'architect' of the defeat of the Iollth."

A glance at the small group of Niyyuuan officers confirmed the dog's assessment. Dazed, Walker turned to his other companions. "I can't do this. I can't be expected to do this. I'm already in over my head with the Niyyuu. Braouk, maybe if you . . . ?"

With a shifting of his lower limbs, the huge Tuuqalian turned his dorsal side on the human—though both eyes, on the ends of their stalks, continued to gaze back at him.

"Not for me, the command of others, for fighting. I am a gentle singer of songs, reciter of sagas, lover of the open plains profound. Better for you, manipulator of clever schemes, to lead."

Desperately, Walker tried another approach. "Listen to me, you puerile purveyor of punk poetry! You're the toughest fighter among us, worth more on the battlefield than any fifty humans *or* Niyyuu. I've seen what you can do, everyone has, and it makes you the master of throwing more than words around! It's your chance to use your true natural abilities, to direct others, to—"

Pivoting on four massive lower tentacles, the Tuuqalian thrust both eyestalks toward Walker so sharply that the human nearly stumbled backward. Even George flinched.

"Not this time, will you incite me, with taunting. We are not now on board the Vilenjji ship, surrounded by captors I was delighted to dismember." A huge tentacle wagged knowingly at Walker. "I am on to you, cunning human." Strong enough to rip off one of Walker's arms, or his head, a second upper tentacle reached toward him—to allow the sensitive tip to stroke the tense commodities trader's right shoulder and drag lightly across his chest.

"You are my friend, Marcus Walker. We have been, through very much together, we two. But in your anxiety you forget that my size and strength does not make me stupid." Withdrawing, the tentacle joined the other on Braouk's right side to wave in the direction of the patiently waiting Iollth.

"These have pledged themselves to you, according to their own custom. Such traditions are no less legitimate than those of my own people. Or those of the Niyyuu, who have done the same." One eye dipped so close that Walker could study his own reflection in the perfectly spherical ocular. "Our objective here, for all of us, is homegoing. If that means that you must show the way for Iollth as well as for Niyyuu, it must be so. Accept this new burden with the grace and skill of which I know you are capable, Marcus Walker." The eye retracted. "And maybe later, you can make dinner, for all."

Rebuffed by the Tuuqalian, a troubled Walker turned to the

K'er-emu. Raising several tentacles of her own, Sque fore-stalled him. From the center of her body, her pinkish speaking tube danced as she spoke.

"I anticipate what you are about to say, friend Marc. That as your intellectual and moral superior, I should be the one to assume this obligation. That, there being no comparison between your level of native intelligence and mine, I should be the one to assume the onus of command of these rapacious but conciliatory folk. That given your inborn obtuseness and ignorance, I should—"

He interrupted dryly. "Granting for a moment the validity of the never-ending comparisons between your species' abilities and mine, Sque—how about it?"

Silvery eyes regarded him unblinkingly. "I wouldn't think of challenging you for command, Marc. You are clearly the one best suited to stand in the line of fire and—wait, allow me to rephrase. You are the designated nominal commander of our expedition. It's only right and proper that you ultimately give direction to these simple folk as well as to our humble friends the Niyyuu." A tentacle wiped meaningfully at one eye. "As ever, I shall be available to offer constructive advice, should you have the sagacity to seek it."

As a last hope, Walker turned to George. Except that George was no longer lingering in the vicinity of his feet. The dog had wandered off and was conversing with the astronomer Ussakk. Seeing Walker staring at him, George raised one paw and waved cheerily.

Ki-ru-vad took a step forward—which, given the size of Iollth feet, constituted no small advance. "You *must* do this thing, Marcus Walker. It has been true throughout the modern history of the Iollth that those who are strong enough to defeat us inevitably lead the defeated on to greater glory and triumph."

"That'd be you, I reckon," observed George, who had trotted back to rejoin his companion. "Or you could offer to lead them to the food synthesizers, though I expect when Ki-ru-vad here speaks of 'greater glory,' he's thinking of something on a somewhat more meaningful scale." Walker glared down at the dog, then turned back to the expectant Iollth officer.

"What if I say no? What if I simply refuse? Won't you go on as you have before—taking your new treaty with the Hyfft into account, of course?"

A small hand executed a gesture Walker could not interpret. The eyes of the Iollth had turned, of all things, limpid.

Surely, an aghast Walker told himself, this leader of murdering invaders, this representative of a species of raiding, killing sentients, was not going to stand before him and cry?

Ki-ru-vad did not. But his reply was undeniably impassioned. "You and your allies have beaten us. We cannot return thus to Ioll. The shame would require that we step, one by one, every member of every caste, naked into the space through which we traveled. Some new victory, however modest, must first accrue to us before we can go home." Though the squat, powerful form straightened, the head of the Iollth still reached no higher than Walker's neck.

"You have to understand, Marcus Walker, that this is how it has always been for the Iollth. You are not of any caste, so your defeat of us carries with it no permanent stain. It is only the weight of the downfall we must remove. This can only be done by replacing loss with triumph, and this must be initiated by the conquerors themselves."

"You again," George reminded his friend helpfully.

"I'm not a conqueror," a frustrated Walker protested firmly. "I'm a cook. And a commodities trader."

"A trader!" The revelation (though Walker felt it to be more of a confession) seemed to please Ki-ru-vad. "Then you must understand what is at stake here, and how it must be resolved. Defeat *must* be replaced by triumph. You are not in the forefront: you are in the middle. A trader true. An honest broker of downfall and resolution." One foot rose up toward him. Sensing that some sort of response was in order and not knowing what else to do, Walker reached down and grabbed the foot. The material of the slipper-like covering was sand-papery rough. The alien sustained the one-foot-in-the-air pose seemingly without effort.

"You accept."

"No, wait," Walker began again. But Ki-ru-vad had already lowered his right foot.

"It is done. The Commitment has been bestowed." While Walker sought urgently for a way to object further, the Iollth was already speaking into his communicator. Next to him, his three companions had raised their own right feet and were showing the fabric-clad soles to Walker and his friends. A salute, a gesture of fealty, a sign of acquiescence—he had no way of knowing the deeper meaning of the dramatic podal gesture. In fact, he was increasingly certain of only one thing.

He was stuck with it.

Feeling a demand for attention at his left leg, he gazed morosely down at where George was pawing his knee. "Congratulations, Marc."

The trader-chef-conqueror sighed heavily. "What am I going to do? I can't even call in to a radio talk show for ideas."

"Don't panic. You've got us." The dog nodded in the direction of the meditating Braouk and the quietly satisfied Sque. "You've got me. We helped you deal with the Niyyuu. We'll help you deal with these turnip-shaped assassins as well." His ears drooped slightly. "I'm not sure any of this will help us get any closer to home, but I am sure of one thing."

Kneeling, an unhappy but increasingly resigned Walker began stroking George's head, front to back. It was debatable whether the action made the dog or himself feel better. "Nice to know somebody's sure of something. What is it?"

Turning his head, but not so far that it moved out from beneath Walker's massaging hand, the dog indicated the gathering of alien beings that surrounded them: resourceful Hyfft, war-loving Niyyuu, ferocious Iollth.

"Wherever we go from here, we're a lot less likely to be picked on."

Sharing similar martial philosophies, if not predatory behavior, the Niyyuu accepted the presence of the five Iollth ships far more readily than Walker had their overall command. Of course, it was Gerlla-hyn and his staff who were actually in charge of the practicalities of integrating the Iollth force and coordinating their movements with their own. Walker's "command" was a useful fiction. As interaction and exchange increased, the Iollth became aware that the human was at once more and less than he seemed. But if the Niyyuu, whose skill and tactics had actually defeated them, were willing to accept the strangely hesitant biped as their ostensible leader, the Iollth were more than willing to go along.

The Niyyuuan ship that had become home to Walker and his friends was once more speeding through the interstellar realm by means he still could not fathom. Or rather, the fleet was. Did eight ships constitute a fleet? What would the enlightened Sessrimathe have thought had they been able to see the four oddly-paired former abductees now? For that matter, he mused, what would his friends and coworkers back home think?

Don't get carried away, now, he warned himself. *You're only the "nominal" leader of this escalating force. Gerlla-hyn is really the leader of the Niyyuu, and Ki-ru-vad's caste is in charge of his people. You're no more than a figurehead.*

A figurehead who was listened to, however.

He wasn't worried about losing perspective. To dominate, to rule, one had to want to do so. He wanted exactly the opposite. This invented command had been forced on him. He'd only taken it on, twice now, to mollify others, to satisfy their cultural needs.

After all, as Sobj-oes had explained it to him once she and the rest of the Niyyuu had been informed of the turn events had taken, the Iollth were a space-going species just like the

Niyyuu, or the Sessrimathe, or many others. They had traditions deserving of respect, even if the manner in which their traditions were sometimes executed were to be deplored.

Initial requests for Walker and his friends to visit the Iollth ships had been politely declined. At first offended, the Iollth were informed by their former foe and new allies the Niyyuu that as commander of such an extensive force, the human Walker had far too much on his mind to devote any time to such frivolities, pleasant though they might be. This excuse the Iollth understood. At speed, of course, any kind of physical ship-to-ship transfer was impossible. So the Iollth would have to wait until the ships emerged back into normal spacetime before they could further venerate their new leader.

Though she was as fully Niyyuu as any warrior of her kind, Sobj-oes, for one, was relieved that the fighting had been resolved with so little loss of life and that all available resources could once more be devoted to trying to carry their four guests homeward—and to the pursuit of science.

"As has been discussed, given what we know about when each of you was taken by the Vilenjji, when we reach world of Tuuqalia we will ask information of their astronomers and try work out vectors for Earth and K'erem from there."

"*If* we can find Tuuqalia." From his cushion on the other side of the cabin, George spoke without raising his chin from the fabric. "As I recall, you don't have an exact course to the nearest port. Just a line on the general area."

Sobj-oes's neck frill flared. "We confident that once in spatial vicinity of advanced world like Tuuqalia, will be able locate system of singer-warrior Braouk. Work of Hyfftian astronomers correlates well with initial calculations made on Niyu." Towering over the dog, she bent toward him. "You should have more confidence in yous friends, friend George." Straightening, she gestured toward Walker, who lounged nearby trying to unravel the secrets of a Hyfftian play-globe and its concentric spheres of electric color. "You should try be more like your companion Walker."

"You mean, 'dim'?" Unreassured, the dog sank his face even lower into the cushion.

From the far side of the cargo cabin that had been modified for their personal use, Braouk parted vertically aligned jaws and displayed saw-edged teeth. "There is a sub-saga that specifically addresses your apprehension, friend George. If you like, I will recite it, for you."

The dog looked over at the vast hill of flesh that was the Tuuqalian. Braouk had been less melancholy than usual lately. And no wonder, George mused sourly. It was *his* homeworld they were heading for.

"Thanks, Braouk, but I'm not in the mood."

"Set your mind at rest, sardonic quadruped." From her resting place in a misting fountain that had been installed specifically for her comfort, Sque squinted across at the cynical canine. "So long as you have my enlightening and didactic company to enjoy, you are being well looked after. Probably more so than in your entire life."

Raising his head slightly from the soft artificial material, George gazed thoughtfully at the K'eremu. What would it be like to have a creature like her as a master? he found himself wondering. Of course, Sque doubtless felt she was master of them all already.

Master. Though they had taken him as a captive, the Vilenjji had also given him higher intelligence and the power of speech. In addition to allowing him to communicate with others, these "enhancements" had saddled him with the ability to reflect.

Born a street dog, he'd never had a master. Eking out an existence on the back streets and in the alleys of Chicago, he'd sometimes envied, in his primitive, uncognitive canine fashion, the pampered appearance of dogs on leashes and in cars. They smelled of food, rich and thick. Now he was able to understand why. They lived in houses or apartments with humans. As pets, who had masters. Having been granted intelligence, he knew he now could never suffer such an existence, no matter how cosseting. Not only had he seen too much and experienced too much: he knew too much.

What if, upon some still tenuous and possibly dubious return to Earth, his alien-imparted enhanced intelligence failed, leaving him once more as incapable of advanced cognition as the other mutts with whom he had roamed the rough streets, fighting and breeding, only dimly aware of the greater reality through which they moved? The prospect made him shudder. If it happened, would it occur instantly or as a slow, agonizing diminution of consciousness? When it finally happened, would he even retain enough awareness to be conscious of the loss?

He found himself staring at Walker. Wholly absorbed in trying to puzzle out the workings of the Hyfftian toy, the human ignored him. They had been through much together. Unbelievable experiences. Did that guarantee that in the event of intelligence loss Walker would take him in? As a *pet*? Would Walker have him fixed?

There were times, he brooded gloomily, when he regretted the involuntary modifications the Vilenjji had made to him. While his enhanced intelligence had opened him to, literally, a universe of experience, it also simultaneously forced him to contemplate the horror of its possible loss. His was no longer a dog's life, simple but content, ignorant but mentally at ease. With a sigh, he rolled onto his side and stretched, all four legs quivering slightly as he did so. In this position he could see one of the many floating readouts that populated the interior of the Niyyuuan ship. At present it was displaying the view outside, precisely adjusted for spatial-temporal distortion. Stars and nebulae shone in the heavens, an unimaginably impressive blaze of ferocious light and dazzling color. Before, they had only been points of light dotting the night sky. Now, he knew what they were. That knowledge simultaneously enhanced and diminished his view of them.

He felt a sudden urge to howl, and caught himself barely in time.

Hyperspace, doublespace, inside-out space: the name for the continuum they were passing through translated differently depending not only on whether one was speaking with Niyyuu as opposed to Iollth, but on specific moments in time and transition. Elsewhere, George took to calling it. Whether standing still or traveling at speed by starcraft, it was the place he and his human had been consigned to ever since their abduction from Earth.

"It doesn't matter, Marc," the dog declared as they made their way toward the central command room. "Wherever we are, it's someplace we shouldn't be."

"Not true." Walker nodded to a passing Iollth avatar as the perambulating image of the squat creature floated past them. Similar ancient and traditional martial interests had gone a long way toward relaxing the initial tension between the tormentors of the Hyfft and their Niyyuuan conquerors, so much so that electronic avatars of both species were now allowed to visit one another's ships.

"We are someplace definite," he told his friend. "We're on our way home."

The dog let out a derisive snort. "*Our* way home? We're on our way to Tuuqalia, and that if we're lucky. Earth is still nothing more than a word. And if we don't find Tuuqalia, we'll probably have to go all the way back to Hyff and start all over again—or even back to Niyu." He snapped at an imaginary passing fly. "Intellect notwithstanding, what I wouldn't give for the comfort of a sweet bitch and an old bone."

Mentally drifting, Walker nearly murmured, "Me too," before the detailed meaning of his friend's words sank in. "Steak," he mumbled. "Real coffee. No more synthetics."

"We've arrived," George prompted him, breaking into his companion's reverie. "Better pack in useless thoughts. No drooling in the command center."

Gerlla-hyn and Sobj-oes were waiting for them. The Niyyuuan Commander-Captain's frill was taut and his tails were quivering, while the astronomer was clearly straining to contain herself. Above them, multiple levels of Niyyuuan technicians worked at mobile consoles, the design of their workspace reflecting the vertically inclined aesthetic of their kind. A Niyyuuan worker was more comfortable above or below colleagues than beside them.

Though no more unpleasant than that of any other of his kind, Gerlla-hyn's voice still grated on Walker's ears. He was not used to the sound of Niyyuuan voices—and never would be. Such acceptance was beyond the aural tolerance of any human. But he and George had both learned to endure the persistent scraping noises that emerged from the slender Niyyuuan throat to form the terse, brusque speech of their kind.

"Wonderful news!" The Commander-Captain's obvious enthusiasm somewhat allayed the shock to Walker's ears. "We have pick up strong signals that yous large friend Braouk has identified as belonging his people." Twirling gracefully, Gerlla-hyn gestured toward a large floating readout. It responded to his prompting with symbols and ideographs that were as alien as ever to Walker. But there was no mistaking the diagram of a star system upon which all manner of lines devolved.

George sniffed the readout. It had no odor. "Tuuqalia?"

"We hope so. Signalings have been tracked to the fourth world in." Thrusting one of the two long fingers on his left hand into the readout, the Commander-Captain stirred the promising mix. "Am informed by Braouk signalings could be coincidental, or from visiting Tuuqalian ship, but volume and strength of same suggests planetary origin."

"Latest available schematics have been provided yous oversize companion," a visibly pleased Sobj-oes informed them. "Distance makes impossible for him to render opinion on surrounding starfield. Is complicated by fact that he not astronomically inclined himself."

"A simple soul, our Braouk," Walker murmured as he watched George wander around behind the readout. "I'm sure I couldn't identify my own system from a light-year or two out." He eyed Gerlla-hyn. "So what you're saying is, essentially, we won't know if this is for real until we get there?"

"Ably put, Marcus." Sobj-oes consulted the slim reader that resided in her hands so often Walker would not have been surprised to learn it was surgically affixed to its owner. "Will emerge into normal space soon and initiate formal contact. Friend Braouk says his people a developed, spacegoing species, though not as avid travelers as Sessrimathe. Must ensure upon emergence that is no confusion as to our intentions."

Walker frowned. "Why would there be? As soon as they learn of our purpose in coming here, they're sure to—"

George interrupted him, his words sage and knowing. "When a strange dog wanders into your neighborhood, Marc, you check him, or her, out. When a strange *pack* wanders in, you raise your hackles, show your teeth, growl, and prepare to run or stand your ground." One upraised paw indicated the small sphere that represented their destination. "Not being able to run, the inhabitants of this world, be they Tuuqalian or anything else, are likely to do the latter."

The dog's opinion was supported by Gerlla-hyn. "If one

ship is detected emerging into normal space of system, would be likely no notable reaction on part of locals. But are now eight ships escorting you and yous companions. Is number unusual enough to be intimidating." He cast an approving glance down at George. "Would be atypical if locals not show teeth and growl at such an appearance." His tone then changed slightly to indicate mild puzzlement. "What are 'hackles'?"

"Think your frill," the dog suggested.

Three days later, the inhabitants of the fourth world of the system they were entering raised something somewhat more impressive than hackles or frill.

Braouk's joy knew no bounds when the first transmissions aimed at the arriving Niyyuuan and Iollth ships were not only determined to be Tuuqalian in origin, but that they indeed emanated from that long-sought homeworld itself.

"So long away, from my own world, almost forgotten." Braouk did not cry, but both eyestalks and upper tentacles trembled in tandem. It was an astonishing sight. "I can hardly believe we are actually here, nearing the homeworld."

"After all we've been through," George observed perceptively from the far side of the converted cargo area, "I can hardly believe we're near *anybody's* homeworld."

Everyone turned their attention to Sobj-oes. The Niyyuuan astronomer had entered their private quarters to deliver the good news in person. Her frill was flushed maroon, a sure sign of excitement. It made Walker think, even at that joyful moment, of Viyv-pym-parr. An episode in his increasingly improbable past. One best forgotten, yet one he seemed unable to shake. He forced himself to focus his attention on the astronomer.

"You're certain? We've been disappointed before."

Wider even than normal, tarsier-like eyes of yellow and gold turned to him. The round, muscular mouth flexed, the words it emitted mitigating the ear-tormenting timbre of the sound.

"There no mistaking response, Marcus. Utilizing translation facilities, communications staff have already had conversation with inhabitants of fourth world this system. Is without question Tuuqalia." Turning away from the human, she faced Braouk. "Has been explained one of their own is with us and relevant recording has been transmitted to provide credulous with proof."

"Essential that is, to reassure my brethren, of amity." Lowering both tentacles and eyestalks, Braouk rose from his crouch and advanced his tonnage toward the astronomer. "Nevertheless, they will not allow these ships to approach nearer than the orbit of the outer moon Suek. A natural precautionary measure." Though they were nowhere near enough yet to Tuuqalia for the large external readout screen to show anything other than empty space, he turned longingly in its direction.

"My people should be arriving soon. All those on Niyyuuan and Iollth vessels should be forewarned. The coming confrontation is a normal response and not a hostile gesture." While one plate-sized eye remained focused on the hovering readout, the other turned back to Sobj-oes. "It would not do to have the forthcoming greeting misinterpreted. The results could be catastrophic."

The depth of their friend's concern was soon illustrated by the nature of the Tuuqalian greeting to which he was referring. According to Berred-imr of the Niyyuuan command staff, no fewer than forty ships had risen from the vicinity of Tuuqalia to intercept the incoming force of Niyyuuan and Iollth vessels. It was by far the largest single grouping of starships Walker and his friends, or for that matter the Niyyuu, had ever encountered. Even on their arrival at Seremathenn, they had not seen so many interstellar craft assembled together in one place. What was even more impressive was their first glimpse of one such craft when it arrived and positioned itself fore of the *Jhevn-bha*. Even the intrepid Iollth confessed themselves to be more than a little impressed.

Being big people, the Tuuqalians had constructed big ships.

Taken together, the chain of huge blocky shapes that comprised the three conjoined lines of the Tuuqalian vessel massed more than any three individual Niyyuuan or Iollth craft. Realizing that forty of them now formed an englobement around his own ships was a daunting thought. Almost as daunting as the realization that Walker had come to think of them as "his" ships. The possessive was unintentional, he told himself. He was a nominal leader, not really in charge of anything. Gerlla-hyn was the real commander of the Niyyuuan force, and Ki-ru-vad's dominion caste the controllers of the Iollth quintet.

First, irrepressible thoughts of an inaccessible alien female, and now an absurd mental repositioning of individual importance. He definitely needed to get home. Quickly, before his reasoning splintered any further. More than anything, he needed Tuuqalia to be Earth. But it wasn't, any more than Seremathenn or Niyu had been, and he was going to have to deal with that.

Concentrate on your happy hulk of a friend Broullkoun-uvv-ahd-Hrashkin, he told himself. *Be delighted for him that he, at least, has finally found his way home. Share in his joy. Take your mind off ridiculous and improvident thoughts. And worry about what those forty ships are capable of and might do if someone drops a wrong word or makes a wrong move.*

Though the tension generated by the confrontation did not evaporate entirely on board the ships of the Niyyuu and the Iollth, it diminished considerably once the commanders of the Tuuqalian vessels were able to see and communicate directly with one of their own. As Braouk told his story, suitably embellished with the emblematic oratorical flourishes of his kind, Walker and George found themselves growing increasingly weary from the impassioned but interminable recitation. They had heard it all before, not to mention having experienced it for themselves. Eventually even the Niyyuuan staff in the command room turned to other pursuits as the energized Tuuqalian in their midst rambled on and on. Meanwhile the audience of his own kind listened raptly and apparently without boredom to the never-ending transmission.

Once again, Sque had been ahead of her friends. Envisioning the nature of the initial communication that was likely to take place between Braouk and his kind, the perceptive K'eremu had remained behind in their quarters, happily brooding in her custom-rigged misting pool. The longer Braouk rambled on, the more Walker wanted to join her himself.

Feeling a tug at his lower leg, he looked down to see George pulling at the hem of his pants. As soon as he had the human's attention, the dog released his grip and whispered urgently.

"At this rate we'll all die of old age before loopy eyes here finishes his story—let alone before we can start looking for Earth again."

Walker crouched down beside his friend. "We can't just cut him off in mid-speech," he murmured softly while the Tuuqalian orated on. "This is *his* story. His saga." He indicated the main viewer, which showed several senior Tuuqalians hanging in evident ecstasy on Braouk's every word. "Interrupting wouldn't only be impolite; it might damage our relations with his kinsfolk. We need to get off on the right foot here. We're going to need the help of their astronomers if we're going to have a chance of locating Earth from here."

"Yeah, yeah, I know," the dog muttered sullenly. His gaze returned to their oversized companion. As Braouk held forth, his four massive upper tentacles gestured energetically enough to generate a small breeze in the command room. When combined with the movement of his eyestalks, the effect was almost dizzying. "But if he doesn't shut up pretty soon, I'm going to pee on one of those four lower limbs. Let's see how he works that into his 'saga.' "

Fortunately, George never had to carry out his threat. After only another two hours of endless declamation, Braouk's floridly embellished tale of abduction and final return reached the point where he and his friends and allies had entered the Tuuqalian system and encountered the wary armada sent forth from his homeworld to meet them. All that remained, Walker supposed, was for them to be escorted into orbit around Tuuqalia itself, for Braouk to be warmly received by his brethren, and for the visitors to make application to whatever passed for a professional association of local astronomers to ask for their help in locating distant Earth.

Ignorant as he was of Tuuqalian society, he could hardly be blamed for being so sanguine. Or so wrong.

From orbit, Tuuqalia was an attractive oxygen-infused world. Though slightly larger than Earth, less area was covered by ocean and sea. There were mountains, and modest ice caps, but the dominating features were endless stretches of flat plains fractured by enormous meandering rivers. Unlike Hyff, whose population was evenly dispersed among thousands of towns and small cities, Tuuqalia boasted some extensive urban concentrations. While serving as centers of manufacturing and culture, however, they were not home to the majority of citizens.

Long centuries of the population management that had allowed Tuuqalian society to thrive without having to deal with the threat of overpopulation had also allowed the majority of its people to spread out across its endless plains. Advanced technology made work from a distance possible. Even more than the villatic Hyfft, the inhabitants of Tuuqalia favored a life in the countryside. This was no surprise to Walker and his friends. More hours than they cared to remember had been spent listening to Braouk natter on about the joys of roving his homeworld's vast open spaces, and how he could not wait to indulge once again in that wandering that was so dear to every Tuuqalian's heart. It was understandable, Walker knew. A species as individually outsized as Braouk's needed plenty of room in which to roam.

Well, their hulking friend wouldn't have to wait much longer to enjoy himself in that regard. As soon as they received proper clearance, they would all be able to stand once more on the solid surface of a habitable world, real earth under their feet and open sky above their heads. The difference was that this time, both earth and sky would belong to one of their own. After all they had been through together, it was still difficult to come to grips with the fact that one of them had actually made it home.

Which made the continuing delay in the granting of the necessary clearance all the more puzzling. Almost as puzzling as Braouk's seeming avoidance not only of Walker, but of George and Sque as well—though Sque was just as content to be ignored as not.

Walker wasn't. The same could be said not only for his canine companion, but for everyone else on board the *Jhevn-Bha*. Not to mention the Iollth, whose inherent limited capacity for tolerance and understanding threatened to destabilize an increasingly ambiguous situation. Despite being heavily outgunned by the fleet of massive Tuuqalian vessels that continued to shadow the arrivals while traveling toward their homeworld, Ki-ru-vad's prickly caste of characters threatened to commence landings without permission and dare the locals to react belligerently. The longer they sat in orbit without that permission, the edgier became the Iollth in particular.

Walker could hardly blame them. He wanted down as much as anyone, especially when the citizens of the world below were presumed to be friendly and welcoming. But if that was the case, then why the excessive delay?

At the risk of irritating his friend, he finally felt compelled to directly confront the only Tuuqalian in their midst.

"What's behind the continuing delay in granting us permission to visit, Braouk?" Though he tried to make his manner as forceful as possible, he knew there was no way a hundred humans could intimidate a Tuuqalian.

In spite of that reality Braouk's reaction smacked, if not of intimidation, at least of embarrassment. All four upper tentacles drew in close around his mouth while both eyestalks contracted until the Tuuqalian's eyes were flush against opposite sides of his trunk-like body. In that pose, he looked not only smaller, but far less alien—such a description, Walker knew, being a highly relative term.

"Yeah, what's the holdup?" George demanded to know from somewhere in the vicinity of Walker's knees. "We've had better receptions on worlds where all of us were strangers." The dog made a rude noise. "You offend somebody important before the Vilenjji snatched you?"

Powerful tentacles fluttered in four different directions. To anyone not familiar with the three-meter-tall Braouk, the effect would have been terrifying. Walker and George were merely surprised. Despite all the time they had spent in the Tuuqalian's company, this was a gesture they had not seen before. They did not know it, but their hulking friend was expressing extreme discomfiture.

"Seeking have I, a way to explain, this circumstance." Eyestalks contracted even tighter into the Tuuqalian's sides, the bulging orbs at their tips disappearing partway into matching recesses in his yellow-green, bristle-covered flanks. "It has been tormenting me even before we entered the heliosphere of Tuuq."

"Even before . . ." Walker's voice faded briefly as he digested the implication. Though no match in size for the basketball-sized orbs of the creature before them, his own eyes widened slightly. "You knew this was going to happen! How long have you known, Braouk?"

"And not told us," George added in a huff, using a hind leg to scratch at one ear.

"Since the day we left Seremathenn with thoughts of returning to our homes," the Tuuqalian rumbled apologetically. Seeking to soothe his companions' injured feelings, he added hastily, "No reason needed, to inform you then, of details. A requirement is demanded of all who wish to visit Tuuqalia. None are being singled out here; not inhabitants of Earth, or of Niyu, or of Ioll." Tentacles extended toward them, a reach for understanding. "Though desperate-dying, to touch my home, I remain. It is why I have stayed with you since our arrival, knowing that I could explain this aspect of my kind's culture better than any who might come to greet you."

"Some greeting." George stopped scratching and flomped disgustedly down onto the deck.

"I see that I cannot delay any longer, no matter the cultural repercussions that may arise."

Walker had been listening intently. He had also been thinking. "Wait a minute. What 'requirement'? What 'cultural repercussions'? Are you saying that unless we fulfill some kind of demand, your people won't let us make touchdown on Tuuqalia?"

One eye, the left one, extended slightly on its stalk, reaching toward him. In the center of the massive body, the fluttering central nostril twitched in agitation. "Not only will you not be allowed to touch down if you do not comply, no Tuuqalian scientist will lift a tentacle tip to help you on your way."

That implied threat was more than discourteous, Walker realized. It represented, potentially, the end of their journey. Without additional assistance from the Tuuqalia, he and George and Sque would have no new astronomical leads to follow. They had only managed to find Tuuqalia with the aid of the Hyfft. Without fresh insight from inhabitants of this part of the galactic arm, they would be left to search hundreds of star systems essentially at random—a task that was more than daunting. How long he could rely on the Niyyuu, much less the volatile Iollth, to continue such voyaging on behalf of him and his friends was an imponderable whose limits he devoutly wished not to have to test. Having a specific stellar destination in mind might make all the difference between being able to continue their search and its complete abandonment.

For that, they needed the help of another sophisticated star-traversing species like the Tuuqalia. And to gain that, they had to fulfill some as yet unexpressed requirement.

He took a deep breath, looked down at George, who shrugged resignedly, and put the question.

"Delaying this won't make implementation any easier, Braouk. What does this requirement consist of? What do George and I have to do to satisfy the appropriate authorities among your people that we're deserving of their hospitality and their help?"

The ton of Tuuqalian hesitated. Despite his size, strength, and daunting appearance, the huge alien looked for all the world like a self-conscious child who had just been caught raiding the cookie jar.

"You have to, to the authority's satisfaction, prove yourselves."

Though George had long ago moved beyond easy intimidation, he was ever suspicious. "Prove ourselves? How? Some kind of contest? Not wrestling, I hope. If that's the case, I'm out." He raised a forepaw. "No opposable thumb. Sorry, Marc."

"Let's not jump to conclusions," a suddenly concerned Walker responded. Addressing himself once more to their reluctant companion, he pushed the question. "Aside from the fact that everyone on these ships wants—no, needs—to feel solid ground under their feet again, we have to have the help and assistance of your people's astronomers. So—what is it that we have to do? To 'prove' ourselves?"

Emboldened by his friends' evident willingness to comply, Braouk was moved to explain. Time had run out anyway. The authorities had granted him more than enough time to put the demand diplomatically.

"The K'eremu are not the only species capable of unsociable behavior. My kind, too, have their pride. They do not accept, far less agree to assist, just any self-declared civilized sentients who come calling. Those who do so must demonstrate beyond doubt that they are capable of more than the construction of interstellar ships and advanced technologies. They must show that they are civilized. And not just civilized. They must demonstrate"—Walker's implanted Vilenjji translator struggled with what was unusually complex and Tuuqalian-specific terminology—"sensitivity."

Walker was taken aback. It was not what he expected. But whatever this required proof consisted of, he told himself, it had to be more amenable than wrestling.

"I'm sensitive." George rolled onto his back, all four feet in the air, tongue lolling out of the side of his mouth. "See?"

Having at last put the requirement into words, Braouk was visibly as well as verbally more relaxed. "More than physical submission is required. Much more. It has always been so among my people. The Tuuqalia grant their friendship without reservation, but not easily. Furthermore, one cannot satisfy for all. A representative of each species wishing the amity and assistance of the Tuuqalia must reassure individually." Both eyes were once more fully extended on their flexible stalks. One focused on Walker, the other on George.

"You, Marcus Walker, must act on behalf of not just yourself, but all your kind. And you for yours, George." The eyes retracted slightly, glistening. "Sequi'aranaqua'na'senemu for the K'eremu. Perhaps Gerlla-hyn, or possibly Sobj-oes, for the Niyyuu, and someone also for the Iollth. One of each."

One time, Walker reminisced, he had been called into the office of the vice president for operations of the firm for which he worked. On arriving, he had been rattled to find not just Steve Holmes, the officer, there, but representatives of several of the firm's major clients. Asked to give his opinion on half a dozen current world situations as they related directly to the firm's business, he'd been subjected to half an hour of intense questioning. Even though no one said so later, he was sure his ability to survive such intense interrogation on such short notice had led directly to his last promotion.

Now he found himself in a similar situation. Only this time, much more than an increase in salary and an office with a slightly better view of the building across the street was at stake. How not only he but how George and Sque and others performed would likely decide whether he would have any chance of ever seeing that office again.

Sque's frequent sardonic comments to the contrary notwithstanding, he felt reasonably confident he could prove that he was civilized. But—how to prove that he, and by inference humankind, was sensitive?

On later reflection, he realized he should have guessed.

"Now that I have finally been able to say these things to your faces," Braouk was telling them, "I will make the necessary arrangements. One each will be conveyed to the surface. One each to represent their own species. One each to prove they are fit to touch Tuuqalian soil." Eyes drew back and tentacles stiffened. "There is no way around this requirement."

"And if we blow it?" George asked.

Both orbs swiveled in the dog's direction. "Then you will have to go on your way, wherever that may be, without impacting Tuuqalian society, and without the aid of its eminent scientists. Companions though we are, companions in adversity though we have been, there will be nothing more I can do for you."

Tuuqalian first, friend second, Walker reflected. Would it have been any different had their situations been reversed? What would wary humans have demanded of someone like Braouk to prove that he was as civilized as they? Or as sensitive?

"I cannot explain, to newcomers in advance, the requirement." Their oversized friend was apologetic but unrelenting. "You will be informed of the details at a suitable time, subsequent to your arrival."

"That doesn't seem very fair," George protested, having regained his feet. "How can we get ready to comply with a requirement when we don't know what it is?"

Having lumbered forward, Braouk now gently rested the end of one tentacle on George's shoulders. The flexible limb was quite capable of reducing the dog's entire skeleton to splinters.

"Your ability to extemporize will comprise a significant portion of the proof," the Tuuqalian explained unhelpfully. "One way the authority will be able to judge both your degree of civilization and species sensitivity will be by observing your reaction to their demand."

"Thanks," the dog replied dryly as the tentacle tip stroked his back, ruffling his fur. "I feel so much better now. Why me?" he muttered under his breath. "Why not a mastiff, or a poodle?" He cast a wan look on his human. "All I want is a bone and a warm bed."

Walker's lips tightened. "We're stuck with this, George. Each of us gets to stand up not just for ourselves but for our entire species. As for me," he drawled, "I'd rather be in Philadelphia."

There was no one present to recognize or understand the reference, but it lightened his mood a little to say it anyway.

There was some hasty discussion among both the Niyyuu and the Iollth as to who among them might best be suited to complying with the still unspecified Tuuqalian demand. Without knowing its nature, it was impossible to determine which of their number would have the best chance of satisfying the enigmatic requirement of their gruff but hopeful hosts. Prove that they were civilized and sensitive, Walker and George had informed them. Who best among the crews of the three Niyyuuan vessels and the five Iollth ships to do that? Who was the most adaptable? Were the chosen representatives going to be expected to fight? Having watched Braouk dismantle tall, muscular Vilenjji as easily as he would a figure fashioned from Popsicle sticks, Walker preferred not even to consider that option. It wouldn't make much sense for them to gain the approval and cooperation of the Tuuqalians if all five of those selected to justify that gain perished in the process of acquiring it.

Though Braouk was not allowed to in any way prepare or coach them for the forthcoming ordeal, it was clear that his old friend desperately wished to do so. If anything, the Tuuqalian who had been their companion during their long journeying seemed more nervous than the human, his canine companion, and the respective Niyyuu and Iollth who were eventually selected to undergo the test.

Each being the sole representative of his kind, Walker and George were spared the discussions among Niyyuu and Iollth that followed the announcement of the Tuuqalian requirement. Of course, Braouk explained, it was not necessary for a representative of either species to participate. But if Sobj-oes and her small but vital contingent of astronomical specialists were to be allowed to consult with their Tuuqalian counterparts, at least one Niyyuu also had to satisfy the unbending local tradition. Learning that one of the tall, multi-tailed beings who had defeated them at Hyff was going to make the attempt, the Iollth felt it imperative that one of their own kind participate and meet the Tuuqalian criteria as well.

Discussion among both groups led to debate, and debate to open argument. There being only one of each of them, human and canine had no choice in the matter of who was to stand for their species. That was not the case among Iollth and Niyyuu. Internal conflict threatened to delay the business further, until an exasperated Walker pointed out to both groups that they were not exactly displaying the kind of sensitivity the Tuuqalians were looking for, and that if word of the ongoing dissention reached their erstwhile hosts, the original invitation itself might be withdrawn.

Abashed by an alien whose species had not even mastered the rudiments of interstellar travel, Niyyuu and Iollth settled down to the selection of one individual to represent each of their kind. Neither recognized that Walker's admonition to each had been based on the possible failure of the other. It was only one in a litany of techniques he had borrowed for use from his days as a trader of commodities. Tell one group that their competitors were acting in an acceptable manner while the other was not, and the first group was likely to comply with the teller's needs. Then reverse and apply to the other, and so gain the cooperation of both.

So it was that De-sil-jimd of the communications caste was chosen to join the group that would descend to the surface with Braouk as their guide and sponsor, while Sobj-oes's assistant Habr-wec was elected to represent the Niyyuu. Ignorant of what they were about to face, Walker thought them both good choices. It would be good to have a communications specialist among the group, as well as a representative of the astronomical team in the event the occasion arose to ask a pertinent question or obtain potentially useful information.

And while Iollth and Niyyuu had argued among themselves, and Gerlla-hyn had been forced to inform the outraged Niyyuuan media contingent that none of them would be permitted to record the confrontation, Walker strived mightily to convince Sque to participate.

"No, absolutely not." From within the mist cloud of her perpetually damp resting place, the equivalent of a human couch, the K'eremu adamantly refused to having anything to do with the upcoming challenge. Metallic gray eyes regarded the crouching Walker mordantly. "Am I wrong in assuming that despite my continued company and occasional tutelage you have progressed insufficiently far to recognize a negative when it is presented to you?"

Gritting his teeth, Walker held his temper and persisted. "Sque, we don't know what we're facing here. This is as important to you as it is to the rest of us. You know what'll happen if we don't gain the respect and approval of Braouk's people. No help in locating a possible line on Earth. No help in finding a vector for K'erem."

One limb adjusted a strand comprised of bits of colored glass that ran from the smooth crown of the K'eremu's head down her right side. It was beaded with moisture and radiant with reflected light.

"It has all the intimations of a cheap carnival, this 'requirement.' I refuse to debase myself to gain the sanction of a lot of bloated saga-spouting carnivores." Half her ten slender tentacles promptly entwined themselves in a complex knot no doubt fraught with ambiguous significance.

"Technologically advanced bloated saga-spouting carnivores," Walker reminded her coolly. "Astronomically competent bloated saga-spouting carnivores." He straightened, looking down at her. "The bloated saga-spouting carnivores whose help we need if any of the rest of us are going to have a prayer of getting home."

The K'eremu was unmoved. "You may perform for them however you wish and obtain the required assistance."

Walker rolled his eyes and tried to contain his exasperation. "You know that's not going to work. They want to pass on every species, and they already know there's a K'eremu on board because Braouk told them about you."

An unoccupied tentacle splashed water on argent eyes. "Always noise-making, that one." Bubbles formed at the end of her speaking tube, eventually to break free and wander off into the enclosed atmosphere of the room; visual punctuation. Another tentacle swung to the right and picked up a small, tightly sealed square container. An integrated readout on its exterior divulged the contents. It was where Sque kept her stock of si'dana drugs—or rather, stimulants, as she preferred to refer to them.

"It would appear that I have on hand a sufficiency of synthesized chemicals to enable me to tolerate such a degrading ordeal. Even in a fog of my own making I would expect no difficulty in satisfying the stipulations of our garrulous friend Braouk's demanding relations." Her entire body expanded and relaxed, like a momentarily inflated balloon. "I suppose I will have to do this."

Walker smiled. "Braouk will be delighted. He's anxious to show us his world. All of us."

"The lumbering sputterer of interminable singsong may not find my reluctant company quite so vitalizing. In any event, I am glad that one of us, at least, has been returned to their home." She climbed, or rather slithered, out of the misting pool. "His kind had better be able to render unto us the kind of scientific assistance we need, or I am certain I will regret this decision for the rest of my natural days."

"Oh, for heaven's sake," Walker snapped as he turned to leave. "You don't even know what the Tuuqalian requirement for entry consists of. It might require us to do nothing more than swear some kind of mild oath not to harm local interests, or to fill out in person a form or two." Feeling a tentacle questing along the back of his leg, he kicked it gently away. Back home, a rubbery, ropy contact like that might have made him jump a foot straight up. Over the past couple of years, he had grown used to and relaxed with touches that were even more alien.

"And stand off—I'm not Braouk, and I'm not going to carry you."

Slithering out of the cabin and into the first corridor on all ten tentacles, Sque blew a large bubble that, when it popped, disseminated a particularly malodorous aroma. Linguistic sophistication notwithstanding, the K'eremu were perfectly capable of venturing an opinion in a nonverbal manner.

10

The Tuuqalian shuttle that carried the representatives of the five visiting species—human, canine, K'eremu, Iollth, and Niyyuu—to the surface was itself larger than some interstellar craft the travelers had seen. A lot of the interior seemed to consist of empty space. No doubt when it was transporting the much bigger Tuuqalians, it was packed full.

Similarly, the interesting high-speed, multi-wheeled ground transport vehicle that transported them from the landing site into the city of Karoceen was plainly not designed for visitors. Everyone except the solicitous Braouk had to be helped to reach the vehicle's high entrance. Everyone, that is, except Sque. Using her suckerless tentacles, the most reluctant among the visitors was able to find sufficient purchase on the exterior of the transport to climb aboard by herself. This achievement had unintended unfortunate consequences, as her four companions were subsequently forced to listen to a patronizing discourse on the superiority of K'eremu physical as well as mental skills all the way into the metropolis.

Karoceen was of a size befitting the dimensions of its inhabitants. Far larger than any urban complex Walker and George had seen on Hyff or Niyu, it reminded them of the great metropolitan concentrations on Seremathenn itself. With one notable exception: few of the buildings were more than five or six stories (albeit they were Tuuqalian stories, he reminded himself) high. The Tuuqalia, Braouk explained in response to his question, were not fond of heights. So while Karoceen and its sister cities were enormous in extent, their skylines failed to impress.

Structures tended to have rounded corners, in keeping with Tuuqalian aesthetics, and large windows. Many appeared to be composed entirely of reinforced polysilicates or similar transparent materials. When the visitors exited the transport vehicle and were ushered into one notably tall building of five stories, Walker felt dwarfed by their native escorts. Being around one Tuuqalian, Braouk, had often been intimidating enough. Finding oneself on their world, surrounded by dozens of the multi-limbed, sawtoothed giants, would be enough to make anyone paranoid. He found himself staying close to the tall young Niyyuuan astronomer Habr-wec. The normally bold George was also intimidated to the point where he threatened to walk under Walker's feet and trip them both.

Only Sque, who had not wanted to come at all, appeared unimpressed, traveling in the manner to which she had become accustomed atop one of Braouk's powerful upper limbs, her own tentacles providing her with a grip Walker could only envy. She was spared the anxiety that afflicted him and the others by her unshakable innate sense of superiority, the knowledge that while all space-traversing species were sentient, the K'eremu were just a little more sentient than anyone else.

Senescent, more likely, Walker grumbled to himself even as he envied her feeling of invincible self-confidence.

Not knowing what to expect, he was taken aback when Braouk and their escort of four massive armed Tuuqalians finally halted before a pair of towering doors.

"We are here," their friend informed them, before adding cryptically, "With luck, this will take a long time."

Walker did not have the opportunity to ask what Braouk

meant by that before the doors folded into opposing walls and they were conducted inside.

The chamber was immense, a gilded hall with a floor that sloped upward instead of down as would have been the case in a comparable human facility. There were no chairs. Like the Iollth, the Tuuqalians neither used nor needed such furnishings. Climbing the slight slope that appeared to be paved with a single continuous strip of something like varnished lapis lazuli, they approached a waiting semicircle of Tuuqalians. The distance between doorway and dais being equally Tuuqalian-sized, Walker felt as if he was hiking across the floor of a vast indoor sports arena instead of simply from one side of a meeting room to the other. Silence save for the muted *slap-slap* of their escorts' lower limbs against the floor and a steady cool breeze whose source he could not discern made the distance to be traversed seem all the greater.

Braouk's people had no more use for clothing than they did for chairs, though the dozen or so figures did flaunt various pendants and other identifying devices that encircled their uppermost limbs like massive bracelets. Twenty-four bulbous, unblinking eyes regarded the approaching visitors, bobbing and weaving at the ends of muscular, flexible eyestalks. The sight was as hypnotic as it was unnerving.

The last time Walker had been so intimidated by rank size was when he had been forced to confront the Ohio State offensive line his senior year at his university. There was no basis for actual physical comparison, of course. The smallest of the aliens squatting before him on its four lower tentacles massed as much as the entire State line. The number of writhing, gesturing tentacles arrayed in front of him reminded him of a horde of pythons leisurely contemplating potential prey.

One of the unabashedly curious officials bade the arrivals and their escort halt. Silence ensued while additional stares were exchanged. Standing in a hall that seemed large enough to manufacture its own weather, surrounded by alien giants, some of whom were even bigger than his friend Braouk, Walker waited for whatever might come. There was no backing out now, he realized. No changing one's mind and asking to be returned to the safety of the *Jhevn-bha*. And he didn't think offering to prepare dinner for the dozen officials squatting before him would allow him and his friends to avoid having to satisfy the still mysterious, unstated "requirement." Right now, the only thing available to cut with a knife was the tension.

It was broken by the Tuuqalian squatting at the far left end of the line. Walker's implant had no trouble translating the straightforward local singsong.

"Let the nearer biped begin first!"

With the representatives of the Niyyuu and Iollth standing to his right, it struck Walker that the speaker was referring to him. Dozens of eyestalks immediately coiled in his direction. He could have done without the attention.

Turning to Braouk's familiar, reassuring shape, he whispered, "What are we supposed to do? What am *I* expected to do? How do we go about satisfying this demand of your people to prove that we're sufficiently civilized and sensitive enough to be allowed to visit your world?"

Each nearly the size of his head, both eyes curved close to him. It was a measure of how far he had come and how much he had changed that their proximity did not unsettle him in the least.

"You must do, the same as I, friend Marcus."

Seeking clarification, he'd hit upon only bafflement. Aware that he was now the focus of the attention of everyone in the vast hall, from Tuuqalian escorts and officials to his own companions, he struggled for understanding.

"Do the same? The same what?" He spread both hands. "You know as well as anyone what I can do, Braouk. I can broker trades, and I can cook."

His massive friend was unrelenting. "You must do one

more thing, Marcus. You must do as I." A pair of tentacles swept down the length of the assembled. "Show them the level of your civilization. Show them your sensitive nature. Recite to them, as best you can, a saga. Intonation is important, inspiration is foremost, format is forgiving."

Near Walker's feet and oblivious to the significance of the moment, George was snickering. "Go ahead, Marc. Sing them a saga of humankind. You could use your own original kindly, polite, human profession as a springboard."

"You're not helping," Walker hissed at his canine companion. Furiously, he tried to think of a subject that would satisfy the demands of those assembled to pass judgment not merely on him, but on his entire species. If he failed, it might not mean a crisis: one or more of his companions might proceed to satisfy the Tuuqalian requirement. But it would not be a good way to begin. Besides, now that he was here, he very much wanted to see something of Braouk's homeworld. There was also a matter of pride involved. When faced with a challenge, he had never let his firm down. Could he do no less for his entire species? Fortunately, he didn't have to sing—only to recite. Choosing his words carefully, modifying them to fit the traditional Tuuqalian saga-pattern, he cleared his throat, took a deep breath and began.

"Big blue blot, floating out in space, so far. Very far away, too far for me, to reach. Blue with water, green with growing plants, white clouds. One special city, by a big lake, my home. It miss it, the good and bad, so much. My heart hurts, every time I think, of it. It's your help, that we really need, right now. To find Earth, and my friend Sque's, homeworlds."

He rambled on, sometimes without effort, at other times having to pause as long as he dared to think furiously (did speed count?). The longer he scribed the story, the easier the words came. Having lived alongside Braouk for so long made settling into the proper speech pattern simpler than he would have believed possible.

Amazing what one could pick up over the years, depending

on the company one kept, he thought even as he continued to churn out words and phrases of parallel pacing. The longer he spun narrative without interruption or objection, the more confident he felt that he was at least being listened to, and the wider the field of acceptable subject matter that occurred to him. Then, with unexpected abruptness, he hit a mental wall. With no more reminiscences to share, no further hopes to declaim, and growing slightly hoarse besides, he just stopped. If the Tuuqalians who had been watching and listening to him had been expecting or waiting for a big finish, it was denied to them. The stress of fulfilling the demand had exhausted him physically as well as mentally.

A wet nose nudged his leg. George looked up at him with as solemn an expression as he had ever seen on the dog's face. "That," his friend informed him somberly, "was as eloquent a collection of words as I've ever heard dribble from your protruding lips, man."

"Thanks, George." Both the Niyyuuan and Iollth representatives also crowded around him to offer muted congratulations, while Braouk threatened to smother his much smaller friend with a complimentary lashing of tentacles. As usual, Sque vouchsafed offering anything like a direct compliment. But neither did she hiss her usual ration of denigration. In fact, when he happened to glance in her direction, the size and shape of the bubbles she was casually burbling from her flexible breathing tube suggested a certain modicum of nonverbal approval.

None of which mattered, of course. Ignoring the continuing congratulations of his friends, he shifted his attention to the line of massive, convened adjudicators. They, too, had been conversing quietly among themselves ever since he had finished. Now the Tuuqalian on the right end of the line, farthest from the one who had instructed Walker to begin, fluttered its single nostril as beartrap-like jaws parted.

"Is good enough, to allow for welcoming, your kind."

Walker's spirits rose as if he had just pulled off a three-way trade involving dollars, euros, and a shipload of raw mahogany. Since at present his kind referred only to him, he assumed he was in.

He was given no time to savor his accomplishment. It was the turn of the young Niyyuuan astronomer to saga-spin on behalf of his people. Having had time to prepare, thanks to Walker's inspired bit of homesick spieling, Habr-wec declaimed in proper Tuuqalian the configuration of stars and planets, of his hopes for learning more about them, of how this journey was the fulfillment of a dream held by every fellow astronomer relegated to observing the heavens only from a planetary surface, and of his hopes that his counterparts on this beautiful world would help him and his friends to realize their goal of returning to their homes the victims of unwarranted abduction presently stranded in their midst. As he spoke, his neck frill flared fully erect, and like a quartet of furry metronomes, his tails kept time to his speaking. Nothing could be done about his Niyyuuan voice, however, the sandpapery nature of which grated even on the recessed hearing organs of the tolerant and attentive row of Tuuqalians.

Despite that unavoidable awkwardness, the concise saga spun by the unexpectedly expressive young scientist also passed muster.

In spite of having been granted far more time to prepare, De-sil-jimd of the Iollth seemed hesitant to begin. Not nervous, Walker thought. Just uncertain. As fidgeting became noticeable among the impatient line of Tuuqalian adjudicators, Walker and his friends gathered around the reluctant communications specialist.

"What's wrong?" Walker whispered. "Can't you think of anything to say?"

"Iollth good fighters, but maybe that all," Habr-wec suggested tactlessly. Walker threw him a dirty look, which did no harm because it was not understood.

De-sil-jimd straightened on his powerful hind legs. "That

is not the problem. I can think of much to say, and the form of speaking is not difficult for my kind." Small dark eyes met Walker's. "The problem is that I can only think of one subject to speak strongly about, and it is nothing like the subjects to which you or the skinny Niyyuu have spoken. I am worried it might offend our welcomers."

Walker frowned. "What subject were you thinking of using as a basis for your saga?"

De-sil-jimd turned on his oversized feet to better regard the taller human. "Predation. The Hyfft would understand."

Walker nodded knowingly. It was certainly a contrast with the serene, peaceful subject matter which he and Habr-wec had addressed. But if it was all the Iollth could think of around which to spin the requisite saga . . .

How *would* the Tuuqalians react? There was only one way to find out.

"Might as well give it a try," he suggested to the bottom-heavy alien. "All they're likely to do is refuse your people landing rights. Habr-wec and I are already in."

The Iollth gestured tersely. Turning slowly, he faced the line of increasingly impatient Tuuqalians and, in a high-pitched voice that was a welcoming contrast to the Niyyuuan discordance that had preceded it, began.

To everyone's relief, the pugnacious nature of the communications specialist's short narrative was in no way off-putting to the attentive jury. If anything, they appreciated its robust nature more than did any of De-sil-jimd's mildly appalled companions. Thinking back to the unrestrained ferocity Braouk had exhibited on board the Vilenjji capture ship, Walker realized he ought not to have been surprised. The Tuuqalians were as open to aggressive saga-spinning as they were to more tranquil reminiscing.

That left only two among the visitors to gain their hosts' tentacle-wave of approval. Her initial reluctance to even participate now appeared in direct contrast to Sque's dynamic verbal invention on behalf of her kind. In fact, after half an hour of tale-telling in perfect Tuuqalian form accompanied by much waving of tentacle tips and blowing of bubbles, those who constituted the imposing array of judges were starting to squirm once again, though this time not from impatience. It was left to Walker to approach the energetically orating K'eremu, crouch down to eye level, and make gentle shushing motions.

Halting in mid-declamation, four tentacles held aloft and preparing to gesture dramatically, she peered over at him. "Something is wrong, Marcus Walker?"

He had long since learned that delicate diplomacy was wasted on a K'eremu. "I think you've sagaed enough, Sque. Time to let our hosts pass judgment. Superb invention, by the way."

"Of course it is," she replied, lowering two of the four uplifted tentacles. "All of my vocalizing is superb. As to letting our hosts pass judgment, their approval of my modest efforts was a foregone conclusion as soon as I began. But I am far from finished." She turned away from him and back to the line of exceedingly tolerant adjudicators. "In point of fact, I have barely concluded the introduction I have composed, and have not yet commenced the body of the recitation."

"And a wonderful recitation it was!" Walker declared loudly, so that all present would be certain to hear him. At the same time, he was gesturing to Braouk. No other Tuuqalian would have understood the significance of that gesture. But to Braouk, who had spent as much time in the company of the K'eremu as had Walker, its meaning and significance were clear.

Stepping forward, he promptly picked up the paused Sque and raised her high. This was her favored mode of travel, carried aloft above everyone else by the prodigiously strong Tuuqalian. She therefore did not object to the unrequested ascension, until a second massive tentacle folded itself gently but firmly around her midsection, collapsing her speaking tube against the slick maroon flesh of her torso. The closest human physical equivalent of Braouk's action would be pinching someone's lips together.

Slitted eyelids expanded. Unable to speak or blow bubbles of protest, she remained elevated above her companions but quite speechless. A necessary interruption, Walker felt certain, lest they find themselves forced to endure her clever but interminable verbal invention for hours on end while trying the patience of the adjudicators.

Despite the surgical delicacy of the intercession, it did not go unnoticed by the assembled panel. Eying the effectively muffled Sque, a Tuuqalian near the middle of the line rumbled inquisitively, "Why is the small many-limbed one now silent, and why is she gesticulating so actively with her appendages?"

Looking back, Walker watched as Braouk promptly passed a second massive tentacle across Sque's body, stilling much of the activity that had drawn the adjudicator's attention.

"It's part of a private ritual of hers," Walker hurriedly improvised. "She likes to be carried. As you've been informed, the four of us who were abducted have been together for some time. Despite being of different species, we've come to an intimate knowledge and appreciation of one another's needs and habits." Gesturing in the direction of the now scrupulously restrained Sque, he lowered his voice slightly. "Our K'eremu's high intelligence is balanced by an unfortunate addiction to certain herbal supplements. Nervousness at the need to satisfy the traditions of Tuuqalia probably led her to . . . well, surely you understand." Repeatedly, he put the fingers of one hand up to his mouth.

Some discussion among the Tuuqalians finally led to the one on the far left announcing, "The presentation of the representative from K'erem is accepted. Only one remains." All eyestalks promptly inclined in the direction of the only quadruped among the visitors.

Walker crouched down beside his friend. "You don't have to do this, George. I know you didn't really want to come."

He gestured toward the others. "Everyone else has satisfied the requirement. That means all the crews, from their scientific compliments, to the salivating media representatives, to those who only want to rest and do some sightseeing, have been granted access. You can go back up on the shuttle and relax on board until we're ready to leave this system. You don't have to stay down here."

Cocking his head to one side, the dog looked over at him. "You think I suffered through another atmospheric roller-coaster ride just to turn around and slink back with my tail tucked between my legs? Now that I'm here, I damn sure wouldn't mind a roll in the local grass, or its equivalent." So saying, he took a couple of steps toward the row of expectant Tuuqalians. Walker straightened and, after one more glance to ensure that the irate Sque was still being held firmly in check, waited to see what the dog would do.

It was impossible to tell whether George had been rehearsing while everyone else had been addressing the Tuuqalians, or if his saga was spontaneous. Whichever, he did not hesitate.

"I'm alone here, if I get home, still alone. The only one, of my small kind, who speaks. Gave me intelligence, did our wicked captors, without asking. Gave me speech, not as a gift, or present. To help them, to easier sell me, to others." Lowering his head, his ears falling limp, the dog pawed evocatively at the lapis-blue floor. "I can't decide, if it's a blessing, or curse. I can't decide, if I should return, to Earth. Being a freak, however affecting and admirable, is hard."

As George continued, the immense hall became utterly silent. The small dog-voice bounced off walls so distant the words barely reached, returning as echoes that rarely rose above a whisper. Even Sque, unable to do more than listen and watch, stilled the outraged writhing of her tentacles and paid attention to the small speaker.

When George finally finished and turned to rejoin his friends, it was all Walker could do to repress the tears that had begun to well up at the corners of his eyes. In their place, he did the only thing he was sure would not be misconstrued. Kneeling, he smiled and patted his companion gently on his head.

The Tuuqalian on the far right of the line spoke in a rumble that might have been ever so subtly different from all that had preceded it.

"An exemplar of sensitivity and saga-composing, the small quadruped is accepted, as are any others of his kind."

"I'm the only one," George replied quietly, clearly affected by his own wistful words. "But thanks anyway."

Walker bent over. "That was beautiful, George. I didn't know you had it in you."

"Why not?" Shielded from view of all but his human, one fur-shaded eye winked unexpectedly at the man. "It was only a bit of doggerel."

Grinning, Walker straightened and looked over at Braouk, who as a preventative measure still held the no-longer-struggling Sque in his grasp. "Then we're done here, right? We can let Gerlla-hyn know that it's okay to send his people down, and De-sil-jimd can inform his caste, who'll so notify the rest of the Iollth."

Braouk started to reply. Before he could, a Tuuqalian near the center of the line pistoned erect on his four supportive tentacles and shuffled forward. All four massive upper limbs thrust straight out, the tips coming together to form a pyramidal point. It struck Walker with sudden disquiet that the point was aimed directly at him.

"*Challenge!* I claim challenge!" the Tuuqalian thundered. Unlike George's plaintive opus, the stentorian Tuuqalian phrases boomed repetitively off the high, perfectly curved walls of the hall.

"Challenge?" Walker turned quickly to Braouk. "What is this? I thought we'd all, individually, satisfied your people's requirement for admittance. What's this 'challenge' business?" Though he spoke to Braouk, he found himself staring

as if mesmerized at those pointing tentacle tips. There was
no question about where they were aimed. When he moved
toward Braouk, they followed him.

His hulking companion gently set Sque back down on the
floor. Though the body of the livid K'eremu had swelled
with fury to the point where her skin threatened to split, she
somehow managed to internalize her rage. Only the serious
nature of the demanding Tuuqalian who had trundled forward swayed her to contain the flood of vituperation that had
been building up within. Her quivering restraint allowed
Braouk to respond without having to raise his voice.

"It is a, right reserved to the, first greeters," he rumbled
apologetically. "It can only be made one time. A challenge
between one representative of Tuuqalia and one visitor. It appears that you are the one to have been so honored."

Walker swallowed, his attention switching rapidly back
and forth between the Tuuqalian who was his good friend
and the other who was—his challenger?

"Somehow I don't feel especially honored. What does this
challenge involve?" His tone was hopeful. "More saga-
spinning?"

"I am afraid not." Braouk explained as George, De-sil-
jimd, Habr-wec, and even a softly sputtering Sque gathered
around to find out what was going on. "By your excellent individual recitations, you have already demonstrated that
your respective species are sufficiently civilized and sensitive. To complete the requirement for access, one of you
must additionally demonstrate bravery. It is a great honor to
be the one so selected to participate in such a demonstra-
tion." Though it weighed forty kilos or so, the tentacle that
reached out to rest kindly on Walker's left shoulder did not
seem half so heavy as the imponderable that continued to
hover menacingly in the air.

"How do I do that," he finally muttered uneasily, "if not by
spinning a saga?"

"Is not complicated," Braouk assured him, "and not take

long, to accomplish." While the one upper appendage still rested on the human's shoulder, another pair indicated the Tuuqalian who had stepped forward and was waiting expectantly. "You and the adjudicator who has issued the challenge will fight."

11

It took only seconds for the full import of Braouk's words to sink in. Walker's response was immediate. "If it's acceptable, I wouldn't mind if someone else received this great honor."

Braouk's eyes rose slightly on their stalks. "That is not possible, friend Marcus. For example, if it was possible to do so, I would gladly accept the challenge on your behalf. But the challenge was made to you. To alter it in any way would be to severely diminish its significance."

"I can live with that," he assured his friend. *Literally,* he thought frantically.

"I understand your concern." Braouk tried to reassure him. "Everything will be all right, friend Marcus. You must trust me."

"I do trust you," Walker told him. With one hand, he indicated the looming mass of his patiently waiting challenger. If anything, the Tuuqalian who had spoken was bigger than Braouk. Like Walker's friend, the challenge-issuer weighed well over a ton. Nor did his size make him slow. Walker had previously seen ample evidence of what a rampaging Tuuqalian could do, when Braouk had finally been freed from captivity on board the Vilenjji capture ship. He had no desire whatsoever to expose himself to similar berserking.

"I just don't trust that one," he finished.

A second tentacle tip fondly stroked Walker's side as both bulging oculars dipped close. "You must do this thing, friend Marcus. It is a requirement."

How many more requirements do your people expect us to fulfill? Walker found himself wondering apprehensively. He eyed the huge Tuuqalian who had issued the challenge. Having observed his friend Braouk in action, he knew that the Tuuqalians' size belied their quickness. But they moved around on four thick, stumpy, lower tentacles. Would he have any kind of an advantage there?

Rather than seek an advantage where none presented itself, maybe he would be better off just relying on Braouk's assurances. There seemed no way around it.

"All right. If I have to do this to obtain the aid of your species' scientists, then I'll do it."

Braouk's eyestalks withdrew and he turned toward the line of waiting adjudicators. "The human accepts the challenge!"

Fight that monster? Walker mused. How, and with what? Was he expected to contest the challenge with weaponry? There was none in evidence, and no sign of any being brought forth. That, at least, was some small relief. Not that the Tuuqalian would need anything more than its natural ability and strength to reduce him to a pulp, if it was so inclined. Surely he couldn't be expected to go one-on-one with it from a purely physical standpoint? Such a matchup was ludicrous on the face of it. And where was this contest supposed to take place? He quickly found out.

Leaving a hole in the line of adjudicators, the Tuuqalian who had issued the challenge bellowed thunderously and came lumbering off the dais directly toward him.

De-sil-jimd and Habr-wec backed quickly away from the human, the Niyyuun's tails twitching in agitation, the Iollth using its oversized feet to retreat with commendable swiftness. Sque scrambled right back up into the same strong limbs of Braouk whose embrace she had so energetically fought to escape only moments earlier. George rushed to take cover behind their Tuuqalian friend.

"You were a good friend, Marc. Been nice knowing you!"

"Wait, everybody slow down a minute!" Walker protested.

No one paid either his native English words or their respective simultaneous translations the least attention. The rest of the adjudicators had brought forth an array of small instruments and were monitoring the sudden activity with undisguised interest. Was his performance being rated? Walker started to back up and begin a desperate search for someplace that might lie beyond the reach of the advancing Tuuqalian.

The official welcoming examination had taken an unexpected and even irrational turn. Everything had suddenly and without warning been turned upside down. What had happened to the brusque but courteous Tuuqalians who had been so concerned with measuring the level of their visitors' civilizations and their degree of sensitivity? From the lofty intellectual endeavor of creating saga-stories he now found himself thrust into the shiny, polished equivalent of little more than a crude arena. It was as if Virgil had suddenly been ordered to stop composing odes and pick up the armor and weapons of a gladiator.

In his college days, Walker had been something of the modern equivalent of a gladiator. But facing the oncoming Tuuqalian who had challenged him, he did not even have the benefit of helmet and pads. Not that they would have been of much use, anyway.

Needing time, he started running. Shorn of hiding space and bereft of any weapons, he could do nothing else. His friends did their best to cheer him on and uphold his spirits. Hailing as they did from martial societies, both the Niyyuu and the Iollth were more energized by the confrontation than Sque or George, who feared for their companion instead of urging him onward.

Their support was not missed in any case, because there

was nowhere to urge him onward to. The walls of the great hall were smooth and gently curved, all lighting and electronics having been fully integrated into the building material itself. Breathing hard, he reached the portal through which they had originally entered. Unsurprisingly, it was locked, but checking it out had been worth a try. With his Tuuqalian challenger looming up fast behind him, Walker bolted to his right, racing around the circumference of the room. In the center of the room, several of the adjudicators were chatting amiably with one another. As he ran, Walker found himself wishing for a couple of small nuclear devices: one for his pursuer, the other for the line of local observers who appeared to be enjoying themselves at his expense. As arriving supplicants, naturally neither he nor any of his companions had been allowed to appear armed before the adjudicators.

At least there was no furniture for him to trip over. Having circled half the oval hall, he found himself nearly back where he had started, close to his friends but at the far right-hand end of the line of adjudicators. He fancied he could feel hot breath on his back and saw-edged teeth clamping down on his skull and spine. He could not linger. Having no time to think, he acted.

He ran straight toward the nearest Tuuqalian.

Busily manipulating a pair of enigmatic devices, it eyed him in surprise, both eyestalks rising upward and as far away as possible from his small but determined onrushing form. The two adjudicators nearest the one Walker was rapidly approaching shifted their position for a better view. Meanwhile, Walker's pursuer had extended all four upper tentacles in an attempt to bring him down.

Darting behind the nearest adjudicator, Walker saw that his risky guess had been correct. Not having challenged him, they did not interfere. They did, however, try to get out of his way. Had there been two or three of them, they might have managed it. But filled with a dozen of the huge creatures, the dais was too crowded. No matter how hard his pursuer tried to envelop the human in its questing tentacles, Walker managed to dart nimbly behind one or two of his hunter's colleagues.

How long could this go on? he wondered wildly. Was there some kind of time limit, or was the contest expected to continue until one or the other combatant fell? Noticing that one of the adjudicators had set its recorder, or whatever the device was, down beside its lower limbs while it worked intently on a second device, Walker nipped in and picked up the instrument before its startled owner could react. The Tuuqalian-sized device was comfortingly heavy in his palm. It was no gun, but it was solid and well-made. Though he'd played linebacker and not quarterback, he'd always had a good arm. Winded now, his expression grim, he turned to face his pursuer.

Tentacles waving, jaws clashing, the challenger came roaring toward him, forcing a path through the milling adjudicators. Evidently it either had not seen Walker pick up the small device, or did not care that the human had done so. Without giving his pursuer a chance to reflect on possibilities, Walker took aim and hurled the apparatus as hard as he could. It struck the oncoming Tuuqalian solidly in its right eye before bouncing off and landing on the floor.

Immediately, the hulking alien halted, its lower limbs scrambling to bring it to a stop. All four grasping tentacles reached up and over to cradle the bruised eye, which had retracted completely into the ocular recess on the same side of the Tuuqalian's body. Several fellow adjudicators rushed to aid their injured colleague.

The others, who heretofore had been milling about indifferently while working with their own individual instrumentation, now proceeded to cluster around Walker. Their massive, menacing forms towered over him.

Well, it had been a good run, he told himself. It wasn't as if he and his friends knew Earth's location and were about to embark on the homeward journey tomorrow. At least George might still make it. He hoped the dog would remember him fondly, and how Walker had sacrificed himself, albeit without having been given a choice, to satisfy the demands of the Tuuqalians and thereby allow his friends to gain access to Tuuqalian scientific knowledge.

It struck him that no one was striking him. The assembly of Tuuqalians who had gathered around him were, in fact, making noises that his implanted translator insisted on deciphering not as threats or curses, but as compliments. The majority of the comments were directed not at him, but to one another.

"Well rendered . . . ," one was saying. "Intelligent decision, to run and not try to stand its ground . . . unusually well-balanced for a creature with only two such spindly limbs and no tail." Walker, who was proud of the effort he had expended in the weight room while in college and who had subsequently worked hard to maintain as much of an aging football player's physique as he could, had never before heard his legs referred to as "spindly." The comments and observations continued.

"Excellent manipulative digit to ocular coordination . . . demonstrated courage by running in among us not knowing what our individual reactions might be . . . clear ability to make use of ordinary objects as weaponry . . ."

It went on in that vein for a while. If nothing else, it gave him time to catch his breath. None of it made any sense. One minute he was being chased around the hall by one of their number whose apparent intent was to do him grievous bodily harm, and the next they were all standing around praising his flight and paltry counterattack. His confusion only deepened when the one who had challenged him approached anew. The eye he had struck was darkened, but Tuuqalian oculars were apparently as tough as the rest of their massive bodies.

"Nothing but sensible and effective reactions. I thank you," it rumbled.

If it hadn't been embedded inside his head, Walker would have tapped his translator to make sure it was still working. "You're thanking me?" he mumbled as an excited George ran up to rejoin him. "For hitting you in the eye?"

The orb in question described a small circle on the end of its strong, flexible stalk. "Admirable inspiration! As was your darting and weaving. You have more than satisfied the final requirement." All four upper tentacles crossed one another in front of the huge, hirsute body to form a precise geometric pattern. "Allow me to be the first to formally welcome you and your companions to Tuuqalia." Having delivered the official welcome that Walker and his friends had been so anxiously seeking, it turned away from him to resume chatting with its fellow adjudicators.

"You all right?" He became aware that George was squinting up at him.

"Yeah, I'm fine. More emotionally exhausted than anything else." Walker gazed at the gathering of huge Tuuqalians. All seemed completely at ease now. No further questions were directed his way, nor was there any indication revenge would be sought for the injury he had inflicted on one of their own. With George at his side, he tottered down the slight slope to rejoin his waiting companions. "Otherwise, just a little a dazed, I guess. What just happened here?"

It was left to Braouk to explain. "Enriching ennobling sagas, since Tuuqalian civilization's beginnings, we create. Reverential tales and inspiring stories. After thousands of years of composition, even the most inventive composers among us have difficulty imagining new themes, new subjects, new visualizations worthy of their efforts. Seeks fresh inspiration, for ideas and composition, every Tuuqalian. New stimulation can, be difficult to obtain, and recognize." Upper tentacles gestured meaningfully. "I am sure you can understand, friend Marcus, that when such presents itself, it is eagerly seized upon."

Walker remained doubtful. "I'm still not sure I understand . . ."

"You," George cut in. "The whole challenge and chase thing—stimuli." The dog nodded in the direction of the milling adjudicators, some of whom had begun to depart but all of whom continued conversing animatedly among themselves. "No wonder the one you hit in the eye thanked you. Not only will he—I think it was a he—get inspired to compose from chasing you, you provided an additional and unexpected incentive when you fought back so effectively."

"Then it was all a sham." Surrounded by his companions, a worn-out Walker stood mumbling to himself. "Just a charade designed to provide new material for saga-spinning."

Braouk eyed his friend gravely, one eye hovering on either side of the human's head. "Your palpable fear, was while being chased, most inspiring. It will no doubt provide the basis for many stirring overtures."

Settling his attention on one eye, Walker regarded the Tuuqalian hesitantly. "Then I was never in any real danger?"

"No."

"What would have happened if I'd just stood still and waited? If I hadn't run or resisted?"

"Nothing," Braouk admitted. "You and the others would have been granted the access to Tuuqalia that you seek. But many here today to pass judgment on you would have gone away disappointed."

"Disappointed, hell!" Walker blurted abruptly. "I was scared to death! I thought that thing, the one who had challenged me, was going to tear me to pieces!"

"Yours was not, the only inspirational source, here today," Braouk replied blithely. "The one who was chosen to challenge you was not only fortunate in being so selected, but played his part well. An eye can heal of its own accord, but the shock of your response provided inspiration that is rare. Ours is a civilized world, wherein the unforeseen is always a delight, because it is so uncommonly encountered."

"You could have told me," Walker grumbled. "You might have warned me."

"Did I not say that everything would be all right?" Both eyes drew back, a gesture that made focusing on the Tuuqalian easier mentally if not physically.

"It's hard to trust anyone's opinion, Braouk, even yours, when you've just been challenged to combat by something ten times your size."

Edging closer, the Tuuqalian placed a comradely tentacle thick as a tree root around Walker's shoulders. "If I had explained fully, and you had been made aware in advance of the purpose of the challenge, would you have reacted similarly? Would you have run as hard and fast as you did? Would you have fought back, to the point of lightly injuring your challenger?"

Braouk had him there, Walker had to admit. "No, of course not. I probably wouldn't have done anything."

"Doing nothing is, a poor foundation for, saga-writing." Like a lazy anaconda, the tentacle slid slowly off his shoulders. "Now, not only will you be able to visit Tuuqalia and confer with our astronomers and other scientists, your name and presence will go down in contemporary saga-telling."

"I'm so pleased," Walker commented dryly.

"Ask him if you're entitled to royalties." George nudged his friend irreverently.

"I'll settle for being alive and in one piece." He took a deep breath, finally at ease.

"I knew it all along."

"What?" He turned in the direction of the familiar mocking voice.

Sque scrambled forward. "You are all of you blind as cave-dwelling *zithins*. The signs were present for anyone to see, and to interpret correctly." She blew a single, disdainful bubble. "If any of you had taken the time to study the body language of the one Tuuqalian in our midst, you would have been able to apply that knowledge to the understated movements of the rank of adjudicators." One tentacle tip cleaned the linear surface of a steel-gray eye. "To anyone who had troubled to do so, interpreting the gestures and tentacle twitches that were rampant among those deigning to pass judgment on us would have been a simple matter."

"I've got a gesture you could try to interpret," Walker groused. "If you had some idea what was going to happen, why didn't you say something? Why didn't *you* warn me?"

While the one tentacle tip continued with its eye cleaning, a different pair gestured in Braouk's direction. "My rationale for not doing so was similar, if not identical to, that of our overlarge friend. I could see no purpose in intervening in a custom that was so clearly important to those locals whose ultimate opinion would decide whether or not we would find assistance here. Also, even had I expressed my opinion to you, it would not have changed anything. The challenge would still have been issued, and would still have had to be met."

Advancing toward him, she halted at his feet, her eyes and speaking tube at the level of his waist. He felt her grip his sides with first one appendage, then another, and another, until all ten had secured a firm grip. Climbing up his front like a logger ascending toward the top of a tree, she halted only when she was eye to eye with him. Though nowhere near as strong as Braouk, he was still sturdy enough to hold his ground even with her hanging onto him. He was more startled by the unexpected intimacy than by her modest weight. She had never before touched him with anything more than a tentacle tip or two. Now, unexpectedly, she was close enough for him to see the fine gray-pink cilia inside the end of her breathing tube. Those strange, horizontal black pupils gazed deeply into his own.

"You are my friend, Marcus Walker. We have been together for a very long time indeed. We have relied on one another to continue living. Despite your unyielding internal skeleton, your stiff and gangly movements, your awkward gestures, your deficiency of limbs, and an intelligence that even after much time spent in my company can still only properly be described as minimal, I would not let anything untoward happen to you that it was in my power to prevent." So saying, she climbed back down off him, leaving only a faint scent of damp mustiness clinging to his clothes.

"You should know by now, if you have learned nothing else, that I do nothing without first considering all possible ramifications. Concerning your recent problematic confrontation, I think you will admit that it has all turned out for the best." Drawing herself up to her full four-foot height, she made a show of adjusting several of the strands of reflective metal and crystal that decorated her body.

He stood staring at her, slightly stunned. In nearly two years of traveling together, it was the closest she had come to expressing anything deeper than wan tolerance for his existence. Sarcasm and the customary jibes about his appearance and mental capabilities aside, what she had just done and said bordered on actual affection. He hardly knew what to say.

Perhaps she sensed his shock, or his discomfiture. "I did not bite you, and even if I had, I suspect there is nothing in my saliva capable of inflicting paralysis on a lifeform so primitively resilient. You may, as soon as you wish, confirm the reality of this observation by moving one or more of your inadequate quartet of appendages, or if the effort of coordinating the requisite muscles and organs is not too much of a strain, by speaking."

"I—thank you, Sque. I won't question your motives again. Either for doing something, or for not doing anything."

Swelling up halfway, she exhaled a stream of aerial froth. "Does a modicum of intelligence begin to show itself? With much continued effort, you may in truth some day achieve an adequate level of common sense. At your current rate of maturation, I should estimate that you might reach that stage in only another two or three hundred of your years." Pivoting on her central axis, she wandered over to ascend Braouk, in order to utilize him as a platform from which to address several of the remaining adjudicators.

George had been no less taken aback by the decapod's unanticipated affirmation. "Whataya know? The squid likes you."

"I never suspected," Walker mumbled, "I never *expected*..."

"Not exactly demonstrative, is she?" The dog snorted softly. "No wonder her kind don't mate very often. Aside from conversing via casual insult, if it takes one of them two years to admit to something as low-key as ordinary friendship, think how long it must take two of them to decide to mate."

Ears erect and alert, he nodded in the K'eremu's direction. She was once more comfortably ensconced on one of Braouk's upper limbs, several of her appendages gesticulating in support of whatever edict of the moment she was currently handing down to a pair of attentive Tuuqalian adjudicators.

Everything she had said to him was all very nice, Walker told himself. Welcome, even. But he labored under no illusions. Her admission of friendship notwithstanding, he knew that if the opportunity to return to K'erem presented itself and required that he be sacrificed to make it possible, she would not hesitate to forfeit his hopes and dreams. That was the canny, experienced trader in him talking. He did not mind admitting it to himself.

Of them all, certainly Sque herself would have understood his caution, and no doubt approved.

While Sobj-oes, her young colleague Habr-wec, and the rest of the Niyyuuan astronautics team joined with members of the Iollth science caste in compiling a list of formal requests for information to be presented to the Tuuqalian astronomy establishment, a relieved and exuberant Broullkoun-uvv-ahd-Hrashkin reveled not only in the sights and sounds and smells of a homeworld he thought he might never see again, but in the opportunity to share them with the companions of his Vilenjji captivity.

"Come with me, we are going north, this dawning!" he boomed the following morning as he lumbered into the port facilities that had been made available for the visitors' use for the duration of their stay on Tuuqalia.

A sleepy George looked up from his oversized pillow and barked softly before adding, "What's 'north'? If it isn't something unique and special, I'm staying right here 'til it's time to leave again." Mumbling to himself, he rolled onto his other side. "Seen one alien world, seen 'em all."

He let out a sharp bark of surprise as one massive tentacle, its grip gentle as a prehensile feather, picked him up and tossed him playfully into the air. Since Braouk was some nine feet tall, rather high into the air.

"Don't *do* that!" the dog yelped. Panting hard, he cast a re-proachful eye on their hulking friend as Braouk set him care-fully back on his pillow. "What do you think I am—a cat?"

As the Vilenjji implants could not translate subjects for which there was no viable counterpart, Braouk admitted that he was at a loss to answer. But his enthusiasm was un-dimmed.

"To the north, lie the fabled plains, Serelth-idyr."

George refused to be impressed. "What's fabled about them?"

The massive, yellow-green torso bent toward George while both eyestalks dipped closer still. Each vertically pupiled eyeball was nearly as big as the dog. "Therein lies my home, that I have not seen since I was taken by the Vilenjji these all too many planetary revolutions ago. My family, all those I left behind, memories of whom were all that sustained me and kept me from going mad while I was alone in isolation aboard the Vilenjji ship."

"Maybe you wouldn't have been left in isolation," Walker pointed out judiciously, "if you hadn't gotten into the habit of trying to dismember everyone on the ship who made an attempt to talk to you. Remember?"

Both eyes arced in his direction. The multi-limbed giant was visibly abashed. "I was half-mad with despair for my situation and hardly to be held responsible for my actions. *You,* friend Marcus, should remember that." As he straightened, the buoyant eagerness that had accompanied his arrival returned. "You please come, to meet my friends, in Serelth-idyr. My friends and my family, who when they hear all of the saga of our meeting and our traveling, will welcome each of you as one of their own."

"Okay." Hopping down off his pillow-platform, George trotted over to stand next to Walker. "But only on two conditions. One, we don't have to listen to you recite *all* of the 'saga of our meeting and our traveling' that I don't doubt you've been slaving over ever since the Sessrimathe rescued us from the Vilenjji, and two, no matter how friendly your friends and family, no backslapping or hugging." By way of emphasis, he arched his shoulders and back. "I have a particular fondness for my spine."

Braouk gestured understandingly. "It is true, that Tuuqalian welcomings sometimes, become physical. I will see to it that you survive." Pivoting on his under-tentacles, he turned to Sque. "Will you come, purveyor of practiced invective, to Serelth-idyr?"

The K'eremu peered out from beneath the small fountain that had been brought in to provide for her comfort. "While the notion of spending time on 'plains' as opposed to a nice beach is not one that I would normally consider inviting, I confess that I am curious to see how oversized beings such as yourself coexist in a social environment. I will come and stay awhile, at least until the usual ennui begins to set in."

"Then it is settled." Braouk turned one eye on George and Walker and the other on Sque. "I will keep two of you safe and dry, and the other safe and wet. Prepare yourselves, my friends, for an outpouring of exorbitant good feelings the likes of which you have never experienced and cannot imagine. Because to our very good fortune, on all the plains of the north it is harvest time!"

12

Though it seemed the size of a small ocean liner, Walker knew the vehicle that was carrying him and his friends northward from the port where they had been granted entrée to Tuuqalia was nothing more than the local equivalent of a cargo and passenger truck. It was also an impressive example of advanced local technology. Built to accommodate Tuuqalian-sized freight as well as Tuuqalians themselves, it emitted little more than a sonorous hiss as it streaked northward barely thirty meters above the ground at some three hundred kilometers an hour.

Once clear of the city and its port, the craft traveled over terrain that alternated between gently rolling and pancake flat. Though he glimpsed them at speed, Walker was able to see enough of the occasional villages they passed to recognize that they were both larger and more technologically developed than their counterparts on either Hyff or Niyu, though for sophistication they were still surpassed by the stylish, organically integrated municipalities of Seremathenn.

They traveled for several days, stopping occasionally to discharge or take on passengers and cargo. Walker and George looked forward to these pauses, not only because it gave them an opportunity to step outside the confines of the transport, but because they were able to see and experience something of their friend Braouk's homeworld outside a major city. Sque settled for studying through a port the numerous stops that were to her becoming increasingly repetitive. She was anxious to reach their destination, make her observations, return to the port where they had landed, and be about the business of finding her own way home. Xenology, she explained, was all very well and good, but it was no substitute for being among one's own kind. Walker did not disagree. With Sque, it would have been a waste of time to do so anyway.

There finally came a morning when Braouk told them to prepare to disembark. Little in the way of preparation was required, since Walker carried everything he and George needed in a single small satchel of Sessrimathe manufacture. A change of clothing, some hygienic supplies, dried emergency rations, vitamin and mineral supplements, and a remarkable spherical storage device that contained, among other things, not only all the recipes he had pored over and devised himself but three-dimensional recordings of his cooking performances. Together, these comprised the bulk of his "luggage." It made traveling easy, if not homey.

Led by Braouk, they exited the craft onto an unloading platform. It projected outward from two modest structures, a receiving building and a tall, windowless tower of unknown purpose. They were the only passengers to disembark at this stop, though they were joined by several large shipping containers. After a brief conversation among themselves, these split up and went their separate self-propelled ways, scooting along just above the ground on their own integrated propulsion units. When the transport craft finally departed, the four travelers were left alone on the dull bronzed, semicircular metal platform.

It was suddenly very quiet.

How the transport, or anyone else for that matter, could locate such unloading platforms was a matter of some interest to Walker and his friends. No roads led to it, no tracks or markers. It was completely surrounded by flat plains whose only distinguishing features were slightly different varieties of low vegetation. To the south and north, endless fields of something like three-meter-tall purple asparagus marched off toward opposite horizons. To the west, undulating rows of bulbous concave shapes thrust upward from manicured soil like thousands of nut-brown bathtubs balanced precariously on their drainage pipes. As Braouk explained, the bathtub-shaped growths consisted of solid, edible protein while the "pipes" were the stalks and stems from which they blossomed.

Eastward, the flora was neither as tall nor as intimidatingly bizarre. The *pirulek* that dominated that direction was reassuringly green and no more than knee-high. However, the vine-like growths existed in a state of constant motion that was rendered more than a little eerie by the complete absence of any breeze. Despite their garish, unnatural colors and alien shapes, the asparagus trees and bathtub vegetation were less unsettling, Walker decided. At least they had they decency to remain still. Gazing at the twitchy, spasming field of *pirulek* was enough to unsettle even someone who had already spent time on several alien worlds.

A hum grew audible and suddenly Braouk was pointing excitedly. "My family comes, hardly daring to hope, so long."

The vehicle that slowed to a halt and hovered level with the raised edge of the unloading platform consisted of three flat congruent discs whose alignment formed a triangular shape. Domed on top, flat on the bottom, a large passenger-cargo compartment bulged upward from the point where the three discs intersected. From it emerged a quartet of Tuuqalians who threatened to trample Walker, George, and a sputtering Sque in their rush to wrap powerful tentacles around Braouk. There was much fulsome spouting of poetry. So much so that by the time Tuuqalia's sun had slipped below its horizon and a definite chill had begun to creep into the air, human, dog, and K'eremu had been rendered half-insensible by the interminable outpouring of greetings.

They were roused by Braouk's introductions that, mercifully, were unusually brief for their usually loquacious companion. They were tired, he explained to his family members, and unused to proper recitation. At this explanation, his welcoming relations became by turns apologetic and solicitous.

Bundling the returned abductee (whom none of his thankful family members had ever expected to see again) and his alien companions into the unusual craft, Braouk's relatives conveyed them to the family residence. Being built to Tuuqalian scale, this very modest (as Braouk had described it) center of cultivation struck Walker as no less than a small town. He was assured it was the home of only one family. On Tuuqalia, however, that was a more elastic term than on Earth. Some sixty multi-tentacled souls of varying age and experience lived and worked at the facility, and it seemed that every one of them wanted to personally congratulate not only the returning Braouk but his peculiar friends as well.

In addition to congratulations, much local food was proffered. Some of it his and Sque's personal Sessrimathe analyzers pronounced fit for human, canine, or K'eremu consumption, some the compact units declared inedible, and some the guests themselves rejected for reasons of taste or visual aesthetics. As the Tuuqalian diet was now largely vegetable based, though with significant infusions of synthetic and gathered meat proteins, Walker found there was quite a lot he could eat. George pronounced a good deal of it not only suitable for consumption, but tasty as well, while Sque nattered on about the need to eat to survive regardless of the incontestable insipidness of the nourishment that happened to be available.

When the Tuuqalians were informed that one of Braouk's friends was a professional chef whose talents had been recognized on multiple worlds, there was nothing for it but that Walker had to demonstrate his skills in a food preparation area the size of a small concert hall. By keeping it simple, he was able to prepare a couple of dishes using regional ingredients that did not outrage local palates, whereupon he was promptly anointed a hero as well as a guest. There was little the inhabitants of Tuuqalia enjoyed more than food, a trait Walker had recognized from the first time he had seen a hungry Braouk chomping down food bricks on board the Vilenjji capture ship. Little more, except the composing and reciting of a proper saga, of course.

It was when everyone had finished eating that Braouk was persuaded (without much effort, Walker noted) to tell something of the story of his experiences subsequent to his abduction from a sowing field one night years ago. As his implant translated his oversized friend's reminiscences, Walker was reminded of his own last evening on Earth, when he had been taken from his campsite by those sucker-armed, pebble-skinned, pointy-headed dissolute creatures called the Vilenjji. His and Braouk's experiences, if not the degree of resistance they had put up, were strikingly similar, notwithstanding that Walker's abduction had taken place under one moon, Braouk's beneath three, George's below a flickering neon sign advertising a local beer, and Sque's in relative darkness.

Having heard it all before, more times than any of them cared to count, the guests were excused from Braouk's never-ending ramblings.

Though all were members of one extended family, each individual Tuuqalian had their own dwelling. No two, mated or otherwise, lived under the same roof.

"At last," Sque commented upon learning the details of the local living arrangements, "some small hint of true civilization."

They were given the living quarters of a member of the family who was presently away on business. As the huge resting depression in the floor with its computerized reactive underbase reminded George of a time when he had been caught in deep mud and nearly suffocated, they elected to sleep instead on strands of the self-binding material that was used to fasten bundles of the purple asparagus-like growths for shipment. The cosseting material was pale blue and tough as spun titanium. A pile of it was supple as silk. The trick, Walker told himself as he fluffed up his makeshift bed, would be not to toss and turn too much in his sleep, or he was liable to strangle himself with the stuff.

Perhaps it was the unexpected softness that woke him. More likely it was the noise. Blinking, rubbing his eyes, he observed in the dim light that issued from the floor that both Sque and George continued to sleep soundly. Surely he had heard something?

There it was again. Rising, shaking off several strands of the fluffy binding material, he walked over to the other side of the enormous resting room. As he approached the wall beyond which he thought he heard the noise, the barrier detected his presence and unexpectedly went transparent. Since he was still half-asleep, the effect startled him into taking a nervous jump backward. When he warily retraced his footsteps and extended an arm, the pressure against his open, upraised palm assured him that the wall was still there. He wondered if anyone outside could see in as easily as he could see out.

The resting chamber of the dwelling was located on the top floor of the residence they were occupying. Thus, the now transparent wall provided him with a sweeping view across the nearby plain. Collectively, the family dwellings formed a giant circle, so that each one looked inward to family meeting, working, and dining areas and buildings, and out onto the family's extensive fields.

All three moons were up, with the result that it was quite bright outside. Though the light was wan and more than a little ethereal, he found that he could see clearly. One gibbous satellite was slightly larger than Earth's while the other two were considerably smaller. They cast an otherworldly, tripartite alien glow on the pastoral scene spread out before him. Stretching to the far, unpolluted horizon was an impressive field of the tall, purple-tinged growths he had first seen upon arriving at the disembarkation station.

Lowering his gaze and working it along the interior of the building's now transparent wall, he came to a softly radiant point of blue light that appeared to be fixed in place just above eye level. His eye level, he reminded himself. Fascinated by the steady glow, reasonably confident he was unlikely to encounter anything dangerous in an area designated for sleeping, he extended a finger toward it. A quick glance backward showed that George and Sque were still fast asleep, George nestled deep into a bed of silken wrappings similar to but less voluminous than Walker's own, Sque atop material not unlike an oversized damp sponge that had been improvised for her comfort.

As his finger slid into the blue glow, cool air enveloped his nude form. Large enough to pass a Tuuqalian, the opening that appeared allowed him egress to a small, curved balcony outside the sleeping chamber. Whatever had rendered the wall transparent had done the same for the balcony area, but once he stepped outside, both the flat extension beneath his feet and the wall behind him turned opaque. He could not see back inside the sleeping area. Only the blue glow of the activator, or doorknob, or whatever it was, remained to show him how to get back inside.

While the mellow ruddiness of the three moons casting their magic on the endless field was what had initially drawn his interest, his attention was quickly caught by a rush of motion off to his right. Moving to the edge of the porch, whose spidery plasticized railing was fortunately low enough for him to see over, he stared in awe at the busy nocturnal activity whose distant sounds had teased him awake.

Several streams of tightly baled purple stalks converged on a large, dun-colored structure far enough out in the fields so that the noise of the activity was little more than a distant buzz. Even at a distance and watching by moonlight, he could tell that there were hundreds of stalks in each hefty bundle, and hundreds of bundles in each line. Each self-propelled bundle remained equidistant from the one in front of it and the one behind. Tuuqalians mounted on individual scoop-shaped vehicles soared and darted among and around the parading streams of trussed vegetation. That much he could comprehend. But what unseen mechanism was supporting the truck-sized bales?

Suddenly, one of the vehicles broke off and came toward him, both craft and driver rapidly increasing in size. Other than exposing him to the slight and not unpleasant chill in the air, his utter lack of apparel did not trouble him. Any alien interest that might be shown in his naked anatomy would be purely academic. For that matter, unlike the Niyyuu or the Sessrimathe, the Tuuqalians themselves had dispensed with clothing.

He considered retreating back into the sleeping chamber, or at least waking George. Was it possible he had inadvertently intruded, even at a distance, on some restricted ceremony? As a visitor, he decided to hold his ground and plead ignorance. Besides, he'd already been seen.

Then he recognized the figure riding astride the scoop ship, and relaxed. It was Braouk. Emitting a deep, unwavering hum, the powerful little vehicle pulled up alongside the porch where he was standing. Eyestalks inclined toward him.

"The human night, as I observed it, means sleeping." A pair of huge upper appendages extended toward him. "You are awake and outside. This contradicts your normal activity. Is something the matter?"

"Not at all." Strolling to the edge of the intricate railing, he raised an arm and gestured in the direction of the ongoing activity. "I heard a noise and got up to see what was going on."

Touching controls, Braouk adjusted the scoop ship's position. As it pivoted on its axis, Walker took the opportunity to examine the vehicle more closely. With its smooth ivory-

colored surface and lack of external instrumentation or orna-
mentation, it was simple and straightforward. Even the concave forward portion where Braouk rode was devoid of all
but the most basic instrumentation. The local equivalent of a
bicycle, Walker mused. Or a motorcycle, or ATV. Working
transport.

Like a fast-growing tree branch, a pale yellow tentacle
fluttered skyward. "In sky together, Teldk, Melevt, and Melaft,
are simultaneously. Here in the northern plains, that means it
is harvest time for the mature *chimttabt*. A special time, for
all who live, near here." Descending, the limb gestured toward
the ongoing streams of activity off to their right. "Would you
like to see better?"

Walker didn't hesitate. Over the past couple of years, he
had learned not to hesitate. He who hesitates might miss
something. Besides, for a commodities trader, who knew
what opportunities might one day present themselves? Perhaps even the chance to trade in bulk *chimttabt*. He had never
been one to pass on an opportunity to learn about a new raw
material.

"Sure, let's go," he told his hulking friend.

Braouk made room for the human between his own mass
and the upward curving control area that was built directly
into the material of the scoop ship itself. Snugging back
against the bristle-like yellow-green fur of his friend kept
Walker warm and, surprisingly, Braouk's hair was not as
itch-inducing against his bare skin as it appeared. To think,
he told himself, that at one time he would have fainted in terror if he had been compelled to endure such close proximity
to a being like Braouk. Friends with him now for years, he
had changed so much that he actually sought the close contact.

I have *changed,* he thought as the scoop ship accelerated
toward the area of greatest activity. Changed in ways that as
recently as three or four years ago he could not have imagined. But then, no one could. Three moons gazing down on

him from high above, he sped in alien company aboard an
alien craft toward a harvest of foodstuffs that more than anything else resembled lavender lightpoles. The food preparer
half of him was intrigued by their culinary potential.

As they drew nearer, he saw that attached to the underside
of each bale was an individual drive device that both propelled and guided it. Keeping perfect time and interval between one another, one bale after another made its way from
distant field to local processing unit under the active supervi-
sion of scoop ship-riding Tuuqalians. The system was far
more advanced than anything back home, he realized. Why
load a truck with tomatoes and further burden it with a driver
when you could set the load of vegetables to drive and guide
itself to the intended destination?

A new sound reached him. Rising above the hum and
whirr of technologically advanced reaping and processing
machinery, it was at once familiar and new. New, because of
the volume that was involved. Swooping and darting among
the gigantic bales of recently harvested *chimttabt,* busy
multi-limbed Tuuqalians burst out in boisterous song. No,
not singing, he corrected himself. They were collaborating in
an a cappella choir of alien saga-spinning. Their strangely
pitched, collective voices boomed and echoed like velvet
thunder across the unreaped vegetation below, rising and
falling almost in concert with their vehicles as they managed
the complicated business of *chimttabt* harvesting.

Massive alien muscles swelled against Walker's back as
Braouk joined in the joyous chorus. After a few moments, he
paused. While the scoop ship hovered, both eyes hooked
around in front of Walker to look back at him.

"Will you join, in the communal recitation, my friend? I
will provide you with the words. Your system of sound-
making is smaller than ours, but the mechanics are not so
very different."

"Why not?" After a few tries, listening and repeating,

Walker felt he could mimic the Tuuqalian timbre near enough not to embarrass himself.

When next Braouk resumed his work, it was two voices that rose from the scoop ship: one local, the other imported. Human and Tuuqalian. Dipping and darting among the cumbersome bales, they occasionally passed close by other workers. Tentacles waved in their direction and astonished eyes extended fully on stalks as one worker after another goggled at the sight of the small, furless alien not only riding in tandem with one of their own, but joining lustily in the saga-spinning that accompanied the mechanical ballet of scoop ships and bales and multi-limbed operators. And all the while the three moons Teldk, Melevt, and Melaft beamed down from an alien sky on the festive commotion below, in which one lone and lonely human was a most unexpected participant.

The cool air, redolent of growing Tuuqalian things and pungent mechanical smells and the musky body odor of the methodical giant behind him, washed over his face and naked form. Moons and multi-limbed monsters, truck-sized bales of plum-hued plants and deep-throated processing devices, danced before his now night-adapted eyes. What was the expression? "Never in your wildest dreams . . ."

It was, he mused as their scoop ship shot close enough past another for him to note with glee the surprised reaction of the other's operator, a long way from motoring boredly through the cornfields south of Chicago to visit friends in Springfield for the weekend.

Tuuqalia's benign sun was just showing itself over the horizon when a jovial Braouk returned an exhausted but exultant Walker to the residence that had been assigned to him and his companions. As he stepped off the powerful little vehicle and back onto the building's upper-level porch, Marc expressed his gratitude by giving the Tuuqalian a punch be-

TITLE: Before the blues [sound recording
BARCODE: 34567014699456
DUE DATE: 08-04-14

TITLE: state of grace [sound recording]
BARCODE: 34567015216225
DUE DATE: 08-04-14

TITLE: the candle of distant earth
BARCODE: 34567014197134
DUE DATE: 08-18-14

tween upper and lower right-side tentacles, hard enough that he hoped his oversized friend might actually feel it.

"What a great night! I can't thank you enough, Braouk. I've attended some all-night parties in my time, but nothing like this. The diving and swooping, the massed saga-chanting, the colors in the moonlight: it's something I'll remember forever."

"Was just harvest," the alien rumbled diffidently. "But I was, glad you could participate, friend Marcus. At such times, sharing is always best, with friends." One huge appendage curled fondly around Walker's shoulders, then withdrew.

Squinting against the rising alien sun, Walker waved as the scoop ship angled away from the balcony. Turning and walking back to the wall, he casually inserted a couple of fingers into the blue glow of the control and stepped through the opening it produced. As it sealed behind him, a familiar voice barked sharply from the dim depths of the temperate sleeping area.

"Where have you been all night? I've been worried sick."

"Good dog," Walker murmured as he made his tired way toward his crib of silken wrappings. Between the excitement of the nocturnal experience and a complete lack of sleep, he was thoroughly bushed. The makeshift cot with its glistening bale of alien padding called to him.

A fast-moving, small brown shape blocked his path and refused access to the beckoning bed. "Don't 'good dog' me—bad human. Where were you?"

"Carrying out research on local agriculture. And making friends." Lurching to his left, he tried to dodge around his companion. George scampered quickly to cut him off. Behind them, Sque slumbered peacefully on, oblivious to the overwrought confrontation.

"In the middle of the night? On an alien world?" Something caught the dog's eye. Leaning to his right, he tried to peer behind his friend. "What happened to your back?"

"Hmm?" Half-asleep now, Walker tried to look over his shoulder and down at himself. "I don't see anything."

Trotting around behind him, George stood up on his hind legs and rested his forepaws against Walker's thigh. "You look like you've been whipped by a dozen angry pixies."

"What? Oh, that comes from leaning my bare back against Braouk's front all night and being thrown all over the place. You know how bristly his fur is. Almost quill-like. It was to be expected after a night of hard riding." Shrugging George off his thigh, Walker made a beeline for the looming bed and slumped gratefully into the mass of alien wrapping material.

" 'Hard riding'?" George was now able to look his prostrate friend in the eye. "If you tell me you were out rustling alien cattle, I'm going to have to raise serious doubts with Gerlla-hyn's medical staff about the state of your sanity."

"Not cattle," Walker murmured sleepily. "*Chimttabt*. The big, purplish striated stalks we've seen growing in several regions. Self-propelled bales of the stuff." He snuggled deeper into the welcoming mass of soft but strong pale blue strands. "During harvest time, the Tuuqalians of these northern plains work around the clock."

"I see," George observed dangerously. "Really dove into local custom, didn't you? Next time I'd appreciate your letting me know when you're going to do something like that. You might keep in mind that I, at least, have a reasonable phobia where unannounced disappearances are concerned. One you ought to empathize with."

"Sorry." By now almost asleep, it was all Walker could do to mumble a reply.

Standing up and leaning over, George dragged his tongue wetly across Walker's eyes. It was sufficient stimulus to keep his friend awake. "What were you thinking, Marc? You doing all-night research because you're planning on going native? Thinking about settling down, hiring a few tentacles, and raising some orange and purple outrages of your own? Or have you forgotten that we're supposed to be focusing all our efforts and all our energies on trying to find a way home? Which right now means getting our four-limbed, flex-eyed hosts to dig through their astronomical charts and records in hopes of doing that?"

Raising his head slightly to meet George's gaze, Walker responded irritably. "That's what Sobj-oes and Habr-wec and their Iollth counterparts are doing. Our job is to continue diplomacy by further cementing our relationship with the locals. That's what I was doing. That's essentially what we did on Seremathenn, to a greater extent on Niyu, and to a lesser one on Hyff. Don't fret, George. I'm sorry I made you worry about me. Next time I'll wake you up." He nodded in the direction of the still sleeping Sque. "Take a hint from our decapodal female friend and don't lose sleep."

"Sure," George snapped. "Like she'd care if you went out in the middle of the night and never came back. In contrast, I *do* care."

"I know you do, George, but I was never in any danger, and I know what I'm doing. I *like* these people, even if they do have twice the appropriate number of limbs, eyes that weave around on stalks like balloons on strings, mouths that run north to south instead of side to side, and enough mass and muscle to out-sumo a grizzly. You need to relax." Lowering his head, he burrowed into the hospitable, cushioning alien material. "And speaking of relaxing, leave me alone. Not to put too fine a point on it, but I'm dog-tired."

"Just don't lose yourself, Marc." George was more worried than he let on. "Just don't let an appreciation for the new and exotic make you lose sight of our real goal." Standing on his hind legs with his forepaws on the edge of the makeshift bed allowed him to poke his snout almost into Walker's upturned left ear. "Steaks and pasta, Marc. Not purple and blue pâté. Ice cream and coffee. Football. The sights and smells of the river. Old friends talking. Making money. Going to the movies." Unfinished and discarded popcorn being one of

George's own favorite snacks. Using his snout and neck, he nudged the back of his friend's head.

"Don't forget all these things when you're overcome by some new, alien sight or sound or sensation. Don't forget about home. *Females in heat,*" he added as a last resort.

It did no good. His human was fast asleep, wheezing contentedly into the depths of the supportive alien pile.

Stay here if you want, then, he thought angrily as he turned and trotted away. *Or go back to Niyu and try to establish some kind of relationship with your scrawny alien admirer. Or return to Seremathenn and live off the largesse of the Sessrimathe. I can get home without you.*

But he couldn't, he knew. Walker was the titular leader of this voyage, having so been anointed by the Niyyuu and accepted as such by the Iollth and the Hyfft. Without him, if only as a unifying figurehead, it was unlikely even Sque was capable of persuading the Niyyuu, in particular, to continue with the journey.

Probably he was worrying unnecessarily. Hadn't Marc expressed an equally strong desire to find their way back home? The human had just enjoyed an exhilarating nocturnal experience, that was all. George began to feel he was being unduly suspicious. Doubtless it stemmed from all those years of being chased down back alleys by marauding abandoned rottweilers and bastard half pit bulls.

Dog-tired. Come to think of it, all the pacing and worrying about his two-legged friend had left him notably short on sleep himself. Wandering over to his own bed, which was nothing more than a much smaller, less densely upholstered version of Walker's, he stepped into it, paced off three increasingly tight circles, and flumped down into a warm, furry, self-contained pile.

When Sque eventually roused herself, the first thing she did was spend several minutes pondering possible new ways to describe the unremitting laziness of the two semi-comatose specimens from Earth, whose respective consciousnesses she was unable to rouse despite the application of repeated prodding and inventive invective.

As Tuuqalians ate their communal meals only twice, once in the morning at sunrise and the other at night during sunset, the vast dining hall was empty save for a few stragglers when Walker and George eventually woke up enough to stumble in and request food. Having by now learned which local victuals were tolerated by their system and which would induce, among other things, uncontrolled vomiting, it did not take long to choose a couple of the smallest of the shallow divided bowls the Tuuqalians utilized. Despite the fact that it was not a recognized mealtime, there was more than enough leftover food to satisfy them both. Together, they ate less than a single Tuuqalian would consume as an appetizer.

Sque accompanied them. Not because she was hungry, which she was not, but out of the usual mixture of boredom and curiosity. One could only slumber for so long in the temporary sleeping quarters that had been assigned to them. Also, thanks to the nature of Tuuqalian cuisine, the interior of the dining hall was just moist enough for her to be comfortable. The cool, dry air of the atmosphere outside was much less to her liking.

Climbing up onto the now largely empty curved table, she settled herself down to examine her surroundings. Occasionally she would glance down at her primitive companions, marveling at their ability to consume almost anything with apparent enjoyment. But then, one could not expect even an educated food preparer like the human Walker to possess the educated palate of a K'eremu.

His snout buried in the bowl that had been placed before him, George lay on the floor next to his friend. Walker sat with legs crossed and the food bowl balanced between them. It did not matter that the Tuuqalians did not use chairs because the table was too high for him to reach comfortably anyway. Designed for grasping by massive, powerful tentacles, the single all-purpose Tuuqalian food scoop was equally useless. This deficiency did not trouble George, who had no grasping limbs anyway. As for Walker, he was content to eat with his fingers.

As he did so, he admired the gentle arc of the table edge above him. Its curvature was similar to that of the balcony on which he had stood last night, as well as the fluid lines of the scoop ship he had ridden with Braouk. Tuuqalian design was surprisingly relaxed and sophisticated, all gentle curves and smooth surfaces. It contrasted rather than clashed with the hearty, rough-hewn nature of the Tuuqalians themselves. Like the floor of every local building or room he had entered, that of the extended family dining hall rose gently toward the center. So did the ceiling, giving every Tuuqalian room the aspect of a fried egg.

He realized with a start that local architecture set out in physical reality the same kind of undulating meter that characterized Tuuqalian sagas. All of a unified whole, the subtleness of it had escaped him until this moment. It was something he would never have noticed back on Earth. His travels, his encounters, were sharpening his perception in ways he could never have imagined.

He was no longer the same person he had been when he had been taken, he knew. Whoever had said that travel was broadening could never have envisioned what he had experienced these past couple of years. Not that he had ever been prejudiced, for example, or looked on others who were slightly different from him with anything other than the usual jaundiced urban eye. But even any subconscious vestiges of suppressed disapproval of other ethnicities or cultures had vanished due to the company he had been compelled to keep.

Look at the Tuuqalians. The first one he had encountered had struck him as a ravening monster, best to be avoided if not killed outright. True, Braouk had been suffering from the effects of his captivity and at the time had not been quite himself, but that still did not wholly excuse Walker's initial revulsion. He had reacted without trying to understand, like a threatened chimp. Now Braouk and his kind were not only friends, they were, as the Tuuqalian had recently informed him, family.

Family. He munched on something bulbous and blue that back home he would instinctively have thrown into the trash. It was sweet and flavorful. What constituted family? Was it only blood? A straightforward genetic linkage? Or could it be expanded to encompass shared ideals, other intelligences, different desires? Who did he really have more in common with? His cousin Larry, who thought farting was the epitome of witty humor and who lived only for inhaling the fumes at Chicago-area racetracks? Or Braouk, thoughtful and creative, if characteristically long-winded? As he chewed, letting alien sugars satiate his system, his attention shifted to where Sque reposed on the table just above him.

Five serpentine limbs dangled lazily off the side of the table while the other five maintained a grip on its surface. From the center of these serpentine coilings rose a tapering, maroon-hued mass that gently expanded and contracted with the K'eremu's breathing. Set in slots of silver, her pupils were horizontal instead of round or vertical. Like a butterfly's siphon, the pinkish speaking tube lay coiled against her body, just above the round mouth. She was about as far from cousin Larry as anything animate he could imagine. And yet, for all the sarcasm and inherent condescension of her kind, she was a better friend and companion than his blood relation. On more than one occasion her intelligence and, yes, caring, had gone a long way toward sustaining his life. All Larry had ever done was borrow money.

How then should one judge intelligence and amity? By the number of limbs and eyes something possessed, by its manner of speaking, or by skin color or hair style? The more experiences he endured, the more he learned, the greater the shallowness of his own kind weighed on him.

When I get home, he vowed, *it's going to be different. I'm going to be different.* He would not have to work hard at it, he knew. Travel was broadening.

They were almost finished when a familiar figure lurched into the hall, searched with scanning eyes, and found them. Lumbering over, Broullkoun-uvv-ahd-Hrashkin thrust one eye in George's direction and the other at Walker.

"Still you enjoy, food of my family, for eating?"

Rummaging around in his bowl, an unsqueamish Walker held up something that back home he would have consigned to his condo's garbage disposal. "The *poatk* is delicious, and so is everything else."

His muzzle stained dark blue, George looked up from his bowl and burped reflectively. "Not bad, snake-arms. In fact, everything here has been good."

Braouk's fur-quills stiffened slightly with pride. "Everything you are eating is of local manufacture. Fresh food of the northern plains is the best on all Tuuqalia, and that of my family famed as among the finest. It is a shame you will not be able to enjoy it any longer."

Frowning, Walker let his stained fingers drop to rest on the edge of the bowl. "I don't follow you. Is something wrong?"

Flexible, muscular eyestalks brought both eyes so close to him that he could see little else. "On the contrary, everything is very right, for you."

From the curving tabletop above, Sque withdrew from her contemplation of distant automatonic machinery to focus on their host. "You have news." Bubbles of excitement burbled from her speaking tube. "Sobj-oes and the astronomics team have found something."

Setting aside the bowl, Walker rose and wiped his mouth with the back of a sleeve. "They've got a direction! They've plotted a way for us to get home!"

Braouk gestured encouragingly. "I am led, to understand that is, the case. That by working together with the scientific opposite number among my people, our Niyyuuan and Iollth friends have managed to divine a Tuuqalia-K'erem vector."

Both eyes retracted. "I insisted on bringing you this wonderful news myself."

On the table, every one of Sque's limbs had contracted up against her body. "I am swollen with excitement. Given the inadequacies of those with whom I had to work, this is a moment I was not sure I would live long enough to see."

"And Earth?" Walker asked eagerly. Sitting attentively by his feet, George was wagging his tail rapidly enough to generate a small breeze.

Both of Braouk's eyes curved around to focus on him once again. Some of the initial keenness had faded from the Tuuqalian's voice. "They have what they believe to be a Tuuqalia-K'erem vector."

The kindly Braouk's lack of a direct response spoke volumes. Walker slumped. The energetic back and forth flailing of the dog's tail slowed. The Tuuqalian did not have to say anything else.

Everything of significance was contained in what he did not say.

13

Returning to their quarters in the company of their companion and guide, they gathered together their few personal belongings prior to departing the northern plains. Walker tried to put a brave face on Braouk's revelation.

"I guess it would've been too much to expect that your people would know where Earth was. We're still isolated, somewhere out on the galactic fringes. It's tough for travelers to find you when you're isolated and alone."

"I think the lyric you're looking for is 'Don't get around much,'" George chimed in. His gaze drifted to Sque, who in her usual fashion was already several steps ahead of them and ready to depart. "I can't see the future." He snorted. "Usually, I can't see beyond the next bone. But one thing I do know: no matter how this ends, I don't see myself spending the rest of my life on K'erem. It's hard enough being around one K'eremu. I can't imagine what living with a whole planetful of them would be like."

"'Maddening' is the word I think *you're* looking for," Walker replied understandingly. Though she plainly heard everything that was being said, Sque took no offense at the comments and offered no riposte. She was as used to their sarcasm and occasional jibes as they were to hers. For a K'eremu, it was all part and parcel of a normal conversation.

"You are always, welcome among my family, any time." Discerning the discouragement he knew would greet the deficiencies in his announcement, Braouk did his best to raise the spirits of his two friends. "Or you may choose to return with your friends the Niyyuu to their world, or even all the way back to distant Seremathenn, of which we recall so many good things."

All the way back, Walker ruminated. After everything they had undergone, it was a discouraging possibility to have to contemplate. A touch made him turn. Sque had come up silently behind him. She was chewing her morning treat of synthesized joqil, one of the two drugs (herbs, Walker dutifully corrected himself) she needed. Evening time would see her luxuriating in a dose of its complement, the pungent and perversely tempting si'dana. Reluctantly, she had once let the curious human taste the latter. To her disgust, he'd quickly spat it out. The powerful alkaloid tasted like powdered sulfur.

"Do not give up hope, Marcus Walker. How many times these past years would it have been all too easy to do so? I admit to having suffered from intermittent discouragement myself. Who would have not, given the odds arrayed against us?" A triplet of tentacles rose and gestured for emphasis. "Yet here we are on bland, bucolicTuuqalia, having returned friend Braouk to his homeworld. Now it seems that it may be possible for I to do the same." Three more slender, whip-like appendages wrapped encouragingly around his waist.

"By what we have accomplished we have already several times rendered impotent the word 'impossible.' Half of us are to be returned home. I promise, that when we reach K'erem, I will intercede with the relevant authorities on your behalf." The tentacles that had slid consolingly around his waist now withdrew. One arced down to pet George gently on the back of his head, mimicking the gesture she had so often seen Walker perform. The dog flinched, but did not retreat. A pet was a pet.

"Your people have never heard of Earth," a dejected Walker muttered. "We haven't found a single space-traversing species that has."

"Just so," she hissed softly through her speaking tube. "But if the Niyyuu can find Hyff, and Niyyuu and Hyfft working together can succeed in locating Tuuqalia, then who is to say what the K'eremu can and cannot find? Would you put the deductive capabilities of all those species up against that of the K'eremu?"

Aware that Braouk was standing right there with them, Walker composed his reply carefully. "I certainly would not be the one to cast doubt on the scientific capabilities of the K'eremu."

"A proper response," she replied in her whispery voice. "My people have achieved many wonderful things. Even finding a primitive, out-of-the-way, backward world such as your own is not necessarily beyond them. I do admit the fact that no one has ever heard of it or visited it tends to complicate the matter, but where my people are concerned, there are no absolutes. Presently, I envision only one problem."

"Why doesn't that overwhelm me with optimism?" George growled softly.

"Finding your world will doubtless require cooperation among the most eminent researchers in several fields," she explained. "As you know, the K'eremu relish their individual solitude. Persuading the germane scientists to work together to try and locate your Earth may prove more difficult than actually doing so." She swelled slightly, increasing her height another centimeter or two. "But as you know, I am not without persuasive skills myself. As a measure of our friendship, I shall exert myself to the utmost on your behalf."

"Thanks, Sque." Walker smiled down at her. "I'm really happy for you, that you're going home. Once we get there, we'll be glad of any help you can give us. We're glad of any help anyone can give us."

"Excellent it is, to hear that said, by you." Looming behind the three of them, Braouk raised all four upper tentacles in a gesture Walker thought he recognized. It seemed inappropriate at that moment, until the Tuuqalian continued. "Because I will still be able to render what aid I can, since I will be accompanying you."

Turning, Walker gaped at the multi-limbed giant. "*What?* But you're home now, Braouk. You're back among your own kind." Raising an arm, he gestured toward the far wall and the distant fertile fields beyond. "Back with your family. Back where you wanted to be." He shook his head wonderingly. "Why would you want to leave all this? George and I aren't asking it of you. We wouldn't expect it of you. We wouldn't expect it of anyone."

"Hell, no," George agreed readily. "I'm not ashamed to say that if our situation was reversed, I'd be staying home in Chicago and waving you a fond farewell. Shoot, I'd settle for staying *anywhere* on Earth." He thought a moment, added, "Well, maybe not Korea. Or Vietnam. But pretty much anywhere else."

"This I do, as much for myself, as you," Braouk informed them solemnly. Walker had shared the giant's company long enough to recognize and interpret certain movements, gestures, and inflections. What he was sensing now, more than anything else, was embarrassment. "I am afraid," Braouk continued, "that I have not been completely forthcoming with you."

Frowning, George trotted up to the base of the Tuuqalian. Though the dog was not much bigger than one of Braouk's eyes, he showed no fear. "That sounds suspiciously like you've been hiding something from us."

Tentacles thick as tree roots swayed a bit aimlessly. "All Tuuqalians dream, of composing a saga, vastly beautiful. But in a mature society such as ours has become, inspiration is often lacking." One eye dipped down to regard the dog while the other gazed at Walker and Sque. "It is said that out of bad things there oftentimes emerges some good. If you had asked it of me when I was a frustrated, introverted prisoner on board the ship of the Vilenjji, I would have replied that such a statement was not only untruthful but heartless." Now all four upper limbs stretched wide to encompass them all.

"But our travels, and the comradeship that has developed between us, has proven the wrongness of that notion and the truth of the ancient adage. From our experiences I have derived much material for, and have been quietly working on, linking together the stanzas and strains of a grand saga that I believe will go down among my kind as one of the better of its recent type. But in order for that to be true, it must have closure. There must be a conclusion that provides sufficient justification for all that has gone before. I thought my returning home would provide that. But since I have been here, I feel it is not so.

"The conclusion to the saga can come only when all of us, when all of *you,* have also been returned to your homes. That will be my coda. A half-completed saga is no saga worth spinning at all. As for the fulfillment of my personal desires, now that the location of Tuuqalia is known to the ships of the Niyyuu and the Iollth, there will be no problem returning me home. It will always be here for me to enjoy. Whereas true inspiration comes but rarely." The massive torso inclined toward George, teeth like serrated spades locking and unlocking with an audible clicking sound as their owner spoke.

"I hope you will all forgive me this small deception."

With a dismissive grunt, George turned tail on the Tuuqalian. "Why didn't you just tell us that's how you feel? It's no big deal."

"If you had known what I was about," Braouk responded, "it might have altered your behavior. To serve as the basis for such an extended composition, the actions described therein must be entirely natural."

Initially tense, Walker's expression melted into a slight grin. "So that's it. 'Smile—you're on candid saga.' It's all right, Braouk. You can compose about me all you want. I'm just glad we'll be having you along for the rest of the ride."

Stepping forward, he extended a hand. One flexible tentacle tip wrapped around his fingers in the human gesture of friendship Braouk had mastered early in their relationship. There was a time when it would have concerned Walker that the appendage grasping his hand could have effortlessly ripped his arm from its socket. No longer. Braouk might have the look of a nightmare, but he had the heart of a poet.

"Would you like to hear the first quotidian stanzas?" his friend asked eagerly.

Withdrawing his hand, Walker hastily composed a reply of his own. "Still some preparation, we have to do, before leaving. Surely you have arrangements to make, things to see to, as well?"

"Some few," the Tuuqalian admitted. "Also, measures must be finalized for the others who will be accompanying us. It is important, that everything be coordinated, for travel."

That brought Walker up short. " 'Others'?"

Braouk executed the equivalent of a Tuuqalian shrug. "Though your visit has been confined to the territory of my family, the notoriety of your experiences has been widely disseminated and appreciated. I am not the only one who finds inspiration in our history together. Others wish to experience something of it as well and, if possible, gain stimulation from the unique circumstances of our continuing encounter. Also, the government of the conjoined extended families of Tuuqalia is always grateful when one of its citizens is preserved from harm, and now wishes to express its gratitude in tangible terms.

"From both a need to acquire fresh artistic inspiration and a desire to reward you for helping in my salvation, the government has decided to provide four ships to escort and assist you all the rest of the way back to your homeworlds." He straightened proudly. "As you may have observed, Tuuqalians do many things by fours." Again, a single tentacle reached out, to rest its flexible end on Walker's shoulder.

"To avoid confusion and conflict, the four vessels and their crews will participate in and agree to the existing command arrangement. I have spoken with the relevant authorities and explained the particulars to them. The response was amenable. They foresee no difficulty placing the ships under your nominal command."

Walker swallowed. This was getting out of hand. All he had hoped for, when leaving Seremathenn for Niyu, was to find one ship crewed by one sentient species that might be willing to help him and George, Sque and Braouk, find their respective ways home. Now, like some rolling galactic stone, they had gathered to them a very impressive cluster of twelve starships. With him as the ostensible head of operations. He might in truth be little more than a facilitating figurehead, but even that responsibility was growing daunting.

"That's very kind of the extended families." More than a little overwhelmed, it was all he could think of to say.

George was more openly delighted. "*One* Tuuqalian ship would be enough to scare off any troublemakers. Four of them should be enough to scare anybody. And if that doesn't work, we can always sic the Iollth and the Niyyuu on anything that happens to get in our way. They'd both enjoy the digression."

"We're not siccing anybody on anybody," Walker warned the dog sternly. "This is and will stay a peaceful expedition, no matter how many decide to join in."

"As a show of force," Sque opined from behind them, "the number and diversity of vessels that will now be traveling with us should be more than adequate to stop any confrontation aborning. Even a K'eremu will acknowledge that an overwhelming display of strength is sometimes an adequate substitute for lack of intelligence."

* * *

There was no impressive ceremony of departure. For all their individual size and strength, and for all the accomplishments of their advanced society, the Tuuqalians were a modest folk. Accompanied by a Braouk reenergized by his return to his homeworld, the travelers were farewelled simply and efficiently and waved on their way. All of it recorded for posterity and with suitably breathless commentary by the ever effervescent representatives of the Niyyuu media, of course.

But there was nothing modest about the four vessels that had moved into orbit proximate to those of the Niyyuu and the Iollth. Even the combative Iollth were impressed, if not actually awed. Each of the arriving Tuuqalian craft was larger than any several Niyyuuan or Iollth ships combined.

Perhaps it was inevitable that a certain tension ensued. It did not last long, as representatives of both of the travelers' allies were immediately invited to tour the newest additions to the expedition. The blocky, multi-cube component designs of the Tuuqalian craft reflected the needs of their oversized crews rather than any military excess. Noting this, Iollth and Niyyuu alike were quickly able to relax and enjoy the educational visits. In turn, crew from the Tuuqalian quartet were invited to visit their counterparts. While this was manageable on the larger Niyyuuan craft, including the *Jhevn-Bha,* all visits to the five Iollth ships had to be conducted virtually, since none featured internal corridors expansive enough to allow the passage of even a small Tuuqalian.

The exchange of visits and information was followed by a small designated chorus of composers on board the Tuuqalian vessels who commenced creating a special saga to commemorate the unusual coming together. By the end of the first day of continuous and unrelenting recitation, Iollth and Niyyuu alike were more than ready to begin the next stage of the journey.

Navigators provided the necessary equations to ensure that the ships from three different worlds maintained constant speed and contact during the crossing from Tuuqalia to

K'erem. When these were executed, the consequences would have been an impressive sight to observe from any other vessel in orbit. Twelve ships featuring the most advanced engineering skills of three different sentient species, all departing simultaneously from the vicinity of Tuuqalia. There would be no noise, of course, but Walker was informed that the synchronized ignition of a dozen interstellar drives should be bright enough to be visible from Tuuqalia's surface.

He was not in a position to witness it, choosing to while away the time in his living quarters on board the *Jhevn-Bha* until the galactic flotilla was well under way. Though soon cleared to move about, he found that he had no urge to do so. Far more sensitive to his companion's frame of mind than anyone else, George leaped up onto Walker's makeshift bed and settled himself down beside his friend.

"Okay—*now* what's wrong?" One paw rubbed down an ear. "I swear, it's always been a wonder to me that the whole human species hasn't died out from a surfeit of excessive moodiness."

Walker had to smile. Reaching down, he ruffled the fur on the back of George's neck. In response, the dog rolled over onto his back and presented for attention his far less hirsute belly. Without thinking, Walker obliged, staring at the blank, pale beige ceiling as he caressed the dog's underside. On the far side of the living quarters the Niyyuu had modified to suit the needs of their singular guests, Sque lay flattened out in her makeshift artificial pond with only her head and upper body visible above the dark, brine-infused water.

Though there was room enough for Braouk to join them, their Tuuqalian companion was not present, having understandably chosen to spend time aboard a ship of his own people among his own kind. He would rejoin them again, Walker had been assured, as soon as they entered orbit around K'erem. After all, it would do nothing to advance the work on his ongoing saga if he remained separated from them at such moments.

"I'm just tired, George. Tired of traveling, tired of strange places and peoples. Tired of trying to keep my spirits up when nobody has ever heard of Earth or has any idea where it might be."

"That is not entirely true."

As he turned onto his right side, Walker forced a grumbling George to adjust his own position accordingly. Slinking silently, Sque had emerged from her pond and ambled over to join them. Reaching over the bed, the flexible tip of one tentacle rested against the human's sternum.

"C'mon, Sque," Walker murmured. "You really don't think your people know where Earth is, do you?"

"I admit that there is no reason why they should." The pink speaking tube wove and danced as she spoke, like the wriggling bait of an anglerfish. "Your world has no contact with the civilizations of the galaxy, therefore the civilizations of the galaxy have no contact with it, save for the occasional isolated and highly informal visit by such as the Vilenjji. But you must not underestimate the abilities of the K'eremu. My people are, as you already know, intellectually superior in every way to any species you have thus far encountered."

"Sez you," declared an unapologetic George, unwilling to let the blanket avowal go unchallenged.

As usual, it was left to Walker to maintain the peace. "You've frequently demonstrated your own cerebral gifts to us during the time we've spent together, Sque. And I'm not doubting that there are individuals among your kind who equal and even exceed your own abilities."

"One must not concede to excess," the K'eremu corrected him primly. "However, there are certainly specialists in such fields as astronautics whose experience in those areas is greater than mine. Strive as one might, one cannot claim to be an authority on everything."

As George was about to respond, Walker gently but firmly used his right hand to cover the dog's snout and clamp his jaws together. He continued the conversation, ignoring the claws that pawed irritably at his grip.

"You really think there's a chance that your scientists can find Earth?"

She drew herself up and swelled importantly, bubbles of emphasis spewing intermittently from her speaking tube. "Remember that I remarked a moment ago that it was 'not entirely true' that no one had any idea where your homeworld lies." Several limbs gestured toward the hovering image that supplied the room's only external view. "We know that we are in the right region of the galaxy, because the Vilenjji took the Tuuqalian Braouk, myself, and the two of you from worlds in the same general vicinity. We know that from comparing the relative elapsed time between our abductions."

"A 'vicinity' hundreds, if not thousands, of light-years in extent," George pointed out crustily as he finally succeeded in twisting his jaws free of Walker's constraining grasp.

"That is still something," Sque argued. "Better to have hundreds or thousands of light-years to search than a million. Better to know that such a search is commencing on the correct side of the galaxy. I reiterate: do not underestimate the skills of my people."

"I'm not underestimating them," Walker insisted. "I'm just trying to be realistic about the scope and difficulty of the undertaking." His voice dropped to a murmur. "No matter what happens, it ought to provide more good material for the saga Braouk is composing, anyway."

She gestured with a pair of appendages. "That attitude, at least, is sensible."

"What about you, Sque? I've been watching you ever since we left the Tuuqalian system. You don't seem to be very excited at the thought of finally returning home."

"I am thrilled beyond imagination," she responded in her usual measured tones. "I am eager to the point of self-voiding. Every sentient reveals such feelings in the manner unique to their species. The K'eremu are not what you would call overly demonstrative. But I assure you that I have, since the day of my abduction, not failed to count the moments until I might once again sprawl tranquil and flaccid in the bowels of my own dwelling." Her lengthwise pupils regarded him unblinkingly.

"Having in the course of the time we have spent together learned enough about me and my kind, you will understand, of course, when I do not invite you to share that particular space with me for more than the least amount of time that is considered minimally polite."

Walker nodded understandingly. "The K'eremu passion for individual privacy. We wouldn't think of intruding." He looked down to his left. "Would we, George?"

"Why would anyone want to?" the dog muttered. "I can find damp, dark, stinky, and claustrophobic on my own. I don't need an invitation."

"Then all will be well." Sque slipped backward a body length or so, the end of her limb withdrawing from contact with the human's chest. "Though it may be difficult and time-consuming to assemble together a sufficiency of authority to render the necessary decisions to assist you in your search, I am confident that I can do so. By aiding me in my escape from the Vilenjji . . ."

"Now just a minute," George began angrily, "just who aided who?"

". . . you have caused my society to incur a corresponding debt. As every K'eremu life is unique and irreplaceable, the munificent gesture you have made must be reciprocated. It constitutes a debt that cannot be ignored. Appropriate assistance will be forthcoming. I will see to it." Leaving that assurance hanging in the air, she scurried rather magisterially back to her tank.

Walker rolled over onto his back again. Though Sque was an insufferable egotist, she had more than once proven herself a true friend. He had no doubt she would be as good as her word. The uncertainty that nagged at him revolved not around her, but her kind.

On a world populated entirely by insufferable egotists, how did anyone, including one of their own kind, persuade them to cooperate long enough to help anyone besides themselves?

14

As with all journeys between star systems, that between Tu-uqalia and far-flung K'erem was interminable and boring. *How quickly we become jaded to the extraordinary,* Walker thought. It was no different with his own civilization. Each generation came to accept as normal and natural, if not a birthright, the unqualified miracles of its predecessor. As for himself, he was privileged, or cursed, to have come to accept as ordinary such things as interstellar travel, a multitude of sentient nonhuman races, the ability to perform gastronomic wonders with some judicious waving of his hands, and other marvels any one of which would individually have been regarded back home as the discovery of the age.

A real cup of coffee, he mused. Brewed from beans as opposed to being synthesized through advanced alien chemistry. Now that truly would be a miracle he could worship.

Having spent so much time in the company of the redoubtable Sequi'aranaqua'na'senemu and listening to her never-ending descriptions of her homeworld—the finest and most engaging in the galaxy, of course—he was not surprised by his first sight of it on the internal viewer when the flotilla emerged from deepspace several AUs out. Shrouded in mostly low cloud broken only occasionally by open sky, it was a maze of thousands of small, low-lying landmasses.

Not one of them was larger than Greenland, and few appeared, at least from space, much more hospitable.

Sque, on the other hand, was quietly ecstatic. "That I should have survived long enough to see such a sight once again," she murmured as together she, Walker, and George viewed the images that central command caused to be relayed to all operative imagers. In front of them, efficiently mimicking the appearance of solidity, hovered a vision of K'erem about a meter in diameter; all gray terrain, scattered seas, and brooding cloud cover. "Is it not beautiful beyond all others, my home?"

Walker hastened to concur, leaving it to George to add, "Reminds me of a particularly gloomy alley I once had to seek shelter in during a winter storm." Raising a paw, he indicated a lower corner of the image. "There's something that's not a geographical feature. It's moving too fast."

Sque approached as close to the image as she could without actually entering and distorting it. "A ship of my people, I should expect, coming up to meet us."

"Wouldn't there be orbit-to-ground communication first?" Walker queried her, frowning slightly.

She turned toward him. "I am sure the redoubtable Commander-Captain Gerlla-hyn, his contact team, and the committed communications caste of the Iollth have been attempting to do exactly that ever since we arrived within suitable range. They are, however, not as familiar with the customs of my kind as are you. Establishing contact from the surface would imply acceptance of arrival."

"In case you and your aloof kinfolk haven't noticed," George commented dryly, "we've already arrived. It's a fatal accompli."

"You have only arrived physically. Until proper communication is established, you have not arrived in the minds of the K'eremu. Hence the custom of making first greeting an extra-atmospheric one." Pivoting once more to face the suspended planetary image, she studied it anew. "Definitely a ship."

"One ship?" A curious Walker also focused his attention on the lower corner of the image.

This time she replied without looking over at him. "One ship is enough. One ship is always enough."

He was not surprised by her observation. From the years he had spent in her company, Walker knew that irrespective of the situation, Sque was unable to make a distinction between being completely self-assured or unreservedly over-confident. There was no in-between. Evidently, it was the same with all K'eremu.

What did surprise him, not to mention take his breath away, was the appearance of the K'eremu ship. While those of the Tuuqalia, Niyyuu, and Iollth differed in design, all were at heart functional and efficient, the end product of work by mathematicians and engineers. Rising from the cloudy surface of the planet below, the single approaching K'eremu craft was—unexpectedly beautiful.

It was not simply a matter of execution. The attention to external aesthetics was deliberate. Svelte and slippery where the construction of the visiting starships was blocky and rough, the ship looked more like the focal pendant of a gigantic brooch. Multi-hued lights of every color flashed in imaginative patterns from its molded flanks: a detail, he realized, that duplicated stylistically if not functionally the strands of metal and other materials with which Sque daily adorned her own person. Just as they contrasted sharply with her own mottled maroon skin and shape, so the artistic affectations that encrusted the gunmetal gray-black body of the K'eremu starship stood out sharply against its glossy-smooth sides. Compared to the singular sleekness of the new arrival, the space-traversing vessels of the three visiting races looked ungainly and bloated. The sheer beauty of the K'eremu craft was intimidating. He could not help wondering if the effect was intentional.

Despite its gratuitously lustrous appearance, he had no doubt it was fully functional—as would be any weapons it carried. Whether the latter could hold their own against the combined firepower of, say, twelve visiting vessels representing the apex of science as practiced within three different systems he did not know. But if it was all in the last analysis an exhibition of supreme (or foolish) overconfidence, it constituted a bluff of which any trader on the exchange back home would have been unashamedly proud.

He did not bother to inquire of Sque if that was actually the case. That was a matter for Gerlla-hyn and his fellow tacticians among the Iollth and the Tuuqalia to decide.

Perhaps not by themselves, however. Their living quarters' communicator promptly filled the room with a request for the guest traveler Sequi'aranaqua'na'senemu to please report to ship communications, so that she might aid in furthering formal contact with her people.

"Late," she commented as she turned to comply. "The call for my assistance should have be made the instant the contact craft was detected rising from the surface."

"Maybe sensors didn't pick it up until just now," Walker pointed out as he slipped off his bed and moved to join her.

Turning to look up at him, she continued scuttling on her way. When one is equipped with ten limbs spaced equidistantly around one's body, every point of the compass is equally easy to access.

"The contact vessel would have made its presence known immediately after liftoff, so that there would be no confusion among visitors as to its nature. That there has been no panicky shooting speaks well of our escort." She expanded to twice normal size, then contracted. "Even at this point in time, when contact is imminent, I find it hard to countenance that I will soon be again conversing with my own kind."

"Bet you can't wait for it," George declared, muting his usual cynicism.

"I anticipate it with boundless glee," she confessed as they moved out into the corridor and started toward the section of the *Jhevn-bha* where Command was located. "A day or two of unbridled conversation and contact. Then travel to my own residence, that I can only hope has been preserved, followed by thorough immersion in a period of blissful extended solitude."

Walker shook his head. Their obvious intelligence notwithstanding, it never ceased to amaze him how a species as ferociously introverted as the K'eremu had managed to build a viable civilization, much less one capable of interstellar travel. Strikingly attractive interstellar travel, if the ship that had now joined the visiting flotilla was not a deliberate aberration. Wondering if the interior was as extravagantly decorated as the outside, he hoped they might be offered the opportunity to visit.

They were not. Permission to board was explicitly refused. Indeed, Sque appeared somewhat put out by the Niyyuuan officer who ventured to make the request. The denial was not reflective, she explained, of any kind of overt hostility. As her human, canine, and Tuuqalian companions could attest, the K'eremu simply were not fond of company, under any circumstances.

Though on the face of it that observation seemed to portend difficulty in expanding further contact, the contrary proved to be the case. In fact, it was much easier to obtain permission to land on K'erem than it had been to visit Tuuqalia. While the precise nature of the permission granted was the exact opposite of effusive, the necessary formalities were executed swiftly and efficiently. Anyone who wanted to visit the surface would be allowed to do so—although in the absence of a local guide such as Sque, their movements would be severely circumscribed.

As representatives not only of the visiting vessels but of their own adverse situation, Walker and George were included in the first landing party. So was Braouk, who eagerly anticipated adding whole stanzas to his ongoing saga. Sobj-oes and her assistant Habr-wec were added along with representatives of the Iollth and Tuuqalian scientific staffs, in the hope that work could begin immediately utilizing the knowledge of their K'eremu counterparts in the search for the unknown world called Earth.

Descending to the surface via shuttle, Walker was struck by the dearth of lights on the nightside. While not actually surprised by the lack of any visible proof for the existence of urban concentrations, familiar as he was thanks to Sque with the K'eremu dislike of crowds, the complete nonexistence of any such suggested a primitive and backward society, which he knew for a fact the K'eremu were not. The construction of complex apparatus such as starships, for example, required extensive manufacturing facilities incorporating functioning high technology.

"Like our dwellings, we prefer to sequester such things below the surface," she informed him when he inquired about the apparent ambiguity. "Also, a great deal of our industrial complex is highly mechanized. More so even than what you saw on Seremathenn." Silver-gray eyes only slightly more vibrant than the clouds they were preparing to penetrate looked up at him. "Surely you did not envision my kind toiling away in the heat and repetition of a common industrial plant?"

Secured in a nearby landing seat that had been specially adapted to accommodate his diminutive form, George glanced over. "Yeah, Marc, what were you thinking? Imagine a K'eremu deigning to get its tentacles dirty with manual labor!"

As usual, the dog's sarcasm was lost on Sque, who simply accepted the canine observation as a statement of fact. "Precisely the point. All such activities on K'erem have been automated for a very long time indeed. They are appropriately supervised, and provide adequately for the needs of the population."

It certainly explained the absence of lights, Walker reflected as the rapidly descending Niyyuuan shuttle simultaneously entered atmosphere and daylight. Also the scarcity of any aboveground structures of consequence. Instead of cities, they passed low over rocky, heavily weathered islands and a few larger landmasses. Vegetation was abundant, but tended to be twisted and low to the ground. There were no jungles, no tall forests—at least, none that were visible to the shuttle's sensors. Here and there a single, unexpectedly tall tree or analogous local growth shot skyward like a solitary spire, a dark green landmark isolated in an otherwise endless heath- and moor-like landscape.

Reflecting the want of urbanization, there did not even appear to be a designated landing facility. That only revealed itself when, in response to their arrival and patient hovering, a portion of rocky terrain irised open to divulge a dry and expansive subterranean port. Descending in response to lackluster but adequate instruction from below, the shuttle settled gently to touchdown. Engines died. After years in Vilenjji captivity and additional ones spent in sometimes hopeful, sometimes despairing wandering, Sque had come home.

Almost, Walker decided. No doubt there were still formalities to be concluded. Hopefully, they would not involve anything as intimidating as those they had been forced to deal with on Tuuqalia, or as complex as those they had adapted to on Niyu.

First impressions certainly hinted at a different approach. As they emerged from the shuttle, their formal arrival on K'erem being thoroughly documented by the ever present Niyyuuan media, Walker and his friends were greeted by— nothing. Not only was no crowd or group present to welcome one of their own back to the communal fold, there was not even a single official present to direct them to the proper office. Bemused, Walker glanced upward. Though an unseen, unsensed field of some kind kept the fine mist that was falling from entering the landing facility, the air within was still noticeably cool and damp. Optimum climate for a

K'eremu, he knew, drawing his lightweight clothing a little tighter around him. Of his friends, only he felt a chill. Braouk and George both came equipped with their own built-in insulation. Still, he was not alone in his climatic sensitivity. Both the hairless Niyyuu and short-furred Iollth were similarly affected.

Scuttling to the fore, Sque called back to him and, by inference, to the rest of the landing party as well. "Please wait here a moment. It is necessary that I deal with the formalities."

Halting halfway between the shuttle and a vitreous gray bulge in the nearest wall, she generated from her speaking tube a sequence of perfectly tuned whistles accompanied by a stream of bubbles. A portal appeared in the bulge. Slowly radiating concentric rings of force rippled through the material as the gap widened, reminding Walker of the effect he used to produce as a child by dropping a slice of apple into a bowl of hot cereal. As a first indication of the stature of K'eremu science, the expanding doorway was pretty impressive.

Another K'eremu, only the second he had ever seen, scurried through the opening and moseyed forward to halt directly in front of Sque. Multiple appendages rose and touched, stroked and gripped, executing an intricate pantomime that would have put the most complex human handshake to shame. After several minutes of this, while Walker and the other visitors watched with interest, the newly arrived K'eremu pivoted and retreated back the way it had come. Sque returned to her companions.

"We can move along now."

Walker gaped at her. Behind him, Sobj-oes and the rest of the waiting Niyyuu and Iollth looked uncertain.

"That's it?" he mumbled. "What about formal immigration procedures? Registration? Signifying that we're here only for peaceful purposes?"

"Everything has been taken care of," she assured him genially. Leaning the upper portion of her body slightly to her right, she directed her attention to Sobj-oes and the rest of the scientific complement. "I will initiate proceedings to place you in touch with your superiors here. Meanwhile facilities, of a sort, will be made ready to accommodate you." Her eyes shifted back to Walker, George, and Braouk. "Amenities for travelers are limited. K'erem knows many visitors, but for some reason they do not choose to linger."

Walker let his gaze rove over the unadorned landing area, defunct of life, much less any kind of formal greeting. Overhead, the gray and cloudy sky continued to weep cold damp on a barren surface landscape. "Maybe it's the enthusiastic welcome they get."

"Or maybe it's the balmy weather," George added distastefully. "This I can get at home in March. If it's like this here all year round . . ."

"The climate today is most salubrious," Sque countered, slightly miffed. A pair of tentacles beckoned. "If you will all follow me, your immediate needs will be seen to."

They shuffled across the flat white landing surface. There was little of the excited conversation that normally accompanied touchdown on a new world. Something about the surroundings served to mute casual chatter. The atmosphere in the landing area was not morbid, just gloomy. As gloomy as the perpetually dank weather, Walker decided. He was happy for Sque, who had been returned to her home, but under the circumstances and that leaden sky above, it was hard to be happy for anyone else.

While contact between Sobj-oes's team of astronomers and their K'eremu counterparts (not "superiors," as Sque had so casually claimed) was initiated, their many-limbed companion of the past years invited them to accompany her on her return to her own personal dwelling. Having nothing else to do, and loathe to be left alone at the glum port facility, Walker and his friends agreed.

There was none of the excitement and anticipation that

had accompanied their similar recent visit to the home province on Tuuqalia of Braouk's extended family. Though the interior of the cargo vehicle that was provided for the journey was sparse and thoroughly utilitarian, they had no choice in the matter of transportation. It was the only mover that could accommodate someone of Walker's size—never mind Braouk. As they accelerated outward from the port, following one of the guidance signals that passed for a major transport vector, the Tuuqalian consoled himself by transforming the sights into saga. Needless to say, the stanzas he composed in the course of their journey were notable for their somberness, though they did no more than accurately reflect the dim and overcast terrain through which they were traveling.

Sque, at least, finally showed some signs of excitement. Her abode, she had learned, had not been disturbed during her absence, nor had it been given over to another. It should be, she told them, just as she had left it on the night when she had been abducted by the Vilenjji. Soon they would have the opportunity to experience real K'eremu hospitality.

"Isn't that a contradiction in terms?" George ventured—but only loud enough for Walker to overhear.

His friend hushed him. "It's not Sque's fault that she is the way she is. The K'eremu, her people—they're just not an outgoing type. Not like the Tuuqalia, or the Niyyuu."

"What," the dog countered, "just because they're conceited, arrogant, self-centered, balled-up bunches of slime?"

Leaning over, Walker put a cautioning hand on his friend's snout. "They're the conceited, arrogant, self-centered, balled-up bunches of slime we're going to have to rely on to help us find a way home. Don't forget that."

Shaking off the human's hand, George let out a resigned snort. "Much as I'd like to, I guess I can't." Standing up on his hind legs, he rested his forepaws on the transparent inner wall of the transport. "What a depressing chunk of rock. I bet there isn't a decent place to bury a bone within a dozen parsecs of this place."

At least they weren't confined to the cargo carrier for very long. Sque's habitat lay little more than half a day's travel from the port where they had set down. As they approached the shadowed, churning sea, cool lights began to emerge from the surrounding landscape, shining from within the depths of homes built into the raw rock, or constructed of material that matched their surroundings so closely it was impossible to tell excavation from artifice. As their vehicle started to slow it also began to descend a gentle grade leading toward a small cove and the water beyond. Eventually, it halted not far from the shoreline itself. A visibly energized Sque bade them disembark. As they did so, everything suddenly changed.

The sun came out. And lit an amethyst sky.

Lips parted, Walker gaped at his abruptly transformed surroundings. So did George and Braouk, when the Tuuqalian finally succeeded in squeezing his bulk out of the transport. Sque had advanced a short distance down an artistically winding path before she noticed that her companions were lingering behind as if stunned senseless.

"What is the matter with you all?" Impatient and perplexed, she scuttled back to rejoin them. "What are you all staring at like a bunch of paralyzed *dreepses*?"

Head tilted back, Walker simply nodded slowly without lowering his gaze to look at her. "The sky here. The color—it's not blue. It's—lavender."

"Lilac-like," agreed Braouk euphoniously. For once, he and the human were equally in tune with what they were looking at.

Silvery-metallic eyes glanced upward from beneath protective ridges of cartilage, eying the appearance of the first gaps between clouds. "Ah—I understand now. What is normal for me is apparently quite new to you. I will endeavor to explain in a manner sufficiently simple for your rustic minds to comprehend."

She proceeded to do so, but while the Vilenjji implants performed effectively with ordinary speech, and coped adequately with the occasional colloquialism, their programming for any language was not heavy with scientific terminology. Still, Walker managed to grasp the basic concepts. Something to do with K'erem's sun being different than those of their own homeworlds. As a consequence, more violet light entered the atmosphere of K'erem than that of Earth or Tuuqalia. She proceeded to add something about shorter wavelengths and higher frequencies, and violet light scattering more than blue, after which the lecture descended into details of optics and physics that were not only beyond the ability of his implant to translate smoothly and effectively, but beyond his capability to understand in any case.

It did not matter. He had understood enough. And no special knowledge was required to appreciate the beauty of a sky that was tinted amethyst instead of turquoise.

Naturally, it affected the appearance of everything through which they resumed walking: the rocky, uneven landscape, the hardscrabble native vegetation, even the paved path that worked its winding way down toward the sea. Only when they reached the terminus of the walkway did his attention turn from lavender sky to the purple-hued foam that crested the occasional wave, and to the strange creatures that frolicked along the shore.

More than anything else, the majority of them resembled half-drowned bats. But they were not mammals, and the wing-like projections that extended from their backs had not evolved with flight in mind. Fist-sized and highly active, they scurried back and forth, plowing the dark sand with flexing undershot scoops that were more like tapering shovels than beaks. Bipedal, their muscular little legs drove them forward through and across the sand. Their communal hissing as they plowed the narrow beach sounded more like a swarm of bees than a flock of birds.

"Tepejk," Sque pointed out almost affectionately. "Nice to see them again. Young K'eremu are often told to approach life like the *tepejk*." A trio of tentacles rose and pointed. "Notice the pitch and design of their limbs. They cannot back up; they can only drive, drive forward. To reverse course they must turn completely around. Their legs are designed to enable them to scour the sand that hides their food, tiny silicaceous lifeforms." Turning to her left, she beckoned for them to follow. "Come. Home awaits."

A smaller side path led along the beachfront, past several lights shining from the interior of what appeared to be a low bluff. Sque's abode lay at the end of the winding route. Despite the ease and expertise with which it blended perfectly into the surrounding terrain, she did not have to tell her friends where to stop. All three of them recognized it. Walker sucked in his breath sharply.

The entrance was an exact duplicate of her living quarters on board the Vilenjji capture ship.

"I can see what you are all thinking," she told them, studying the diversity of faces. "You may already have noted that my home lies at the very end of this larger community space." Turning, she gestured up the beach. "Unable to sleep one night, I was out wandering. The Vilenjji abduction took place far enough away from my home to preclude detection. As all of you know, our former captors were quite skilled at their nefarious activities."

Walker gestured back the way they had come. "That must have been quite a walk. It looks like there are multiple residences scattered all through this section of coast."

"Too distant to overhear, or to notice." Her limbs lowered to her base. "Then too, as you should know by now, K'eremu tend to keep to themselves, and to mind their own business. Needless to say, there was no crowd present to witness my abduction."

Flowing easily over the wave-worn rocks that lined both sides of the access path, she worked her way down to the beach, scattering feeding *tepejk* from her path. Her companions followed without effort. George began to trot up the shoreline, holding his nose close to the ground, sniffing out the details of yet another alien world. Braouk settled himself among the larger boulders, not wanting to coat his bristle-like fur with sand. Only Walker felt comfortable sitting down and letting his backside sink slightly into the cool, moist surface. Walker, and his ten-limbed female friend.

"Home." The way even the perpetually acerbic K'eremu hissed the word brought a lump to Walker's throat. How many times had he uttered the English equivalent silently, to himself? At last, and against seemingly impossible odds, Sequi'aranaqua'na'senemu had come home. Squatting nearby, the Tuuqalian Broullkoun-uvv-ahd-Hrashkin composed with silent ferocity, adding to the extension of his monumental ongoing saga that was intended to describe their travels and adventures. Up the beach, George was now digging at the dark, faintly mauve sand in an attempt to expose something small and vigorous that was frantically burrowing in the opposite direction.

Home, Walker mused. Would he and George ever see it? Or were they doomed to be travelers forever, visitors to worlds wondrous but alien, welcoming but unfamiliar? Could Sque's people really do as she claimed? Much K'eremu oratory was backed by accomplishment, he knew. But not all. The K'eremu were arrogant but brilliant—Sque was proof enough of that. Yet, they did not know everything. They were not omniscient. He did not really care whether they were or not.

He cared only if they could find Earth.

Having stopped digging, George had backed slightly away from the excavation he had made and was barking challengingly at the hole. Walker squinted in the dog's direction. A pair of weaving feelers had emerged from the cavity and were fluttering at the dog's face. Sensibly, George kept his distance, but continued to bark. His four-legged friend wanted to get home as badly as he did, Walker felt, but the dog's one-day-at-a-time approach to their situation allowed him to avoid much of the stress that plagued Walker daily.

That's the secret, he told himself. *Dig holes, and don't worry so much about what tomorrow may or may not bring.* But hard as he tried, he couldn't do it. Unfortunately for him, he was a human, and not a dog.

Nearby, Sque lolled in the metronomic wash of the sea, more at ease than he had ever seen her. It began to rain, a heavy mist that aspired to drizzle. Bubbles formed and drifted free from the tip of her speaking tube.

"Excellent. All that was needed to complete my home-coming was for the weather to turn good again."

Walker blinked up at the clammy precipitation, wiping moisture from his eyes. Like hands coming together, the clouds had closed in again, shutting out what had been a briefly glorious purple sky.

"I'm happy for you, Sque," he told her, "but as you know, the rest of us prefer to be out of this kind of weather instead of out in it."

A stream of small bubbles burst from her speaking organ. "I know, yes, I know. Bright sunshine and enervating dryness, that's what you three crave. Desiccation and dehydration." She heaved herself out of the centimeter-deep water. "Let it not be said that I was a poor host. We will retire within."

Sque's dwelling was thankfully larger inside than had been her makeshift abode on board the Vilenjji vessel, though Walker still had to enter on hands and knees and once inside sit on the floor with his head bent to avoid hitting it on the ceiling. George experienced no such difficulty, but there was no way Braouk could be accommodated. Supplied by Sque with a remarkably thin and light but thoroughly waterproof sheet of some glossy fabric, the Tuuqalian sat outside and contentedly compiled stanzas. The chill and dark that would have bothered Walker, and to a lesser extent George, did not affect him.

While the Vilenjji had successfully duplicated the exterior of Sque's home, they had never been inside. The interior was far different from the minimalist décor Walker remembered from the capture ship. In sharp contrast to the rough-hewn, natural coastal setting outside, the interior was lined with instrumentation and devices whose surfaces betrayed a silken texture. Soft light emanated from several locations within the dwelling, their purposes unknown. There were also what appeared to be works of art. All were multi-dimensional. There was nothing resembling a painting or sketch.

There were only two rooms, she informed them. A central, ovoidal living area, and a smaller storage chamber beyond. Everything she—a sophisticated, highly intelligent K'eremu—needed was in this one room and could be accessed by touch or voice command. To prove it, she brought forth several slick-sided mechanical shapes that emerged like gold-hued polyps from the lower portion of one wall.

"What do those do?" George sniffed cautiously of one of the metallic blobs.

"Kitchen," she told them brusquely. She could not smile, of course, but in an unmistakable gesture of the kind of affection she could not quite voice, one tendril snaked out to gently caress Walker's leg. "Don't you think, after all we have been through together, that it is about time that I cooked something for *you*?"

Consigned to Sque's care until some notification of progress came from Sobj-oes's busy scientific team, Walker found himself worrying about Braouk. He need not have bothered. As it developed, the big Tuuqalian did not mind spending all his days and nights outside the residence that was too small to admit him. With the bolt of glossy material provided by Sque to help shield him from the rain, he was quite at home beneath a large rocky overhang nearby. As for the temperature, it was often much colder during wintertime on the plains that were his natural home. He passed the days composing. When it was time to eat the food the synthesizer in Sque's home churned out for her guests, the Tuuqalian would hunch low near the entrance to receive his own massive portion, and also to chat with his friends.

Since Sque herself showed no inclination whatsoever to entertain her visitors, and in fact kept to herself as much as possible, and Braouk was preoccupied with his saga-spinning, Walker and George were left to themselves to wander the stony slopes that surrounded Sque's abode, and to explore the narrow beach of dark sand that fronted the cove like a necklace of unpolished hematite.

Occasionally when they were out strolling along the beach, they would encounter another K'eremu. Apprised of the return of the prodigal cephalopod Sequi'aranaqua'na'senemu and of the presence of visiting aliens in their midst, these locals would hurry to scurry away from oncoming human and dog. When surprised, or hailed, sometimes they would reply with a gruff hiss and an emitted bubble or two before vanishing along the nearest escape route.

"They really don't like company, do they?" George commented one afternoon when not one but two local residents utilized all ten limbs to the max to avoid having to confront him and his tall friend.

Walker watched the second K'eremu disappear over a slight hillock fragrant with what looked like acres of rose-bushes that had been stomped flat. "They don't even like each other, remember? That's why we've never seen more than two of them together at any one time."

The fur on his feet slick with seawater and bearing clumps of black sand, George trotted along easily beside his human. "Despite what Sque told us about how automated their society is, wouldn't they have to congregate together to build things? Like a house, or a path, or maybe civilization?"

Walker shrugged and tugged his shirt collar closer around

him. An intermittent breeze was blowing in off the gunmetal gray sea, and he was cold. "I wouldn't wager against anything the K'eremu try to do, or the way they choose to do it. I guess it's easier for them to deal with automatons than with each other."

George paused to sniff something hard-shelled and dead, snorted, and resumed his walk. "It's their innate sense of superiority. Individual as much as racial. Collectively, they're convinced the K'eremu are the sharpest, smartest species around. And each K'eremu is sharper and smarter than its neighbor. It's a wonder they've cooperated enough to advance as far as they have."

"Yeah, cooperated."

The dog frowned up at his friend. "You said that funny. What're you thinking, biped?"

"Oh, nothing, nothing really." He looked out to sea. A great bluish-green bulk was heaving itself slowly above the waves, as if the accumulated wastes of a million years had suddenly acquired sentience and decided to belch themselves surfaceward. The misshapen mass was festooned with scraggly lengths of scabrous brown growths that writhed and twitched with shocking, independent life. At a distance, it was impossible to tell if they were appendages, parasites, or something unidentifiable.

"You'd think at least one or two of her old neighbors would've dropped by to congratulate Sque on surviving her abduction, and to welcome her home."

George grunted knowingly. "She wouldn't have let them in. I'm telling you, Marc, it's one thing to label somebody as antisocial; it's another to see it applied to an entire species. When a strange dog wanders into your territory, you have to at least make initial contact before you can decide whether it's friend or foe." With his snout he indicated the widespread, artfully concealed dwellings that inhabited the coast they were passing. "There's sure no equivalent of sociable butt-sniffing here."

"No butts, either." Idly, Walker kicked at something half-buried in the sand, jumped back as it shot into the air, spun several times on its longitudinal axis while spraying water in all directions, and landed hard on the sand. Whereupon it promptly scurried on a dozen or more cilia down to the water's edge. There it crouched, looking like an ambulatory rubber glove, and spat at them as it glared up out of a single flattened red eye.

The clouds broke, revealing K'erem's spectacular alien sky. The planet's strange sun beamed down, warming Walker with its eerie violet glow while electrifying the normally dark and clammy landscape with shocking wine-colored highlights. As always, it had a profound effect on Walker, though much less so on the largely color-blind George.

"This isn't such a bad world," the commodities trader observed. "At least, not when the sun is out."

"No, it's not," George agreed without hesitation.

It was enough to halt Walker in his tracks. "What did you say?"

The dog sat back on his haunches and stared out at the alien, lavender-tinted waves. "It's not such a bad place. Reminds me of the city on a late autumn afternoon."

Walker knelt beside him. "Those are about the first kind words I've heard you say about any place we've been. What's changed?"

The light wind racing in off the ocean rippled the dog's fur. He shrugged diffidently. "I dunno. Maybe I'm adapting. Maybe I'm resigned. Maybe I'm losing my mind. They say travel is broadening."

Grinning, Walker reached over to scratch his friend's neck. "The first space-dog. Harbinger of a new species."

"Hairbinger, you mean."

They stayed like that for a long while, man and dog, the former with his horizons broadened, the latter with his intelligence elevated, contemplating a sheet of water that was farther from the familiar wavelets of Lake Michigan than either of them could have imagined as recently as four years ago. Then they rose and, each lost in his own thoughts, made their way back to the compact, low-ceilinged home of their inherently irascible, intrinsically reluctant, many-limbed hostess.

15

Sque was waiting for them when they returned. That is to say, she was in her domicile when they got back. As to whether or not she cared if they returned or if they happened to drown in the merlot-shaded sea was a matter for conjecture.

They were greeted first by Braouk, who was sitting beneath his usual stony overhang letting the occasional burst of purple sunshine warm his fur. Noting their approach, he bestirred himself, rose up on all four supportive limbs, and lumbered toward them.

"The charming Sque, I have been advised, has information. Of what nature she would not tell me, but insisted on waiting until you returned and all could hear it together."

Walker's heart thumped. He glanced excitedly down at his companion. "Finally! Some news regarding the hunt for Earth, I bet."

"Some news, anyway," conceded George, his reaction more guarded than that of his friend.

Wanting all three of her companions and visitors to simultaneously learn the details of what she had to tell them, as Braouk had said, she exited her dwelling as soon as Walker and George alerted her to their return. She carried nothing with her, unless one counted the usual ribbons of personal adornment. Walker was unable to restrain himself from prompting her.

"News of the search for our homeworld?" he asked eagerly.

Metallic gray eyes turned to regard him. Having lived with her for so long, he had learned to recognize certain subtle movements. A swelling here, a tentacle twitch there. At the moment, she seemed ill at ease. That was unusual in and of itself. It did not bode well.

He was right. "No news of the search for your homeworld, Marcus. And I am very much afraid there will not be any news of the search for your homeworld." Her body expanded slightly, contracted more slowly as she punctuated her response with an exhalation signifying resignation. "Because there will not be any search for your homeworld." Reaching up with one appendage, she used it to delicately clean one aural opening. "At least, none that involve the K'eremu."

Walker swallowed. He felt as if someone had kicked him in the throat. "I don't understand, Sque. Why not? What's wrong?"

"Nothing is 'wrong,' Marcus." Though the tone of her voice did not change, the intensity of her feeling was underlined by the fact that she had used his personal name twice in as many responses. "The K'eremu are simply being the K'eremu."

"Slimy bastards." George made no attempt to hide his bitterness.

"I assure you that neither epidermal viscosity nor the composition of individual ancestry has anything to do with the decision."

Walker suddenly felt sorry for her. As much as was possible for one of her kind, she clearly felt disturbed at having to deliver such bad news. She was K'eremu, but she was also their friend.

Putting aside his resentment and frustration, he made himself inquire patiently, "Why won't your people help us? What do you mean when you say that 'the K'eremu are simply being the K'eremu'?"

She gesticulated with three limbs, and this time it was a gesture whose meaning he could not divine. "There is no hostility involved, Marcus. Only characteristic indifference. If the average K'eremu, and those are two terms I assure you are not often used in tandem, is not concerned with his or her neighbor, how can they be expected to involve themselves in the far more alien and complex troubles of others? Especially those of insignificant non-K'eremu primitives?"

"Is that what you told your authorities we are?" George snarled. It had been a long time since he had heard the dog growl like that, Walker reflected.

Sque reacted immediately, and in a manner sufficiently unexpected to startle both man and dog. One flexible appendage whipped out and smacked the dog across his snout. So startled was George that he did not even respond with an instinctive bite. Instead, he was knocked back onto his haunches, where he sat, stunned, staring at their hostess.

"Do you think so little of me, after all this time we have spent in one another's company?" She swelled up so prodigiously Walker thought she might burst, the expression "bust a gut" having a more literal application among the K'eremu than any other species he had yet encountered. To his relief, the furious bloat rapidly subsided.

"That may indeed be what you are," she went on, having brought herself under control once more, "but it is not how I presented you and your case to the relevant segment of K'erem's scientific establishment. Plainly, my account made no difference to those in a position to act upon it."

"What about our part in helping to rescue you," Walker ventured, "in helping a K'eremu to return home? Did you mention that? You said it would be worth something."

"I did indeed allude at length to your humble and unassuming assistance," she assured him. "It seems to have swayed no opinion. Without a compelling reason to do so, no astronomer of K'erem will expend the time or effort to assist your Niyyuuan and Iollth friends in their attempt to locate your homeworld. That if they wished they could do so I have no doubt. The problem is not execution, but motivation." A pair of tentacles reached out to wrap around his right leg and squeeze gently. Apologetically, even.

"I am sorry, Marcus Walker and George. There is nothing more I can do. Rare is the individual K'eremu who can persuade another."

"Because each one feels superior to every other one," a disconsolate George muttered. "A standoff of superciliousness." He looked up at Walker. "That means there's no higher court we can appeal to, because none of these squids recognizes another of their kind as having a superior grasp of any situation. How do you convince a pod of conceited egotists to change their minds?"

"I don't know," a dejected Walker muttered. Wind nipped at his ears. "I don't know."

"I sorrow also, for my good friends, at this." Braouk rested one massive upper tentacle across Walker's shoulders, lightly stroking George's back with another. "The K'eremu are not Tuuqalian."

"Observations of the obvious don't help us much." Shrugging off the caress, George jogged off toward the low alien scrub that dominated the landscape in the vicinity of Sque's residence. Walker didn't try to stop him. Let his friend and companion brood in privacy. They'd had little enough of that during these past years traveling.

He looked back down at Sque. "Is there anything else we can do? Anything that might change the minds of the K'eremu who could help us?"

Half a dozen appendages waved fluidly in a gesture of substantial import. "You can try putting your case to some of them directly; possibly one at a time, certainly not many, since as you know we are not especially fond of one another's company."

Her suggestion wasn't exactly encouraging, he decided, but it was a beginning. Certainly it was better than sitting around helplessly bemoaning the fate to which an unkind, uncaring universe had consigned them. From the time he had been introduced to the Vilenjji capture ship, he had taken a proactive role in his own survival. That was how he had conducted his trading of commodities; that was how he had conducted his life. He would not change that now, not even in the face of seemingly indomitable K'eremu obduracy.

"All right then: we'll start with one. Can you at least line up an initial interview with an appropriate entity? We'll try putting our case to the scientific authorities that way, like you say. One at a time."

She hesitated, but only briefly. "It may take a little while to make the necessary arrangements, but I think it might be possible."

Bending down, he leaned so close to her that she could have touched his face with her speaking tube. "And will you continue to speak on our behalf?"

"Having only recently returned to it, I dislike the idea of being away from my residence again so soon. But"—and she reached up with an appendage to flick him gently on one cheek—"if nothing else it may prove entertaining. A relief from the tedium of everyday existence is always welcome."

"Oh, it won't be dull, I promise you that." Straightening, he cupped both hands to his mouth and raised his voice. "George! Get back here! We're going traveling—again."

The route they took several days later was as familiar as their intended destination. There being no facility on all of K'erem dedicated to the (according to the K'eremu way of thinking) unnatural and downright repulsive enterprise of mass assembly, it was decided to hold the meeting Sque had arranged as well as any subsequent ones at the port where they had first set down. The port, at least, was equipped with facilities for the handling and distribution not only of cargo, which was almost entirely dealt with by servicing automatons, but also the occasional odd guest. Such uncommon visitors had to be very odd indeed, Walker reflected as he and his companions disembarked from their transport and entered once more into the facility, given that the K'eremu were not exactly a warm, wildly welcoming folk.

As he had during the course of his initial arrival at K'erem, he once more had the opportunity to admire and marvel at the smoothly supple bronzed and silvered shapes that comprised his surroundings. Devices and mechanisms extruded silently from or retracted almost sensuously into walls, ceilings, and floor, pulsing with oozing mechanical life. From time to time K'eremu automatons slid, scurried, or shushed past the travelers as they followed Sque deeper into the complex. Walker likened it to strolling through a set of alien internal organs that had been fashioned from several different consistencies and colors of liquid metal.

Infrequently, they encountered another K'eremu. Espying the visitors, these locals would every so often offer a greeting to Sque. Just as frequently, they ignored her. Argent eyes flicked over human and dog and Tuuqalian. They did not precisely drip contempt. They did not have to. If you were not K'eremu, you barely qualified as sentient. And if you were K'eremu, regardless of profession or specialty or age or education, you were superior to everything and everyone else, including your neighbors. Recalling the arrogant attitudes of certain human teenagers he had met, Walker was thankful he had not been forced to deal with any juvenile K'eremu. Doubtless they raised the description "insufferable" to new heights. Or maybe, he thought, adolescence progressed differently among his hosts. When traveling among alien cultures, anthropomorphism was the first casualty.

There were three K'eremu waiting for them in an immigration holding chamber just beyond the point where arrivals officially disembarked from or reboarded visiting ships. All three were bedecked with the kind of trashy, glittering individual bodily adornments Walker and his friends were familiar with from time spent in Sque's similarly gaudy company: K'eremu bling. The slick, shiny skin of two of the aliens was the same yellow-mottled maroon hue as Sque's, though the patterns differed. The third's epidermis was a darker red, almost carmine, and marked with mildly eye-catching splotches of yellow that shaded to gold. Sexual dimorphism being readily recognizable among the K'eremu, and Walker having been enlightened as to the details by Sque, he duly noted that the trio waiting before them consisted of two females and one male.

"You should feel honored," Sque hissed softly up at him. "Rarely do more than two K'eremu come together in person for any purpose."

"Then why aren't there only two?" Walker whispered back at her.

"Two might never come to a decision. When K'eremu desire to reach a consensus, the number involved in the discussion must always be odd, never even."

The trio did not look happy. Dozens of tentacles writhed in annoyance. Introductions were perfunctory and delivered with the same kind of generic irritation Walker and his friends had been subjected to ever since they had made Sque's acquaintance back on the Vilenjji ship. Accustomed to it, he was able to largely ignore it. Adhering to usual K'eremu practice, formalities were, well, brief.

"Speak," snapped the larger of the two females, whose name (greatly shortened like Sque's for the convenience of inarticulate alien visitors) was Alet. "My time passes, and I can think of at least a hundred things that would be better done with it."

Walker looked down at George; George promptly settled his belly down on the shimmering bronzed floor and crossed his front legs. Walker looked at Braouk; the Tuuqalian giant squatted down on his four under-limbs, and Walker realized that yet again it was being left to him to make their case.

Clearing his throat, which caused the male member of the impatiently waiting trio to wince visibly, he took a step forward. After a moment's thought he crouched down, the better to put himself eye level to eye level with the three already visibly indifferent K'eremu.

"I am—" he began. It was as far as he was allowed to get before he was brusquely interrupted by the female called Mhez.

"We know who you are. We know all there is to know about you that is knowable by K'eremu." A pair of appendages waved briskly. "I am of the personal opinion that is more than enough. We know where you came from, how you came to be here, and what you want. Your request has already been denied." A couple of desultory bubbles wandered aloft from the end of her speaking tube. "Our astronomers have a higher calling, and better things to do, than waste their time seeking the location of remote worlds inhabited by boorish primitives."

George sprang to his feet, only to visibly control himself in response to a cautionary wave from Walker. "We're aware of your opinion of us."

"Do you dispute it?" challenged the male, whose abridged name was Rehj.

"I think you underestimate us." Walker composed his reply carefully. He was acutely conscious of the fragile nature of the confrontation, and that the trio of scarcely attentive K'eremu might decide at any moment to bring it to an abrupt and unproductive end. "For one thing, as our friend and companion Sque can attest, George and I are intelligent enough to recognize the innate and unarguable superiority of the K'eremu." Behind him, a rude canine noise sounded. Unfamiliar with the nature of the auditory discharge or its possible import, the K'eremu ignored it.

As a result of Walker's comment, some shuffling ensued among the judgmental trio. "That shows wisdom, if not intelligence," declared Alet. "It also conforms to the opinion of another who has exhibited an interest in this situation."

A frowning Walker immediately glanced over at Sque. Their K'eremu companion raised a pair of appendages.

"I have done nothing more than comment honestly on what I have observed these past several years. You should know that I can be nothing but honest."

"That kind of honesty doesn't seem to be helping us much," George observed tartly.

"The other to whom I refer," Alet continued irritably, "is not the K'eremu Sequi'aranaqua'na'senemu, who has been forced to associate with you in the course of your wandering." Pivoting slightly, she gestured in the direction of the fluid wall to her left. Like chrome jelly stirred by an active hand, a portal appeared in the undulating surface and a figure stepped through to join them.

Walker lost a breath. George growled softly as the hackles rose on his shoulders. Braouk started forward, only to be restrained by Sque.

"There can be no fighting here," she warned their hulking companion. Tentacles gestured simultaneously in several directions. "There are dynamic devices present that will restrain even such an oversized sentient as yourself, and not always gently." At her words of warning the Tuuqalian paused, vertically aligned jaws opening and clashing in frustration.

Advancing on thickened, flap-padded feet, the Vilenjji Pret-Klob came toward them, halting well out of reach of any of his former captives. Huge eyes that nearly met in the center of the tapering, cilia-crowned skull regarded them impassively.

"Greetings to inventory," their former captor murmured with utter lack of emotion. "Tracking you has been one of the most psychologically rewarding if fiscally unproductive experiences of my lifetime."

"How did you find us?" a stunned Walker blurted. "How *did* you track us?"

Cold, calculating eyes met his own. "On every world you visited, you stood out, human investment. By virtue of your uniqueness, you drew attention. The media of Niyu, where you traveled upon entering the service of one minor official there, was constantly full of your exploits: political, military, and culinary. That is how we initially located you there. You will recall that unfortunate confrontation, when this increasingly costly recovery operation would have ended but for the misguided interference of some of the natives. By the way, I congratulate you on your mastery of a new skill. I am always pleased when an item of inventory takes the time and trouble to enhance its own value without the need of additional financial input from my association. You are to be commended on your initiative."

"Keep it," Walker growled, no less gutturally than the snarling dog now standing at his feet.

"As you were journeying in the company of three well-armed vessels, we could hardly attempt to recover you through the use of force. Subsequent to your illicit flight from that world, the Niyyuuan media very usefully indicated in detail and at length the next destination to which you hoped to travel. As you know, the nature of our business requires my association to travel quite extensively. We had no difficulty locating Hyff. Though we arrived there in the wake of your enterprising engagement with the Iollth, by presenting ourselves to the locals as your friends, and making ourselves useful in other ways, we succeeded in learning that you were going to try to reach Tuuqalia." Vast flattened eyes shifted to the barely restrained Braouk. "That being a world whose location in the stellar firmament we already knew, we then traveled there."

Mindful of Sque's warning, Walker was also keeping a watchful eye on the silently seething Braouk. "I hope you had enough brains not to try to abduct another Tuuqalian."

The Vilenjji's response suggested common sense, if not morality. "Actually, as we were already there, and had successfully carried out such an appropriation previously, the possibility was discussed. It was decided, however, that despite the potential profit, since the prior acquisition from that world had proven untenable, not to mention lethal, it fell on the downside of cost-effectiveness. Hence, no: no further acquisition was attempted on that world."

"How fortunate for you," Braouk rumbled.

"We only just missed you there," Pret-Klob continued serenely, "but by the same means that have so greatly facilitated our commerce in the past, we did learn that you next intended to visit K'erem. We were most impressed to learn that you had acquired the assistance and company not only of the original three craft that had accompanied you from Niyu, but by now of Iollth and Tuuqalian help as well." Eyes appraisingly traveled the length and breadth of the enraged Braouk. "You are well and intact, I see. That is good. Throughout the term of our following you my associates and I were much concerned for the state of our long-lost inventory."

"Not your inventory, this particular saga spinner, or friends." Reaching out with the two massive appendages on his left side, Braouk extended them protectively out over Walker and George. Probably correctly, the Tuuqalian was assuming that Sque was in no danger here on her homeworld. Though where the capricious K'eremu were concerned, Walker cautioned himself, nothing could be taken for granted.

"I'd like to know," he pressed their tormentor, "why you continue to bother. In my trade, when a business deal goes sour and costs you money, you don't pursue it." He indicated his friends. "We'd call it 'throwing good money after bad.' "

"For one thing," the Vilenjji told him easily, "in the course of your traveling, you have accumulated knowledge and skills that have greatly enhanced your value beyond that of simply being interesting uneducated specimens from unvisited worlds. More importantly"—and as he spoke, the tendrils atop his tapered head writhed and twisted vigorously—"there is principle involved. The Vilenjji do not willingly surrender inventory without making as aggressive an attempt as possible to recover it. Also, as I may have explained previously, it sets a precedent that is very bad for business if it is learned that inventory has been able to disengage from us without any compensation. That is damaging for customers to know, and damaging for inventory still in retention to know."

"All right," Walker shot back, his tone an uneasy mix of disquiet and defiance, "so you've managed to follow us this far." He jerked his head sharply in the direction of the three inquisitive K'eremu. "Alet says you have an 'interest in the situation.' I can tell you right now that's as far as it's going to go."

"On the contrary," Pret-Klob replied, unperturbed as ever, "I hope, and expect, that 'it' will continue onward to what I consider to be the most desirable and logical conclusion. Unable to recover our absent inventory by force, the members of the association have consistently sought a way to bring other means to bear on this odious and ongoing dilemma. It may be that those means that would not be practical on, say, Niyu or Tuuqalia may have more efficacious application here." The Vilenjji appeared to gather himself.

"In connection with that I have lodged a formal claim for the return of our absent property with the amorphous entity that passes for local authority on this world." A sucker-lined upper arm flap indicated the unblinking Sque. "With the exception of one among you, the rights to whom my association must for obvious practical reasons abjure any claim."

Feeling slightly faint, Walker struggled to hang on to his wits. Turning away from the poised and expectant Vilenjji, he directed his attention to the trio of silently watching K'eremu.

"This is insane. Surely you can't give any credence to this contemptible creature's outrageous claims!" Behind him, Braouk was already searching for an escape route, calculating whether it would be better to try to flee the port complex or take one or more of the three monitoring K'eremu hostage.

Though mindful, and respectful, of Sque's warning, he would readily die without seeing Tuuqalia again and with his grand saga unfinished before he would submit to Vilenjji captivity a second time.

George took a couple of steps toward the trio, nodding in the direction of the ever watchful Pret-Klob. "No matter what this ambulatory vegetable claims, we're all of us here independent intelligences. Capturing and selling a sentient is against the laws and customs of galactic civilization."

It was Rehj who responded coolly. "What galactic civilization would that be? Whichever, it is not one to which the K'eremu belong, nor to whose laws we subscribe."

That was right, Walker thought furiously. K'erem lay far, far outside the boundaries of the culture and society inhabited by the Sessrimathe and the Niyyuu, among others. Undoubtedly Pret-Klob and his loathsome association were counting on that.

"Though no decision has been rendered in this matter," Mehz informed him, "it would behoove you to offer a better argument."

"I have an argument." The Vilenjji waved the flattened, sucker-lined extremity of one limb. "At this moment, there are in orbit around K'erem twelve warships crewed by representatives of three different warlike species, with delegates from a fourth." In what was not quite a bow, his cloaked, purple-tinged upper body inclined in the direction of the three. "While I do not doubt the ability of such superior beings as the K'eremu to defend themselves and their world from any imprudent demonstrations of bellicosity, twelve ships is an impressive number. One that, directed and designed by other intelligent races, might conceivably pose a threat even to K'erem itself."

Standing for a moment on his hind legs, George whispered up at his human. "What's the moldy old eggplant getting at?"

"I don't know," Walker replied honestly, plenty worried in spite of his ignorance.

Both travelers quickly found out, as Pret-Klob continued. "By coincidence and good fortune, the commander of this entire force stands now before you. Neutralize him and his companions while still keeping them alive and well, and you eliminate any motivation for those on board the twelve armed ships to cause trouble. And in doing so, you also make permanent allies and friends of myself and my kind."

Rehj could not frown, but conveyed the impression of doing so. "What 'commander'?"

The arm flap that had been deferring to the three K'eremu now swung around to point directly at the startled Walker.

16

Not only was it a clever ploy, an apprehensively admiring Walker had to admit, it gave evidence of the veneer, if not the spirit, of intelligent thought. But while he was striving not to panic as he sought wildly for a suitable rebuttal, it became evident that the K'eremu, neutral in the dispute though they might be, were not to be easily persuaded to support *either* side.

"We could accomplish the same thing by simply keeping them here on K'erem and preventing them from returning to their ships. Realizing the hopelessness of recovering these three alive, those vessels would eventually depart." Alet focused silver-gray eyes on the much bigger Vilenjji. "Such a course of action, however, would do nothing to satisfy the claim you have made."

Mehz spoke up beside her, the ambient light of the chamber gleaming brightly on his more reflective epidermis. "While not subject to the laws of this distant galactic civilization of which everyone speaks, and indifferent to them, I admit to being personally uncomfortable at the idea that one intelligent species might profit through the buying and selling of representatives of another."

"Keep in mind," Pret-Klob responded greasily, "that by many standards they do not qualify as intelligent. Certainly not by K'eremu standards." He gestured with both arms. "Do they come here in ships of their own people? No. Do they exhibit advanced technology of their own design? No. Have they, since they have been on your world, demonstrated any special insight or ability that would lead you to countenance such higher sentience? I think not." One sucker-lined arm flap stabbed suddenly in George's direction. "As for that specimen, before it underwent an extensive internal adjustment by us, its intelligence was of such a low order it could neither think nor speak properly."

Growling, head down, George started forward. "How about if I think I'll speak about taking a bite out of—"

Whispering urgently, Walker grabbed the dog by the nape of his neck to hold him back. "Don't do it, George. I'd like to take a bite out of him myself, but that's just what he wants: to upset us enough to get proof of what he's claiming." Ignoring the Vilenjji, he turned his attention back to the watchful, contemplative threesome.

"I don't pretend to lay claim to any special intelligence. I'm only a trader in basic commodities—and a chef. If I'm not as smart as the average K'eremu, I'm still intelligent enough to do those simple things, and do them well. Surely that qualifies as sufficient sentience." Releasing his grip on George's neck, he patted the still softly snarling dog on the head. "My friend here can't cook, and he can't arrange complex trades, but he can observe, and analyze, and comment intelligently on what he sees." Jerking a thumb back over his shoulder, he concluded by observing, "And our large friend here is a composer of sagas and sonnets, whose people designed and built the four largest of the visiting vessels that are currently in orbit around your world. I think without a doubt, that even if our level of intelligence doesn't approach that of the K'eremu, it's enough to qualify each of us as intelligent." He glowered at Pret-Klob, who was as usual unaffected by the glare. "Too intelligent by half to be returned to the tender mercies of a third party that intends to treat *us* as nothing more than a commodity."

Distasteful as they found mutual proximity, the three K'eremu moved close together to consult. They said nothing Walker could overhear, but a prodigious volume of bubbles issued from the trio of nearly entwined speaking tubes. After several moments had passed, it was finally left to Alet to explain.

"Clearly, you are at least minimally intelligent." Walker's spirits rose. "By your own standards." They promptly fell anew. "We are not sure that is adequate to allow us to render proper judgment in this matter."

A stalemate? Walker reflected. What did that mean, if the K'eremu charged with dealing with this business could not come to a resolution? The stated ambiguity did nothing to reassure him.

Just when it seemed that the final determination might as easily go one way as the other, Sque stepped, or rather scuttled, forward. Walker glanced over at her in surprise, while George, for once, sensibly kept his mouth firmly closed.

"While the simple nature of the three primitives whose company I was compelled to share these past several years is undeniable, I believe they have demonstrated intelligence sufficient to warrant their continued existence as independent entities."

Walker immediately looked to Pret-Klob. While obviously upset at Sque's intercession on behalf of the remainder of his fugitive inventory, the Vilenjji wisely did not comment. Not with the current speaker having been among the former unwilling detainees held in captivity by his association.

"On what do you base that conclusion?" Alet asked her. Encouragingly, all three of the arbitrators appeared more than usually interested in what the fourth member of their number present had to say.

Sque was now gesturing with nearly every one of her appendages, executing a succession of complex gestures that were as much dance as exclamation. There was far too much for Walker or his friends to follow. But the combination of words and waves was having an effect on the trio who were to decide their fate.

"On their continued recognition of myself as the prevailing intelligence among them and, more critically, on the aid they rendered," Sque declared in response to the question. Functioning with marvelous independence of one another, her gesticulating limbs individually pointed out Walker, George, and Braouk. "Without their assistance, primitive as it may have been, I would not be here now, faced with the need to confront you physically in a manner I am certain you find as unpleasant as do I. That effort on my behalf alone justifies their claim to retention of individual autonomy: the undeniable fact that they assisted a K'eremu."

With that, she retreated from uncomfortable nearness to the three others of her kind. Walker badly wanted to add a comment of his own, but dared not. Instead, he knelt to let his right hand methodically stroke George's back. Recognizing the import of the moment, the dog continued to remain silent. Behind them, Braouk withheld the saga stanza he had just completed, conscious of the fact that it would be better to wait for a more propitious moment in which to deliver himself of his latest lines.

A second consultation among the three K'eremu went on longer than its predecessor. At its conclusion, the trio gratefully separated. Mehz waved three appendages at them, one for each supplicant.

"In the absence of compelling evidence to the contrary, it has been decided that no better way exists to resolve this apparent dilemma than to rely on the word of that paragon of sentient evolution, another K'eremu." Other limbs gestured in Sque's direction. "We accept your reflection. Your primitive acquaintances are free to return to their waiting craft."

Walker wanted to jump up and shout, to fling his clenched fist into the enclosed, perpetually damp air of the port. He restrained himself lest the reaction be thought overtly primal. Certainly it was impossible to envision a K'eremu reacting the same way in a similar situation. He settled instead for giving George a last firm pat on the head, straightening, and letting Braouk wrap the tip of one massive tentacle around his five human digits.

It was only by chance that he happened to notice the weapon gripped firmly in the suckers of Pret-Klob's right arm flap.

"I and the other members of my association have not traveled this long and this far to be denied that which we seek. The inventory is coming with me."

The oddly circular hand weapon, Walker noted without moving a muscle, was aimed at the lone male among the three watchful K'eremu. They did not appear overly concerned by the Vilenjji's unexpected show of force. But then, a K'eremu never did. Feeling Braouk's mass shift subtly behind him, he slowly raised a forestalling hand. His arm could not stop the Tuuqalian if he wanted to make a rush at the Vilenjji. A tank would be necessary. But the gesture was enough. Respecting Walker's insight, Braouk held his ground.

"Interesting aggressive device," Rehj commented thoughtfully, eying the weapon. "By way of contrast, our far more sophisticated equivalents are notably less injurious."

None of the three K'eremu reached for a control, or made an unusual gesture, or took out a concealed device. None spoke a command or called for help. One moment, a large and very determined Vilenjji was standing nearby, his weapon trained on the trio. The next, Pret-Klob went stiff as purple pine, his body unmoving as a flash-frozen crab spat out by the quick-freezer of a Bering Sea trawler. Pulsing softly, a pale aura now enveloped his body, or perhaps emanated from it. Walker couldn't tell.

There are devices active here that will restrain, he remember Sque warning him earlier. For once, their K'eremu companion had resorted to understatement.

"There is one other matter that should be attended to." As if nothing untoward had happened, Alet advanced a few body lengths in Walker's direction. "Now that you know the location of K'erem, if we allow you to depart, what guarantee do we have that we will not be troubled by your annoying presence again?"

"We promise." Walker responded reflexively, just as he would have if he had been in the midst of an important business meeting with any client. "We won't come back. Honestly. Not that your world doesn't have its undeniable charms," he added hastily, the trader in him contriving the necessary tact, "but for us K'erem has always been just a way station, not a destination."

"Just one more hydrant on the highway of life." Fortunately, the K'eremu's translators could not quite manage a seamless interpretation of the dog's comment.

"It be same, with me and mine, forever," Braouk hastened to assure the watchful trio.

"What better way to be rid of them," Sque added conclusively, "than to send them on their way back to the homeworlds they seek?"

A voice issued from the partially immobilized Pret-Klob. "Only the association knows the location of the human and canine world. The Niyyuu do not know it, nor do the Iollth, or the Hyfft, or the Tuuqalia. It is so isolated and distant that none are aware of its location but us. It will not be divulged; not even for a price." While the Vilenjji could move neither head nor eyes, Walker became convinced his former captor was staring directly at him, and him alone. "There is principle involved."

Though Pret-Klob could not have known it, it was exactly the wrong thing to say. If only he had not said "only." Because in doing so, he had unwittingly laid down a challenge to the K'eremu.

This time it was Mehz who stepped forward to confront the visitors—still maintaining a suitable distance, of course.

"Sequi'aranaqua'na'senemu speaks sensibly. In the interests of ridding K'erem's vicinity of you as quickly and expeditiously as possible, it will be recommended that our astronomical facilities be encouraged to cooperate with your own meager equivalents." Silvery eyes glanced indifferently in the direction of the immobilized Vilenjji. "So many of the lesser species suffer from an appalling conviction of their own supremacy."

George could not restrain himself. "A failing that fortunately escapes the K'eremu."

"Yes," agreed Mehz without a hint of irony. "I suspect you will all be on your way sooner than you think."

Walker gestured at the powerless, silently fuming Pret-Klob. "What about him?"

Alet spoke up. "The unpleasant creature will be returned to its own orbiting vessel. Hopefully suitably chastened. Neither he nor any other from his craft will be permitted to return to the surface of K'erem. They have violated our generous hospitality."

Walker wanted to say, "What hospitality?" He did not, and this time George held his peace. Possibly because Braouk had, as he had once done with Sque on his own world, thoughtfully wrapped the tapered end of a very large and very strong tentacle around the dog's mouth.

Sque's condescending brethren were as good as their supercilious word. Working in conjunction with, if not alongside, Sobj-oes and her team of Niyyuuan, Iollth, and Tuuqalian professionals, the K'eremu did indeed locate Earth.

Several of them.

As proof of intelligence could not be detected over such vast distances, the grudgingly helpful K'eremu had been reduced to searching for systems that matched Walker's layman's description. Only their astounding scientific resources and expertise allowed them to winnow down worlds abounding from thousands of potential stellar candidates, to hundreds, to—finally—four. By terrestrial standards the four lay unreachable distances apart. In the advanced ships of the Niyyuu, Iollth, and Tuuqalians, the prospective journey was not an unfeasible one.

As they made ready to depart from the vicinity of K'erem's sun, a last surprise awaited the travelers. It arrived in the form of a communication that materialized within Walker and George's living quarters, and took the form of the avatar of a certain very familiar K'eremu.

"A last farewell, Sque?" Walker faced the projection while George dozed on his pillow-bed nearby. "I know we didn't have much time for leave-taking below." He did not add that the K'eremu had neglected to see them off. While disappointed, he had not been surprised. If nothing else, her nonappearance was characteristically K'eremu. Now, it appeared, she might have had second thoughts, and had decided to project a formal goodbye before the orbiting ships headed outsystem.

"As usual, your perception is inaccurate." The three-dimensional image hovered before him. "This communication represents nothing of the kind. I continue to accompany you, though of course I cannot be expected to tolerate your physical proximity any more than is minimally necessary."

That brought George's head up off his bed. "The squid's coming with us?"

"Not with you specifically," the projection replied, choosing to ignore the dog's impertinence. "It has been decided that there is useful data to be acquired from accompanying you on your return. Just as the ungainly Tuuqalian Braouk has continued to accompany you to acquire material for his pitiable saga, so I and others of my kind have determined to do so in the everlasting pursuit of knowledge." She abruptly vanished, to be replaced by a new image: of one of the sleek, breathtakingly beautiful ships of her kind. The substitution was brief, and she quickly returned.

"There are twenty of us on board," she informed Walker

and George, in reference to the newly arrived craft whose image they had just viewed. "The minimum necessary to supervise the operation of a long-range vessel. Also near the maximum number of K'eremu who can stand to be in one another's company."

"We're glad to have you along," Walker told her feelingly. "I was afraid I wasn't going to get the chance to say a real goodbye."

"Uneconomical frivolities," she replied. "Sometimes to be favored, nonetheless. While we cannot of course greet one another in person while we are in transit between star systems, there will doubtless be opportunities to do so during those times when we are not."

"Wonderful," George groused from the vicinity of his pillow. "I do so miss the comforting caress of wet, slimy tentacles."

As always, Sque did not react to the sarcasm inherent in the dog's response, because to her it was only natural to take his words at face value.

The excitement Walker and George felt as the ships returned to normal space turned to disappointment when it became clear that the system they had entered was not home to Earth. The outer portion was home to the essential number of gas giants, their existence necessary so that their gravity might sweep up planetary dust and debris and allow the formation of habitable inner worlds. The third of these looked very much like Earth, even to the swathes of fleecy white clouds that streaked its very breathable oxynitro atmosphere. There were water oceans, and dry continents, and evidence of life. But it was not Earth. A quick scan revealed that it harbored no intelligence. At least, none that had developed so much as rudimentary electronic communications.

It was an empty, uninhabited paradise. News of its existence would cause a sensation on Earth, where any working astronomer would part with years of his or her life for the chance to be the herald of such a discovery. Instead, it was left to Walker and George to admire it, have Sobj-oes and her colleagues methodically note its coordinates, and watch via the communications system in their quarters as it receded behind them.

"Could have had a world to ourselves," George commented as the blue and white image shrank in the view space that occupied the center of the room. "No one to tell you where to pee, no one to yell at you to stop barking."

"No one to talk to," Walker added. "I'm sure we'll have better luck at the next star."

How far had he come, he reflected. How much had he changed, that he could make a statement like that sound as casual and natural as if he was discussing the next stop on the commuter train that served the Big Windy's suburbs.

But they did not have better luck. While the second system's sun was a near twin of Sol, and the fourth world out was indeed habitable, it was not welcoming. Some unknown disaster or plague had reduced all life on its surface and in its roiling seas to a fraction of what it once must have been. Not even the K'eremu desired to risk encountering what unspeakable virulence might linger on the devastated surface. Their ship and every other departed without penetrating the unnamed world's atmosphere, leaving it untouched, uncontacted, and unknown. Whatever terrible secret it harbored remained inviolate in the wake of their hasty departure.

Having been twice disillusioned, neither man nor dog expected much when the third system of the four identified by the K'eremu was reached. So it was with a mix of shock and delight that they reacted to the news that not only had electromagnetic means of communication been detected emanating from the third planet out from the sun, but that a portion of it matched perfectly the language employed by Walker and his canine friend. Allowed to sample it for himself, a misty-eyed Walker found himself listening to the evening news on the BBC. While not exactly the same language he and George spoke, it was more than close enough to provide the necessary confirmation.

They were home.

After so many years away, he found he did not know how to react. As the ships emerged into normal space somewhere in the vicinity of the orbit of Neptune, he retreated to quarters, leaving George to further query Sobj-oes and her team in their research facility elsewhere on the ship. As he was trying to decide how next to instruct Gerlla-hyn to proceed, indeed, trying to decide how to proceed himself, a Niyyuu announced himself at the portal.

"A moment of you time, human Marcus Walker. I am Qeld-wos. With me is also colleague Nabn-dix. We not formally met. Are members of much respected communicators public of Niyu."

The Niyyuuan media, Walker realized. Ever present, ever alert for a new angle on the return of the peculiar aliens to their homeworlds, and occasionally irritating. Especially at this singular moment, when he wanted, when he *needed,* to be left alone to try to figure out what to do next. Which, he reflected, was probably precisely why they wanted to see him now. Oh well. It would be impolite to deny them a minute or two. He directed the portal to open.

Two had announced themselves. Three entered. The third was not a representative of the energetic Niyyuuan media. Walker's eyes widened, and then he opened his mouth to shout in the direction of the room's communicator.

A flash from the circular weapon clasped in the powerful suckers of the third visitor's right arm flap knocked Walker to the floor. As the pair of obviously surprised Niyyuu turned in his direction, Pret-Klob fired at each of them in turn. The tall, slender forms crumpled. Perhaps they had received a stronger charge from the Vilenjji's weapon. Or possibly Walker's constitution was tougher. Regardless of the reason, while both human and Niyyuu lay stunned, only he remained conscious.

Advancing with the peculiar side-to-side lurching motion that was so distinctive of his kind, Pret-Klob entered farther into the room until he was standing almost directly over the recumbent human. Walker felt as if every part of his body had gone to sleep. The tingling sensation was intense. As he struggled to speak and to move arms and legs, he watched helplessly as the Vilenjji adjusted something on the side of his weapon.

Where was George? he found himself thinking frantically. Paralyzed, he could not call to the communicator for help. Slowly, he felt some feeling, some muscular control, returning. The pinprick, stabbing sensation of returning neurological normality was excruciating.

"Umg . . . unk . . ." He still couldn't form words. Not quite. But soon . . .

"Soon" soon became irrelevant. The Vilenjji was not stupid. His very presence here, on board the *Jhevn-bha,* attested to that. It should not have been. But it was. As soon as he had regained sufficient control of his larynx and tongue, lips and lungs, Walker wondered at it aloud.

By way of response, the calm and composed Vilenjji pointed to the still unconscious bodies of the two Niyyuuan media representatives. "After the unmentionable K'eremu returned me to my own vessel, following my regrettably unsuccessful attempt to repossess property rightfully belonging to my association, I subsequently made contact with the pair who presently occupy the floor across from you. A proper entrepreneur is always alert to potentially useful contacts. Familiar as I was from the time I had been compelled to spend on Niyu with the characteristic excesses of their kind, I devised a procedure that, with luck, I believed might allow me to make contact with my absent inventory yet one more time." The arm flap that held the circular weapon gestured absently. "As you can observe, that possibility has been fulfilled."

Breathing hard, still unable to move his arms or legs,

Walker looked up at his tormentor, his relentless pursuer, his primary abductor, and wished he had enough muscular control to spit.

"You bribed them," he managed to whisper accusingly, in reference to the two inert Niyyuu.

"Not at all." It was difficult to tell if the Vilenjji's tone was reflecting as abstract a quality as pride. "They were traveling on a different vessel, one of their own kind. Less than fully versed in the details of the relationship between myself and wandering inventory, they proved amenable when my representatives suggested that there was an acquaintance of yours who very much wished to see and offer you congratulations before your final return to your world.

"Captivated by the visual and aural possibilities inherent in such a confrontation and knowing that I would be alone and isolated as the only one of my kind to participate in the further progress of this expedition, it was agreed that I could arrange to pay for transport and accommodation on their ship, and that when the opportunity presented itself, they would arrange for me to join them so that they could record the proposed meeting between us. After which, having no other choice, I would return with them to their vessel, thence to be reunited with my own people at some undetermined future date." This time it was the unarmed limb that gestured.

"On board their vessel I kept largely to myself, both from choice and need. With Niyyuu, Iollth, Hyfft, and the occasional Tuuqalian mixing freely during the visits to previous systems, my presence went largely unremarked upon. Each group assumed the other had authorized it. The only risk was that knowledge of my presence might be conveyed to this particular vessel, and thence to you or to someone familiar with our less than genial mutual history." Now there was no mistaking the conceit in his tone. "Thankfully, that did not occur."

The tingling pain coursing through Walker's body was diminishing, but was still prevalent enough to make him clench his teeth. "You're right. You're all alone here. Your association can't help you. There's no way you can—recover your wandering inventory. So—what *do* you want?"

An answer appeared in the form of the muzzle, or business end, of the Vilenjji's circular weapon, as it inclined downward until it was pointing directly between Walker's eyes. As much as it was possible for his muscles to freeze up again, they did so. He gaped at the purple-skinned, big-eyed alien.

"You're going to *kill* me?"

"I am going to kill you," Pret-Klob replied calmly.

Walker struggled for a response. His initial reaction was to say something dramatic, along the lines of "If you kill me, you'll never get off the *Jhevn-bha* alive!" He did not say it because it was patently clear that Pret-Klob had already considered and accepted that inevitability. Walker realized he was neither going to reach or affect the Vilenjji that way. So instead, he retorted, "You're going to destroy valuable stock? Without any possibility of recompense? That doesn't sound like prudent Vilenjji business practice to me."

"It is not. However, more than plain profit is at stake in this now. That is your fault. Your continued existence, and in particular your ability not only to successfully remove yourself and your companions from the association's original vessel, but to somehow orchestrate a return here, to your home system, stands as an ongoing affront to every principle that the association and all related Vilenjji enterprises hold most dear. It is unnatural. It cannot be permitted to eventuate." The muzzle of the weapon descended slightly toward Walker. Instinct told him to close his eyes. Experience and determination told him not to.

Pret-Klob was not finished. "Do you remember what I said to you when last we saw one another on board the ship of the interfering Sessrimathe? 'Be assured that in the realness of time, the natural order of things will be restored.'"

"Yeah," Walker mumbled softly. "I remember that. I also remember you saying 'It's only business.'"

The tendrils atop the Vilenjji's tapering skull writhed forcefully as the huge eyes continued to focus unblinkingly on the human at its feet. "Only business. Part of that is to restore the natural order of things. That demands that an incontestably more primitive creature not be allowed to humiliate one demonstrably more superior."

"What," Walker told him, realizing he did not have much time left and thinking furiously, "if I could prove to you that I'm not your inferior, and that we're equals? Would that satisfy you? Would that fit into your 'natural order' of things enough to satisfy you and preserve this principle you're so concerned about that you're ready to die for it?"

It seemed to him that the Vilenjji hesitated. "You cannot prove such an assertion. To do so would oblige me to admit that it was wrong to take you in the first place."

"That's what I'm thinking, too." Making a supreme effort, Walker found that he could sit up. While he was once more fully in control of his faculties, he knew that to yell at the communicator for help would be futile: the fatalistic Vilenjji could kill him long before any help could arrive. All that was left to him by way of a defense was logic and reason.

It was time, he knew, to attempt to make the trade of his life.

"I can't go home," he said simply.

The Vilenjji stared at him, unblinking as ever. "Of course you cannot. I am going to kill you."

"Even if you don't kill me, even if you weren't here, I can't go home."

The muzzle of the alien weapon wavered ever so slightly. "I do not understand. Do not take my noncomprehension as an admission of equality," he added quickly.

"I won't." Walker found it was surprisingly easy to warm to his task. It was something he'd been ruminating on, had been forced to ponder, for a long, long time. "Finally, actually getting here makes me realize something that's been nagging at me and troubling me for some time now. I've

changed too much." Finding he could once more control his
arms, he made use of them to emphasize his conversion. "I
can't go home anymore."

The Vilenjji stared at him.

"After everything that's happened, after all I've been
through, I just don't think I can do it. I'm not a citizen of one
world anymore. Not of any world. I've been exposed to too
many wonders, seen too much, to go back to living on one
small, out-of-the-way, backward world, however familiar. I
thought that's what I've wanted ever since my friends and I
were rescued from your captivity by the Sessrimathe." He
shook his head in wonder at his own words. "The Sessrimathe. I'd like to see Seremathenn again. Spectacular place,
wonderful people. And Niyu, and Hyff, and Tuuqalia. Maybe
visit Ioll, and a dozen or so other worlds." He met the Vilenjji's much broader gaze challengingly. "I'd even be curious to
see what Vilenj is like.

"But I can't go back. Sure, I can long for a piece of choco-
late cake, or a Sunday football game. And I probably will.
But would I trade a visit to the mountains of Niyu or a performance of the silica-dancers of Seremathenn for them?"
He shook his head. "Not anymore. I've changed too much.
I've *learned* too much." He smiled. Not for the effect it
might have on the Vilenjji, but for himself. "I've learned how
to cook. I can do things no chef back home can even imagine. I might even manage a reasonable facsimile of a choco-
late cake. Or trade for one." With difficulty, he struggled
erect and met the Vilenjji's alien gaze without blinking.

"I've become as much a civilized resident of this galaxy as
the Niyyuu, or the Hyfft, or even the K'eremu. Or you, or
any Vilenjji." That said, with finality, he did close his eyes,
and waited for the fatal shot.

Seconds passed. The seconds stretched into a minute, then
two. A weight descended on his left shoulder and he
flinched. But there was no pain, and none of the agonizing

tingling that had coursed through him earlier. He opened his eyes.

Under-flaps splayed out to both sides, Pret-Klob had squatted down in front of him. The circular weapon had been put away. The weight Walker felt came from one wide arm flap resting on his shoulder. The last time he had felt such a weight, it had been dragging him forcibly out of his rented SUV beside Cawley Lake high in the Sierra Nevada of northern California. Whatever the Vilenjji had decided to do, he suspected that was a place he would never see again.

Because he had told the truth.

As much as he might want to see the lake, or revisit certain haunts and certain friends, he couldn't go back to the life he had known on Earth. Or any life on Earth. For him, Earth had become—what was a suitable term?

Small. That was it. In a galaxy of wonderments, the majority of which he had yet to experience and could not even envisage, Earth was small.

He was aware that Pret-Klob continued to stare at him. "'The natural order of things.' It is not a fixed immutable. Everything can change. One who is adept at commerce learns to recognize such shifts. In abandoning your primitive world, you abandon your primitive self. I cannot countenance this change as being one applicable to every member of your species—but I must acknowledge that with which I am personally confronted." Dragging itself heavily down Walker's arm, the end of the powerful appendage attached itself to his hand. Suckers took hold—but not hurtfully.

"While I continue to remain tentative as to the specifics of this unexpected revelation, I am persuaded to acknowledge at least one of your kind as an equal. Or at least, a near equal. Therefore, I will not kill you, Marcus Walker."

Walker managed to remain as composed as possible under the circumstances. "Much obliged." It was another measure of how much he had changed that he was able to add, "No hard feelings. I understand when you say it was only business. I'm—I was, in business myself. I was a trader in commodities. You know—raw materials?"

Releasing the human's hand, Pret-Klob glanced thoughtfully over at the pair of Niyyuuan media representatives. They were beginning to moan and stir, their brightly colored frills flexing spasmodically, their quadruple tails twitching reflexively. He had not intended to kill them, and he had not. Satisfied that they would recover fully, he turned his attention back to his graduated inventory.

"That is most interesting. Perhaps we might even do some business together ourselves one day. My association is always ready to learn from others."

Walker squinted up at the Vilenjji. "Even from former assets?"

A thick appendage gestured meaningfully. "It is the substance of knowledge that matters, not its source. One seeks profit wherever and however one can find it."

"Couldn't have put it better myself. You know, there was this one time I was offered three containership-loads of processed cocoa and I had to—"

He broke off. Pret-Klob was being polite. The Vilenjji would have no knowledge of or interest in cocoa, cocoa futures, or how the fluctuating political situation in Ivory Coast versus that in Venezuela might affect that particular market. If they were going to do anything together, a prospect that remained questionable, it would have to involve matters of mutual understanding. Could he somehow work his newly acquired culinary expertise into any such problematic equation?

"First thing: no trading in sentients," he told the alien assertively. "Even if they're not as intelligent as Vilenjji—or humans, or Tuuqalians, or K'eremu. Not only does it go against civilized galactic behavior, it's not—nice."

"I respect your self-elevated status," Pret-Klob replied evenly, "but it is not for you to render judgment on the commercial traditions of another species."

They sat and argued for some time. All the while Walker wondered at how far he had come, from being a captive of the Vilenjji to sitting peacefully across from one while discussing the nature and ethics of Vilenjji business.

Displaying the noteworthy resilience that defined their craft, as soon as they had recovered from the muted effects of Pret-Klob's weapon, both Niyyuuan media representatives set aside their distress at having been deceived and mistreated by the Vilenjji in favor of recording the fascinating discussion taking place between it and the solitary human.

While they were not shocked, their feisty aplomb was not matched by that of the four-legged terrestrial who walked in on them. It was difficult to say which George found more shocking: the presence of their former captor Pret-Klob in his and Walker's private quarters, or the fact that man and Vilenjji appeared to be engaged in nothing more confrontational than polite and animated conversation.

"Shouldn't be any abducting of dogs, either," Walker declared, adding a cryptic comment to the conversational brew into which his canine companion had just wandered.

Dazed, George entered farther into his quarters, sparing nary a glance for the two Niyyuuan media representatives who were busy recording everything within range of their pickups.

"Captivating reaction," declared one.

"Very attractive, yes," agreed the other as she adjusted the myriad devices that spotted her slender front like so many electronic boils. "It will be well received when played for audience back home."

"What's going on here?" Sidling up alongside his friend, George continued to keep a wary eye on the looming bulk of the Vilenjji. "What's he doing here?"

Reaching down, Walker stroked the dog's head and back, reassuring him. "Pret-Klob arranged to accompany us here in order to kill me. Probably you, too." He returned his gaze to the big alien. "Instead, we had a chat, and we've come to an understanding. Nobody's going to kill anybody, and his association will quit its claim to us. We might even end up doing some business together." He winked at the bewildered dog.

"No kidnapping and abducting of close relations, though. Oh, and one other thing. I'm not going back to Earth." His voice was steady now, confident. As assured as his words. "It's not home anymore, and I've decided I can't do it. I don't *want* to do it. I want to see, and experience"—he took a deep breath, let it out slowly—"everything else. But I'm sure Gerlla-hyn can find a way to drop you off. Back in Chicago, or anywhere else you might prefer."

Recovering his composure, George stared evenly up at his human. Then he stepped forward—and nipped him on the leg. Letting out a yelp of mixed pain and surprise (more the latter than the former), Marcus gaped at his companion. Pret-Klob looked on with quiet interest, while the two Niyyuuan media representatives could hardly contain their delight at the action they were recording.

"George, what . . . ?"

"You stupid, stupid man. You stupefied hairless ape. Don't you remember anything? Don't you *see* anything?" He paused, then added, "Evidently not, because all you can do is sit there with your mouth open and nothing but seeohtwo coming out." The dog began to pace in an agitated, tight circle. "How many times did I mention that on Earth I'd be a talking freak, or have to live an existence as an enforced mute? How many times did I point out that out here I'm just one alien among hundreds? That not going back would be by far the most sensible and rational end for me?"

Walker found his voice. "But every time we talked about returning, every time it was brought up, you were as steadfast about it as I was."

The dog lunged forward again, and Walker jerked his leg back just in time. "There's intelligence, and then there's smarts. You may be intelligent, Marc." He nodded in the di-

rection of the interested Vilenjji. "Intelligent enough to satisfy our walking eggplant, here. But when it comes to smarts,
you come up shorter than an addled Chihuahua.

"Of course I talked like I wanted to return home. I did that
for *you*. I was supporting *you*. Because your need to do so
was so obviously desperate. Because it was all you talked
about. Because—you're my friend, Marc." The furry head
dropped, then came up again. "Me—I don't care if I ever see
a cold, friendless, empty alley again. As far as I'm concerned, the whole mutt-catching, puppy-abusing, neuter-
happy place can go to the dogs!" He glanced over at the
delighted media representatives. "You get all that? Good!
You can add that because of the changes *I've* undergone, because of the way *I've* changed, I know that I'd be better off on
Niyu than on my homeworld—though Seremathenn would
be better still. Dog-breath, I'd even prefer K'erem. At least
the smells are interesting, and I wouldn't have to spend the
rest of my life being prodded and poked in the service of advancing 'science.' "

It was quiet in the room, the ship silent around them, the
hum of the Niyyu's equipment barely audible.

"Well," Walker finally murmured.

Standing up, George put his front paws in his friend's lap
and stared earnestly into his face. "I don't have anything
worthwhile to go back to, Marc. But what about you? Are
you sure about this? Are you really sure?"

Walker smiled. "I'm sure, George." He reached out to
stroke the dog's back, running his fingers down the dense fur.
"I've hopped the train I want to be on. I got on board some
time ago, I think. It just took a while to admit it to myself."
He shrugged meaningfully. "After persisting and fighting
and struggling so long and so hard to get back here, it turns
out there's no here here for me anymore."

By now at least partly convinced that their former Vilenjji
tormentor really did no longer mean them any harm, the dog
allowed himself to relax. "How you gonna keep 'em down

on the farm once they've seen galactic civilization? I'm glad, Marc. More than glad. I'm happy. I can live out my life without having to hide my ability to talk. Or my intelligence." His gaze narrowed as he eyed the watchful Vilenjji sharply. "You're sure about this 'understanding' Marc says you and he have reached?"

The Vilenjji reached toward George, who flinched instinctively. But the gesture ended in a stroke, albeit one that was rough and sucker-lined. "I am not ready for, nor am I in a position to suggest wholesale changes in the structure and purpose of the association. But if better means of making a profit can be devised . . ." He left the thought hanging, along with a steady look at the human.

Walker found himself thinking back, all the way back to his original abduction that crazy night at his camp in the Sierras. This had all begun with a group of aliens who had abducted him with the intention of putting him up for sale. Of making use of him. For some time now, he had been making use of aliens. Sessrimathe and Niyyuu, Hyfft and Iollth, Tuuqalia and K'eremu and others; all had been caught up and put upon and cajoled in the service of him and his three friends. It was not unlike the ways and means he had employed to great success during his work with the Chicago Commodities Exchange.

He found that he was looking forward to the future with high expectations indeed. As to Earth, he would always have his memories to tide him over any unforeseen bouts of homesickness. Memories, and George. He would forgo visits to Starbucks for adventures in star systems. Instead of keeping tabs on football, he could watch the well-mannered, carefully structured internal wars of Niyu.

Niyu. There was someone there, as thoroughly and truly an alien as any he had yet encountered, whose acquaintance he very much wanted to renew. What would Viyv-pym-parr think if he returned? Of one thing he was certain: the rabid and active Niyyuuan media would have a field day with such a reunion, however biologically platonic.

Could there be anything more? In the spirit of scientific inquiry that had become one of his new motivations, he fully intended to find out.

But not right away. The Tuuqalians would want to go home, but the Iollth had pledged themselves to him—for a while, at least. As for the K'eremu, Sque had said that they had accompanied him in hopes of adding to their immense store of universal knowledge. As he was their nominal leader, the Niyyuu might go along with any decision he chose to render—for a while, at least. Especially if their avid and ever ambitious media had anything to say about it.

There was plenty of time yet before his extraordinary diversity of friends had to return to Niyu, and to their respective other homeworlds. Plenty of time for him to further cement relations with, and try to dissuade from the abduction and selling of sentients, the Vilenjji Pret-Klob. Time to travel, to explore, to *see*.

Rising, he turned and addressed the pair of contented (and now fully recovered) Niyyuu. "We're not going on to my homeworld. My companion and I"—he indicated George, whose tail was metronoming briskly—"have decided that locating it was return enough. We'll be going back to Niyu, I expect."

All four of the female's tails swayed back and forth in a vigorous visual expression of professional contentment. "That wonderful news to hear, Marcus Walker! The longer expedition journeys, the more opportunities we have for making fine and memorable recordings."

Walker nodded encouragingly. "That's what George and I were thinking. As official representatives of the Niyyuuan media, you two might as well be the ones to so inform Gerlla-hyn." He grinned, as much to himself as for the benefit of aliens unfamiliar with the meaning behind the expression. "Tell the Commander-Captain that the fleet"—*the fleet!*

he thought wonderingly—"will be taking the scenic route home."

They did not quite comprehend his words, their own translators functioning shy of the comprehensiveness needed to fully interpret the human's comment, but they would understand soon enough.

"Did you then have particular routing in mind?" the male inquired tentatively.

Walker considered. Untutored and undereducated in astronomy, he would have been forced to confess an ignorance of his own homeworld's immediate galactic neighborhood. That there was much to experience in its vicinity he had no doubt. The galaxy, as he had already involuntarily seen, was replete with endless wonders. A tug at his leg made him look down. As he did so, George released the grip his jaws had taken on a pants leg.

"I don't know about you, man, but as for myself, I've always had a serious urge to see the Dog Star."

Walker smiled. Not too many years ago, and regardless of source, such a request would have been no more than a mild joke. Not, he reflected as he contemplated his astounding and astoundingly familiar starship surroundings and the three aliens who waited on his reply, anymore.

Nor for him and his small and inordinately loquacious furry friend, ever again.

EPILOGUE

Jeron was very proud of the telescope his parents had given him two birthdays ago. In the time since then, he had mastered its use and added one accessory after another to the basic unit. He'd spent hours and days photographing the moons of Saturn and Jupiter, working his way out to those of Uranus and Neptune as well as distant nebulae and star clusters.

But this morning he was confused. The tiny section of night sky he had set his scope to automatically scan had come back with an anomaly. It was one of those distant areas of the solar system where nothing was supposed to exist. Which was precisely why he had been scanning it. Amateur astronomers tended to find the most interesting things where nothing was supposed to be, and thus where the professionals did not bother to look.

The sequence of photographs showed a mass of incredibly small objects where none ought to be. Furthermore, they appeared and disappeared over an all too brief series of sequential images. Present and gone, far too rapidly to be wandering asteroids, or cometary fragments, or anything else for which he could think of a reasonable, rational explanation. Despite checking and rechecking his scope and its attendant devices and finding them in perfect working order, he knew that the objects' appearance had to be the result of a functional irregularity. Had to be, because they could not be anything else. He could just see himself forwarding and reporting to one of the professional organizations that vetted the thousands of reports turned in by dedicated amateurs such as himself a sighting of a tightly packed cluster of baffling, inexplicable objects located somewhere in the vicinity of Neptune's giant moon Triton.

Especially when the number of them totaled thirteen.

FINISHED ALREADY?

LOOK OUT FOR THE NEXT PIP & FLINX NOVEL,

PATRIMONY,

WHERE FLINX FINDS OUT WHO HIS FATHER IS.

**AVAILABLE IN HARDCOVER
SOON FROM DEL REY BOOKS.**

Make the right moves.

Easy for an Ulru-Ujurrian to say, Flinx reflected as the *Teacher* maintained its approach to the world that lay at the end of the decelerating KK-drive craft's present course. Easy for an Ulru-Ujurrian to do. But then, everything was easy for an Ulru-Ujurrian to say and do. Unimaginably powerful, preposterously playful, and possessed of talents as yet unmeasured—and quite possibly unmeasurable—they went about their daily activities without a care in the world—short of keeping busy by way of the unfathomable playtime that involved moving their planet closer to its sun.

Even that bit of outrageous astrophysics seemed simpler to Flinx than unraveling the mystery of his origins.

He had been given a clue. For the first time in many seemingly interminable years, a tangible clue. And even more than that, he had been provided with a destination. It lay before him now, a world he had never considered before, lying the same distance from his present position as his homeworld of Moth or, in a different direction, New Riviera and Clarity Held.

Clarity, Clarity. Under the proficient ministrations and attentive guardianship of his old friends Bran Tse-Mallory and Truzenzuzex, she would be recovering from the injuries she had sustained during the fight that had allowed him to successfully flee New Riviera, also known as Nur. While his love was healing physically, perhaps he could finally heal the open wound of his unknown origins. These chafed and burned within him as intensely as any cancer.

Gestalt.

A word bursting with meaning. Perhaps also a *world* full of meaning, as it was the name of the globe his ship was rapidly approaching. An undistinguished colony world, H Class VIII, with a single large moon whose orbit the *Teacher* was presently cutting. Home to a native species called the Tlel, as well as to a modest complement of human colonists. Rather eccentric human colonists, if the details contained within the galographic he had perused were to be believed. Not that he expected to interact very much with the general population. He was here to find something specific. Something for which he had been searching a long, long time, without any real hope of ever finding it. Now, for the first time in years, he had hope.

That is, he did if what he had been told was not a cynical dying man's final provocation—a last lie intended to exact a final measure of revenge on the youth responsible for his death.

I know who your father is, Theon al-bar Cocarol had wheezed on Visaria just prior to dying. Self-proclaimed sole unmindwiped survivor of the renegade, edicted eugenicist Meliorare Society, he had dubbed Flinx *Experiment Twelve-A* before gasping out *Gestalt!* and then inconveniently expiring. *Experiments are not supposed to have knowledge of their biological progenitors,* he had coldly insisted earlier.

To the Great Emptiness with that, Flinx had decided immediately. In his lifelong search for his origins he had pursued more than his share of dead ends. It would only be one more irony in a life filled to bursting with them if a lead supplied by a dying outlaw turned out to be the right one.

Equally important had been the expiring scientist's choice of words. *I know who your father is,* Cocarol had declaimed before gasping his last. Penultimate breath or not, Flinx had

not confused the tense. Cocarol had clearly and unmistak-
ably said "is." Not *was*, but *is*. So small a word, so full of
promise. Was it possible, Flinx had been unable to keep himself from musing ever since that critical, piercing moment,
that he might not only finally learn the identity of his father,
but actually find him alive? It was too much to hope for.

So he did not hope. He had been disappointed too often
before. But he allowed himself, had to allow himself, space
in which to wish.

Intent on the fate of the galaxy and every one of its inhabitants civilized or otherwise, his mentors Bran Tse-Mallory
and the Eint Truzenzuzex would almost certainly not have
sympathized with his present detour. Much as she loved
him, Clarity might not have sympathized, either. But she
would have understood. Even with the fate of so much and
so many at stake, there were private demons that had to
be put to rest before Flinx could fully focus on external
threats, no matter how vast in extent they might be. Save the
inner universe first, he kept telling himself, and you're likely
to be in better condition to make a stab at saving everything
else.

Sprawled like a length of pink-and-green rope below the
Teacher's foreport, Pip lifted her head to glance across at
him. Epitomizing the empathetic bond that existed between
them, the minidrag's attitude reflected her friend and master's anguish.

"Am I selfish?" he asked the ship, after explicating his disquiet aloud.

"Of course you are." The *Teacher*'s ship-mind had been
programmed for many things. Subtlety was not to be counted
among them. "The fate of a galaxy rests in your hands. Or
rather, in lieu of a cheap analogy, in your mind."

"Uh-huh. Assuming I exist in this hypothetical position to
do anything at all about it, notwithstanding what Bran and
Tru seem to think."

"In the absence of an alternative specifically encouraging,
they seek surcease in the exploration of remote possibilities.

Of which you are, like it or not, ostensibly the most promising."

Flinx nodded. Rising from the command chair, he strolled over to the manual console and absently ran his hand down the length of Pip's back. The flying snake quivered with pleasure.

"What do *you* think?" he asked softly. "*Am* I the last hope? Am I the key to something bigger, something more powerful, that visits me in dreams? Or whatever you want to call that perversely altered state of consciousness in which I sometimes unwillingly find myself."

"I do not know," the *Teacher* told him honestly. "I serve, without pretending to understand. I can take you wherever you wish to go, except to comprehension. That destination is not programmed into me."

Mechanical soul, Flinx thought. Not designed to pronounce judgment. In lieu of the advice of a superior intellect, he would have to judge himself. With a sigh, he raised one hand and gestured toward the port. Soon they would need to announce themselves to planetary control with an eye toward taking up orbit.

"What about this change of course? What do you think of my putting aside the hunt for the Tar-Aiym weapons platform in order to search for my father here, based on what the dying Meliorare told me?"

Understanding of certain matters might not have been programmed into the *Teacher*'s ship-mind, but contempt was. "An insupportable waste of time. I have run a number of calculations based on the facts and variables available to me. The results are less than promising. Consider: the human Cocarol may have simply been enjoying a final, embittered joke at your expense. Or he may not have known what he was talking about. If he did, circumstances may have changed since he was last conversant with the issue at hand. Since then, any knowledge he may have possessed concerning the identity or location of your male parent may have changed radically.

"Meanwhile, whatever lies behind the Great Emptiness

continues this way. It is my opinion that your time would be better spent searching for the absent, ancient Tar-Aiym weapons platform that represents the only hope, thus far, of a device even theoretically powerful enough to counter the oncoming danger. A device with whom only you have had, and can initiate, mental contact." The silken yet tart mechanical voice paused briefly. "Have I at least succeeded in instigating within you a modicum of guilt?"

"The attempt is redundant," Flinx snapped. "No need to refresh that which never leaves me."

"That realization, at least, is encouraging," the ship replied.

"Since logic and reason are having no effect, I search for that which *will* work."

In some respects chatting with the *Teacher* was easier than engaging in conversation with a human. For example, the ship never raised its voice, and if Flinx so wished, he could terminate the discussion with a simple command. On the other hand, unlike with another person, he could not turn away from it. The ship-mind was everywhere around him.

"As soon as I've settled this question, I'll resume the search. I promise." Pip looked up at him quizzically.

The ship responded, "What makes you so certain that you will settle it here? This is a question the answer to which you have sought on many worlds. As I have commented repeatedly, the dying human could have perished with a falsehood on his lips. It would not be overmuch to expect of one who had so long lived a lie himself."

"I know, I know." A pensive Flinx raised his gaze once more to the cloud-swathed new world looming steadily larger in the foreport. As he stared, the port continuously adapted to the changing light outside the ship. Another new world in a long list of those that instead of answers had thus far provided him with only more questions. "But after all these years, it's the most promising lie that I've been told."

Though Gestalt's human population numbered only in the millions, he was still surprised at the informality that infused the exchange of arrival formalities. According to the *Teacher,* the orbiting station-based automatic electronic protocol that challenged their approach did not even bother to inquire as to the nature of his business. This suggested that the planetary authority was either lazy, indifferent, or criminally negligent. As it developed, it was none of these. Orbital insertion protocol was a true reflection of the colonists' attitude and philosophy. It was not quite like anything Flinx had encountered before.

The lack of bureaucratic ceremony meant that he had to conceal only his true identity, and not the configuration of his vessel. The *Teacher* was able to avoid having to employ the complex external morphing he usually had to order it to undergo to disguise its appearance when visiting other worlds.

After equipping himself as best he could from ship stores according to the recommendations that were included in Gestalt's unpretentious but thorough galographics file, he headed down the corridor that led to the shuttle bay. Riding his left shoulder beneath his dark brown nanofiber cold-weather jacket, Pip had gone to sleep. A quick predeparture check indicated that everything was in place for him to take his usual leave from the vessel. The communit that would not only allow him to communicate with the *Teacher* but also allow it to keep track of him was secure in its pouch on his duty belt, which was itself concealed beneath the lower hem of the jacket.

Though not an iceworld like Tran-ky-ky, by all indications the surface of Gestalt was as chilly as a Meliorare's heart. It would, he reflected, be a change from all the temperate, tropical, and semidesert worlds on which he had recently spent so much of his time.

"I'll be back soon," he declared aloud as the shuttle lock door curled softly shut behind him. A slight hiss signified pressure equalization.

"Famous last words," the *Teacher* murmured, addressing the observation as much to itself as to the lanky young human who was now slipping into harness inside the shuttle.

My father, Flinx thought to himself as he felt the subtle jolt that indicated the shuttle had dropped clear of the *Teacher.* My father *is.* So had insisted the dying Meliorare Cocarol. So many years spent searching. So much time lost wondering. Finding his father would not save civilization from the vast abyssal horror that was speeding toward the Milky Way from beyond the Great Emptiness—but it might help to fortify the hesitant, vacillating key that was himself.

In all his traveling he had never seen a planetary surface quite like that of Gestalt. Its waters were blue, its heavy cloud cover mottled white. Normal enough. But instead of ambiguous, perambulating scattering, the numerous continental landmasses ran north to south in roughly parallel, scimitar-shaped arcs, striping the entire globe with mountainous chevrons. Some of the larger bodies of land were loosely connected by wandering, thin strips of terrain, while others were completely isolated from one another by long stretches of open sea.

Each individual landmass consisted largely of rugged mountain ranges that had been squeezed up from the planetary crust by grumbling tectonic forces. There should be active volcanism, Flinx mused as he studied the surface that was rising swiftly toward him. Indeed, in the course of the descent he spotted several confessional plumes, their telltale trails stretching out straight and sharp as white feathers amid the rest of what was an otherwise typically anarchic atmosphere.

As the shuttle automatically leveled off on final approach, he marveled at the landscape that spread out in every direction. Valleys cutting through the incessant mountain chains flashed churning rivers. Bright flashes of alpine lakes lay strung like shards of shattered mirror among the green. And, startlingly, the blue. There was an inordinate amount of undeniably blue vegetation, he saw, in every imaginable shade and variation. In addition, the snow that capped the higher peaks and lay like cotton in shadowed vales and chasms was tinted a distinctive pink that occasionally deepened to rose. There must be something unique in the composition of the local precipitates, he reflected.

Finding one's way around such country would be next to impossible without modern technology. As the *Teacher*'s shuttle sped over valley after valley, dropping gradually lower and lower, he saw that one rocky, tree-fringed gorge looked much like another. Infrequently, a cluster of structures indicating organized habitation impinged briefly on his vision. Even at the shuttle's rapidly diminishing landing speed, these came and went too fast for him to tell if their origin was human or indigenous.

According to Gestalt's galographics, population centers of any kind were few and far between. Both the native Tlel and the humans who had settled among them favored their privacy. It was a trait inborn among the natives and elective among the humans.

The shuttle's voice, a modest echo of its starship parent, advised him to prepare for touchdown. It was a warning he always took seriously, even when preparing to land on a developed world. He had been prepared for touchdown ever since he had first settled into the seat. Sensing his heightened anticipation, Pip tensed slightly beneath the cold-climate jacket.

Only a few valleys on Gestalt were wide and flat enough to allow for the siting of a shuttleport. Tlearandra was located on the other side of the planet. Since it was also home to the offices of Gestalt's Commonwealth representative and the preponderance of potentially inquisitive secondary officials, Flinx had prudently chosen to land at Tlossene, the other principal metropolitan area.

Used to touching down at ports that were located well outside the boundaries of the major conurbations they served, he was startled when it appeared as if the shuttle was heading for the center of the city itself. Though eventually realizing this was an illusion born of descent velocity and angle of approach, he was still relieved when his craft made primary contact with an actual landing strip instead of the cluster of buildings whose rooftops it seemed to barely clear. The shuttleport was situated in a region of hard, dried river bottom that struck him as perilously close to inhabited areas. While it was true that Gestalt exported only small manufactures and conversely boasted only modest imports, thus negating any need for extensive port servicing facilities, the proximity of port to population struck him as irresponsible. He intended to inquire about the choice. Even though he could not think of one, doubtless there was a good reason why the port had been placed so close to the community.

It did not occur to him that maybe nobody cared.

Arrival formalities on the ground proved to be as thankfully unceremonious and perfunctory as they had been when the *Teacher* had first settled into orbit and been contacted by landing control. He had only to state his name (falsified), ship identification (falsified), and purpose of visit (conducting research on behalf of a company that for reasons related to commercial security preferred to remain unnamed—also falsified). It was thus under multiple fictitious pretenses and with considerable confidence that Flinx requested directions to the usual subterranean pedestrian accessway.

"This is Gestalt," an inordinately relaxed male voice informed him via the shuttle's internal communications system. "Nothing is paid for that receives insufficient use. That includes costly underground conveniences. We don't get many private craft here. There are no subterranean amenities for travelers such as yourself. Your landing craft's present orientation is positioned clear on my readout. Step out of your vessel and turn west. You'll see the main terminal. It's a short walk across the tarmac." A brief pause, then, "Weather's good today. If you're not properly equipped for the climate, you shouldn't be here. The valley in which Tlossene is located is almost three thousand meters up, you know. Or you do now, if by some odd chance you didn't prior to touchdown."

The controller's tone suggested someone chatting casually with a friend instead of that of a government official conducting formal business attendant on offworld arrival. The easy tenor, the absence of attitude, the lack of ceremony were truly refreshing compared with the flood of restrictive regulations and formal procedures Flinx so often was forced to follow when landing on other worlds.

But—step out and turn west?

"We only have two subsurface accessways," the controller explained in response to the new arrival's uncertainty, "both of which are currently in use by the pair of cargo shuttles you can see working off to the east."

Peering out the foreport in the indicated direction, Flinx could see the two much larger, bulkier craft parked on the indicated section of tarmac. Clunky robotic haulers and more agile automated loaders swarmed around several gaping service bays. No humans or Tlel were in view, and the industrious mechanicals paid no attention to the new arrival.

"Okay, I'll walk," he informed the controller. "What about Customs and Immigration?"

"Someone will meet you." A tinge of humor colored the rest of the reply. "It'll give SeBois something to do."

Flinx did not have to secure the shuttle—the ship would see to such mundane safety measures on its own initiative. As soon as the landing ramp was deployed, he made sure the skin-sensitive softsealing collar of his jacket was snug around his neck and over Pip, and exited through the lock.

The cold hit him immediately. Prepared for it, he was not surprised. If anything, the ambient temperature was less bracing than the shuttle's readout had led him to expect. No doubt the chill was mitigated by the intensity of Gestalt's sun at this altitude. His well-being was further enhanced by the planet's slightly denser-than-Terranorm atmosphere, which helped to compensate for the altitude. Inhaling deeply and deliberately, he could not tell any difference from sea-level breathing on any Earth-normal world. Beneath his jacket, Pip twitched slightly against him but was otherwise untroubled by the sharp drop in temperature. As long as she could find enough food to power her dynamic metabolism, she would be fine.

At the moment, food held no particular appeal for Flinx, since he had eaten prior to departing the *Teacher*. But he decided that if available, he wouldn't turn down a hot drink. While the emergency reserve that did double duty as a component of his jacket insulation could supply that, he preferred not to access its limited volume unless he had to. Besides, it was always nice to try something local.

Across the pavement and beyond the line of port buildings, the city of Tlossene crawled up a pair of opposing mountainsides that funneled into a sloping canyon in the distance. At the city's higher elevations, poured and fabricated structures gave way or filtered into blue and green alien forest. None of the structures was taller than half a dozen stories. Though a real city with a population in the hundreds of thousands, Tlossene was no grand metropolis. Many of the central buildings he could see clearly looked weathered but tasteful. Their external appearance fit what he knew of the history of Gestalt's settlement by humans. Scattered among them were distinctively dimpled domes and bulging egg-shaped constructions that hinted at a nonhuman sense of design. If these eye-catching edifices had not been built by the indigenous Tlel, they had at least been inspired by them.

In the far distance beyond the city soared peaks whose heights Flinx could only estimate. If he needed to know exact altitudes, he could always check with the communit on his belt that had been loaded with all the information on this world that was available to the *Teacher*. Reaching the bottom of the ramp, he headed away from the shuttle, strolling in the designated direction.

The pounding at the back of his head had nothing to do with the slight change in pressure from ship to surface. Such sometimes debilitating headaches were no stranger. As always, he would ignore the throbbing pain and attendant discomfort unless it became genuinely disabling. Only at such times did he reluctantly resort to medication or meditation. Sensing her master's discomfort, Pip shifted uneasily against his shoulder. There was nothing she could do but empathize.

If he were back on Arrawd, where the locals were in much more than one way of similar mind, his mind would be at peace. Or even if he were somewhere within that strange rain-forest-swathed world Midway—no, Midworld, he corrected himself. In all the Arm, those were the only two planetfalls he had made where he knew he could be reasonably certain of finding mental peace. Lips pressed tightly together against the pain, he strode grimly on. Learning the truth of the Meliorare Cocarol's last revelation would go a long way toward easing any discomfort he felt while on Gestalt.

He forgot about the all-too-recurrent pain in his head as he caught sight of something coming across the tarmac toward him. *Someone will meet you,* the amiable port controller had assured him. Flinx's gaze narrowed. Whatever was coming toward him—and it was coming fast—was no genial representative of local officialdom. It was neither human nor Tlel. As it, or rather they, sped in his direction, they were sending out silent feelings of fear, anxiety, and confusion.

They didn't even have legs.

The lack of visible limbs in no way hampered their progress. In fact, as they loomed larger in Flinx's vision, it was apparent that legs would only have hindered their chosen method of locomotion. There were at least a dozen of the bizarre creatures tumbling and rolling rapidly in his general direction. Tumbling and rolling frantically, if his perception of the primitive emotions they were generating was correct. About the size of a human head, each of the roughly spherical creatures was completely covered in mottled white and brown fur. Longer, denser bristles stood out to the sides like oversized whiskers. They propelled themselves across the tarmac with four arms that terminated in wide, flat, fleshy pads. Working in unison, these grabbed at the hard surface and pushed off powerfully. Somewhere beneath all that fur, he imagined, must be nostrils, a mouth or trunk, and possibly eyes and ears. For all that they appeared blind and dumb, they did not roll into one another.

Pursuing them was something much larger, far more ominous, and uncompromisingly threatening in appearance. As if to reinforce its menacing aspect, it was generating emotions that were as primitive as its obvious intentions. Hulking and bearish, it nonetheless traversed the pavement with a speed and grace that belied its bulk. Unlike its intended prey it did not roll, but instead lumbered forward on several dozen short, muscular legs that terminated in sharp-hoofed feet. White fur decorated with irregular splotches of pink combined to create an incongruously feminine façade. This initially disarming impression lasted only until one noticed the mouth. Almost as wide as the creature was broad, the protruding appendage skimmed along just above the ground, its horizontal maw gaping open. An enormous, trifurcated nostril set atop the blocky skull supplied the necessary air intake and outflow for the galloping carnivore, serving not only to fill its predatory lungs but also to allow the spatulate mouth to suction up anything in its path.

That explained the visible absence of teeth or bony ridges inside the flexible jaws, Flinx realized. The meat-eater didn't bite its victims, or crunch them, or bring them down with fang and claw. It simply, efficiently, and bloodlessly vacuumed them up. This particular alien carnivore, Flinx reflected, sucked.

The distance separating the desperate dozen of the round, rolling creatures and the whistling predator shrank as he looked on. That this frenetic display of local predation was taking place right out on the tarmac of one of the planet's main shuttleports would have been sufficiently surprising all by itself, even without the fact that the entire screeching, howling menagerie was bearing down on him at impressive speed. Perceiving the threat, Pip struggled to take to the air—only to find herself constrained by the soft-seal of her master's jacket.

Quadruple arms flailing wildly, a pair of the rolling furballs bounded past Flinx on his right. A trio shot past on his left. All five stank profoundly, emitting a pungent musk that was an olfactory reflection of their terror. It occurred to him that their route, rather than being arbitrary, might have been chosen with the intent of possibly placing a diversion into the path of their ravenous pursuer.

That, he realized a bit late as he reached for the pistol holstered at his service belt, would be him. He had plenty of time to adjust the weapon's setting. The trouble was, the gun was properly secured in its holster. The holster was attached to his service belt. His service belt was fastened comfortably around his waist—beneath the jacket, whose front was snugly sealed against the local climate. Sharing some of the emotional tumult of the last roller as it swerved wildly past him, Flinx began to fumble a bit more hurriedly with the seal that kept the hem of his coat snug against his upper thighs. Oblivious to his concerns, the lumbering oncoming predator continued to head straight toward him. Flinx felt fairly sure that, unlike the rollers, it had no intention of going around. The broad, flattened, energetically suctioning mouth was more than capacious enough to vacuum him up as easily as it would have any of the fleeing, multiarmed furballs. Fumbling faster with the jacket's lower seal, he tried projecting feelings of uncertainty onto the onrushing meat-eater. When that had no effect, he strove to project fear. Too primitive or too preoccupied with the hunt to respond, the creature took no notice of his increasingly harried mental efforts.

Finally forcing her way free of the jacket, Pip took to the air. In the denser atmosphere, she had to work even less than usual to get aloft. Her iridescent body was a sudden burst of color against the blue sky. A blur of pleated blue-and-pink wings, she needed but a moment to orient herself before diving directly at the charging carnivore—only to hesitate in midair. The poison she spat was lethal when it struck the eyes of a target, and she was deadly accurate from a surprising distance. Only one thing kept her from dropping the whistling predator in its tracks.

She couldn't find its eyes.

Either like the fast-fleeing rollers it had none, an increasingly uneasy Flinx surmised, or else they were so deeply concealed beneath the coat of white-rose fur they could not be seen. As the beast drew entirely too near, suction from its mouth began to pluck at the legs of Flinx's thermotropic pants. Normally steady as sunshine, his fingers were uncharacteristically fickle as they fumbled ever more anxiously for the handgrip of his gun. The deep-toned whistling, he now noted, came not from the gaping cavity of the creature's distinctive, expansive mouth, but from the exceptionally large tripartite nostril set atop its skull. Mouth, nostril. Drawn by what must be an enormous lung, or set of lungs, air was sucked in through the vacuuming mouth and expelled through the bony structure atop the head. If he did not do something to halt or divert the monster, very shortly he would find himself in a position to study this fascinating example of adaptive alien biology from the inside.

As Pip darted and hovered overhead in a frantic but futile attempt to distract the lumbering carnivore, Flinx finally succeeded in pulling his pistol free of its holster and taking aim. Knowing nothing of the creature's anatomy and in any case not having any time to evaluate it, he pointed the beamer's muzzle at the center of the fur-matted skull. Hopefully, the brain that powered the animal was located in the general region between mouth and nose.

It was only when he had the pistol leveled and ready to fire that he noticed it was set on Heat, its lowest calibration, instead of Stun or Kill.